I swear and vow

I swear and vow.

by STEFAN OLIVIER

translated by Helen Sebba

Doubleday & Company, Inc.

Garden City, New York

All of the characters in this book are fictitious,
and any resemblance to actual persons, living or dead,
is purely coincidental.

I swear and vow

I

At some point in his life everyone faces a decision which will determine his fate. He can postpone it; he cannot escape it. It is impossible to stand still at a crossroads.

William Feldhusen, M.D., member of the medical faculty, was at one of these crossroads when the letter arrived—a blue envelope, one of several, but Feldhusen saw it right away. He drew it toward him across the desk, hesitating. For weeks he had been waiting for it; now it frightened him, for this letter was concerned with a matter of the utmost importance to him: a position as Head Physician in the leading hospital of the nearest big city. The height of his ambition. A fresh start. Or had they turned him down?

Feldhusen leaned back. If I'm turned down, he thought, everything will remain the way it is: the practice, sick calls, unwanted children, unfulfilled desires for children, prescriptions, hospital insurance forms, taxes. Month after month, year after year. Four weeks' vacation in the south, forty-eight weeks of work in this sorry little town. Professional journals, evening meetings on new developments in medicine, conventions. Then in due course the heart infarct, the obituary in the medical journal—the end! Gina will survive me ten, twenty, maybe thirty years. If I'm turned down, how will Gina react?

Gina had been waiting for the letter just as eagerly and even more confidently. For her everything was so straightforward. She was young—dangerously young for Feldhusen—and ambitious. "You're the right man, Will," she kept saying. "You're a born gynecologist, with your looks and your manner. And your research publications! They can't possibly ask for anything more. Daddy says the same thing. He's talked to Fehling about you. Fehling has a lot of influence with the right people. He's on the City Council. Right where you need him. He has fabulous connections. Daddy and Fehling will manage it. You're the successful type, and that's all there is to it."

He could hear her voice as if she were in the room with him. What she said was true. Hadn't he always been successful? Well —except for the last few years . . . and the times, not any fault of his own, were to blame for that.

Feldhusen stuck his letter opener under the fold of the envelope. The paper tore. He saw letters, figures, rubber stamps. Something flashed through his head: too long for a rejection, far too long!

. . . happy to inform you that you have been appointed to the position. An investigation of your personal and professional qualifications revealed nothing to prevent the acceptance of the committee's recommendation. May I congratulate . . .

Feldhusen took a deep breath. Appointed! Singled out from all the other applicants. Successor to Professor Weinreich as Head of the Department of Obstetrics and Gynecology at the Paul Ehrlich Hospital. One hundred and twenty beds. Six major operations a week. Three hundred a year, not counting the minor ones.

Operations! Slowly he let the letter fall. It was fourteen years since he had operated. No one but himself knew this. Fourteen years behind. Forty-two hundred operations behind. Could he ever make it up?

He looked at the letter opener, and suddenly he seemed to see before him on the desk a gleaming scalpel, flat, pointed, silent, and deadly. Life and death in one. I can't do it, thought Feldhusen. It's impossible. I'll refuse. He stared out the window. Accept? Refuse? He sat like this for quite a while. Everything was quiet.

Then Gina came in, and in an instant everything changed. She saw the letter in his hand. A few swift, light steps, and she was beside him. She snatched up the sheet of paper and read it.

"Oh, Will!" she exclaimed, sitting down on the arm of his chair. "I knew it all along. With Fehling behind you, they couldn't have done anything else. A man like you!" She put her arm around his shoulders and kissed him.

He felt her youthful body, saw her green eyes, caught the fragrance of her skin, and smiled. He was forty-eight; she was twenty-six. Twenty-two years difference. All the same she had fallen for him in a big way two years ago when he had come to her father, after his escape from the Russian zone, to ask for help. Now she was his wife.

He had no regrets. She was right for him, precisely because of her youth and good looks—right for the image he had created of himself. She was proud of him; she loved him. Women always had loved him; in that respect he had never gone short. But Gina was different from all the women before her; she aroused new passions in him; she pushed him, and he liked it; she worshiped him and yet controlled him. Love at forty-eight is different from love at thirty.

"Have you answered it yet?" she asked.

He stroked her bare arm. "The letter only came two minutes ago."

"You'll reply immediately, won't you? Oh, I'm so glad!"

"Yes, darling." Smiling, he pushed her away from him. "I'll answer it."

She took his face in her hands and kissed him again, her lips parted, her breath sweet, then she was gone. He was alone, but her scent still pervaded the room. He reached for the letter and read it again.

After all, why shouldn't it work? He had done some surgery. Fourteen years ago. He could pick it up again. In gynecology there are only a few procedures, which recur over and over again. After the first time or two he'd know how.

He hastily lighted a cigarette. Before him lay his big chance—his last one. Head Physician of the Paul Ehrlich Hospital. On to a new life.

He put out his cigarette and slowly began to write. He wrote that he considered it a privilege to be asked to assume such a responsible position in so pre-eminent a hospital, and he closed:

> In appreciation of the confidence expressed in me by the City Council and in full awareness of the responsibility . . .

Feldhusen was good at writing letters.

Hans-Heinrich Neugebauer, M.D., Senior Physician at the Paul Ehrlich Hospital, had also applied for the vacant position as Head. Not unhopefully, for he knew his own ability, but not with too much confidence either, for he was a clear-headed man and familiar with the devious ways of bureaucracy.

In his capacity as Acting Head of the Gynecology Department he was sitting this morning at the desk of the late Professor Weinreich.

The room was on the second floor, on the sunny side of the building. The deep-pile carpet absorbed all footsteps, and the leather-upholstered double doors kept out all sound, the groaning of women in labor as well as the first cries of the newborn.

Sunbeams slanted through the window. Neugebauer stood up and pushed the curtains aside. Then he crossed to the washbasin and washed his hands slowly and carefully. He could see his face in the mirror. It wasn't handsome, but he could get along with it. As could several other people. There was a knock, and he turned around. Sister Pia stood in the doorway, neat and white as usual.

She came of good family and had graduated from a good school for girls. She had a nice way with private patients. She held a thin manila file in her hand.

"What is it, Pia?" asked Neugebauer.

"Mr. and Mrs. Maurer. You know."

"I know," said Neugebauer. "Bring them in." A knock interrupted him. His eyebrows came together. "Who's that now?"

The nurse shrugged her shoulders.

The man standing in the doorway had a round face and a malicious smile. The sun caught his red tie. Brütsch, the Administrative Director.

"Herr Direktor," said Neugebauer, hanging the towel back on its hook, "what can I do for you?"

"I'd like a word with you, Doctor," said Brütsch. His smile became more intense. "Won't take a moment."

"Right now?" asked Neugebauer. "Private patients don't like to be kept waiting, you know."

"I know," said the Director. His voice didn't go with his face. "They feel more pain than service patients, too."

The two men looked each other in the eye. Suddenly Neugebauer wondered what the fellow was doing here. For a long time now they had confined their contacts to telephone conversations. And now here was Brütsch in person. There was only one possible reason—the Head Physician appointment.

"All right." Neugebauer glanced at the nurse, who went out, closing the door quietly behind her.

The Director passed a sheet of paper across the desk. A letter from the City Council, Department of Public Health. Letterhead, date, signature, seal—all correct. The last tiny glimmer of hope died in Neugebauer as he read the contents:

Effective July 1, 1956, William Feldhusen, M.D., member of the medical faculty, will take over the Department of Obstetrics and Gynecology as Head Physician.

Neugebauer didn't read any further. He let the sheet of paper fall and handed it back.

"I can see you're glad," said Brütsch. "It really was a bit too much for you. It was time we got a new Head."

"Yes," said Neugebauer. I need a cigarette, he thought. I can't. Consulting hours.

"I'm sorry you weren't the lucky man," said Brütsch and kept on smiling.

"I know you are," said Neugebauer. "Let's hope you get over it. And now I must ask you to excuse me. I'm busy."

The Director's bald head turned pink. His smile vanished. He turned abruptly and walked toward the door. It banged behind him.

Neugebauer had remained seated. His hands lay flat on the desk. The clock in front of him ticked with quiet regularity. The dream was over. William Feldhusen, M.D. *Yes indeed, Doctor. I'll be glad to, Doctor.*

He jumped when the door was timidly opened. He hadn't heard any knock. "What is it?" he asked crossly.

The nurse's eyes were round and apprehensive. "Excuse me . . . I thought . . . Mrs. Maurer . . ."

He pulled himself together. "Oh yes. Yes, of course. Bring her in."

By the time Marianne Maurer entered he was in control of himself again. He stood up, smiling.

Her summer suit was tight-fitting and chic. Its vertical stripes made her look even slimmer. Her face was so young-looking that anyone would have thought she had needed the permission of her guardian to get married. Her eyes seemed to be ceaselessly searching for a protector, and her hands were as restless as those of a young girl on her first date. Neugebauer was suddenly overwhelmed with sympathy and a desire to help her. He took her hand and looked her in the face. "Another big bill at the beauty shop?"

She blushed. "Oh no. I haven't been for ages."

"I don't believe a word of it," said Neugebauer. He gently took her arm and guided her to a chair. "Well, how do we stand?"

She pulled at her glove. "It's just the same," she said, without looking at him.

He nodded slowly. He hadn't expected anything else. "In that case, Mrs. Maurer . . ." he said. "Well, anyway let's have a look first."

While he was examining her and his hands were palpating the tumor inside her he forgot about Brütsch and the letter.

The examination over, he went to the washbasin. While he was washing his hands he asked: "Mrs. Maurer, could you stand seeing me around for three weeks?"

In the mirror he saw the shock on her face. "You mean . . . an operation?"

"M'm-h'm."

She was so scared she could not speak. After a while Neugebauer said: "Is your husband with you?"

She nodded.

He went into the waiting room. A well-dressed young man jumped to his feet.

"Mr. Maurer?"

"Yes."

Neugebauer put his hand on his shoulder. "Would you please come in and join us."

Marianne Maurer was standing up. She came toward her husband. Her face still looked pale.

"I have to have an operation."

Maurer turned to Neugebauer. "Is it essential?"

"Essential," said Neugebauer. "Good advice isn't going to cure this."

"And . . . what is it?"

"A myoma," said Neugebauer. "A benign tumor in the muscular tissue of the womb. It's growing slowly, but it's growing. The sooner we get rid of it the better. And the easier."

Maurer reached for his wife's hand. He was still looking at Neugebauer. "And afterward will we still . . . what about children?"

"Of course you can have children," said Neugebauer. "Better

than ever. My wife had the same thing, and we've got four running around now. They make enough racket too, I can tell you."

He smiled, but Maurer's face remained unchanged. "You wouldn't have to remove the womb?"

"No," said Neugebauer. "Sometimes in serious cases it does have to be removed. Your wife has a relatively small tumor, and it's in a favorable position."

"And suppose it's . . . not benign?" asked Marianne Maurer suddenly.

"It's not cancer," said Neugebauer calmly. "You're far too young, and your health is too good. And the tumor is growing too slowly. And it's not in the right place. And if it were cancer, we'd have to do something immediately. The day after tomorrow."

The objective phrases had their effect. Maurer leaned back. His face relaxed. He turned to his wife. "Well, Marianne, let's get it settled, darling. When are you moving in?"

She tried to smile. "You just want to get rid of me."

"Nonsense!" He already had his appointment book in his hand. "Look. Next Monday. That would be the second."

"Oh—so soon?"

"It's over a week. And you'll be back home with me all the sooner."

"That's right," said Neugebauer from behind his desk.

Marianne looked up quickly. "But, Klaus, Daddy's birthday's on the fifth." She seemed pleased to have thought of a way out. This was an old story to Neugebauer.

Maurer wrinkled his brow. "What do you think, Doctor?"

"I think we can make allowance for Daddy. If it had been Auntie, she'd have had to wait."

Marianne looked at him gratefully. Her husband's finger ran along under the dates. "All right, a week's delay. Monday week then. That's the ninth. And the operation?"

"Probably on the Thursday," said Neugebauer. "The twelfth."

Maurer laughed uncertainly. "Better than Friday the thirteenth."

As Neugebauer was writing the name Maurer under the date in his appointment book he felt the stab of pain again. The same pain as before. Thursday, July 12. It won't be you who does it, he thought. The new man will do it. William Feldhusen, M.D. He looked up.

"Something's just occurred to me," he said. "A surprise. Our new Head Physician will perform the operation, Mrs. Maurer."

Marianne was taken aback. "Yes, but . . . after all, you're my doctor . . ."

"Of course. I'll still be your doctor. But from now on the Head will be taking care of major cases."

"Oh," said Marianne. "And why weren't you made Head?"

"Marianne!" said Maurer.

Neugebauer smiled, but there was a pain in his heart. "My beard isn't long enough yet. But don't worry, you'll be in excellent hands. Probably better than mine. And I'll be there to keep an eye on you."

Her eyes were fixed on his mouth. She was prepared to believe anything he said. *In excellent hands*, he had said.

When Neugebauer got home that night the noise his children were making made his ears ring. They were romping about in their pajamas and crowded around him joyfully as he entered the hall. "Off with you and cut out the racket!" he shouted. The children raced off.

His wife came out of the kitchen. "Hello, Hans." She raised her face for a kiss.

"Hello, Lilo. Listen, do we always have to have so much noise at this time of day?"

Her eyes held no reproach. "What's the matter?" she asked.

"Nothing."

He went into his room and closed the door a little more noisily than usual.

Silence spread through the apartment like a physical substance. Neugebauer noticed it and felt ashamed. After a while Liselotte opened the door quietly and came in. She didn't speak, but simply sat down in her chair by the window. Outside a few cars went past.

He said: "The new Head starts on the first."

She got up and closed the window. The room became even quieter. Slowly the curtains came together. "Who is he?" she asked.

"No idea. His name's Feldhusen."

"Professor?"

"He's on the faculty."

"Do you know him?"

"No."

She went around to him and sat down beside him. "Don't be upset," she said. "We knew it all along. You told me yourself that you're too young and that a man hardly ever gets to be Head in the hospital he works at, and you know how many people are in the running for a job of this kind."

"Yes," said Neugebauer grimly. "Plenty. All the ones who were publishing their junk while we were taking care of sick people. And someone in a municipal office, who has no idea what it's all about, stacks up their publications and measures them with a ruler. The highest stack wins."

He unbuttoned his collar and took a cigarette.

"Give me one too," she said.

Soundlessly the smoke curled upward. "Hans," she said softly, "what about the private patients?"

He shrugged. "I don't know. It's up to him. He'll probably take them over. I would in his place."

"All of them?"

"Yes. Why?"

"The payments on the furniture," she said. "Two more months would have done it. If he'd only let you keep a few of them."

His head dropped. She put her arm around his shoulders and kissed him. "Don't worry," she said. "We'll manage somehow. We've managed everything up to now. You'll get on with him all right, I know. That's the main thing. And someday there'll be an opening somewhere for a Head Physician who can operate. Even if he hasn't published a lot of junk."

They smiled at one another through the smoke.

"And now I'm going to make a cup of tea. Would you like one?"

He nodded.

2

The morning of July 1 arrived.

Dr. Feldhusen entered the Medical Director's office, and the picture which Neugebauer's curiosity and anticipation had created of the newcomer was immediately destroyed. He had imagined a tall, gaunt man, uncommunicative, unworldly, carelessly dressed, and with sensitive hands. He saw what is generally called a fine figure of a man.

Feldhusen's hair was thick and dark with iron-gray highlights. His forehead was scarred with fine dueling cuts, and he had one big, gaping scar on his left cheek. It would have made anyone else look aggressive and daring, but Feldhusen wore his scar casually and nonchalantly, as though he were still regretting this minor accident. He had light, lively eyes and a cleft in his chin. The superlative quality of his suit was not apparent at first glance.

Typical gynecologist, thought Neugebauer. The type that decided on his career after a look in the mirror.

Feldhusen shook hands with all of them quickly and unaffectedly, as if he were greeting old acquaintances. "Only three gentlemen, thank heaven, and no brass band with banners!" he said cheerfully. His voice penetrated the room and filled it—a deep, resonant, superior voice. Neugebauer sensed how this man was taking control of the situation with just a few words, and a fleeting stab of embarrassment shot through him. I could never have done that, he thought. I would just have stood there awkwardly.

When it was over and they went across to the Head Physician's outer office, the secretary jumped to her feet, blushed, stammered, and said nothing. The new doctor took her hand and said cheerfully: "My name's Feldhusen. I hope you're going to like me, Fräulein . . ."

"Rieck," she whispered. "Of course, Doctor."

"Don't be so sure," he exclaimed. "I've heard plenty of complaints." He smiled at her, then with a wave of his hand went into the Head Physician's office. Neugebauer followed him.

Feldhusen dropped into a chair and unbuttoned his coat. "Sit down, Neugebauer. Am I glad that's over! Worse than the first day at school." He opened a silver cigarette case. Neugebauer fumbled for matches, but Feldhusen's lighter beat him to it.

They took several deep pulls. Neugebauer kept silent and waited. He saw the light eyes watching him. He dropped his glance and fixed it on the tip of his cigarette.

Suddenly Feldhusen said: "You applied too, didn't you?"

Neugebauer didn't change his position. A warm flush began to rise in his neck, and he hoped it wouldn't show. That was exactly what he had been thinking about, so obsessively and so intensely that the other man must have sensed it. "Yes."

Feldhusen nodded. "I'm sorry," he said. "I'm very sorry. . . ."

There was no trace of insincerity in his voice.

"It was just a trial balloon," said Neugebauer.

"Sure. Same thing with me. I've put in more years on hospital staffs than you, that's all."

Okay, thought Neugebauer. He's not conceited. He looks like a show-off, but he isn't one. He's a human being like me, with his hopes and his disappointments. Lilo's right. I'll get along with him.

There was a knock.

"Yes," called Feldhusen.

"Oh, excuse me," said Fräulein Rieck in the doorway. "The Head Nurse wants to know if she may come in and meet the Head Physician."

"Please ask her to," said Feldhusen. "Just a second—I just have to button my coat."

The Head Nurse came in. She was fifty years old, and all her feminine illusions were behind her. Her one objective was retirement to the convent; her one joy, power; her one weakness, strong black coffee. The expression of professional friendliness which she was forced to assume day in and day out had worn deep lines into her face and now seemed to be a part of it. But the hard eyes beneath her headdress revealed the truth.

Feldhusen came to meet her and took her arm to guide her to a chair, forcing her to sit down. She didn't get a chance to speak. She looked at him, and her lips parted slightly. For heaven's sake, thought Neugebauer, she's melting already.

"I hope the smoke doesn't bother you," said Feldhusen. "Or perhaps you smoke yourself?"

"No, Doctor."

She's eating out of his hand already, thought Neugebauer.

"Oh. But coffee, what about that?"

"Yes." She cast down her eyes bashfully. "Yes, I like coffee."

"Ah, now we've got it! If it isn't one vice it's another! Would it be too much to ask you to make me a cup every day?"

She was gazing at him ecstatically. "Of course, Doctor. I'd be only too glad to."

"Fine. As you no doubt know, Neugebauer, no one in the world makes better coffee than experienced head nurses."

"I don't know much about that," said Neugebauer dryly.

Out of her rapture Sister Louise darted a glance at him. Feldhusen saw it and Feldhusen understood it. They don't like each other, he thought. That can only work in my favor. Divide and conquer. They'll never join forces to attack me. "How long have you been here, Sister?"

"Sixteen years," she said with feeling.

Far too long, thought Neugebauer.

"That's quite a time. And how long have you been in the order?"

"Thirty-one years."

Feldhusen stood up. "I'm delighted to have acquired such an experienced assistant," he said in a warm tone. "We'll meet again soon." She gave a gentle nod. Feldhusen went to the door and opened it. Sister Louise went out without deigning to look at Neugebauer.

That's the way to do it, thought Neugebauer. I've always handled things the wrong way. I could have saved myself a peck of trouble.

Feldhusen came back. "A pillar of the institution," he said. "She'll do. A slight odor of valerian, though. Did you notice?"

"I'm used to it," said Neugebauer.

Feldhusen began to ask questions: residents and interns, cases, hospital routine. Neugebauer gave answers and explanations. There was hardly anything left to discuss—just two points, and they both had them in mind. But Feldhusen didn't bring them up. The last pause was growing lengthier.

"There's one more thing, Doctor," said Neugebauer. "The private patients. What would you like to do about them?"

"Oh yes, I'd forgotten all about them," said Feldhusen casually. "Of course. The cornerstones of our prosperity. Let's see, what was the old arrangement? With my predecessor, I mean?"

"Professor Weinreich left some of them to me. He couldn't take care of all of them in addition to his practice. Since his death I've been responsible for all of them."

"I see. I see." Feldhusen was thinking, without changing his expression. "H'm," he muttered. "Takes up an awful lot of time, that business. But it can't be helped. Word of a new doctor gets around fast, and all the women want to see what he's like and tell him their troubles. I'll make a proposition. You carry on with the present patients, and I'll take over the new ones. Later on we'll come to an arrangement. Okay?"

That means I'll be through in three months, thought Neugebauer. He couldn't have offered me less. But still it should cover the furniture payments. "Yes," he said.

"Fine. When are consulting hours for private patients?"

"Not till tomorrow afternoon."

"Good. I'll be there. Anything else?"

Neugebauer had kept for the last the thing it was going to hurt him most to give up. He took a slip of paper from his breast pocket. "Here's the operations schedule for tomorrow, Doctor," he said. "Would you tell me which ones you'd like to perform?"

"Excellent!" exclaimed Feldhusen. "Let me look at it." As he read, his lips moved. He repeated the names: "Wernicke: laparotomy. Müller: plastic. Steingräber: ovariotomy."

There won't be anything left for me, thought Neugebauer. He'll get his hands on everything he can. I'd do better to get out of here.

Feldhusen handed him the slip back. "Quite a schedule! Really very impressive. But these are all still your cases, Neugebauer. I'd like to get to know the patients first, and I have an awful lot of things to see to these first few days: the administration, formal calls, hands to shake. You know how it is. You go ahead tomorrow as usual with the operations. On Wednesday we'll do the rounds together, and then we'll see. We're not going to get in each other's hair. I'm sure of that."

Postponed, thought Neugebauer. He doesn't want to get on the wrong side of me. But he was relieved all the same. "Just as you like," he said almost happily.

Feldhusen stood up. "That's fine, then."

Neugebauer was accompanied to the door in the same friendly manner as the Head Nurse. As he stepped into the corridor he heard Fräulein Rieck's purring voice and the new doctor's laugh. I've really been doing everything wrong, he thought once more.

When he stood outside his apartment door that evening, he

couldn't hear a sound. He smiled. Liselotte must have taken drastic steps to insure quiet. She opened the door before he could pull out his key ring. He gripped her by the shoulders and kissed her. Then he went into the children's room.

The tea was waiting when he came back. She didn't wait for him to speak. "What's he like?" she asked.

He stuck out his lower lip. "Very nice fellow. Cuts a better figure than your old man."

"Half-wit! What does he look like?"

"Like an actor after a world première. Speaks like one too. Business will boom."

"How old?"

"Middle forties, I'd say."

"Where's he from?"

"I haven't any idea. I didn't ask." He drank a few sips. "You'll be able to hold onto your furniture. He's letting me keep the old private patients."

"Do you think that will be enough?"

"It'll have to be. I'll stretch it out as long as possible."

She filled his cup. "What's he like otherwise?"

"Otherwise? Charming. Gets on the right side of everyone. I don't think he likes trouble."

"Not like you," she said.

Neugebauer kept silent and stared at his cup.

"Is he operating tomorrow?"

"No. . . . No, he doesn't know everyone yet, has to be introduced . . . all sorts of things. No, he's not operating." He was still staring ahead. He was tired.

"That seems odd," she said quietly.

"What seems odd?"

"That he's not operating."

"What's odd about it?" he asked irritably. "I've told you he has to go chasing about being introduced."

"You would never have done that," she said.

Neugebauer kept silent. He was thinking of the operating room with its cool, white walls. He saw the narrow table, smelled the dry, ether-laden air. The noiseless hands seemed very close to him, and the pairs of eyes showing between cap and mask. She was right. He wouldn't voluntarily have missed a single one of these thrilling episodes.

"I'm surprised," she repeated.

"You won't be surprised long." He laughed and patted her hand. "He's sure to begin on Thursday, and then your old man will be through."

But Feldhusen did not begin, not even on Thursday.

He was introduced all round, had an individual session with each of the residents and interns, took care of considerable paper work, went over every corner of his wing of the hospital plant. For a few days he went along on all the ward rounds and soon knew all the patients and amazed everyone by his memory for cases and histories. His reputation increased; his authority grew; his appointment book filled up. The patients were crazy about him.

But he didn't operate.

And although he was popular and respected he lacked one thing for complete acceptance—something that a surgeon can attain only in the operating room, scalpel in hand, on the narrow border line between life and death, where words can never redeem a mistake. Feldhusen was aware of the test ahead of him. He was hesitating, postponing it.

But the day finally came when he could put it off no longer. The Head Physician's rounds were almost over. The long procession of white coats was dispersing at the entrance to the private wing. Only Neugebauer, the resident surgeon, Dr. Krüger, and the floor nurse, Sister Waltraudt, stayed with Feldhusen.

In the last room at the end of the corridor Marianne Maurer had been installed the day before.

Neugebauer knocked and opened the door. He followed Feldhusen in, and the others came after them. He caught a quick glance from Marianne's childlike eyes, then Feldhusen stepped between them.

"Good morning," he said in his cheerful way. He turned to Neugebauer. "We could hold a beauty contest here, Doctor." And then to Marianne: "How do you like it here, Mrs. Maurer? Everything all right?"

"Fine," said Marianne, responding to his cheerful tone. "Just fine."

"That's good." He looked at her again. The dimple in his chin deepened. "Well, Dr. Neugebauer, why have we forced Mrs. Maurer to leave her husband's bed and board?"

The chart rustled. Neugebauer quietly gave the details. "The patient I told you about the day before yesterday. The myoma. Partly intramural."

"Oh yes, of course. I know. Yes, that's all pretty straight-forward." Feldhusen sat down on the edge of Marianne's bed and placed his hand on top of hers. "On Thursday we'll take a look. I hope you're not scared."

"No, Professor," said Marianne obediently.

"Doctor," smiled Feldhusen. "Just plain Doctor. There's no need to be scared. Thursday noon I'll be around to ask you if it was too bad."

She summoned up all her courage. "Are you going to perform the operation, Doctor?"

For a fraction of a second the smile froze on his face, but no one noticed it. *Are you going to perform the operation?* Four wit-nesses to that question.

"We-ell, my dear little lady," he drawled, "it's like this. You're Dr. Neugebauer's patient. He's taken care of you as if he were your legal guardian. He found out what was wrong and diagnosed the trouble. We really ought to give him the satisfaction of mak-ing you well again. Don't you think so?"

He said exactly the same thing in Room 210, thought Krüger. Five hundred marks, thought Neugebauer. Private patient. Hus-band architect; father building contractor. Five hundred marks. The final payment on the furniture and a bit left over. Will he let that slip through his fingers?

"Yes, of course," whispered Marianne. She was terribly embarrassed. "I was only thinking . . ." She stopped. The room was still. Neugebauer, Krüger, Sister Waltraudt—all kept silent. Feldhusen was as conscious of the turning point he had come to as if it had been a stone wall.

Are you going to perform the operation, Doctor?

Put it off, he thought. Put it off just one more time. I'll do it; I'll make a start. Of course I'll make a start. But just wait a bit, just a few days, just one more day. And it doesn't have to be a private patient.

To gain time he asked about her symptoms. He palpated her abdomen, saw the white skin he would have to cut into the next day. With a beaming smile he straightened up. "In any case I'll be there," he said. "Don't worry. Everything will be all right."

Marianne nodded without speaking.

Two men approached Feldhusen as he left the room. He guessed who they were, and his heart sank.

Marianne Maurer's husband moved like a young boy in spite of his custom-made suit. The other man was broad and thickset. He advanced slowly. Feldhusen saw a massive chin and a face which held no room for a smile. A feeling of physical oppression came over him.

"My father-in-law, Mr. Jensen," said Maurer quietly and shyly. "We . . ."

"Good morning, Doctor," said Jensen, as if his son-in-law hadn't said a word. His deep voice boomed through the corridor. "I'd like a word with you if possible."

Feldhusen knew there was no getting away from this man. Neither now nor later. This was Jensen. A former bricklayer, now the city's biggest building contractor, head of his family and of his business. His will was law.

"Certainly, Mr. Jensen. We've just finished. Please come in here, gentlemen. You too, Neugebauer. Thank you, Krüger. Thank you, Sister Waltraudt."

Krüger and the nurse watched the three men walk away. "Is he going to do it?" she asked.

"I think he'll have to," said Dr. Krüger. "He just wanted to spare Neugebauer's sensitive soul. Now he's going to agree, with a bleeding heart, and rake in the five hundred."

"Seems to me it's about time," she said. "When I think of the Old Man . . ."

"Yes. He'd have performed a caesarean on himself if anyone had handed him a knife."

She looked at him reprovingly.

He grinned. "Haven't you got a bottle of beer left in the icebox, Nursie?"

"You alcoholic!" she said, but it didn't sound unfriendly.

Now the four of them were sitting in the office which no longer belonged to Neugebauer. The visitor's chair creaked under Jensen's weight.

"I'm sure you'll understand, gentlemen," said Feldhusen. "I wouldn't want to cut Dr. Neugebauer out of this operation!" He smiled at the silent faces. "You wouldn't want to finish building a house that somebody else had started."

"A house isn't a human being," said Jensen stiffly and without the least trace of cordiality. "The thing is, Dr. Feldhusen, Marianne is a child. She can't stand on her own feet, but she's obstinate. At first she wasn't going to be ill. Wouldn't go to a doctor. Then she didn't want to have an operation. In the end she got used to the idea and to Dr. Neugebauer. And just when she reached that point he told her he wouldn't perform the operation. And the whole nonsense started over again."

Neugebauer looked at Feldhusen. "I assumed . . ."

Feldhusen stopped him with a glance. He knew what Neugebauer had assumed.

"By this time she refused point-blank," Jensen continued in his blunt way. "We had to talk to her like Dutch uncles. Finally she calmed down and began to have confidence in the new Head. And now you come along and tell her you won't perform the operation." His hand dropped heavily on the arm of the chair.

For a moment Feldhusen lowered his eyes. This was it. It was inevitable, and now it had happened. He couldn't get out of it any longer without arousing suspicion. He lighted a cigarette and looked with a wrinkled brow at its glowing tip. Take it easy, he thought. What is it, after all? A simple laparotomy, that's all. Incision, extirpation, sutures. Perfectly simple. It's nothing but fear, he went on to himself. That's all that makes an execution horrible, nothing else. I'm sick of evasions and shilly-shallying. If it has to be, let it be now. And then another thought flashed through his mind: Gina. She's asked me twice already. By the time she gets here on Sunday it will be over and done with. I'll tell her about it, all the details. I know she'll want to hear every bit of it. . . .

He looked up with his usual smile. "I accept your argument, Mr. Jensen," he said. "I'll perform the operation on your daughter."

"Good," said Jensen. For the first time his face showed friendliness. He held out his great hand to Feldhusen.

Marianne Maurer had been given her injection. Cool alcohol on the skin and a faint prick. She lay there waiting. The curtains were drawn, and the morning light seemed to be dammed up behind them. I don't feel anything yet, she thought. I'm sure they didn't give me enough.

Then suddenly, without any warning, a cheerful, buoyant feeling came over her, a reckless exuberance. She lay still, feeling no inclination to move any more. She needed nothing and wanted nothing. She just felt like being nice to everybody and causing no trouble.

She was lifted up, placed on another bed, rolled away. An elevator carried her endlessly up and up. She could hear whispering voices but didn't understand a word. She came to rest in a brightly lighted room, saw white tiles and shining glass. Then she felt very tired.

When she was lifted up again and carefully laid down she did not know whether a minute had elapsed or an hour. Her sense of time was out of action. She opened her eyes. Through a thin, delicate veil she saw Neugebauer's face.

"Go to sleep," he said. "Everything's going to be all right." She felt something prick her left arm, but it didn't hurt. Everything's going to be all right, she thought.

Neugebauer looked at the clock. Ten-twenty. Another ten minutes, he thought.

Feldhusen sat in his office, reading. He had read half the night through, and he was still reading—the same book, like a student trying to cram a little more in the final hour before the examination. *Surgical Techniques in Gynecology.*

He had been through it all a hundred times, through every detail, step by step, considered every complication. Now he was no longer able to absorb any more. The words before his eyes had no meaning—dead letters signifying nothing.

There was a knock.

The Head Nurse crossed the carpet with noiseless footsteps. There were crow's-foot wrinkles around her eyes. "Your coffee, Doctor."

His smile cost him an effort. "Thank you so much. Put it down there. How much longer have I?"

"Ten minutes. Then we ought to begin scrubbing up."

We? thought Feldhusen. Me, not you.

He drank the coffee slowly. Then he left the room and took the elevator upstairs. He was greeted respectfully, with deferential bows.

The Head's operating. . . .

The swing door closed automatically behind him. The smell of ether and disinfectant rose to meet him like a warm wave. Then he was standing between Neugebauer and Krüger at the basin. He scrubbed up, deliberately, smiling, rubbing each finger separately and carefully just as he had been taught to do long ago. No one spoke. They all stared at their soapy hands.

They put on his gown and tied it tightly. His breath was trapped behind his mask. The edge of the muslin mask pressed into his damp forehead. For just a second he felt dizzy.

I can't do it, he thought. I simply can't. "Thank you, Sister Sieglinde," he heard himself saying.

Then he saw the wide iodine-stained strip on Marianne Maurer's skin. The operating room nurse handed him the scalpel with stylish, experienced deftness, without looking up. He felt the ridged handle, saw the blade. He raised his head and looked into Neugebauer's eyes above his mask—dark, with small pupils, but not hostile.

A good thing he's here, thought Feldhusen.

He made a cut.

Incision's far too small, flashed through Neugebauer's mind. He'll never reach it. Or will he? If he does, he's really good. It seemed as though Feldhusen had read his thoughts. He drew the knife another inch, another inch and a half. The incision ran vertically below the navel, parallel to the mid-line, a thin red streak. Neugebauer sponged the seeping blood and clamped the severed blood vessels. The clamps clung to the two edges of the wound like crab's claws.

Feldhusen went deeper. A thin layer of fat, then muscle. He separated the fascia.

The point of the knife trembled, grazed a few muscle fibers, and cut through them. Neugebauer's fingers reached out as if they wanted to take over. He's unsure of himself, he thought. Let's hope he doesn't mess it up.

There was a faint clink as instruments touched. Krüger, the resident, positioned the wide, blunt retractors and held the gaping cut open.

Feldhusen felt perspiration on his face. His back ached from the unfamiliar position. The worst was still to come.

Neugebauer noticed Feldhusen's wet forehead. He signaled to Sister Sieglinde with his eyes. She dabbed Feldhusen's face with a piece of gauze, and he gave her a grateful glance.

They came to the peritoneum. Feldhusen bent over still further. Neugebauer took hold of the shiny, transparent membrane with forceps. Feldhusen stretched it taut on the other side. Midway between the two forceps he slashed through it and stuck his finger through the aperture.

Carefully he lifted the peritoneum and went on cutting. He had almost finished when the knife grazed his glove. A slit appeared in the rubber finger. For a moment his hand was arrested, but no blood appeared. "Sieglinde," said Neugebauer quietly, "another pair of gloves."

With experienced movements Sister Sieglinde put new gloves on the head surgeon. Feldhusen took up his knife again as though nothing had happened.

Lucky devil, thought Krüger. He had been out on the town the night before and was tired. His mask retained the slight aroma of alcohol which came from his mouth, but he could smell it himself and it bothered him. If only the old boy would get on with the job. And then a long cool beer.

"Krüger," said Feldhusen in good-natured reproof, "assisting means helping with the patient, not sleeping with the patient!"

"I'm sorry," murmured Krüger in confusion and pulled his retractors further apart. Neugebauer smiled behind his mask. That stale old surgeons' joke! Sister Sieglinde didn't bat an eyelid. She was no more upset by surgical talk than an apple seller is by worms.

Neugebauer clamped the edges of the exposed peritoneum. When they carefully walled off the intestines, they could see the myoma: a shiny little ball protruding from the wall of the uterus, about the size of a plum and bluish red.

Just as I expected, thought Neugebauer. It extends well into the wall. Will he be able to get it out?

By the time the next ten minutes were over Neugebauer knew that his wife had been right. There was a reason why Feldhusen had avoided operating. He didn't know how.

Feldhusen had begun to dissect out the myoma. But he seemed not to perceive the outlines of the growth. He cut into the mass, then further into healthy tissue. He severed veins, and the numerous blood vessels in the muscular tissue bled more and more freely. The blood obscured his view. Neugebauer clamped and sponged, and his heart hammered. He wanted to reach out and take the knife away from the other man. He saw Sieglinde's expression and knew she was thinking the same thing.

But he didn't do anything. Bit by bit Feldhusen mutilated the living organ. No one prevented him; no one stayed his hand.

Krüger and Regina Florstedt, the anesthetist, felt the tension, although Dr. Florstedt could see nothing and Krüger only part of what was going on. But they could read Neugebauer's face as if it had been a mirror.

Feldhusen realized that his extirpation was a failure. The defect was far too big. No one could ever sew that up. And even if they did, the scar tissue would never withstand labor.

He looked up. "How's the patient, Dr. Florstedt?"

"Doing well, Doctor," she answered. "Pulse 76. Strong. Blood pressure 135."

"Good." Feldhusen hesitated. Neugebauer's eyes were in line with his own. Earlier his glance had given him support; now he was afraid of it.

He mustered all his courage. "Hysterectomy," he said. "There's nothing else to do." He lowered his head as though to fend off protest. But Neugebauer did not say a word. What could he say? It was too late. He helped remove the uterus. Nothing but a little stump was left. A ruin of living flesh.

When the bleeding had been stopped and the first sutures were in place Feldhusen's confidence returned. He closed the abdominal wall layer by layer. Krüger put aside his retractors. Dr. Florstedt removed the mask from Marianne Maurer's face. Sister Sieglinde passed the needle-holders, quick and accurate as she always was. A final snip of catgut and it was all over.

Neugebauer stood by, numb, while the patient was wheeled away. He noticed neither the heat nor the smell of ether. Finished, he thought. No babies for that little girl. A whole lifetime without children. And no grandson and heir for the old man.

Feldhusen guessed his thoughts. "Yes," he said. "I feel really sorry for the poor girl. There was nothing else to do. The growth extended too far into the wall. A defect like that could never have been stitched up."

Neugebauer did not speak. The others did not speak. Feldhusen sensed their unspoken dissent. He mustn't make any further attempt to get them to agree, he realized that. He threw his gloves down in the basin. "Are you coming?" he asked the Senior Physician.

"I still have a D and C," said Neugebauer hastily. It was an exploratory curettage on an old woman suspected of cancer. No hurry. But Neugebauer was glad of it. Right now he wanted to be alone.

"Oh well . . ." said Feldhusen and turned to the others. "Thank you, all of you. If you need me I'll be in my office."

He went out. A young nurse held the door for him. He thanked her with a smile and gave a wave of his hand to the others. Silently they watched him go.

In his office Feldhusen reached for the book he had been reading earlier. The marker showed him his place.

. . . the size of the field of excision and the number of myomas determine the applicability of this technique. The surgeon must be able to estimate the point at which trophopathy of the uterus is likely to ensue. If the success of the extirpation is in doubt, the uterus must be removed . . .

Feldhusen read it again. There he had his alibi. Who could ever prove that trophopathy would not have ensued? Nobody. He had done the safest thing. There would be no more myomas and no complications. He hadn't distinguished himself, but he hadn't been a failure either. Nobody could charge him with that.

When he heard the knock he was momentarily afraid. Neugebauer?

It was Head Nurse Louise. She set the carefully balanced coffee cup on his desk. Her parchment-colored face was beaming.

"Are congratulations in order, Doctor?"

"I suppose so," said Feldhusen with relief. "Thank you very much."

"Did everything go all right?"
"Yes. Perfectly."

Upstairs Neugebauer was standing before the washbasin. The curettage had been quick and simple. The old woman was beginning to awaken slowly. She was groaning faintly, and her thin hands moved rhythmically in the leather straps. Neugebauer smoothed her lank hair silently. Then with weary movements he took off his gown. Sieglinde helped him. She knew what was passing through his mind. She had seen a lot of operations and a lot of hands. She knew instinctively who could operate. The new man couldn't.

"Poor kid," she said quietly. "That could never have happened with Weinreich."

At this point Neugebauer ought to have backed up the Head Physician's authority. He ought to have said: "That's not for you to judge, Sister Sieglinde." He couldn't do it.

"Not with you either," she said just before he went out.

Depressed, Neugebauer started his rounds in the obstetrical ward. He went from door to door, chatting, congratulating, consoling. He saw exhausted faces, discouraged ones, and happy ones. From the nursery at the other end of the hall he could hear shrill crying. As he stood by the tiny bassinets and looked at the wrinkled, worried little faces which were so young and yet looked so ancient, the thought of Marianne Maurer came back to him forcefully and compellingly.

He had advised her to have the operation.

And afterward will we still be able to have children?

Of course you will. Better than ever.

His eyes fell on the Weber baby. The first child of an oldish woman. Overdue baby. Weak labor. Forceps. But there he is. No happier woman in the whole building than his mother. And Marianne Maurer—when she wakes up?

He took his leave and went over to the septic ward. He was in a hurry to get through. "Everything all right?" he asked the nurse.

"Everything's all right, Doctor, except Mrs. Kirchner. She can't stop crying."

"Is that so?" He opened the door of the first private room. In the bed lay a pale, lifeless-looking woman. Her face was pretty, but it bore signs of exhaustion and an expression of despair. When he came in she covered her face with her hands.

"Now, now, Mrs. Kirchner," he said. "That's enough of that. It was a hard river to cross, but we're on the other side now, you and I together."

She didn't stop crying. "I'm so ashamed, Doctor. I'm so ashamed of myself."

"Nothing to be ashamed of," he said.

She went on crying.

He pulled a chair up to her bed and sat down. On the bedside table, in front of a little bunch of violets, stood a photograph of her children, a boy and a little girl, and next to it one of her husband. Neugebauer knew him; he had talked to him the day before—a store clerk, brisk and hard-working, superficially confident but unsure of himself inside, with high hopes and small prospects.

"I shouldn't have done it," sobbed Mrs. Kirchner. "But I just didn't see how . . ."

"Now you're going to stop crying."

"Yes . . . Yes." She groped for her handkerchief and blew her nose.

Neugebauer had seen hundreds of cases like hers. Two children, not enough money, a crowded apartment shared with the husband's parents. The third baby shouldn't have come along, but it did. The authorities refused the application for termination of pregnancy. The woman tried to take matters into her own hands. When she was admitted peritonitis was imminent.

Neugebauer touched her hand. "I'm not a preacher, Mrs. Kirchner," he said. "But you might have died. And then your children would have been left all alone. It's not very likely that a stepmother could handle them properly."

She began to cry again.

He stroked the back of her hand gently. "Everything's all right now. And there's nothing to be ashamed of any more. You're not the only one. Everybody welcomes the first child, and nobody has any objections to the second one if it doesn't come along too soon. But the third one is usually a bit too much, because of the expense. Everybody's just about a hundred marks short. Same with me. You're lucky that you can still have children—in spite of everything."

"I'll never do it again, Doctor."

"All right, Mrs. Kirchner. We can trust each other." He stood up and put his chair back in its place. "We have a young woman in here now," he said quietly, as though he were telling her something he shouldn't, "who wanted children more than anything in the world. She can't have any. Do you have any idea how glad she'd be to change places with you?"

Tears were coming to Mrs. Kirchner's eyes again.

He straightened her sheet. "Everything's all right now," he said. "Go to sleep."

Then he left, closing the door quietly.

Outside he stood still, hesitating. It was lunchtime. But he went back downstairs to the private wing. Silently and carefully he opened the door to the end room. Marianne Maurer lay motionless, her hands still. Her breathing was regular, easier and quieter than before. Narcosis had changed into natural sleep from which she would soon awaken. She still knew nothing; she was still happy.

Keep on sleeping, thought Neugebauer. Sleep as long as you can.

No operations were scheduled for the next day. Neugebauer was thinking about this as he sat in his office before starting on his rounds. But it meant no more than a postponement. The day after tomorrow there would be more, a never ending stream of them, and Feldhusen would have to face up to it, and he himself would have to be present. The telephone gave one shrill ring.

"Neugebauer speaking."

"This is Feldhusen. Good morning, my friend. Did you get a good night's sleep? Excellent! Er, Neugebauer, I'd like to ask you a favor. I've a letter here in my mail from the Health Department, and I'm afraid I'll have to tackle that business over there this morning. Yes . . . yes. So I'd appreciate it if you'd take over my rounds in the private wing. Just for today. Awfully good of you. Fine! Thanks, Neugebauer, thanks a lot. Good-by."

Neugebauer stood up and went over to the private wing. While he was going from room to room, chatting with the patients, joking with them, looking at their case histories and charts, he could still hear Feldhusen's resonant voice in his ear: *Fine! Thanks, Neugebauer.* Funny! Something sounded fishy.

He came to the end room, number 213. Marianne Maurer. The moment he put his hand on the doorknob he knew why Feldhusen had asked him to take over. Feldhusen was a coward. A quitter.

Marianne Maurer looked up and smiled when Neugebauer came in with Dr. Krüger and the nurse. Neugebauer immediately sensed that she had been expecting Feldhusen, not himself. "Sorry to disappoint you first thing in the morning," he said. "Unfortunately the Head is tied up. He'll be along later. In the meantime I've come to tell you how pleased we are with you."

"Pleased with me? What for?"

"For being such a brave girl. The whole operating room says so."

Her eyes shone happily. "Oh, you're just telling me that."

"No, I'm not. Krüger, isn't that right?"

Krüger nodded. "Absolutely. Your Good Conduct Medal's been ordered."

Neugebauer sat down by the bed and moved the sandbag. His fingers pressed the bandage. He gave a few short instructions. Then Marianne asked: "Is everything all right, Doctor? I mean . . . did they . . . get it out?"

He managed to retain his smile. "Yes, it's out," he said. "But you must go on co-operating with us and keep your abdomen quite still. And sleep all you can. When the Head gets here later on we want you to look as glamorous as a fashion model."

"I'll try."

He patted the back of her hand. "Has your husband been to see you?"

"Yes, twice. He's waiting for Dr. Feldhusen outside."

"Aha," said Neugebauer and held out his hand to her. "Well, just go on being a good girl." Then he was gone.

As he was walking down to the next room Maurer hurried over to him. "Ah, Dr. Neugebauer, I'm glad I caught you. I was here earlier, but the secretary told me the Head wouldn't be in this morning."

Wouldn't be in? thought Neugebauer. That hurried explanation and then not in? His secretary's covering up for him. But if he thinks he's going to make me pay for his mistakes, he's wrong.

Maurer looked at him inquiringly. "Perhaps you could——"

Neugebauer didn't let him finish. "If you can come in this afternoon," he said hastily, "you'll be sure of seeing him. He'll tell you all the details then. I don't want to anticipate . . . I'm sure you understand."

"Of course," said Maurer acquiescently. "Everything's all right, isn't it?"

"Yes," replied Neugebauer. His heart rebelled at the lie. "Your wife is doing excellently. You can go in for a few minutes if you like." He shook hands, then walked quickly down the hall. He had to make an effort to hide his anger.

He heard nothing from Feldhusen until late afternoon. By the time he had finished his work it was half past five. Would Feldhusen try to get out of it again?

He picked up the telephone and dialed the Head Physician's number.

Feldhusen was standing by the window in his office. He jumped when the telephone buzzed. Then he crossed over to the desk and picked it up. "Yes?"

"Neugebauer speaking."

"Yes, Neugebauer. What is it?"

"Nothing much. I just wanted to know if you were back on account of the private wing rounds."

Feldhusen frowned. That sounded co-operative enough—a bit too co-operative. The private wing—Mrs. Maurer. Was that it? "I don't quite understand," he said coldly. "Back? I haven't been out. I told you——"

"Yes, you told me. But Mr. Maurer was told you weren't in."

Feldhusen thought he detected derision in Neugebauer's voice. Anger rose up in him. "Sure he was," he said. "You know how it is when you don't want to be disturbed."

"I certainly do, Doctor."

That sounded better. Feldhusen pulled himself together and went on in a friendly tone. "Er, did you tell Mr. Maurer that we had unfortunately been forced to . . ."

"No, I thought I'd better leave that to you."

Again that slight suggestion of derision. "H'm," said Feldhusen. "Oh well, that's all right. Although . . . you could perfectly well have told Mr. Maurer . . . Oh well, never mind." He paused. "By the way, there was something else . . . oh yes, the operating schedule for Tuesday. Is it ready?"

"The opera——" Astonishment showed in Neugebauer's voice. "Yes, I have it here."

"Fine," said Feldhusen coolly. "Please send it over to me. It's time I took some of the load off you."

"Certainly. And the rounds? Would you like me to go with you?"

"No, don't bother, thanks. I'll take care of it myself. Thanks very much, Neugebauer. Good-by."

As Feldhusen was hanging up it occurred to him momentarily that he would be too late by this time to meet young Mrs. Maurer's husband. A good thing too.

Neugebauer still had the receiver in his hand. Operating schedule? Some of the load? "Well I'll be damned!" he said aloud.

He took off his white coat and put on his suit coat. He was looking forward to the weekend with Liselotte and the children.

Krüger was on duty. He wouldn't have to worry about anything until Monday morning.

I'd have every weekend free if I were Head Physician, he thought as he left his office. I wonder if I ever will be. He always took the stairs two at a time. I'm much too awkward for that, he thought, much too awkward.

3

Feldhusen postponed his talk with Maurer until Monday. The weekend came in between. And Gina's visit. There was so much to talk about, especially in connection with the apartment. Gina had the most fantastic plans, and they were all going to come true. The thought of Gina put the Maurer case out of his mind. And then there was the new car. He wanted that to be a surprise for her. The dealer had called that morning.

Feldhusen left the hospital with a light heart. Two o'clock. If he went to pick up the car he wouldn't be able to meet Gina at the station. Never mind. She knew the way to the residential hotel where he was living, and she would wait for him there. Gina could stand on her own feet. Quite different from Trude. Trude, good God! A good thing he was rid of her. A fine woman but absolutely without charm. A homebody. She was a long way off, in the Russian zone. If it hadn't been for the children . . . he thought about them sometimes. Peter must be as tall as his father by now. A senior in school. Better not think about that. Think about Gina.

The car was standing in front of the showroom, new and shiny, with the dealer smiling beside it.

"Pretty good timing, eh, Doctor?"

"Excellent. Registration, license plates, everything taken care of?"

"Everything."

"You wouldn't think to look at her that she'd take so many payments."

The dealer laughed. "Doctor, if you had any idea how many of the cars in this town aren't paid for!"

"I can imagine."

"And not so likely to be paid for as yours."

"Really? Well, I'll do my best to live up to your faith in me. Is she ready to go?"

"She's ready. Good luck, Doctor."

"Thanks." Feldhusen got in and started the motor. It purred. He put it smoothly into gear. Gently the car began to roll. Black and silver. "You must get a black one, of course," Gina had said. "It has to look dignified, but stylish too." He smiled, drove carefully out into the street, and picked up speed.

The residential hotel was in the Gartenstrasse—a bit old-fashioned but quiet and a good neighborhood. Feldhusen had the best room. Not quite his own taste, and certainly not Gina's —the massive furniture and the china and cut glass behind the crystal panes of the mahogany cabinet—but he had to put up with it. It was only temporary. The new apartment would seem all the more up to date.

Frau Grün, the proprietress, greeted him at the door, beaming, with an ill-concealed motherly air. Long-staying guests like Feldhusen were dear to her heart. "Good morning, Doctor. I'm so glad you're back. Mrs. Feldhusen just got here." She came a little closer and dropped her voice. "What a charming wife you have!"

He smiled indulgently. "Would you make us some coffee?"

"It's on already, Doctor. And Mrs. Feldhusen's bed is all made up."

"Good." He bestowed a friendly glance on her and went up

to his room. Gina came to meet him, young, beautiful, affectionate. He drew her close to him, and for a while they joked and chatted about things of no importance. Then Frau Grün served the coffee. "I hope it's the way you like it."

"Of course it's the way we like it," said Feldhusen. "You make better coffee than my Head Nurse."

Frau Grün smiled happily.

"Won't you have a cup with us?" he asked.

Frau Grün declined. "Oh no, Doctor, I couldn't do that. I don't want to take up your time when you have so little of it to spend with your young wife." She disappeared.

"She matches the furniture," said Gina.

"Shsh," he said. "But she takes good care of me. Come on, pour out."

Gina did so. "What about an apartment, Will?"

"Darling, I haven't had a chance to do a thing."

She smiled. "I thought so. Well, just wait. In a couple of weeks I'll have the practice all wound up, and then I'll move over here for good, and you'll see how soon we find a place to live."

He bent over and kissed her. "You're a clever girl. I'll leave it all to you."

"You do that," she said. Then she reached for her handbag. "Mercy, I nearly forgot. A letter from your wife. I've read it. Do you mind?"

He felt a slight ache in the region of his stomach. Letters from Trude always gave him this feeling. Ridiculous, really. He hid his annoyance. "You can read all my letters," he said, "if you'll only get out of the habit of talking about 'my wife.' She's not been my wife for the last two years. You're my wife now. And I hope you don't regret it."

She laughed. "I certainly don't. And I like it better than ever now that I'm the wife of Head Physician Feldhusen. Okay, a letter from your divorced wife. Or simply: a letter from the Russian zone. Is that better?"

"That's better." He took the letter out of the envelope and skimmed through it indifferently.

Dear William,

I have to write to you again . . . Life here isn't easy . . . everything so hard . . . If you could send an extra package from time to time, not for me, for the children . . . You have a well-established practice now. . . . The children are so big now, growing out of everything and costing more and more. Peter takes his final school exams at Easter. He'd like to go to a university in the Western zone . . . his love of medicine . . . Please don't be cross with me for . . . With best wishes,

Trude

He let the letter fall. The boy! He would have to do something for him. No getting around that. He had no feeling at all for Trude. But the boy. Suppose someday he was confronted with him. . . . He'd have to find some way . . .

Gina's voice broke into his thoughts. "Will, that bit about your son is out of the question. You see that, don't you? It would cost far too much. You have so many obligations. He can go to a university over there. In fact that would be much simpler for him."

He frowned. She was right. And another thing: Gina and the boy. That would only lead to complications. On the other hand . . . again that discomfort in the region of his stomach.

Gina took his hand and stroked it tenderly. "You poor man! So much to worry about."

He quickly put the letter in his pocket. Get rid of it. Put it off. It would be quite a time before the boy was through with all his exams. And there was Gina sitting in front of him, consoling him. "Oh, never mind it," he said briskly. "We'll deal with that somehow. With a wife like you I can handle anything."

She smiled and played with his fingers. "Surgeon's hands," she said. "You've got real surgeon's hands. Funny, it's the first time I've noticed it." She looked at him. "Say, how many operations have you performed?"

"One," he said.

"Only one?"

"Darling, have you any idea of all the things a brand-new Head Physician has to see to before he can get down to work?"

"Was it a major one?"

"Pretty major."

"What was it? Come on, tell me."

"A myoma of the uterus."

"Serious?"

"Not at all. Half an hour. She'll soon be up and about again."

"Really!" she said. "When I think of the things you do nowadays! A myoma of the uterus!" She took his hand again and looked at it. "You know," she said, "I'd love to watch you operate someday. It must be marvelous. You must look wonderful in your mask and white cap. And then your hands."

He laughed. "They've got gloves on, and in my mask and cap I look like a convict with hay fever."

She gazed at him with admiration. "Oh no, you don't, Will. If I were a nurse I'd fall in love with you immediately in your mask and cap and rubber gloves." She let go of his hand. "Tell me about it. I want to hear all the details. I think it's terribly interesting. And to think that the life of that poor woman depends on you and your skill!"

Suddenly Feldhusen saw Neugebauer's eyes before him, dark and questioning. He shook off the haunting image, jumped up, took hold of Gina by the waist, and lifted her up. "You're crazy. Absolutely crazy. I'm just another doctor, except that perhaps I've had a bit better luck. Especially where my wife is concerned. Come on, let's go. I've got something to show you."

She put her arms around his neck. "What is it, Will?"

"It's down the street."

"The car!" she shouted. "The car!" She ran out, and he followed her. Frau Grün stepped out of the kitchen with a motherly nod. "Dear Frau Grün," he said, "I'm afraid we'll be home rather late. I hope we won't disturb you."

"Of course you won't, Doctor."

Gina was on the steps already. "Will," she called. "Come on." He winked at Frau Grün and went out.

Frau Grün closed the door behind him. Suddenly her eyes were quite moist. What a couple, she thought. Such a quiet, refined, distinguished gentleman and such an enchanting little wife.

Young Mrs. Maurer's husband was not able to see Feldhusen on Monday morning either. Annoyed and restless, he went home. He was behind in his work, but nevertheless he went back to the hospital at four o'clock and waited until he saw Feldhusen in the hall after his afternoon visits.

Maurer had prepared a few well-phrased remarks in which to express his irritation, but when he was confronted with Feldhusen, his white coat open, grave and yet friendly, followed by a swarm of interns and nurses whom he dismissed with an absent-minded gesture, all he could bring out was a halting "Good afternoon."

"I'm so glad," said Feldhusen in a tone which sounded as though he were really very glad to see Maurer at last. "We've missed each other several times, haven't we? I'm awfully sorry, but a man's not master of his own time. Absolutely snowed under. You know how it is." He took Maurer's arm and opened the door to the ward office. It was empty. "Do sit down."

Maurer sat down on the proffered chair. Feldhusen leaned against the window sill. His face was in the shadow. "You've seen how well your wife is doing?"

Maurer was overwhelmed again with nervous restlessness. "Yes. Yes, she's quite chipper again. But now I'd like to know . . ."

"Certainly." Feldhusen cleared his throat discreetly. "Everything went perfectly, Mr. Maurer," he said, looking at his fingernails. "Absolutely perfectly. Only—the growth was bigger than I had expected."

"Cancer?"

Feldhusen made a gesture in the air. "Certainly not. Who's talking about cancer? No, no, not that at all. No, the tumor was too big, that was all. We had to . . . remove the uterus."

At first Maurer did not understand, but then the enormity of it began to dawn on him.

Feldhusen went on quickly. "I did what I could, Mr. Maurer. There was no alternative. My colleague, Dr. Neugebauer, had slightly underestimated the size. To err is human. Everybody does it sometimes."

"But you examined her too."

"Certainly I did. I was a bit dubious, but I kept it to myself. Why should I destroy your hopes? It wasn't until I began to operate that I saw that the extirpation would not be successful."

Maurer leaned back. Despair was enveloping him like a dark-colored cloth.

"The danger of another myoma has been permanently averted," said Feldhusen like a salesman listing the selling points of an article. "Only . . ."

"No children," said Maurer.

"No."

No children. I can get over it, thought Maurer. But Marianne? And her father! He could not think any further. "You haven't told my wife yet?"

"No, Mr. Maurer. I thought it would be wiser to let her get a bit stronger first. And then we'll tell her. You're the one," he went on in a tone of deep sincerity, "you're the one who can do that better than anybody else."

A brief blaze of hatred flared in Maurer. He? Why should he do it? But grief overwhelmed the other emotion and extinguished it.

"You have my deepest sympathy," said Feldhusen in his resonant voice. "I wish things had gone differently. Time will heal a lot." With this closing phrase he glanced at the clock. "And now I must ask you to excuse me, Mr. Maurer. Duty calls. And please feel free to ask for me any time you . . ."

Maurer nodded absently. He scarcely felt the pressure of the hand which had destroyed all his hopes. He stepped into the hall and saw the door to Marianne's room. He couldn't go in there again. Not now. He went back the way he had come so many times in the last three days. Outside he was bathed in the red of the sunset, but he did not notice it. He went home mechanically, feeling nothing.

Feldhusen was standing by the window in his office. So that's over with, he thought. Thank God! It had been easier than he had feared. And everything had been all right. He had operated like plenty of other men, neither better nor worse.

He was thinking: I can operate. I'll get better every day. I need a bit of practice, that's all. He looked at his hands. Surgeon's hands, Gina had called them. Wasn't that a nice thing to say? She's so sweet. And still romantic. I won't let her down. I'll show her she's right. He went to his desk and picked up the schedule Fräulein Rieck had brought him.

Tuesday, July 17:
1. Gerstenberg, Erna. Prolapse with cystocele. Repair of anterior vaginal wall.

Ah yes. He remembered the woman. Elderly, plump, and talkative. Social insurance patient. Good. They don't make as much fuss as private ones. Displaced womb and a bladder hernia too. Has to be put back and secured. Not easy, but I'll manage it. I'll manage everything.

The next morning he was the first one in the operating room. He wished them all a cheerful good morning, scrubbed up slowly and with enjoyment. After a little while Neugebauer and Warzin, the intern, came in. "Good morning, gentlemen," said Feldhusen.

"Morning, Doctor," they said. The water trickled over their hands. Warzin saw Feldhusen's Roman profile in the mirror. That's the way I should look, he thought. Warzin wasn't as handsome as he would have liked, though he was never short of girl friends. Apart from his professional career he devoted himself solely to the female sex between the ages of eighteen and twenty-five.

Feldhusen turned his head toward Neugebauer without looking directly at him. "By the way, I talked to Mr. Maurer yesterday." He was waiting for an answer, but none came.

"Yes. The young fellow took it pretty well. He's going to break it to his wife. Not too easy for either of them."

Not too easy. No.

"Too bad they haven't got a child already," Feldhusen went on. "One man wants one; the other doesn't. And it's always the wrong man who gets it. I remember a case . . ."

He went on talking as he soaped and scrubbed. Neugebauer listened in silence, and slowly a loathing rose in him. He thought of his four children and of Liselotte. Suppose Liselotte had fallen into the hands of a man like Feldhusen when she . . .

The patient was brought in, a flat form beneath white sheets. Feldhusen finished his story. Regina Florstedt began the anesthetic. Then they set to work. After a few minutes Neugebauer knew that Marianne Maurer had not been an isolated case or just beginner's bad luck. Feldhusen didn't have the technique. His movements were uncertain, his cutting timid. He spared minor structures and cut through major ones and was soon groping around in a mess of blood and tissue.

When he came to detach the bladder from the cervix he had reached the limit of his ability.

With a hammering heart Neugebauer followed the course of the blade in Feldhusen's hand. He edged the bladder aside and stretched the tissue as tight as he could to show him the way. It did no good. The next stroke of the scalpel took its point deep into the bladder wall.

Feldhusen's hand jumped back. "Damn!" he exclaimed. In the first moment of shock he glanced up at Neugebauer, then back to the field of surgery.

Neugebauer's fingers clenched as though he wanted to snatch the knife from the other man. Warzin frowned. Sister Sieglinde's eyes grew large and round.

"Suture," said Neugebauer over his shoulder. A moment later the needle-holder was in his hand. "Just a minute." Without waiting for permission, he took three stitches in the cut. He worked fast, and they held.

"Thank you, Neugebauer," murmured Feldhusen. "Too bad."

He became more careful. Again and again he glanced at Neugebauer's fingers, which were guiding his hands as though with invisible threads, exposing the outlines to his knife. He had already taken far too long. Sister Sieglinde and Dr. Florstedt exchanged looks. Warzin cursed under his breath and glanced at the clock more and more often. The line of empty ether containers grew longer. The woman's breath rattled.

Feldhusen sensed the impatience around him. It made him angry and nervous. He was new; he wasn't used to the team yet. They weren't making allowances for him; they weren't giving him a chance. They'd better watch out.

When the last suture was finally in place Neugebauer felt worn out and depressed. Sister Sieglinde helped him out of his gown, without bothering about the Head Physician. Feldhusen didn't seem to notice. He tossed his cap and mask into the basket and went out without a word, his hands in his coat pockets.

When Neugebauer had left Warzin said aloud: "Thank God that's over. I thought I'd grow roots into the floor. If he always takes this long, I'll send my landlady to him. She has a weak heart. She'd never live through an anesthetic like that. Sieglinde, you old army sergeant, let's take a break! Haven't you got a Coca-Cola on ice?" Laughing at his own jokes, he went over to the doctors' lounge.

Upstairs in his office Neugebauer sat down at his desk and propped his head on his hands. He needed time to think things out slowly. He can't operate, he thought. And it doesn't look as if he ever will be able to. Good grief, how could the man ever have applied for the job? He lighted a cigarette, and as he smoked his tension relaxed. He'll never learn, he thought, judging by what he's shown up to now. Some people simply don't have the knack—like driving a car. When's he going to realize it? Never. He's not the type that goes in for self-analysis.

But what's to be done? thought Neugebauer. Am I to shut my eyes to it indefinitely?

He sat silent and still for a while. Then with a slow movement he pulled open the desk drawer. He groped around until he found a narrow notebook with a shiny black cover. He opened it and leafed over the pages to the middle. He hesitated a moment, then he picked up his ball-point pen. "Feldhusen: Operations" he wrote and underlined the words.

Thursday, July 12. Marianne Maurer, 22. Myoma. Intramural. Size of a pigeon's egg. Hysterectomy for no cogent reason.

Tuesday, July 17. Erna Gerstenberg, 52. Prolapse. Cystocele. Repair of anterior vaginal wall. Bladder perforated. Time: 1¾ hours.

He saw his own writing as though it were that of a stranger. Where was this going to lead him? Abruptly he slammed the notebook closed, put it back in the drawer, turned the key, and stood up. Then he left the room.

When he stepped into the corridor Marianne Maurer's husband came up to him. Neugebauer slowed down. "Good morning, Mr. Maurer, how's everything going?"

Maurer stared past him. "Good morning, Doctor," he said and walked on.

Neugebauer looked after him in astonishment until the door of the private wing closed automatically behind him. He's at the end of his rope, he thought. I would be too in his place. I wonder if she knows yet. What's she going to do when she finds out?

Marianne Maurer found out ten days after her operation, on a Sunday.

She was sitting up in bed, leaning back on her pillows. She had slept well and felt on top of the world. The sandbag was gone, the wound almost healed. Two days ago Feldhusen had taken out her stitches, with a lot of jokes and compliments. She could eat and drink whatever she liked. Sister Waltraudt was as nice as she could possibly be, and Dr. Krüger stopped in more often than necessary, made her laugh and called her "Miss Private Wing."

Only her husband wasn't his usual self. He looked at her; he smiled; but his lips felt cold, as if he were chilly.

"Sit down," she said. "No, not on my sweater! Hang it up here. That's it. And now tell me everything that's going on at home. What do you do all day long?"

"We're waiting for you," he said.

"I'll be home soon. Dr. Krüger said so. I'll certainly be out early next week. You know, he's awfully nice. They all are. Especially Dr. Feldhusen." She took his arm and drew him closer to her. "Klaus dear, when I have a baby I'll come back here."

Maurer shrank. He crumpled as though hit by an invisible bullet.

"Whatever's the matter?" she asked, confused. "You're always acting so strangely nowadays. Is anything wrong?"

He put his hands over his eyes without answering.

"Klaus dear," she said impatiently. "Don't make me worm everything out of you bit by bit. What's wrong? Is it something at home, something about Father?"

"No," he said, between his fingers. "Something about you."

She flinched. A tiny frown appeared above her nose. She pulled his arm down lower. "About me? What is it? Tell me, for goodness' sake."

God help both of us, he thought. His words came out faltering and husky. "Marianne . . . maybe I should have told you sooner, but we . . . I wanted to wait till you were better."

Her eyes widened. "Why? Whatever is it? I'm fine. Is it anything—serious?"

He tried to smile but it was a miserable failure. "Serious—serious . . . well, it's not exactly serious, but . . ."

She was getting annoyed. "Don't make such a fuss, for pity's sake. Just tell me."

He moistened his lips. "Listen, Marianne. On the whole everything went perfectly all right. You're well, and you're not going to get sick any more. Only . . . Neugebauer made a wrong diagnosis. The growth was much bigger. I'm thankful it was Feld-husen who did the operation. But . . ."

She had a sudden inkling, like some terrible omen in the sky. "Klaus, what is it?"

Every word weighed a ton. "Children . . . that won't work any more."

She turned as white as snow. He bent over her, but she pushed him away. Everything he loved in her had vanished from her face. Her mouth was twisted.

He stretched out his arms. "Marianne!"

"Leave me alone," she shouted. "I never wanted this, and Fa-ther never wanted it. It was your fault and yours alone. 'Just go to the hospital, Marianne dear. It's nothing. Just a minor oper-ation.' Yes, so minor that none of you had the courage to tell me the truth! Pussyfooting around, the whole lot of you, patting my hand and lying to me! You too! You of all people—my husband!"

She could tell from his face how much he was suffering; she was conscious of her own unfairness, but something compelled her to hurl herself into the very depths of this abyss until she touched bottom.

"Get out," she screamed. "Get out. I simply don't want to see you."

She buried her face in the pillows, and her words were smoth-ered. Waves of sobbing shook her body. Everything melted in a flood of tears—her anger, her desire to hurt him, her unfairness. There was nothing left but overwhelming sorrow.

No children. No children, ever. All the riches in the world could never make up for what had been denied her: the prospect of walking along the street with a son two heads taller than herself.

Klaus Maurer sat still and silent. He did not dare to touch her; he scarcely breathed. He forgave her even before he felt any re-sentment, but her outburst had kindled in him a fierce hatred of Neugebauer, and it clung like a poisonous weed.

The door opened soundlessly. Sister Waltraudt appeared. She

saw, and she understood. She took Maurer's arm tactfully. He followed her, unresisting.

"Go home now," she said. "I'll give her something. Tomorrow everything will look different."

He nodded. He left without looking back.

Across in the other wing Feldhusen was in the middle of his private consultations. He was in magnificent spirits. This was his element, the role Gina wanted for him: the Man in White in all his glory.

The woman sitting opposite him was going through the change of life. She was dressed with tasteful elegance; her make-up was sophisticated, her diamonds large and expensive. But she took no pleasure in these things any more. She took no pleasure in anything since this extraordinary change had cast its shadow over her life, something she had hitherto regarded with indifference and reassuring clichés. The lines of her face had grown sharper, her eyes had lost their brilliance. It was an expression Feldhusen had seen often enough before, a mixture of tiredness and distrust, nervousness and envy. She was no longer attractive, either to herself or to other people. She didn't want to submit to this fate and accept the inevitable. She made an illness of it and began to play the part of a martyr. The doctor's office became her refuge, doctors her confessors. She had been one of the first to come to the new Head Physician.

Feldhusen listened to the complaining account of her symptoms with utter seriousness. It was as if he had never seen a case like this, as though it were the most important and interesting case in the world. She had money, he could tell, and her file card confirmed it.

The way he listened did her good. Here was a doctor who had time to spare, who didn't interrupt, who had understanding and sympathy. She had realized it even during her first visit.

She left feeling more contented than she had for a long time. His treatment was no different from the standard one. But that didn't matter. She had found a new refuge on the painful road to old age—this office and this man with wisdom in his eyes and warmth in his hands.

"You must come and see us sometime," she said as she left. Feldhusen bowed with a smile and closed the door behind her.

From the desk came the subdued buzz of the telephone. He heard Sister Waltraudt's voice. Mrs. Maurer had just suffered a shock, and she could not calm her. Would the doctor perhaps . . .

Feldhusen hated interruptions like this. He would have liked to leave it to Neugebauer or Krüger, but in this case he would have to go. "I'll be right over," he said.

Sister Waltraudt stood up as he entered the room. She placed the chair for him and went out without waiting to be asked.

He smoothed Marianne's tousled hair. "Cry all you want to," he said.

Marianne was ashamed that he should see her like this. She swallowed a sob, groped for her handkerchief. Feldhusen handed it to her.

"I know how you feel," he said. "As far as a man can possibly know, I do. No one would be as glad as I if you could be happy. Please believe me."

Marianne turned over on her back. Feldhusen's voice was caressing her.

She nodded with closed eyes. How good of him to come! He sympathized with her and understood. "Please excuse me," she said hesitantly. "I'm behaving like a child. It's so silly of me . . ." Her tears began to flow again.

Feldhusen looked up at the ceiling as if in search of inspiration. He took out his own handkerchief and dabbed her face. She opened her eyes and tried to smile.

"Now you're going to take a nice little pill and go to sleep," he said. "Sleep heals. Tomorrow the sun will be shining again. You must be thankful that at least you're well again." He gestured toward her abdomen. "It wasn't so easy, that."

Slowly she turned her head. "I didn't want to have the operation. It was my husband who wanted it."

"Your husband was right," he said. "You weren't a normal human being any more with that thing. The growth was too big. You should have been told that in the first place." He stopped, and his unspoken words laid the blame on Neugebauer.

"No more crying," he said. "You're my favorite patient, after all. And my bravest. But you mustn't cry any more. Or do you want to make things even harder for me?"

"You're so kind," she whispered.

He smiled. "Now you're going to sleep. And tomorrow I'll be in to see you first of anyone." He gave her a fatherly nod and went out.

In his office he hastily washed his hands and sat down at his desk. When the next patient came in all thought of Marianne Maurer vanished.

She was tall, with a full but supple figure. Her suit was stretched tightly over her body, which seemed somehow to resent the fabric. Her movements were self-confident and full of energy. Her gray-green eyes looked him over without shyness or embarrassment. Above her forehead was a mass of hair like a helmet of red gold.

Well, well, he thought. Might be dangerous if it weren't for Gina! He laughed and dropped his eyes quickly to her card. Mrs. Vera Manders, he read. She was thirty-three and lived in the wealthy section of town. Manders? Manders? The name was familiar; it was a well-known one in the city. Ah yes, a huge manufacturing corporation. Ball bearings or something. Plenty of money. Good connections all over the place. His reaction was prompt and accurate. He looked her full in the face, laughing. "You look perfectly healthy, Mrs. Manders. Are you sure you want to see me?"

She smiled spontaneously. "Of course I do."

"And do you mind if I ask how you happened to come to me? After all, I've only been here three weeks."

"That's just it," she said frankly. "That sort of news travels fast. A friend of mine recommended you."

A friend of hers. So that was it. She probably had plenty more friends too. "Thank you for your confidence," he said. "That's what keeps us going. I'll try to live up to it." She looked at him. Nice, she thought. And good-looking. Even better than Karla's description. Marvelous eyes. She looked at his hands. Nice masculine hands that you wouldn't mind being touched by. Married? No matter. Men like him were often married to nice, plain homebodies.

He understood her glance. He knew the type. Bored with her marriage; too much money; too much time on her hands. Husband always on the go and endlessly overworked. Children—if there were any—away at boarding school. Time was he would have been attracted to her. Now he had Gina. Thank God. Now he was free and invulnerable. He could flirt with her a bit, and whatever happened he must make sure of her. "I don't see how I'm to get a chance to prove whether I'm a good doctor or not," he said. "You look the picture of health."

"But I get pains," she said, pouting.

Feldhusen shook his head. "That's bad. That's bad. Where?"

"In my back." She stretched and gripped her back with her hands. "Here. I've been to an orthopedist. He said I ought to be examined by a gynecologist. Just to make sure." Her voice was coy and full of a calculated innocence. "When I play tennis or when I'm doing my setting-up exercises . . ."

"Setting-up exercises?" queried Feldhusen.

"Well, you can't skip those, can you?" she said seriously, though not quite sure of herself.

"Oh, can't you? H'm. I can think of some setting-up exercises that wouldn't give you a backache."

She drew herself up slightly. Her eyes never left his. What was he going to say next?

What he said was: "Ear lobes down. Shoulders up. Ear lobes up. Stop!"

For a moment she didn't react. Then she began to laugh, loud and unrestrained, and she laughed and laughed and couldn't stop. Feldhusen watched her with unconcealed benevolence. Another permanent patient, he thought cheerfully.

He quickly discovered that there was nothing at all wrong with her gynecologically. Her body was limber from exercise. Nothing organically wrong anywhere. She immediately thought up something else and complained of a painful cough which bothered her at night. He examined her lungs and percussed with impressive solemnity. Nothing there either. A private patient with plenty of money who would give him no trouble. She would be back, he knew, and several of her friends would follow her.

He prescribed some medicine which did no one any good except the manufacturer. "I don't want to contradict the orthopedist," he said. "But come back in a couple of weeks and let me know if you feel better."

She made a pretense of considering whether she would be able to come back in a couple of weeks. She would. "All right," she said. "Same time?" She shook his hand with a strong, warm grip, and he accompanied her to the door. Her expensive perfume pervaded his office for a while and aroused an eager longing for Gina.

By evening the longing was still with him. He called Gina up and had a long talk with her. She told him about three apartments the agent had suggested, all of which were possible. Expensive, very expensive, but Daddy was willing to help out. "Good-by till Saturday, Will. I'm looking forward to it so much. And take care of yourself. Don't work too hard. Love and kisses, darling."

Now he was in a mood to answer the letter from the Russian zone. He wrote:

Dear Trude,

I'm afraid you have a false impression of conditions here in the West. We have to work hard for every pfennig. I have recently given up my practice and taken a hospital position. For a man of my age it's not easy today to make a fresh start. Bear this in mind when you ask me for help. In future I'll try to send something extra for the children. I've been thinking about Peter's plans, but so far I don't see what I can do. But there's no hurry. Give the children my love,

                                                    William

Thoughtfully he folded the letter, wondering if he hadn't perhaps committed himself too far. Perhaps it would be better not to answer at all. The alimony she had been awarded was paid regularly anyhow. Trude would only take the letter as a justification for writing to him again. Despite the divorce and the unpleasantness it had involved, in some peculiar middle-class way Trude still felt she was inseparably bound to him. This bothered him considerably.

He hurriedly put the letter in an envelope and left it there for the time being, unaddressed.

4

The next morning Feldhusen performed his first major, radical operation.

Ilse Zenker was the woman's name. She was thirty-five. She had borne three children and never been ill until her last birthday. But six months ago she had begun to be frightened.

She started to bleed between her regular periods. Not much, just a faint trace of red. No pain, no feeling of indisposition. "A show," people used to call it in her part of the country. It happened twice, then stopped. She waited, and nothing happened; she felt relieved and forgot about it.

Then it happened again. The dread, which had left her, overwhelmed her anew. She told her neighbor about it, but not her husband. The woman reassured her and gave her some medicine which had been lying forgotten among countless other boxes and bottles in the drawer of her bedside table.

Ilse Zenker took a few doses, then stopped. Again things seemed to improve. New hope was born, only to be destroyed again within a few months. And that same day she read a magazine article on cancer. She had never given it a thought before; now the word tangled round her heart like a death-bringing net, tightening and settling in her dreams. The dread drove her to the doctor.

He was a young man, new to the neighborhood, not yet approved for appointment to the local health insurance panel. He earned his living by substituting for other doctors, treating a few rare private patients and taking over other doctors' night calls. His ambition and his wife's desire for worldly goods both intensified his fanatical preoccupation with his work. He had had little experience and was still unsure of himself. He tried to use medical school techniques in general practice, did a lot of things that were unnecessary, and omitted a lot that were important. He examined his new patient thoroughly and loquaciously, found nothing wrong, and prescribed an antiseptic.

Could it possibly be cancer?

Nonsense! At her age? Of course not. On her card he wrote: Carcinophobia—morbid fear of cancer.

She went away, but her suspicions persisted. She did as she had been told. For a long time everything was all right again. Then all of a sudden the disease showed its alarming mark once more. With fear growing at her heart Ilse waited three months until she could get a new health insurance permit for an examination. Then she went to another doctor. Perhaps it really was something serious. He was old, with a small practice. He listened patiently, until she stopped talking of her own accord. He examined her, confirmed the findings of his young colleague, and backed him up. Nevertheless he sent her to a gynecologist he knew.

This was a big, up-to-date practice. The waiting room was crowded, but every case was dealt with quickly. Ilse took no part in the conversations in which the women gave detailed descriptions of their symptoms while they waited. She was frightened now, really frightened. Beneath his white hair the doctor had a young face. He didn't let her talk much, but he spent longer examining her than either of the others. However he found no growth and no suspicious areas in the mucous membrane. Everything seemed normal. Nothing wrong in the connective tissue either.

The doctor was overworked. More serious cases were waiting. He decided against a curettage for the present. He told Ilse Zenker to be sure and come back regularly.

This time she felt reassured. She had no pain of any kind. But in the depths of her body the cancer cells were proliferating.

When she came back after four weeks for her routine examination the doctor experienced a violent stab of shock. The cervix was hard, lumpy, seriously distended. To its right a thick, painless cord led into the connective tissue. This was one of those treacherous cancers that undermine the mucous membrane without immediately becoming palpable or visible.

Now everything proceeded as fast as it should have proceeded a year earlier. The D and C took place the following day. Within the gleaming focus of the microscope lay the deadly cells: still, immobilized, harmless; a vivid, chaotic mosaic; immature, varying in size, with numerous juvenile cell nuclei. Cancer in its most malevolent form, which grows fast and destroys the tissues like a devouring flame.

Her husband was told the truth. Ilse was told what everyone is told in similar cases: "A suspicion. Just a suspicion, Frau Zenker. Don't worry. But you'll have to have an operation. Just to be on the safe side."

The operation she faced was major and dangerous. The surgeon would be obliged to go as far as was humanly possible so as to leave no place for dispersed cancer cells to establish themselves. Any tissue he left behind would be a source of new danger.

Feldhusen sat up half the night before his book. Wertheim's operation. The biggest and most serious gynecological intervention that existed. If he brought this off, he was over the hump. It had to be successful. The next morning he was in good spirits, although he had hardly slept. His optimism was encouraging, his confidence contagious. Neugebauer scrutinized him. It's going to be all right, he thought.

Neugebauer and Krüger were assisting. Feldhusen began vigorously, with marked self-confidence. The field of surgery was soon exposed. Luck worked in his favor. Everything was clear and plainly to be seen. No abnormal misplacement of organs, no serious adhesions. The further they progressed, the more relieved Neugebauer felt.

But suddenly Feldhusen faltered. The delicate work was taking all his energy; the terrific tension was exceeding his reserves. He grew impatient, unsteady. His hands refused to obey; his eye lost its precision. He had overrated himself. It was too much for him.

Everybody saw that Feldhusen was not exploiting the technique to the full. He failed to cut to the very limit, left far too much tissue behind, worked sloppily, without precision. Time was pressing him; he must get it finished and vindicate himself, both in his own eyes and the others!

He summoned up all the strength in him. Get on with it. Finish. That was all that mattered.

And so it happened that he missed his objective. The operation was incomplete, not radical as it was meant to be; the danger was not removed once and for all. The cancer could keep on proliferating in every lymph node that Feldhusen had failed to find, in every fiber that had escaped his knife. Neugebauer watched in silence. The vein in his temple had swollen to a blue cord. What was the point of it? What was the point of this senseless half operation which was totally useless? What sort of man was he, this man he was helping instead of hindering?

Feldhusen began the sutures.

"Sister Sieglinde," asked Neugebauer without raising his voice, "are all the sponges accounted for?"

Sieglinde looked mortified. The long duration, the silent tension, had confused her. She had forgotten to count. In trembling haste she checked the bloodstained pieces of gauze.

". . . four, five . . ."

She counted again. "There's one missing, Doctor," she said in a husky voice.

Feldhusen's forehead grew red. "Please be more careful," he shouted at her. "What are you here for anyhow?" There was no trace left of his courteous, superior manner. Without a word Neugebauer went into action. His hand felt its way quickly and gently through the gaping aperture. Deep down in the narrow pelvis he found the sponge. Feldhusen dropped his head and kept on grimly taking sutures.

Then Ilse Zenker was wheeled away. Feldhusen left, pale, exhausted, sticky with perspiration. No one looked him in the face, but in all their minds there was one single thought: he doesn't know how. He's failed.

Slowly Neugebauer untied the tapes of his gown.

"I'm terribly sorry, Doctor," Sieglinde was murmuring at his side. "I've never done a thing like that before—never."

"There always has to be a first time," said Neugebauer hoarsely. "From now on each of us will have to be doubly careful. Do you see what I mean?"

"Yes, Doctor."

Then he left too.

The pages of the black notebook curved as he flicked them over noiselessly. Neugebauer could feel the draft they made. He had entered Ilse Zenker as the third case. He looked at the words his hand had written, and he did not know what he ought to do. Was this treason? Was it right to collect evidence against one's own boss?

But the blunders were there. Three blunders. An unnecessary hysterectomy; an incomplete radical operation for cancer; perforation of a bladder. Not to mention uncertainty and inadequate technique.

Where was one to draw the line?

At what point could one assume the right to accuse a colleague of incompetence and to destroy him? Failures were not uncommon. He had made mistakes himself. Should he cast the first stone? Wouldn't people say: "He's jealous of the man's position"?

He closed the book abruptly and hid it in the drawer, far back under some other papers, as though he wanted nothing further to do with it.

Outside it was getting dark. While Neugebauer was washing his hands he saw his tired face in the mirror. His life had gone so smoothly up to now. Why couldn't it continue the same way? He changed his coat and left the office.

Slowly he went downstairs, out through the main entrance and along the walk leading past the lawns and trees of the garden to the rear exit. Before he reached it Marianne Maurer came toward him on one of the side paths. She was walking in the middle between her husband and her father, the thick-set Mr. Jensen. They saw him before he saw them. Marianne dropped her eyes. The men's faces took on a stony expression. The group turned aside to let Neugebauer pass.

Now he remembered Maurer's cool greeting in the hall of the private wing. A prickling nervousness came over him. He wanted to know what they had against him. He turned to his left, blocking their path. "Good evening, gentlemen," he said. "Good evening, Mrs. Maurer. I'm glad to see you looking so well."

Marianne did not answer. Her lips began to quiver. She jerked her head around to her husband's shoulder.

Neugebauer was startled. "Now, Mrs. Maurer," he said, "whatever's the matter?"

"Klaus." Jensen's tone permitted no resistance. "Go on ahead with Marianne." Maurer walked protectively on with his young wife without paying any attention to the doctor.

Neugebauer saw Jensen's face. They were standing close to each other, as though one of them was about to tell a joke which he didn't want overheard.

"You know very well what's the matter," said Jensen in a hard voice. "Or don't you?"

"Of course I know," answered Neugebauer. "And I'm extremely sorry."

The other man's jaw jutted forward. "And so you should be."

Neugebauer took a step backward, more astonished than annoyed. "May I ask you to express yourself a bit more clearly, Mr. Jensen?"

"Certainly, Doctor. Your diagnosis was wrong."

"What?" A surge of rage welled up in Neugebauer. "Who says so?"

Jensen drew his head back slightly. He was becoming less sure of himself. He was remembering doctors' sensitivity about things of this kind. It might lead to a slander action, and then they would all gang up on him. "At any rate it was inaccurate," he said.

Neugebauer exhaled between his teeth. His voice was harsh and somber. "Oh? Inaccurate? And where did you get this interesting information?"

"This interesting information is the opinion of your Head Physician."

Feldhusen? Was it possible? Neugebauer turned pale. "I'd like an explanation, Mr. Jensen. What is the opinion of the Head Physician?"

Jensen did not dare to go any further. He had said enough. "I suggest you ask him yourself. Good evening, Doctor."

He walked past Neugebauer, who stood stock-still. Curious glances were directed at the doctor. He went back into the hospital with hurried steps. But Feldhusen was no longer in the building.

The next morning at twenty minutes to twelve Neugebauer entered Feldhusen's outer office. "Is the Head in?"

"Yes, Doctor. Shall I tell him you'd like to see him?"

"Yes, please."

Fräulein Rieck spoke on the telephone. Feldhusen's cheery voice asked him to come in. He was sitting at his desk smoking. "Good morning, Neugebauer. Do sit down."

Neugebauer remained standing, with threatening eyes.

"Why, is anything wrong?"

"Yes. I met the Maurer family last night in the garden. Mr. Jensen accused me of making a wrong diagnosis on his daughter.

When I pressed him he said that was your opinion." Neugebauer's voice was husky with anger.

Feldhusen's reaction was not what he had expected. He smiled indulgently and intimately. "Wrong diagnosis! Oh my, what a tragedy! Now, Neugebauer, first of all, do sit down. You look so uncomfortable."

Neugebauer hesitated. Then he sat down, stiff and straight.

"Of course that's utter nonsense," said Feldhusen.

"Dr. Feldhusen," insisted Neugebauer, "I'd like to know what you told the Maurers."

Feldhusen maintained his benevolent attitude, although there wasn't a trace of deference in Neugebauer's tone. "Certainly," he replied. "I told them exactly what you would have told them. What else could I do? She was desperate—understandably. I talked to her as if she'd been a sick child . . ." He stood up and walked back and forth across the room. He kept his left hand in his pocket; with the right he made gestures in the air as if he wanted to emphasize every word, like a general expounding his strategy to a not very bright officer. " 'Mrs. Maurer,' I said, 'the growth was too big. The defect could never have been repaired. Do you think we don't realize what that meant for you? There was no other way out.' " He looked at Neugebauer. "Those were my words. Wrong diagnosis was never mentioned. You know as well as I do what patients can make of such an episode when they're upset. 'My dear child,' I said to her, 'we were mistaken. Dr. Neugebauer was mistaken, and I was mistaken. We're human after all——' "

"I was not mistaken, Doctor," said Neugebauer coldly.

Feldhusen remained standing. For a moment he was seized with the same feeling that had overwhelmed him when his acceptance had arrived from the Health Department and he hadn't dared to open the letter: the haunting knowledge of his lost years, the terror of not being good enough, the fear of failure. But he obliterated it all. The warmth disappeared from his expression. "Oh, you weren't mistaken? Never in your life? I must congratulate you, Doctor, on your infallibility."

Neugebauer felt the blood rush to his forehead. "That's not what I mean . . ." he stuttered. Why did he have to feel embarrassed, damn it? Anger rose in him. He searched for words, cold, pointed, devastating words, and couldn't find them.

But Feldhusen had already undergone another transformation. He went to his desk, sat down, pressed his well-cared-for hands together. "Now, Neugebauer, what about it? Are we going to let our valuable partnership be ruined by a few stupid words? A man like you, a surgeon of your ability, such a reliable colleague, really ought to be above that sort of thing!" He sat at his desk like a school principal giving a misguided child a friendly talking-to.

Neugebauer sensed this and felt humiliated. "No, of course not," he said hastily. "I simply wanted——"

Feldhusen interrupted him. "My dear Neugebauer," he said in his ringing voice. "I know your ability better than anyone else. You applied for this job too—and with good reason, although you're so young. Well, you didn't get it, and I did. That's the way it worked out. But now the last thing either of us wants is any kind of talk about your resenting someone being brought in over your head. Isn't that right?"

"But, Dr. Feldhusen——"

Feldhusen made a fatherly, restraining gesture. "My dear fellow, that sort of thing gets started more easily than you think."

Helpless rage overwhelmed Neugebauer. What was the man talking about? Had he come here to listen to stuff like that? "You've misunderstood me," he exclaimed. "I wanted to talk to you about the Maurer case, nothing else."

Feldhusen was growing impatient and annoyed, yet his face remained unruffled. "But, my dear Neugebauer, that's just what we are talking about."

Neugebauer stared at him in amazement. "Not so far as I can see," he said brusquely.

Feldhusen wrinkled his handsome brow. "Dr. Neugebauer"— it sounded icy—"I think everything has been said that needed to be said. With all due respect for your professional ethics, discussions of this kind can be carried too far, don't you agree?"

"Just as you like," said Neugebauer slowly. "I won't keep you any longer, Doctor."

He was once again amazed at how Feldhusen's facial expression could change. Feldhusen was smiling. "You're not keeping me. A man-to-man talk is better than bearing a grudge. Let's carry on on the same basis as before, shall we? All right. Good morning, then."

Neugebauer stood helpless for a second, then quickly turned and left. He crossed the outer office without seeing Fräulein Rieck. He didn't see any of the people who said good morning to him in the hall either. A man-to-man talk? Feldhusen had evaded him in that damnably smooth way of his. Nothing had been achieved. He hadn't even found out what Feldhusen had actually said to the Maurers. What a fool I am, he thought angrily. Letting him butter me up like that. What a moron!

Feldhusen sat at his desk staring at the glowing tip of his cigarette. A fanatic, he thought. And one who's got his eye on me. You have to be careful with fanatics: they'll demolish the whole world rather than give in. This one's going to make plenty more trouble for me too. Why do people like this exist who have to dig and dig to the very bottom of things?

He put out his cigarette with a decisive movement. So what? he thought. He's my enemy. For every enemy you need two friends. I'll get them. He stood up and went to the door. The secretary swiveled her chair around and jumped up as he opened the door.

Feldhusen raised both hands. "For goodness' sake, don't get up, Fräulein Rieck. I just wanted to know . . . what's the setup here when it's one of the staff's birthday? Do you have a party or does everyone offer his congratulations separately or what? Look, please sit down."

In some bewilderment she did so. Her cheeks flushed visibly. "I'm not sure. . . . Sometimes Professor Weinreich would congratulate them, and sometimes he wouldn't. . . ."

"I see. And Dr. Neugebauer?"

"Oh, he never does. He's never paid any attention to things like that."

"Really?" Feldhusen's eyes twinkled. "We'll have to do better than that. Will you make me a list of everybody's birthday? No hurry, no hurry at all. Any time in the next few days. All the names and dates. With the signs of the zodiac too if you can manage it. What sign are you? The Crab or the Twins?"

She dropped her eyes. The flush deepened on her skin. "I'm . . . I'm a Virgin."

"A Virgin!" Feldhusen's expression was one of the utmost respect. "Imagine that! That's really something! Well, anyhow, write down your birthday too, so I won't forget it. Will you do that for me?"

"Certainly, Doctor."

"Fine. Thank you."

He disappeared.

For a few moments she sat there. Then she ran out the door. Head Nurse Louise had her office diagonally across the hall. She was just coming out on her way to lunch.

"Can you imagine, Sister . . ." Fräulein Rieck poured forth all that had just happened. "What do you think of that? Isn't that marvelous of him?"

Sister Louise didn't get a chance to reply. Feldhusen stepped into the corridor. He walked past quickly, with a friendly word to them. They looked after him enchanted.

"Isn't he the nicest man?" sighed Fräulein Rieck, the Virgin.

"Absolutely charming," said Sister Louise.

That evening Neugebauer went home worn out. His conversation with Feldhusen had haunted him all day, and the thought of it was still worrying him when his children came noisily to greet him.

Antje and Sibylle were each clutching one of their father's legs. Impatiently he shook himself free. "That's enough now, children. Leave me in peace now. I need a bit of quiet."

Liselotte pushed Uli, the eldest, forward. "Tell Daddy," she said encouragingly. "Go ahead and tell him."

Uli stood in front of his father without raising his head.

"Well, what is it?" asked Neugebauer irritably.

Uli glanced up. "I got an A in math."

"Did you now?" answered Neugebauer absently. "That's fine. Anything else new?"

"No," said the boy, disappointed. He hunched up his shoulders and went to his room.

"What's wrong with him?" asked Neugebauer.

Liselotte sent the other two children away and then took his arm. "He expected you to be a bit more pleased about it, that's all. And now tell me what's the matter with you."

"With me? Nothing." He followed her into the kitchen. "Have you got any beer or anything?"

"Yes. In the icebox. It's good and cold. Just a minute."

"I'll do it," he said. "Where's the opener?"

"Here in the drawer."

He let the beer drain slowly into the glass. Then he drank it in small swallows.

His wife stood at the kitchen table slicing bread. "Rosel called up."

"She did?" Rosel was the wife of Brinkmann, a friend from his medical school days. A G.P. Nice people both of them, but at the moment they didn't particularly interest him.

"She wants us to come over two weeks from Monday," she said. "I'm looking forward to it. We haven't seen them for ages. We haven't even seen their new house."

He went on drinking in silence. He could hear the sound of her words, but he wasn't taking them in. Feldhusen's voice intervened. *The thing was too big. There was no alternative. A man like you . . . such a reliable colleague, really ought to be above that sort of thing.* Above what sort of thing? Feldhusen's bungling?

Liselotte looked at him. "You're not listening."

"Yes, I am. Go on. What about Rosel?"

Patiently she repeated the whole thing.

"Yes," he said. "Next Monday then?"

"No, two weeks from Monday. They've left for Grado today for the convention. They're going to combine it with a few days' vacation."

"Oh," he said. "All right, two weeks from Monday. That's a long way off."

"That's just it. Rosel gave me plenty of notice so you could arrange it."

"All right," he said. "I'll make a note of it." He emptied his glass and banged it down on the table.

She put her knife aside. Then she came close enough to put her hands on his arms. "Can't you get along with him?" she asked gently.

He suddenly stiffened. "What put that into your head?"

"I know you, don't I? I know all about you."

"Yes, you know me," he said in annoyance. "Inside and out. If I'm not in the best possible temper you see some kind of a demon haunting me."

"Feldhusen's the demon," she said.

He recoiled involuntarily. "What's all this about Feldhusen?"

She knew she was right. Her eyes searched his face, the face she knew so well. And a thought occurred to her, one which had often bothered her before: suppose he can't reconcile himself to Feldhusen's getting the job? Suppose his disappointment turns into jealousy and envy? "You mustn't be unfair, Hannes," she said. "It's not his fault they appointed him over your head. If it wasn't him it would be someone else. You'll just have to get along with him."

"It's not so easy," said Neugebauer. His voice was sharp, as though he were speaking to an inferior.

"What's not so easy?"

He didn't answer. Again she came closer.

He was defenseless against her gentle approach. "Isn't he a good enough surgeon for you?"

Astonishment spread across his face and softened its gloomy

expression. Then he laughed aloud, but without any joy. "Not good enough? You can say that again. I'm expecting him to kill someone any day now." He turned and went out.

She watched him go. Poor old Hannes, she thought. It's not going to be as bad as all that. He's not going to kill anyone. It's your disappointment, that's all. But suddenly fear filled her heart. She knew his dedication to his profession. She had always been proud of it. But suppose he was going beyond the point of no return? Suppose he was taking a microscopic view of everything the new man did, thinking the worst of him, not giving him a chance? That could only lead to trouble. No one would put up with that for long. If she only knew what this Feldhusen was like. I've got to find out, she thought. He mustn't get caught in a situation like that. I must keep him out of it.

The following Monday, one of the last days in July, Marianne Maurer was discharged.

She was glad to be going home, but she was not happy when her last day came, and a slight feeling of sadness overcame her. The time she had spent here was a vital part of her life, never to be eradicated, and from now on that life would be a different one, with relinquished hopes and one joy beyond her reach forever.

The whole wing came to say good-by. Half an hour before Marianne was to leave they came in with a small bottle of brandy contributed by Dr. Krüger. They had assembled soundlessly, then came a timid knock. They swarmed into her room, and Marianne's eyes grew round with surprise.

Krüger with the bottle, Sister Waltraudt carrying a tray of medicine glasses, the two young nurses, the aides—they were all present.

"My dear Miss Private Wing," said Krüger solemnly. "Permit me to make the following speech. Today you are leaving us and this excellently run wing."

Sister Waltraudt gave him an oblique, skeptical glance, and he looked at her reprovingly. "To a man we are jealous of your husband. The only remedy for this distressing feeling is alcohol. Since

I'm way overdue for my dose in any case, let's all drink a fitting toast to your good health—against all hospital regulations."

He filled the glasses.

"My dear Mrs. Maurer," he said. "Stay well, but come back just the same. I end with the best-known word in any language: Cheers."

Marianne stood up. She drank up quickly so as not to have to say anything. The liquor burned her throat. She acted as though that were the reason for her moist eyes, then she felt easier, and there was no time to be sad. Laughing, she shook all the hands that were offered. She spoke to Sister Waltraudt and the other nurses. Krüger made his jokes. Their laughter drifted out the window. Then suddenly Marianne's husband was standing in the doorway.

Krüger went up to him. "Don't be alarmed, Mr. Maurer. We've just been wishing your wife a fond farewell. This bottle didn't contain liquor, as you might suspect. It was intended as a receptacle for our tears."

Maurer came in and lifted up the bottle. "You haven't been doing much crying."

"We've only just got started. Will you join us?"

"Yes, please."

They had a drink together. Then one after another they took their leave and went out. A vague smell of brandy remained.

"Wasn't that touching?" asked Marianne when she was standing beside her husband at the main entrance.

"Yes. Did Feldhusen come too?"

"This morning. He stayed a long time. He's quite a doctor, you know! He was wonderful. He said I'm to feel free to come and see him any time. He'll always be glad to see me."

"H'm. And Neugebauer?"

She winced. "Not him. He hasn't showed his face again—of course."

"Really? Well, it's better that way. Shall we go?"

Maurer had brought his father-in-law's big car. Marianne rolled down the window. The air was hot. She closed her eyes and turned her face to the sun. She was thinking about the day her husband had driven her to the hospital. How much had changed since then! She herself was a different person, she knew. The old times would never return, and neither would the old Marianne Maurer.

The car stopped at the little house which her father had given them and which her husband had had built for her. While he was getting her suitcase she stood at the garden gate. Against the green of the lawn she saw the flagstone walk intersected by veins of earth branching in all directions. In the background were small groups of evergreens, which cast no shadow in the midday sun. In front of the big living-room window shone a bed of lupines, blue, yellow, and pink.

The ground-floor rooms were finished and lived in, but the upstairs wasn't yet. It had been intended as the nursery, and Marianne had imagined to herself hundreds of times how she would decorate it. Dainty and colorful, with a wallpaper showing scenes from fairy tales.

Her husband came up to her. "Well, do you like our little nest?"

She nodded absently.

"What are you thinking about?"

"The upstairs," she said. There were tears in her voice but not in her eyes. "We'll never need to finish it now."

He took her arm gently and pushed the door open with the suitcase.

At this time Neugebauer was standing by the bed of the patient whose name he had also entered in his book. "Well, Mrs. Gerstenberg," he said cheerfully. "You seem to be feeling fine."

"Yes, Doctor." Her roundish face beamed. "That's what Dr. Feldhusen said this morning."

He can thank his lucky stars, thought Neugebauer. Hope he's not forgotten the perforated bladder. "Good," he said. "In that case you can get up this afternoon. But only for an hour. And don't go trying any push-ups."

She was very pleased.

He saw the third case too.

Ilse Zenker's face was pale and sickly. She moistened her lips before she spoke. "May I get up too?"

Neugebauer put his head on one side and shook it slightly. "We have fixed prices—no reductions, Mrs. Zenker. A week's not long enough. But you'll be surprised how fast you'll get better. In a few weeks you'll be doing Phys. Ed. with your children."

The thought of her children brought a smile to her face. "I'm so glad I'm going to get well. I'm so grateful to Dr. Feldhusen. And to you, too."

Neugebauer could taste the poison of his fury. Grateful to him! He hacks around in your insides like a butcher and you rave about him!

Anxiously she asked: "What was actually wrong?"

"Not too much," said Neugebauer. "Not as bad as we feared. You're rid of it now."

"That's good," she said listlessly. "You know, my little boy is just twelve. He's doing so well in school. We want to send him to college. I've got to live until he's grown."

"You'll live to see your great-grandchildren," said Neugebauer.

"Do you really think I will?"

"Sure." He shook her hand and left. Anxiety for her lay heavy on his heart.

Feldhusen's lucky star was in the ascendant that week. His private practice was thriving. Patients were coming and bringing their money with them. He was able to pay the first installment on the car without any difficulty. He ordered two custom-made suits and a dozen white shirts.

Gina called up about the apartment. She had two wonderful prospects. He would have to help her decide. He was glad to do so. He had had enough of living at Frau Grün's. The apartment hunting took up quite a lot of time, and he left the difficult operations to Neugebauer. He did this as though he were bestowing something on him. "I'm awfully sorry, old chap, but if you had my worries! Trying to find an apartment we'll be comfortable in—

phew! I hope this is the last time. Would you mind? Okay? Fine.
I'll do the same for you sometime."

Neugebauer jumped at the opportunity. Was this the turning
point? Had Feldhusen realized his limitations? It was all right
with him. There was even a private case included. At least two
hundred and fifty marks. Liselotte would be pleased.

Feldhusen had a long conference with the real estate agent. In
the end he decided in favor of a four-room penthouse in a big
apartment building, brand new. A vast view of the city. Perfect
quiet. Convenient to transportation. He called Gina up.

"Let's look at it carefully once more, Will. I'll come over at the
weekend."

The whole week he looked forward to seeing her.

That Friday evening, as his private consultation hour was drawing to its close, his prize patient, Mrs. Vera Manders, was sitting
opposite him, well groomed and fragrant. He was smiling at her.
She had already sent three of her friends to him, all straightforward cases and none of them exactly impecunious. He was
determined to keep Mrs. Manders as a patient for a long time to
come. "My medicine's done wonders," he said. "I'm going to take
it myself from now on."

"Why?"

"Because you look even better than you did last time."

"Really? Oh, I don't know. When I play tennis, I still . . ."

"All I hear is tennis. You should try not playing for three weeks.
It's nothing but overexertion."

"Is that so? And what about my figure?"

He made an objective face while he looked her up and down.
"Your figure, Mrs. Manders? I'd say that physically you are an
attractive mixture of types: athletic-leptosomatic. With or without exercise, you'll never get fat."

She was extremely flattered.

The telephone buzzed, and he picked it up. Fräulein Rieck's
faint voice: "Doctor, Mrs. Feldhusen is here. She doesn't want to
disturb you. She's waiting in the hall."

He was pleasantly surprised but didn't show it. "Thank you,

Fräulein Rieck. That's fine. I'll be right out." He hung up and immediately turned to his patient. "So you don't need to worry about your figure."

"Then I don't need to come back any more?" she asked.

"Of course you're to come back," he said cheerfully. "Any time you feel like it. The major function of modern medicine is preventive."

He's really got a good face, she thought, and decided to come back soon.

"Then I'm through for today?"

"All through. And I am too." He escorted her to the door. "Good-by, Mrs. Manders. And as I told you, don't overdo the exercise."

She looked him in the eye as she held out her hand. "I believe you're really a good doctor."

When he was alone his consulting-room mask vanished. He thought about Gina, and this time his smile was genuine. He hurried over to the ward. The swing door closed behind him. She came out of an alcove to meet him. "Hello, darling. What a surprise! I didn't expect you till tomorrow."

"I know. But I had nothing else to do, and I simply couldn't wait."

He took her arm gaily. "Come along. Just a few letters to sign, and then I'll be through." He drew her along the white-painted corridor and opened the door of his outer office. "You've met Fräulein Rieck, haven't you?"

Fräulein Rieck half rose. "Yes, Doctor," she whispered.

"The most efficient secretary I've ever come across in my life," he said breezily.

Fräulein Rieck blushed deeply. Gina gave her a sympathetic nod before entering the office.

He closed the door, took her in his arms, and kissed her.

"Dr. Feldhusen! In your office!"

"You're not a patient, thank God. And Fräulein Rieck's on guard."

"She's in love with you, you know."

"Don't be silly."

"Yes, she is. The look she gave me when I came in and said I'd like to see you! No, you were busy. What was it about? 'I'm Mrs. Feldhusen,' I said. Did she get a shock! She turned purple. She's in love with you all right. They probably all are."

"Don't be silly. We have other things to think about here. Here there's work to be done." He sat down at his desk and reached for the pile of papers to be signed. "Did you have to wait long?"

She sat down close to his side. "No, not at all. I watched the people passing in the corridor. You know, I think I saw your Senior Physician."

"How come? You don't even know him."

"From your description it couldn't have been anyone else. Lord, what an oaf! I was just touching up my lipstick a bit as he went past. He looked at me and frowned as if he'd never even seen a lipstick before. Didn't say a word, turned around to look at me again and then walked on, looking glum." She laughed. "Is that who it was?"

Feldhusen smiled. "That's Neugebauer all right. He's not so bad. You must be nice to him, won't you? He's a good man. A big help to me."

She stroked his hair. "You and your ethical attitude! You won't even let anyone criticize a colleague. He probably needs your help much more than you need his."

"Darling," he said seriously, "we're a team which has to work together. Each of us depends on the others."

"I know. I know. Don't worry, I'll treat him nicely if he ever comes to see us." She slipped off the arm of his chair. "Are you ready now?"

He signed his name to the last form and stood up. "Ready," he said happily. "Come along. First of all we're going to have a decent meal."

They had dinner at a first-class restaurant where he was already known. Gina enjoyed the attentiveness of the waiter and of the proprietor. "Certainly, Doctor. Yes, madam." She was so proud of him. She stroked his hand.

"Are you very busy?"

"Terribly."

"And the private practice?"

"Coming along nicely." He was thinking of Mrs. Manders. "I have one patient who's unloading all her friends on me."

"Is she rich?"

"She isn't, but her husband is."

"Is she pretty?"

"My dear child, I haven't the vaguest idea. A good doctor never notices anything of that sort when he's dealing with someone who's ill."

She looked at him in delight. "I'm glad you're such a good doctor!"

It was a wonderful weekend, and Feldhusen felt so free and self-confident that even the thought of the operations coming up could not dampen his high spirits.

On Saturday they went to see the apartment in the new apartment building. The plastering wasn't finished, but Gina was enchanted with the view over the city and with the layout of the rooms. They closed the deal with the agent. They could move in in four weeks. "That fits in perfectly," said Gina. "Mother wants to go to the beach, but she doesn't want to go alone. I'll go with her for three weeks. And when I get back we can move in. Okay?"

He agreed. He agreed to anything Gina planned.

5

In the following week only one single major operation came up. Unexpected and sudden, it could not have been foreseen by anyone. A young woman having her first child was admitted, already groaning with labor pains. She had a narrow pelvis, and the bony girdle was holding back the baby's head and preventing it from making its way out into life and the light of day.

There was no choice and no time. The rhythm of the baby's heart was already accelerating. Every contraction squeezed the tiny body more tightly; every minute diminished the narrow margin of time at their disposal.

Feldhusen heard Neugebauer's voice on the telephone. "Will you operate, Doctor?"

A caesarean. The classic, ever-new method, which never fails to leave anybody who witnesses it breathless with wonder. The premature delivery of the child by cutting open the womb. The most rewarding operation the obstetrician can ever perform, the intervention which demands the most accurate indications and the fastest technique, the race against time and death.

Will you operate, Doctor?

And no time to think about it; no way out. It had to be done now, with no hesitation or delay.

Suddenly, in the midst of the danger, he saw the opportunity offered to him. It had to be done fast, but it wasn't difficult. Much easier than the endless, precise detail involved in other operations. And he needed a success. That was all it would take to make Neugebauer retreat. "I'll be right over, Neugebauer," said Feldhusen.

It was all or nothing. It had to succeed. And it did.

The time was right, for Neugebauer had made the decision. The mother was healthy and strong; the child still unharmed. There was no infection, no abnormality. The wall of the uterus pressed against Feldhusen's knife as though nature itself were showing him the way, and Neugebauer's hands left him no room for a false move with the scalpel.

Feldhusen heard the baby cry and saw it draw its first breath. The relief which overwhelmed him was so infinite that he felt suddenly dizzy and had to lean against the table. It passed away without anyone noticing. Then he saw the faces surrounding him, saw appreciation and satisfaction, even on Neugebauer's.

The feeling of victory relieved his tension and calmed him again. Confidently and neatly he took stitches and closed the incision. The head midwife was attending to the baby. The pallor of its skin gave way to a rosy color; its voice grew stronger. This was the reward that no other branch of medicine could offer a doctor.

A wave of gratitude and happiness enveloped Feldhusen, and it was hard for him not to let his emotion become too obvious. He shook Neugebauer's hand. There was warmth in his voice. "It would have been too bad if anything had happened to the little brat. I'll leave the next one to you"—he laughed to hide the irony of his words—"so you won't get out of practice. Thank you very much, gentlemen. Thank you, Sister Thea."

Neugebauer stayed behind, dubious. It was okay, he thought.

A bit clumsy, but okay. Maybe he'll be all right. Maybe things will work out. Maybe not. Let's hope for the best.

The next morning the Senior Physician did not come to the hospital. He had left for a minor gynecologists' convention. For the first time Feldhusen was entirely on his own. He felt liberated, unsupervised, free from the feeling of inferiority which came over him when he operated with Neugebauer, and his triumph of the previous day strengthened this impression.

If only he'd stay away for good, he thought.

There was nothing major on the books. Only four women awaiting curettages and biopsies. They were none of Feldhusen's business; he could have left them to the residents; but he was eager now to show what he could do, and this was an extra chance to win over his young colleagues to his side. He took over one of the curettages. Warzin, who had a stack of uncompleted work to finish, was grateful to him.

Feldhusen set to work with a relaxed hand, determined to get it done in the shortest possible time. The woman was sixty years old. She had borne many children. Now, as so often happens, they wanted to rule out the suspicion of cancer. Feldhusen worked easily, with style and a confidence he had never shown before. And yet he was only putting half his mind to it. He was thinking about Gina, about the new apartment and all the happiness in store for him.

It was quite straightforward. He finished in less time than the others had taken. He left the operating room, joking. The old woman slept on for a long time. There was nothing to indicate how soon Neugebauer's doubts were to be turned to sinister certainty.

That same night the patient's sleep became restless. The evening temperature showed a slight rise. The student nurse noticed it and mentioned it to the floor nurse when she handed in her TPR charts.

"Nothing to worry about," the nurse said. "They always run a slight temperature after a D and C. Give her an aspirin."

But the fever did not drop. It rose still further during the first half of the night, and from time to time a pain seared through the old woman's body like a singeing flame.

Warzin came in to see her on the Saturday morning. He saw the chart and palpated her abdomen. The abdominal wall had hardened in painful reactive tension. The pulse was faster. The face was yellowish and sunken.

Warzin prescribed more aspirin and waited. There was no external change. But that evening the temperature line on the chart first went above 102, a jump of two degrees above the morning temperature. Intermittent fever—a sign of general septicemia. Warzin did not overlook it. Where the devil had that come from? Did she have peritonitis or what? And where did she get it?

He prescribed large doses of penicillin. He was on duty, and it would be dangerous to wait any longer. This would hold her until Monday, and then the other doctors would be there. Including Neugebauer.

The fever did not go away. The curve shot up and then dropped again, varying between normal and 104. It looked like a sawblade with red, jagged teeth snapping at life itself. The abdomen remained hard and still as death. There was not the least movement in it.

On Monday morning the Head Physician made his rounds. He had systematically and deliberately built up these visits into a weekly demonstration of his ability and popularity. He laughed, joked, told stories. His success was directly connected with his appearance; his method of treatment was based on encouraging words. He painted rosy pictures of the future, aroused hopes, made serious things appear trivial and assumed a grave expression over unimportant cases.

He came up to the old lady's bed. He had forgotten who she was. Her dry, cracked lips were moving as if she were speaking soundless words, and her hands moved restlessly over the sheet, as if she were picking flowers which no one except herself could see.

Feldhusen's brow wrinkled. With a casual gesture he took hold of her wrist. In the throng surrounding him no one spoke. "What have we here?" he asked.

Warzin stepped closer. He held the clipboard with the temperature chart flat against his lower arm. "Peritonitis, Doctor. D and C on Thursday for suspected malignancy."

"H'm." There was no change in Feldhusen's face. The other five patients in the room had turned round to look.

Feldhusen gestured with his hand. The nurse turned back the sheet, pulled up the gown. The still, old body was revealed to all of them. Feldhusen's fingers palpated superficially, applying no pressure. He saw the chart with the steep red peaks. The pulse line, too, was far higher than normal.

No possible doubt now. His eyes met Warzin's. "D and C normal?"

"Perfectly normal, Doctor. No complications. The report's already been . . ." He faltered. His eyebrows contracted. Then he said quietly in some embarrassment: "Excuse me, Doctor. This is the D and C you performed yourself."

Neugebauer heard Warzin's words and was horror-struck. What had caused the peritonitis? He looked at Feldhusen. Feldhusen withdrew his hand slowly. He was smiling. "So it is," he said. "It's quite clear. H'm. What do you know!" He felt the skin of the distended abdomen very gently, pulled the gown down with his own hands. Then he turned to Warzin. "You've taken all appropriate measures, have you?"

"Right away, Doctor," said Warzin eagerly. "I was on duty over the weekend, and I immediately——"

"Good, good. Excellent. Please keep me informed."

"Yes, Doctor."

Feldhusen took the woman's hand and held it between his own. "Don't worry, Mom. Everything's going to be all right. We'll get over it." He picked up the temperature chart, which had registered its lowest point that morning—100.6. "See, it's coming down already. Fine, fine. Just keep on like this."

It would be up to 104 by evening, Neugebauer knew.

How nicely he cheers her up, thought the woman in the next bed.

The old woman lay still. Feldhusen went over to the next bed. His performance was not yet over; he must exude confidence; but his mind was only half on the role he was playing. Nobody noticed except Neugebauer. The Senior Physician was perturbed. What the devil had happened here? While he was following Feldhusen from bed to bed on the remainder of the round he kept glancing back at the old woman. She had her eyes half closed and was blinking apathetically at the ceiling.

Outside Feldhusen with a friendly wave of his hand dismissed the group that had accompanied him. He nodded at the Senior Physician with a smile. "Thank you so much. That's all for today. See you."

Neugebauer walked away in silence.

When he was back in his office, sitting down, the telephone rang. It was Liselotte. "Is that you, Hans? You haven't forgotten that we're supposed to go to Rosel and Helmut's tonight, have you?"

"Oh, Lord, yes, of course. I'd almost——"

"I knew it! Good thing I called up."

"Oh no. I'd have remembered."

"You'll really try to be early, won't you? Rosel always goes to so much trouble, you know. We mustn't be late. They're waiting supper for us."

"Okay, okay. Don't worry. Good-by, darling." He hung up. The woman in Room 28 had in fact driven the invitation out of his head. He was really in no mood to go to the Brinkmanns'. He could talk shop here, and he had children of his own. Helmut was a nice guy though. Liselotte was right, one shouldn't neglect old friendships. He'd get into the mood without even trying.

He hurried and was through by five o'clock. Before leaving he took a look in Room 28. He said good evening very quietly and stepped softly. The whispering voices fell silent.

The critically ill patient lay there unchanged. Her fever had risen sharply to 104.5. From time to time her body shuddered faintly. Her breathing was shallow and panting. Her hands were still now, as though she had found what she was looking for.

When was our last case of peritonitis after a curettage? thought Neugebauer. I can't even remember. Ages ago. What are we coming to?

Neugebauer was still thinking about the woman in Room 28 when he left his apartment with Liselotte at half past six.

He had put on a dark suit, as if for a rather formal party. Might as well go the whole hog! With surprise and concealed satisfaction he noticed how pretty Liselotte looked. Suddenly his spirits rose. Now he was glad they were going to have an evening out. She doesn't have much fun, he thought. Nothing but the kids and cleaning house and worrying. I ought to be nice to her.

They walked to the nearest streetcar stop, about five minutes away. It was turning cooler, and the trees looked exhausted by the blazing heat of the day. Here and there windows were beginning to light up. In front of one house stood a tiny car, a Goggomobil, basking in the splendor of its shiny new paint. "That's what we need," said Liselotte. "It looks cute, and it doesn't cost too much. Would all the kids fit into it?"

Neugebauer laughed good-temperedly. "For our crew we need a Mercedes 300. And a luggage trailer as well."

"It would be nice though," she said.

"You can count yourself lucky that your furniture's paid for."

"I do. I was only thinking . . . just imagine, we could go abroad now if we had a car. To Italy or Austria."

"I can imagine anything," said Neugebauer, staring straight ahead down the street.

She linked her arm in his. "There's no hurry, Hans. Someday you'll be a Head Physician too. Then we'll make up for lost time. You can have a great big car, and I'll have a little one for shopping."

He laughed. In the distance the yellow streetcar came into sight. They walked faster.

When they got out of the streetcar the city had a different look. There were rigid rows of houses, all made of the same kind of brick and with the same kind of windows. On some of the balconies hung limp washing; television antennas stuck out like metal coat hangers. Teen-agers clustered in the doorways. The stillness was broken by a shrill voice: "Karin. Come in now."

Helmut Brinkmann had his practice on the outskirts of this subdivision. Neugebauer had known him since they were students. They had attended the same university for three semesters, then their ways had separated. But their friendship had lasted, and despite their differences they valued each other. Brinkmann had started a practice as soon as possible. The prestige of the specialist held no attraction for him; he wanted to start earning money and make himself independent.

It hadn't taken him long to work up his practice to fifteen hundred health insurance cases per quarter. He worked all day long and got no rest at night. He was always available and never turned anybody away. His reputation grew. Men thawed out in his presence; women poured out their hearts to his wife, and there was candy for the children. Everyone was happy.

Brinkmann knew that these were the best years of his life. House, car, major appliances, the children's education, debts to be paid off, old-age insurance—all this had to be taken care of at once, in these years of highest productivity.

His house was a little distance away from the red brick ones, separate but near enough to be one of them. It was a house worth a hundred thousand marks, built on a seventy-five-thousand-mark savings bank credit. Rosel Brinkmann had occasionally seen her husband high, but never as drunk as the day the roof was raised.

It was a welcoming, unusual house with an extra wing for the professional rooms and a pretty garden. Brinkmann invested whatever he could in tax-deductible items. His equipment was all the latest model. His patients were impressed by it and told other people about it as evidence of his skill and success.

When the Neugebauers reached the garden gate they saw the Brinkmanns' car standing in front of the garage. It was a light gray Isabella with a radio antenna, a little pennant, and his round doctor's badge. Neugebauer's glance took in the car, but he did not say anything. Neither did Liselotte. They pressed down the latch of the garden gate.

Brinkmann came out almost before they had entered the little front garden. He greeted them with his customary mixture of weariness and enthusiasm. "Give me a kiss, my beauty. Hi, Hans. Come on in. I just got rid of the last patient a minute ago. Another one of those days like the Christmas rush at the post office. Go on in to Rosel while I put the horse in the stable."

"No more house calls?"

"Don't mention it or there will be!"

Brinkmann's wife appeared in the open doorway, dainty and animated as a spinning top. She was never out of sorts, and her cheeks were always as fresh and red as the apples in her garden. As usual, her hard day had left no trace on her face. "Come on in. I'm glad to see you," she said and kissed Liselotte.

"What about me?" asked Neugebauer. She stood on tiptoe and kissed him on the forehead. Then she took them both into the living room.

Liselotte looked around at the furniture.

"Don't look too closely," said Rosel with ill-concealed pride. "There's still a lot to be done. I want to change this whole corner. But the fireplace is nice, isn't it?"

"Wonderful."

Brinkmann came in. "Roselie, suppose you two see to the supper. I'll show Hans the X-ray equipment. And then that will be done with."

"X-ray equipment?" asked Neugebauer.

"Yes, indeed," said Rosel. "Thirty-five thousand."

"If it was only paid for!" said Brinkmann. "Would you like to look at it?"

"I'll look at anything so long as it's not color prints of Mediterranean sunsets."

"Oh, I'm well past that stage."

They went out. The ladies went into the kitchen, passing through the foyer where Liselotte noticed the wallpaper with big stylized flowers. She stroked them with her hand. Pretty, she thought and could not quite suppress a tiny twinge of envy.

The kitchen was fairly big, square, with everything easily accessible. The upper part of the walls was almost entirely taken up with built-in cabinets. Pastel and white, clean and light. Liselotte was reminded of her own kitchen and again had to fight a little battle with her emotions. She looked at the dishwasher and the mixer. "Say, do you do anything by hand any more?"

"I certainly do. The kitchen's not the whole house. And Friedel left a week ago."

"So soon?"

"Oh, these maids—they quit every three months. They get married or take jobs in industry or Lord knows what. And there's too much work for them here. It's easier to get a new baby than a new maid."

"Well, let's get to work," said Liselotte.

They prepared everything they needed. Rosel passed dishes and bread through the service window to the dining area next to the kitchen. And as they exchanged stories about their children and laughed about the idiosyncrasies of their husbands, the last faint trace of dissatisfaction vanished from Liselotte's heart.

"Come on, let's bring in the ravening beasts," said Rosel.

They went through the waiting room and the treatment room into the office. The tubular steel chairs stood there, gleamingly functional. Fish swam around slowly in an aquarium. "Relaxes people like anything," said Rosel as she went by. "Just watch them for a bit and you fall asleep."

She opened the door of the X-ray room. Liselotte remained standing on the threshold in amazement. Her husband was standing against the screen, with the upper part of his body naked and his arms bent upward at right angles. He was not breathing, and his cheeks were distended.

"Keep out!" shouted Brinkmann, who was invisible in a corner. "We're taking pictures."

Rosel pulled Liselotte back and hastily closed the door. "He's doing his lung," she whispered.

"Whatever for?"

"Just for fun. Let them play a bit."

"Heavens, what a procedure!"

"Ever since he's had the equipment he does this with anyone who knows anything at all about it. Like a little boy with a new train."

They waited until they were called in. Brinkmann took the slide out of the frame and carried it into the darkroom. Hans was standing beside the screen putting on his shirt.

Liselotte went up to him. "Hannes," she said reproachfully, "how can you wear a shirt like that? There's a button missing."

He grinned like a young kid. "See how you neglect me?"

"But I checked them all before I put them in your drawer."

Good-naturedly he raised her chin and kissed her. "Forget it, madam. You're a model housekeeper. It couldn't be your fault. It must have come off just now. Here it is."

Brinkmann came back and tapped Liselotte proudly on the shoulder. "Well, what do you say to this? I've just immortalized your old man's insides. Pretty nice, what?"

"Does it bring in a lot of money?" asked Liselotte.

"It certainly does. I do all my own lungs and fractures. I had a pretty rough time at first—naturally the radiologists take a dim view of it. But I have a restricted radiologist's license and a thick head."

"You surely have," said Rosel.

"And I enjoy it. I was fooled by a kid's pigtail again the other day. She had it hanging down over her shoulder. It cast a marvelous shadow, and I was congratulating myself on my eagle eye when she pulled it up and all her symptoms disappeared."

Liselotte laughed. "You've got a nice setup here," she said.

"Take it easy." Brinkmann put his arm around Rosel. "It's not all paid for yet. Build yourself a house, and you can count on worries."

"I wish I had a few."

"What I'm worried about right now is some tea. Senior Physician Neugebauer, aren't you ready yet?"

Neugebauer was tying his tie. "You could at least be polite to your patients. Where's the tea?"

In high spirits they went back.

The telephone shrilled while they were at supper. "You go," said Brinkmann with his mouth full. "You're the physician on duty. I'm not here."

His wife came back in a few minutes. "Old Frau Schöndube," she said. "Is she to go on taking the tablets? Her fever's down."

"Yes, let her. It will give her something to do."

"That's what I told her."

"Am I supposed to look in tomorrow?"

"No, I told her to have somebody call up if she gets any worse."

"Clever girl."

They finished their meal in peace.

"Suggestion!" said Rosel as they were stacking the plates. "I'll wash the dishes, and we can chat a bit. I'll show Lilo the changes we've made upstairs. You go in with Hans and start a fire."

"Very good, milady," said Brinkmann.

From his chair Neugebauer watched Brinkmann get the fire going with a pair of creaking bellows. Soon little tongues of flame were licking the kindling. The reflection danced on the walls. There was a smell of resinous wood. Brinkmann filled whiskey glasses. "Cheers, old chap," he said.

They drank. The ice cubes clinked gently against the glasses.

"It's nice, the fireplace," said Neugebauer. "Goes well with the whiskey. Makes me feel quite English."

"Yes. We don't use it very often though. The ashes and the mess, you know." Brinkmann stretched out his legs to the fire. Neugebauer sat up straight, holding his glass in both hands.

"Well, how's everything with you?" asked Brinkmann comfortably. "How's the new boss behaving? Are you satisfied with him?"

Neugebauer took a drink before replying. "Okay," he said.

"You don't sound exactly carried away."

"I'm worried."

"Worried? Does he bother you?"

"No more than the old one did. No, it's something else."

Brinkmann kept silent. He knew Neugebauer. He played with the bellows and waited.

Neugebauer emptied his glass and half of a fresh one. Suddenly, without leading up to it, he began to talk about Feldhusen's surgery. The words came to him without pauses or hesitations, as though he were reading them from print. His every fiber was so absorbed in what he was saying that it gripped the cynical Brinkmann's attention and prevented him from interrupting. Marianne Maurer. Erna Gerstenberg. Ilse Zenker. The interlude of the successful caesarean. And finally the old lady who was close to death and about whom Neugebauer was racking his brain in vain.

"What would you do, Helmut?"

Brinkmann raised his head and looked at his friend. Yes, that was Neugebauer all right. He'd always been like this. Either—or. Never give anything time. Everything immediately became a question of life and death.

Nevertheless Brinkmann was moved; he couldn't harden his heart completely. These were problems which fortunately didn't affect him. He was his own master. But he could imagine it: a boss who couldn't operate, making you want to snatch the knife out of his hand, and not the least chance to do anything about it. To have to stand there time and again, watching the patients being butchered. A ghastly situation, especially for a man like Neugebauer. But what could you do? To get carried away would be fatal.

"Well, Hans," he said finally. "What would I do? For the present I'd try not to get excited. He's slaughtering them, not you. There are washouts everywhere. The medical profession has broad shoulders, thank God. I hear enough dirt about my colleagues, I can tell you. And at the same time I'm absolutely sure they take me for the same kind of a jackass. Don't you remember the story old Bärwitz used to tell in his course? About the man who in a premature separation of the placenta perforated the uterus and pulled out something white. He snipped off a chunk and sent it to the Pathological Institute. He got a letter back: 'Dear Colleague, your umbilical cord contained a lot of excrement and in fact looks more like small intestine. . . .'"

He caught sight of Neugebauer's face and stopped. "I'm sorry, Hans. Maybe the story isn't in the best of taste in your situation, but . . ."

Neugebauer interrupted him with an impulsive gesture. "I've got to do something," he said hoarsely.

Brinkmann sat up straight in alarm. "Do something? What, for example? Write to the Health Department? 'Dear Sirs, My boss can't operate. He's slaughtering people. I consider him incompetent.' And what can you prove? You can't make anything out of the hysterectomy. Any expert opinion would back him up on that. The perforated bladder? It's healed now. The unsuccessful Wertheim? They're not going to crucify him for that."

"And the peritonitis after his D and C?"

"You're still not sure what's wrong. It happens to everyone sometime, not excluding you. Do you think you'll make a good impression by attacking your boss? Professionally unbecoming conduct is the least thing they'll charge you with. I hope you don't mind my speaking frankly, Hans. The world's full of senior physicians with an eye on their bosses' jobs. I know it, and those Health Department boys know it. Anybody who's got to the top is safe unless he's caught stealing silver spoons. Don't go looking for trouble."

"If she dies, I'm going to do something," said Neugebauer.

Brinkmann felt his irritation rising. "Good God, Hans, you're really incorrigible."

"It's a matter of responsibility!" Neugebauer exclaimed. "The great doctors all have a lot to say about that. They started indoctrinating us in college. And I'm supposed to look on and keep my mouth shut?"

Brinkmann quickly regained his self-possession. He shrugged his shoulders. "Well, if you have to do it, go ahead. But think it over three times first."

Neugebauer did not speak. They stared at the fire. The reflection flickered on their faces. They were more reserved than they had been, and there was a visible trace of something that would stand between them forever.

From outside the room came the sound of the women's voices. Liselotte and Rosel bounced noisily into the room. Liselotte was bubbling over about everything she had seen. Rosel devoted herself to Neugebauer. She sat down on his lap and drank out of his glass. He cheered up. But his depression was still there and the feeling that he would always be alone. No one would help him in this battle.

He was almost glad when the telephone rang and Brinkmann had to answer it. This time he had to go out. An old man having a heart attack, all alone, with only the neighbors to take care of him.

"Well, my friends," said Brinkmann, "I see it's after eleven. The question is: will you wait until I get back? I'd like you to. Or shall we call it a day and I'll take you to the streetcar? What do you say?"

"Whatever the girls decide," said Neugebauer.

"You might as well stay. Helmut won't be long."

"No, Rosel. No," said Liselotte firmly. "You're going to have a hard day tomorrow. Hans has to operate. Let's call it a day. We've had such a good time, and we'll be glad of the lift."

"Oh, I'll take you home," said Brinkmann. "I might just as well."

"No, Helmut, there's no need. You've got to get to bed. Think of the payments due on your house!"

"That wouldn't be so bad," said Rosel, "but once he gets going there's no stopping him. Three bottles at least. And I have to deal with him the next day. One day's drinking, three days sick. He's not the man he used to be!"

"Why not come right out with it and say you don't drink?" shouted Brinkmann. "Just look at Madam Temperance. The word 'liquor' horrifies her. And yet I have to make pencil marks on the bottles to keep a check on her!"

They stayed on for a few minutes, laughing, then put on their coats and said good-by to their hostess, while Brinkmann brought the car out of the garage.

"See you soon," said Rosel.

"It's our turn next," called Liselotte. "It really is."

"Jump in, boys and girls," said Brinkmann. He gave it a little too much gas as he started, and the motor raced. His pride in his car was unmistakable.

At the nearest streetcar stop he pulled up with a slight jerk. "Good-by, Liselotte. Good-by, Hans. Let's get together as soon as possible. And, Hans," he continued after a pause during which he pressed his friend's arm, "think it over three times."

He got in and turned around. The car rolled quickly away.

She watched the red rear lights. "What happened between you two?"

"What do you mean? Nothing."

"Oh yes, there was something. I noticed it even while you were sitting by the fire. And then: 'Think it over three times.' It was about Feldhusen, wasn't it?"

Neugebauer looked at his wife. There was anxiety in her eyes. Suddenly he felt sorry for her. Did he have to bother her with these things? She had enough to worry about. He drew her toward him and introduced a cheerful tone into his voice. "Yes, it was about Feldhusen. I got everything off my chest."

"And Helmut? What did he say about it?"

"That I shouldn't make so much fuss. It'll work out in the end."

"He's right, isn't he?"

He kissed her. "Absolutely."

She sighed with relief and returned his kiss. They stood at the stop like a pair of young lovers until the streetcar came screeching along.

Neugebauer's first concern when he finished operating the following morning was for the woman in Room 28. He found her as apathetic as the previous day, with the same jagged temperature line. But the response of her abdomen to palpation was different. The tense rigidity had decreased; the pain was all concentrated in one single spot. His hand found it, and the sick woman groaned faintly.

He took his stethoscope and listened to her heart. Its beats were weak and fluttering, her circulation poor. He still hadn't made up his mind. He prescribed injections of various heart stimulants at regular intervals. Then he turned to his routine work.

In the afternoon he came back and made another examination. This time his last doubts were dispelled. He went over to the ward telephone.

Feldhusen was in his private office facing a patient who had begun to get on his nerves the week before. She was doing it again today. The torrent of her words flowed over him like a waterfall. But Feldhusen reminded himself of the fee and put up with her bravely. Vera Manders had sent her, and everything that originated with Vera Manders was good.

"I don't know if I ought to take up so much of your time, Doctor . . ." she was saying, leaving not the slightest doubt as to what she expected of him.

"That's perfectly all right," he said kindly, hiding his distaste as he looked into her rapturous eyes. "Just tell me everything that's on your mind. The most trivial details are important."

She smiled, took a deep breath, and started over.

The hell with the stupid old cow, he thought. He went through the motions of taking notes on her history, but his pencil produced a gallows with a little figure dangling from it, its legs kicking and struggling.

Near Feldhusen's left hand lay two letters: one white with the printed heading: Max Fehling—city councilor and influential friend of his friend and father-in-law. An invitation to come over to Fehling's apartment for a glass of wine.

The second letter, on lavender-colored handmade paper, was from Gina in Westerland:

Darling,

I miss you so much. It's marvelous here. Heavenly weather. Mother looks a whole lot better. So do I. But I'd rather be with you. If only they'd get the apartment finished! Be good and don't work too hard. Leave some of it to the others. Thousands of kisses . . .

Those few lines, written in big, round letters, filled the whole page, generously, with no space left over. Gina often wrote notes of this kind although she could call up at any time. Nice of her. He felt pleased the whole day, and it made everything easier, even the chattering of this hysterical half-wit.

He was wondering how to stem the spate of words. Fortunately the telephone buzzed and solved his problem.

It was Neugebauer. The peritonitis. Abscess. Ripe for opening and draining. No time to lose.

"Is that so?" drawled Feldhusen. "Well, if you think so . . . No, no. I'll rely entirely on you. Go ahead and operate. Yes, of course. Thanks, Neugebauer."

He hung up. It was a good thing, after all, that he was there —old Neugebauer, with his sense of responsibility and his delight in surgery. Like a faithful watchdog.

"Please go on," he said to his patient in a warm voice. She did so. Feldhusen began to draw a goose with a terribly long neck.

Neugebauer was already upstairs, Warzin with him.

A general anesthetic was out of the question. The heart would stop. They gave her a spinal anesthetic in which the drug is injected through the hard membrane which envelopes the spinal cord like a tube. The body and limbs become insensitive, but consciousness remains, and the lungs are not affected.

After the injection they scrubbed up. Neugebauer did not speak, and Warzin asked no questions. Warzin felt a tension inside him but also the carefree feeling of the outsider who is not involved and has nothing to fear. Neugebauer operated quickly and meticulously. He made a small incision in the area where he suspected the abscess to be. Sooner than they expected, it bulged against their hands. The diagnosis was confirmed. Abscessforming peritonitis. What from? thought Neugebauer. An idea struck him, a suspicion, and he bent lower.

He scrupulously cleaned out the cavity, sponged the peritoneum with wet compresses. It had lost its healthy sheen and was dull and streaky. But it seemed that the force of the inflammation was broken.

Gradually they began to see more clearly. Neugebauer wanted to proceed cautiously and risk no further focuses of infection. Carefully he moved the intestinal loops about, feeling them. A few manipulations and the uterus was exposed.

Then they found what they had been looking for.

The posterior wall of the uterus was perforated, just beneath its summit. There was a star-shaped aperture with fibrous edges, which were now touching one another. Like a tear in a sheet of parchment. The womb was a thin sac of flabby muscle. It had offered no resistance; Feldhusen's curette had torn it, and he had felt nothing. From this starting point the peritoneum had become inflamed; from this starting point the pus had spread like a ravening beast, and the poisonous bodies had broken into the blood stream.

Warzin did not dare to make a movement. He heard the Senior Physician exhale through his nose. His face was all dark planes in the harsh light of the reflectors, and his lips were bloodless. Thank God it wasn't me, thought Warzin. He'd tear me apart.

Neugebauer felt a wave of fury surging over him. He perforated it, he thought, shuddering, perforated it and never noticed it. Or else he pretended he hadn't noticed and left the old woman to die, the bastard! I've got to go down there. Right now. This is the last straw. I'm going to shout it in his face. I'll let him have it with both barrels. But he was holding the scalpel. He saw the helpless, injured body, heard the woman's faltering breathing. This life, which he wanted to save, kept him chained to the spot. The seconds ticked by. His rage collapsed like burned-out embers. The blood was oozing, and he had to sponge it away. And Warzin was awaiting his decision.

"Excision," said Neugebauer. The safest thing was to remove the womb. It was useless and dead.

Warzin watched the incredible swiftness with which the Senior Physician removed the torn muscular structure. Neugebauer was operating mechanically, as if his fingers were attached to invisible wires moved by some higher power. "Save the specimen," he said in the silence of the room.

Save the specimen? thought Warzin. What for?

Neugebauer worked on without a word. They inserted drainage tubes in the abdominal cavity and cleaned up the field of surgery. Then Neugebauer sewed up the incision, layer by layer.

It was over.

Exhausted, he peeled off his gloves. Despite the powder his fingers were shiny with perspiration. As he dried them he saw the old lady's gray, sunken face in its dreamy semiconsciousness.

"We've finished," he said in a loud voice. "Everything's all right, Mrs. Säbisch. Thank you for co-operating with us so well." But she made no reply, and her features showed no sign of understanding.

Is she better off if she dies now? Neugebauer asked himself. What would she stand to lose? What would she be spared? Is my help depriving her of peace and making new trouble for her? Am I operating to help her or to show off to myself? Is it vanity? Am I like Feldhusen only more dishonest?

He felt the woman's pulse. Faint, barely perceptible. No, he thought. Any way you look at it, you can't just let a person die. It's not for us to decide. Not for me anyway.

"Warzin," he said. "Intravenous drip. Heart stimulants as before. Call me at once if the circulation gets worse."

"Yes, Doctor."

"Sister Sieglinde, please give me a jar of alcohol for the specimen. I'll take it down myself."

She nodded, with a glance at Warzin. Their eyes met. Neugebauer took the jar and left without another word.

"A pack of trouble," said Warzin aloud.

"What's he going to do?" asked Sister Sieglinde.

Warzin wrinkled his freckled brow. "I wouldn't put it past him to leave it on the Head Man's desk." He glanced at the patient. "Come on, roll her over. And let's be quick about it."

Warzin went on ahead to the ward. A bed had been prepared

for the surgery patient in one of the private rooms. She did not go back to the ward. The whispering curiosity of her roommates was not to be satisfied.

Warzin looked in every half hour. He had inserted the drip needle into the vein in her arm. The drops of saline solution dripped soundlessly through the glass bulb hanging down from the frame between the tubes. There she lay, isolated and alone, as though she no longer belonged among the other patients.

In the afternoon she grew restless and began to groan. Her pulse became faster and fainter; she struggled painfully for breath. Neugebauer came in a hurry. They rolled a container of oxygen up to her bed. The gas escaped from the steel cylinder and streamed through the tube and mouthpiece to her bluish lips. Just as Neugebauer was attaching the needle to a hypodermic of strophanthin the sick woman opened her eyes. All the life left in her concentrated in her helpless, beseeching expression. She saw the farther shore and did not want to go.

Neugebauer smiled at her. "Just breathe deeply. Don't worry."

Her eyes held onto him tight. He saw the pale ring of old age around the iris; the pupils were dark and dilated. Dying people have dilated pupils as if trying to soak up the last light before the final darkness.

It was all for nothing, thought Neugebauer. She's dying. Across the way a child's being born. You keep on working. In a few days you'll have forgotten her. There'll be nothing left. A concluded case history and a fresh grave somewhere.

The strophanthin flowed slowly into her blood. When the plunger reached the bottom of the syringe she closed her eyes. Warzin, checking her pulse in the other hand, was waiting for her heart to stop beating. But suddenly his face became more confident and he nodded encouragingly at Neugebauer. The pulse beats were growing slower and stronger. Her breathing was easier under the stream of oxygen. The blue of her lips was changing to a faint, pale red.

Neugebauer rubbed his forehead nervously. "Keep on with the oxygen," he whispered. "Adrenalin and sodium benzoate alternately every half hour." He inserted the drip needle again and removed the clip. "Don't leave her alone. Call me if there's any change."

Noiselessly they left the room. Neugebauer went on his way, his head bowed.

"Where am I supposed to get a special nurse, I'd like to know?" said Sister Mathilde gloomily.

"It won't be for long," said Warzin. "I don't think she's going to make it. Oh yes, leave me a couple of death certificates out. Last time I hunted high and low and never did find any." They separated.

Warzin was in a hurry today. He had a date with Brigitte at seven, for supper.

For years these suppers had been a standing weekly engagement. Warzin had met Brigitte while he was still a medical student, in the hard postwar years. She was the only daughter of a baker, a fact which the hungry Warzin had turned to good account. But that wasn't the whole story. She was pretty, good company, uncomplicated. She liked him and looked up to him, and they had gotten used to one another. Warzin remained her lover even after he graduated and became a doctor, partly to save himself the bother of finding another girl friend who could cook home-fried potatoes, partly out of reluctance to break things off decisively. So he kept on seeing her. Every Monday for supper, and in between at movies, swimming, or in bars.

The most convenient girl friend in the world, he thought on his way to her house. The only one up to now who's not got on my nerves. Sure, Tilly and Suzanne were prettier, better dressed —different types entirely, girls you could take out on the town, but they were exhausting, caused a whole lot of unnecessary trouble. Brigitte was like the bread from her father's shop: wholesome and reliable.

He didn't particularly like the section of town where she lived. Houses with crumbling stucco façades, little people hanging out of windows, swarms of children. Brigitte now had the third floor all to herself, which would have been fine except that the house smelled of yeast and hot ovens. At one time he had liked the smell, but not any more.

Brigitte opened the door right away. "Almost on the dot, *Herr Doktor*."

"You're lucky it's not midnight," said Warzin. "Just finished operating." He shook hands and gave her a quick kiss. She had brown hair and gentle eyes of the same color. Warzin had never seen any other expression in them. He couldn't remember a single quarrel, a single complaint. Not like Tilly. Lord, no!

He went into the living room where he had been so often before. Attractive and comfortable—the ideal place for home-fried potatoes, but with the slightly plebeian touch that people like her never quite get rid of and which would be permanently hers. He saw the old-fashioned upholstered chairs at the table on which the plates were already laid. A can of herring in aspic, bread and butter, teacups.

"The potatoes will be ready in a minute. Do you want a drink to warm you up?"

"You know I don't drink! Let's have it right away."

While she was out of the room he drank the shot of liquor and walked back and forth. He looked out the window into the dusty courtyard where garbage cans stood in a long row. He glanced into her bedroom with the wide wooden bedstead which had been her grandmother's. He was acquainted with it. A bit on the short side.

She came back with a frying pan heaped with a golden-brown mound of home-fried potatoes. He ate slowly, with enjoyment, until he had had enough. Brigitte watched him, pleased. They smoked a cigarette and had some more drinks from the bottle.

Brigitte was quiet today. Funny. Usually she always had something to tell him, about the shop or the customers; she would laugh and chatter. Today she hardly said a word.

"Aren't you well?" he asked.

She shook her head gently. Then she edged her chair closer

to him and reached for his hands. He felt slightly uncomfortable. Did I forget her birthday or what? he thought.

"Werner, may I ask you something?"

"Go ahead and ask. I'll answer like a quiz contestant."

"You're not cross?"

"How could I be cross after a meal like that?"

He saw her brown velvet eyes resting on him. "Would you like to stay with me forever, Werner?"

Warzin didn't understand. "Of course I would, Brigitte darling. Why shouldn't I?" He counted on his fingers. "I've had you for almost seven years. A heck of a time, isn't it? Let's have a drink to celebrate it."

As he was drinking she said: "I mean—we could get married."

Warzin choked. He barked and coughed, and his eyes protruded. The brandy dripped down his chin. She wiped the drops away with her hand. "Is the idea so terrible?"

Sure is, he thought. "No! No, the drink went down the wrong way, that's all. Say, what put that into your head all of a sudden?"

"We've been together six years, Werner. I've never had anyone but you all that time. No other man. I don't want anyone else, either. I want you."

Warzin sat with the empty glass in his hand. His mouth was open. He had never seen her like this. What had gotten into her? "Yes, but, Brigitte dear, you've got me. Why . . ."

"So I'm not good enough for you to marry? Just because I never went to college and didn't finish high school?"

He pulled her onto his knee. "Now don't talk nonsense, baby. You know I don't give a damn for women with college degrees. You're exactly what I want. I've no objections to you. I have objections to getting married."

"Why? Do you want to carry on like this forever?"

"Not forever, but for a while. Look here, I'm still in training. I'm an intern. I can't possibly manage on what I earn. It will be at least ten years before I have a practice and a decent income. We can't even think about it before then. Do you really want to wait that long for a poor fool like me?"

"I've waited six years already."

"That's bad enough."

She put her arms around his neck. "But I love you."

"That's nice of you. I love you too, Brigitte darling. If I didn't I wouldn't have kept on coming here so long. Please believe me."

"It wasn't just the home-fried potatoes?"

"Don't be silly. You can get those anywhere. It's you. But it's no good talking about marriage."

"Even if you found a really rich girl?"

Please God! thought Warzin. "For Pete's sake! That's the last thing I want. Spend the rest of my life listening to her tell me how her money pulled me through. Worse still."

She didn't speak. Her hair lay against his cheek. He didn't move, waiting to see what was going to happen.

"Are you cross now?"

"Of course not. No harm in talking about it. You asked a question, and I gave you an answer. Come on, let's have another drink."

He clinked glasses with her, then kissed her on the lips. "You're not cross either, are you?"

"No." She stroked his hair. Then she began to twist a button on his jacket. "Are you going to stay?"

He thought about her question, and momentarily the sense of an imminent danger came over him. But then his usual attitude of irresponsibility returned, chasing away all misgivings. "At this time of night? And with a single lady? I don't know what I'm to make of that."

"Don't make anything of it," she said.

Later they lay side by side in the darkness. Brigitte was already asleep, but Warzin was awake, thinking.

Get married? Did she have to start on that tack too? H'm. It would be too bad if it had to end. The whole setup with her was fine. Couldn't be better, in fact. It would really be too bad. But marriage? To all this, to the bakery, to these people? To have her around his neck forever—her and her relations? No, he thought. What she needs is a baker. That would be the right thing for her.

Then Warzin fell asleep.

Neugebauer finished earlier than usual that afternoon. He went to his office and waited until shortly after six. Then he took the jar containing the uterus and asked to see the Head Physician.

Feldhusen greeted him in his usual friendly manner. He noticed the jar immediately. "What have you got there?"

"I consider it my duty to tell you," said Neugebauer bluntly. "It's the Säbisch case, the peritonitis. I did an excision."

"An excision?" asked Feldhusen, bewildered. "Why?"

Neugebauer pushed the jar right under his nose. "Perforated. Please check if you wish."

Feldhusen looked helplessly at the specimen floating inert in the colorless alcohol. Delicate fibers of flesh waved like tentacles around the torn area. Neugebauer too looked at the specimen jar.

Feldhusen reached for it. He held it tilted, looked at it closely. His eyes narrowed. "Unbelievable," he said in a tone of grave reproach. "I'd never have believed that I'm still capable of such a thing. No, no, Neugebauer, don't try to make excuses for me——"

Why would I ever do that? thought Neugebauer in amazement.

"But it just shows how the same mistakes keep cropping up, even if we live to be ninety. I remember a fantastic case a colleague of mine . . . endless trouble . . . a terribly unpleasant business . . ." Feldhusen pushed the jar aside. "I'm sincerely grateful to you for taking over this case, Neugebauer. If I'd had the least idea, of course, I'd have closed the perforation. How's she doing now?"

"She's still alive," said Neugebauer.

"H'm, h'm. Peritonitis. Your operation—which was necessary of course . . . always some risk to the circulation. We'll just have to wait and hope. I'll simply have to take all the blame myself if things go wrong. But I'm glad I can count on you, my dear

Neugebauer. I won't forget this." Feldhusen's eyes shone with candor and benevolence.

Neugebauer sat there, confused and bewildered. Once more he experienced that feeling of helplessness which he was beginning almost to fear whenever he entered this office. What else was he waiting for? Feldhusen had pleaded guilty before being accused. He had expressed gratitude which Neugebauer had neither asked for nor expected. Without any struggle he had admitted something he could not deny.

Feldhusen pushed up his sleeve over his wrist watch. "Oh dear, please excuse me, but I'm in rather a hurry today. I'll check tomorrow myself, and then we can discuss the case again." He reached for the jar again, picked it up, and smiled. "Leave the corpus delicti here with me to remind me to be ashamed of myself! Thanks again, my dear Neugebauer. And you go home now too. I think you've done enough for today."

He stretched out his hand across the desk. Neugebauer took it. He did not feel its pressure. He felt nothing but helplessness and shame at the latest retreat he had been forced into. He could have sworn that Feldhusen was secretly laughing at him.

Feldhusen was not laughing. When the Senior Physician had left he suddenly collapsed, put his hand before his eyes, propped his elbows on the desk top. They'll have to give me time, he thought, exhausted. I'm only human after all. I wasn't loafing all those years. I was working just as hard as they were, perhaps even harder. Only I didn't do enough surgery. But I'll learn. I've got to learn until I'm absolutely tops. God, if only I had someone I could count on! If I only had one person I could talk to about all this! Gina. Ah, Gina had no idea of his difficulties. Gina thought him perfect.

He was gripped by fear. Suppose the old woman died? Neugebauer knew the case history, and the others would know it too after the autopsy and the general pathological conference. He could already hear the whispered murmuring which would die away when he appeared. He could already see his colleagues' gloating, Neugebauer's triumph.

He was suddenly seized with hatred for the Senior Physician, and the hatred left no room for his depression. He took his hands away from his eyes and stared at the specimen jar. Just like Neugebauer to leave the thing on his desk. Damned impudence! He hadn't meant the old woman any harm. He'd had bad luck, that was all—bad luck. Everybody made a mistake from time to time, even Neugebauer.

Gradually he calmed down, and the old Feldhusen returned. He thought things out coolly and objectively. He had never had a long run of bad fortune; his luck had always held. He was still the same person: the Head Physician of this department. And he would remain the same person in future, in spite of Neugebauer.

With a decisive movement he picked up the specimen, went to the door, and opened it. "Oh, Fräulein Rieck, would you do me a small favor? Have the lab pick this up. It can be thrown away. I don't need it any more."

"Certainly, Doctor."

"Thank you so much." He closed the door, looked at the clock. It was seven o'clock. He was supposed to be at Fehling's at eight. He had to go home first, change, and buy flowers. What a good thing he had accepted the invitation, even without Gina! Right now he needed a man like Fehling. Not for his advice, but for his sympathy—and he would make sure of that.

He took off his coat and washed his hands. He smiled at his face in the mirror. I'll handle it, he thought. I'll handle this too.

His car was in front of the building. The paint gleamed. Feldhusen let down the top and switched on the radio. Smoothly he drove beneath the window of the room in which an old woman was fighting death.

6

City Councilor Fehling lived with his wife and daughter in a
modest, respectable, upstairs apartment in a new development on
the edge of town. Modest and respectable—this was also the key-
note of his role in political life, and to this he attributed his success. He was only on the City Council and chairman of the Public
Health Committee; he was also his party's spokesman in the City
Assembly and party chairman for the electoral district.

Feldhusen rang at the pink-enameled apartment door, and
while he waited he carefully began to remove the tissue paper
from the flowers he had brought.

Fehling opened the door himself. "Here we are," he exclaimed
good-humoredly. "Come on in, Doctor." He took Feldhusen's
arm and drew him into the small entrance hall.

The city councilor had a fleshy, jovial face and a military hair-
cut. He wore a blue and green striped tie with an ill-fitting dark
suit. A solid citizen. Only his sea-blue eyes betrayed the hardness
he needed in his fights in the political arena. He took Feldhusen's
hat and hung it on a hook.

A door opened, and his wife and daughter appeared.

Feldhusen took them both in at one glance. The councilor's wife reminded him unpleasantly of Trude: grayish-blond, rosy-cheeked, homey, wearing a print dress with a big design which unnecessarily emphasized the stoutness of its wearer. The daughter thin and pale, with pointed elbows and shy eyes. In her early twenties. A secretary at party headquarters, Feldhusen knew. This was exactly the way he had always imagined secretaries at party headquarters. He smiled and looked into Frau Fehling's eyes. "My dear Frau Fehling, I'm so glad to get to know you personally at last. And I'm terribly sorry I couldn't bring my wife along."

Frau Fehling already had her arm full of flowers so that she was able to peer graciously at him from among the blooms—big, feathery, tea-colored dahlias, selected with great care. "Oh, what beautiful flowers!" she exclaimed.

Feldhusen's smile did not diminish as he shook hands with the daughter. "If I weren't a professional man, Frau Fehling, I'd have said it was impossible for you to have such a grown-up daughter."

"Oh really?" said Frau Fehling in a naïve way. She passed the flowers to her daughter. "Jutta dear, would you . . ." Jutta went off to find a vase. Her relief at having something to do was obvious.

"Do come in, Doctor," said Frau Fehling.

Feldhusen touched her plump lower arm as if by accident. "I left the Doctor at home, or rather in the hospital. Just Feldhusen, if you don't mind, without any handle to the name."

Frau Fehling beamed. A charming man. And so natural. "Honor to him to whom honor is due," she smiled.

"Oh, not that!" he exclaimed, and they entered the living room laughing.

Feldhusen glanced quickly at the furniture. "Antique," upholstered in green plush. A carpet with a design which hurt your eyes. Everything fairly new. Gina should see this, he thought, and said: "What a nice room! So comfortable."

"One does one's best," said Frau Fehling, not without pride. "Unfortunately my husband isn't the least bit interested in our interior decorating."

"I don't have the time for it," said Fehling. "What's a wife for?"

"Yes," said Feldhusen, "if every man had to pay his wife a salary for all the things she does in the house which we never notice I think we'd get a shock."

"You see," said Frau Fehling to her husband. "That's what I always say."

"Oh, Uschi," said Fehling. "You really can't complain about me. But let's sit down." He picked up a bottle of wine and filled their glasses.

Feldhusen sat down in the chair offered to him beside his hostess. Carefully he selected a cigar from the silver box Fehling handed him. Daughter Jutta appeared with the flowers, which she had arranged in a cut-glass vase. She sat down opposite Feldhusen and looked at him surreptitiously.

Fehling sat down too, noisily. He raised his glass. "Welcome, Feldhusen! And to a long residence in our beautiful city."

After they had drunk the toast they sat back in their chairs, and the conversation took its expected course. After a few introductory sentences the hostess told the guest with perfect frankness about all the illnesses she had ever had. True to his principles, Feldhusen listened attentively.

Even Daughter Jutta's chronic anemia was discussed, although she was obviously not very happy about this. Nevertheless Feldhusen managed to give Fräulein Fehling the impression that only unusually sensitive natures are subject to this disease and with a peremptory glance at her father also prescribed an immediate vacation of not less than three weeks at the beach. This concluded the medical theme to the satisfaction of all. Fehling opened another bottle. The wine was excellent, as were the cigars. Daughter Jutta quietly refilled the bowl of cheese pastries.

Fehling turned the conversation to his own field of interest:

the hospital. Did Feldhusen feel at home there? Was everybody co-operating? Was he happy?

Feldhusen had been expecting this. He was quite happy and had begun to feel at home very quickly. He should be grateful to his predecessor, Professor Weinreich, for having bequeathed him such an excellently run department. All in all he really had nothing but praise for everything, apart from one little problem. And after all you came up against problems everywhere and he'd solve this one too.

Fehling took the bait. What problem? The administration perhaps? Brütsch?

"Good heavens, no," protested Feldhusen. "A fine man, Herr Brütsch. No, no . . . and the word 'problem' is really an exaggeration. I meant my Senior Physician, Dr. Neugebauer. He's extraordinarily capable, as you know, but . . . a bit complicated. . . ." He watched Fehling's face and realized that he didn't need to beat his head against any wall, so he began to praise Neugebauer. An absolutely first-class, reliable doctor. Awkward sometimes in his contacts with the staff, but a real diamond in the rough. "And we mustn't forget the human side. He applied for the job too. It must have been a terrible blow to the poor fellow to have an outsider brought in over his head, you understand."

"I understand," said Fehling, "but I wish he had a little of your generosity."

Feldhusen laughed. "That comes with old age, worse luck. Don't worry. Good old Neugebauer won't stick in my throat."

"I'm sure he won't," said Fehling. "And I can't tell you how glad I am we managed to get you. We need men like you. Your health, Feldhusen!"

They clinked glasses and drank. Then Fehling began to talk about the war. This seemed to be one of his favorite subjects, for his wife immediately raised her hands in protest. "Oh, Max, please!" she exclaimed. "Do we have to listen to this?" She turned to Feldhusen. "I can't stand hearing about the war. For me it was the worst time of my life."

Feldhusen nodded sympathetically.

"It wasn't exactly easy for us either," said Fehling. He looked his guest in the face. "Your father-in-law and I . . . well, you know . . ."

Feldhusen knew. During the war Gina's father had commanded a national guard battalion, and Fehling had been his top sergeant. This was the origin of their friendship, which had been consolidated in politics after the war. Patiently Feldhusen submitted to a story about fighting guerrillas in Russia.

"That's how it is," Fehling concluded. "Common danger is a great bond. And what about you?" he asked Feldhusen. "As a doctor you must have gone through plenty of experiences at the front."

Feldhusen smiled. "I can't oblige with any heroic exploits, I'm afraid. Since the war was waged chiefly by men there wasn't much call for gynecologists at the front."

"Oh, Lord, of course not! I'd forgotten." Fehling was suddenly overcome by merriment. He had to get it all out of his system, and the ladies joined in his laughter. A gynecologist as a front-line doctor with all those uncouth men! What a comical idea!

Where had he been then during the war? Daughter Jutta inquired quietly, when the general merriment had died down.

"In uniform too," Feldhusen replied, smiling. "Staff surgeon, reserve status. Finally adjutant of an army corps surgeon, if that means anything to you."

Jutta nodded vigorously, although it meant nothing to her.

"The war," said Feldhusen, "destroyed many of my hopes. And then the long spell afterward as a British prisoner of war. At that time I still had ambitions. I wanted a career in university teaching. Yes, that dream's over."

"Oh well," said Fehling. "Head Physician isn't too bad a position. Especially in this town."

His wife agreed and related a severe disappointment she had suffered in connection with a doctor.

Feldhusen looked furtively at his watch. He had stood this long enough; he had said what needed to be said. He stayed another fifteen minutes, then took his leave on the grounds that he had to operate the next day. This was an argument no one could resist, although Frau Fehling would gladly have kept him a little longer.

They said good-by elatedly but with dignity. Feldhusen undertook to repay the invitation at the housewarming for his new apartment. The Fehlings were looking forward to it.

When the city councilor had closed the door behind the Head Physician he turned to his wife and said: "Well?"

"A charming man," she said. "And so conscientious. A doctor I'd have complete confidence in from the first. Don't you think so, Jutta dear?"

Jutta nodded with conviction.

"You haven't any idea," said Fehling, "of the fight we had in the committee to get him approved. But I knew he was the right man. And I was doing my former chief a terrific favor."

Down in the street Feldhusen was getting into his car. As he started the engine he whistled quietly to himself. He felt jaunty and relieved. He knew now how secure his position was. Neugebauer would not be able to shake it, and he himself would have to learn, to make up everything he had missed. As far as he was concerned Neugebauer could stay on as Senior so long as he left him in peace. He was a capable man, after all. And you never knew when you might need a capable man.

Neugebauer slept badly that night and got up earlier than usual. He left the bedroom quietly and dressed in the bathroom. Then he went to the telephone and dialed the number of the hospital. "Ward 3, please." He was connected, and Sister Mathilde answered.

"This is Neugebauer. Good morning. The patient in Room 36, Mrs. Säbisch . . . how's she doing?"

"Better, Doctor."

"Temperature?"

"A hundred and one point five last night. A hundred this morning."

"Circulation?"

"Pulse 105. Pretty strong."

"Much accumulation in the drain?"

"Not much."

Neugebauer did not speak for a moment. Things seemed to be going all right—even well. So far. But disappointment was still hovering in the background. "Fine, Mathilde. I'll be right in to see her. If she relapses give her oxygen again immediately."

He hung up. He looked out the window and saw the gleaming summery morning. He would have liked to go to the hospital then and there and have a look at the woman, but that was a childish idea. He left the house and took a morning walk. When he came back the two older children had already left for school and the little ones were still in bed. Liselotte had made this arrangement so that he could have breakfast in peace.

She was still in her bathrobe, but there was no trace of fatigue on her fresh face. He glanced at her hair-do, which looked pretty. Dark, shining hair, stylishly done, not waved.

"What are you staring at, Grandpa?" she asked.

"You're pretty."

"Oh, go along with you."

"Yes, you are. And you've got a figure like . . . like . . ."

"You don't go to the movies enough or you'd be able to tell me like who."

"Like Greta Garbo for instance."

"She looks like a string bean. She takes size ten in shoes, and she's at least twenty years older than me."

"Well, like what's-her-name then . . . Gina Loren."

"For heaven's sake, you've got two of them mixed up! Never mind. You'll never keep their names straight."

"I don't have to as long as I have you."

She blushed slightly. "Get a move on or your coffee will be cold. Where have you been anyhow?"

He sat down at the breakfast table. "For a walk."

"Sounds fishy. And before that you were on the phone. Who were you talking to?"

"A patient."

"Really? Is she pretty?"

He cracked his soft-boiled egg and reached for the salt. "What are you talking about?"

"What am I talking about? You never call the hospital this early, and then you go out for a morning walk like a high school boy supposed to be going to dancing class, and then you tell me I'm pretty."

"I really do think you're pretty," he said peaceably. "I probably don't tell you so often enough, seeing that you're so excited about it. And sometimes I'm as much in love with you as back in the old days. Today for instance. But maybe it's just something to do with the weather."

She stroked his hand and laughed happily. "I hope not. I like you to be in love with me even in rainy weather." She poured his coffee carefully. "But that doesn't alter the fact that you call up women patients at seven o'clock in the morning."

"I didn't call her up, I just inquired about her. She's sixty. I was dreaming about her all night. She's got peritonitis. I operated on her yesterday afternoon. I hardly dared hope she'd pull through."

"And she did?"

"Apparently."

She got up to bring the coffeepot. "How did she ever get peritonitis?"

She wasn't expecting him to answer. He was usually reserved about anything professional. Today he was different. He stopped eating, and his reply came prompt and angry. "Your friend Feldhusen performed a curettage on her. Her uterus looked like an umbrella that's been blown inside out. All in record time and all in the day's work."

She sat down slowly on the couch in speechless amazement. Her bathrobe was open, showing her breast. She didn't notice it and bent forward. "What?"

"You heard me. He perforated a uterus." He put down his spoon, reached for the top button of her bathrobe, and buttoned it. Instead of letting her go, he pulled her gently toward him and kissed her on the mouth.

"You're catching cold. Wake up."

Only now was she able to speak. "What are you going to do now?"

"Find out if she's still alive," he said sarcastically.

"And Feldhusen?"

"I haven't any idea. I left the uterus on his desk so he could take a good look at his masterpiece."

"On his desk!" she exclaimed, horrified. "You shouldn't have done that! Was he . . . was he very upset?"

"He acted that way."

She did not speak. There was a deep wrinkle in her brow as though she were making a great effort to think. Neugebauer wiped his mouth. He leaned back and looked at the clock. "Time to go, baby. I've got to be on my way."

When he tried to get up she caught his arm and held him tight. "Hans, I'm sure you're making a mistake. I know you are. Let him alone."

A withdrawn look came over his face, the beginning of anger. "A mistake? Me? He's the one who made the mistake. Are you worried because he's got to pay for it?"

"I'm worried about you. I know you. It must have been an accident."

"Oh yes, an accident!" he said scornfully. "Some accident! He has no idea how to operate, that's the accident. Weren't you the first to wonder why he didn't get started? Putting it off from day to day. I know now what he was up to: postponing his disgrace as long as possible, that's what he was doing."

She followed him when he stood up. She stood close beside him and held the lapel of his coat tight. "Even so, Hans—even if that's the way it is—don't do anything foolish. That can happen to anyone, you said so yourself. Let him alone. We're not responsible for him."

"Maybe we're not, but I'm responsible for the patients. And

do you think I'm going to stand by indefinitely and watch this and say amen to it?"

"You don't have to do that. You only have to think carefully about what you're going to do. He's got the upper hand. He can make more trouble for you than you can for him."

"I don't want to make trouble for him," said Neugebauer, furious. "I want him to operate decently, that's all. Apart from that he can do what he likes."

"You have to take him all in all," she said gently. "Maybe he has other qualities."

He pulled away from her reluctantly. "Other qualities aren't much help to people in the operating room. He has to be able to operate, that's all. Now I must go."

She did not try to prevent him, but stood there with her arms hanging limp. The button of her bathrobe had come open again. She felt helpless and sad, and he seemed to sense this. He turned around at the door and smiled. "Your button's open again." He rushed back to her and kissed her. "I'm sure of one thing. I'd never let him operate on you."

Then he left. She heard the door click behind him.

On his way to the hospital his conversation with Liselotte kept running through his head, and as usual when he came to think things out carefully after an argument with his wife, he found himself ready to see the situation through her eyes. There was no doubt that she was right on one point. He mustn't make a mistake. But in this case what was right and what was wrong? Perhaps he'd been wrong to leave the jar on Feldhusen's desk. What was the use? It was a humiliation for Feldhusen and a cheap triumph for himself. Never mind. It certainly wasn't a mistake to save the specimen.

When he had changed his coat he went up to the Head Physician's office. He knocked and went in. Fräulein Rieck had just arrived. She was standing in front of the mirror, putting on her white coat. Neugebauer made a gesture to restrain her even before she spoke. "Don't bother, Fräulein Rieck. The doctor's not in yet?"

"No, he usually doesn't get in until . . ."

"Okay. I just wanted to ask about a specimen I left here yesterday. I'll come back later."

"Oh, that? The jar with the—with that . . . The doctor had the lab pick it up yesterday."

Neugebauer turned back from the door and let go of the handle. "He . . . what?"

"He had the lab pick it up," she repeated. "Fräulein Reinhold came up. It was to be destroyed, I think."

Neugebauer had trouble controlling himself. Picked up? Destroyed? Had Feldhusen got through being ashamed of himself so quickly?

"Oh," he said in a hoarse voice. "Did he? Then the matter's taken care of. Thanks."

The secretary looked after him in astonishment. He's getting more and more peculiar all the time, she thought.

Neugebauer went down to Room 36 where the old woman lay. If she dies, he thought, if she dies he's got something coming to him!

He met Krüger and Warzin in the hall. "Good morning, Doctor."

"What? Oh yes, of course. Good morning. Good morning." Neugebauer had already walked on.

The intern and the resident looked after him. "What's wrong with him?" asked Krüger.

"He's still on the warpath. Haven't you heard the latest?"

"No. What?"

"The Old Man perforated. During a D and C. A terrible boner. Messed everything up completely. She almost died. Neugebauer did a laparotomy, and then she just pulled through."

"Honestly?"

"I was there. I saw the trophy in the jar."

Krüger looked over Warzin's shoulder down the corridor.

"Have you told anyone?"

"No."

"I wouldn't if I were you. Some things are best forgotten. Let other people take care of their troubles and you take care of yours."

Warzin laughed. "I haven't any to take care of."

"Just wait," said Krüger. "You soon will have. Well, so long, pal." He stuck his hands in his pockets and left.

"So long, Resident Physician Krüger," Warzin called after him.

Neugebauer had reached Ward 3. Cautiously he opened the door of Room 36.

The old lady looked at him. She recognized him and smiled. A little color had returned to her face, and her breathing was deep and quiet. On the temperature chart above her bed the jagged peaks had straightened out into a curving line like waves calming down after a storm. She was going to live.

Neugebauer thought of Liselotte and her words. And now he was glad he didn't have to do anything about Feldhusen.

"That's how it is, Mrs. Säbisch," he said. "Things never go quite as smoothly as we'd like. But the operation had one advantage: we know now that everything's all right inside. You keep on like this and you'll soon be back home again."

He went through the other rooms quickly and cheerfully, joking. His good temper lasted all day, and that evening when he was leaving their wing and in his hurry bumped into Feldhusen in the corridor, he smiled at him. "Excuse me, Doctor. I was halfway home already."

Feldhusen seemed to be in a hurry too, but he stopped. Impulsively he put his hand on Neugebauer's shoulder. "Congratulations on Mrs. Säbisch, Neugebauer. It's really fine. Whatever would become of me if it weren't for you?"

Neugebauer fingered his tie in embarrassment. What could he say now?

Feldhusen let him go. "By the way, thanks so much for the invitation. It's awfully nice of you. I've been wanting to meet your wife for ages. Too bad mine's not here yet. But we'll make up for it later. I'm really looking forward to it. Well, see you Friday evening then. Good-by." He waved his hand and hurried on.

Neugebauer looked after him, speechless. He didn't understand a word of it. Invitation? Friday evening? Liselotte! he thought. That's just like her.

Liselotte met him down in the lobby. "How's the old lady?" she asked.

"What's this about Feldhusen?" he asked.

"Tell me first how the old lady is."

"She's alive. He can thank his lucky stars."

"Or you can. See now who was right? A lot of fuss and nothing came of it in the end."

"Maybe, but it might have ended differently. Now you'd better explain what gave you the crazy idea of inviting Feldhusen. I just met him in the hall and he thanked me. I must have looked like a half-wit."

She stood facing him, her hands on her hips, a don't-care look in her eyes. "The crazy idea came to me a few days ago. And this afternoon I simply called him up."

"You didn't think there was any need to ask me?"

She came up to him and put her arms around him. "No, my lord and master. I didn't want you to talk me out of it."

He couldn't be cross. "Is that so? And what do you hope to get out of it? Is he supposed to tell you about his triumphs?"

"I just want to get a look at him. I want to know what he's like. I have an eye for people. He won't take me in."

"I hope to God he won't," said Neugebauer.

On Friday they had supper earlier than usual, and Liselotte put the children to bed in good time. Neugebauer was sitting in the living room. He had changed, and he was skimming through the newspaper. From time to time he glanced at his wife, trotting back and forth between the kitchen and the living room. "You don't know if you're coming or going, do you, sweetheart?" he said, teasing her good-naturedly.

She had already left the room. When she came back she was pushing the tea cart. The wineglasses on it were clinking faintly, and the platter of appetizers looked really appetizing. "If I were as lazy as you," she said, "Feldhusen would find himself sitting at a bare table. Come on, don't be so lackadaisical. Get to work. After all, he's your boss, not mine."

He stood up clumsily and lifted the tea cart over the edge of the carpet and up to the table. "I didn't invite him. You just couldn't rest till you'd seen him." He picked out a square of pumpernickel with cheese, garnished with a tiny piece of pineapple. "For heaven's sake! Dainty! You never made anything like this for me."

"I got the idea from Rosel. Only don't polish it all off before he gets here." She had brought a dish towel with her and began wiping the glasses with it. "What time is it?"

He sank back into his chair and looked at the clock. "Quarter past seven."

"Lord, and I'm not dressed yet."

"Well then, stop fiddling with the wretched glasses."

She put the glasses down. "You'll see about the wine, won't you? But let it be something good."

"All right. I'll pick the best bottle from our extensive cellars. What shall it be? Moselle, rhine, bordeaux, burgundy, or just champagne?"

"Nuthead!" she said and rushed out of the room. As he was fetching the wine he could hear her impatient exclamations from the bedroom. Then everything grew quiet. He opened the bottle and sank down again behind his newspaper.

After a short time Liselotte came back. She was wearing a turquoise linen dress with a becoming round neckline; he had never seen it before. Her face was pink and fresh and bore no trace of her hard day's work. He put his paper aside, took her hands, and drew her to him.

"Just look what a treasure I have within my walls. And it took you such a short time too. What a wonderful dress! I've never seen it before."

"You couldn't have. I bought it yesterday. Don't worry, it only cost forty-nine marks."

The doorbell rang shrilly. "He's certainly punctual," said Liselotte.

Neugebauer opened the door.

Feldhusen was beaming with good humor and elegance. He was wearing a dark gray raglan topcoat and a matching suit. He winked at Neugebauer confidentially. "Am I a bit too punctual? You get so out of training when you're a summer bachelor. And Neugebauer, let's drop the 'Doctor' for tonight if you don't mind."

He remained standing by the mirror and smoothed the hair back from his temples. Then he followed Neugebauer into the living room. His eyes swept the room, took in the furnishings, and finally came to rest on Liselotte.

She was sitting on a chair by the table, and she couldn't quite manage to look casual. Feldhusen came over to her. Her hand was kissed as it had never been kissed before in her life, and she was given the most expensive flower she had ever seen. One single, huge, fiery-tongued bloom.

"Oh, what a beauty!" she exclaimed. She held it up to her face. "You really shouldn't have done that, Mr.—Dr. Feldhusen."

"I have though," said Feldhusen with a smile. "In any case there's something more beautiful right here in this room."

She blushed still more and cursed her own embarrassment.

His eye fell on the label of the wine bottle: *Mosel, 1951, Spätlese.* They've gone to some trouble, he thought.

"Won't you sit here, Feldhusen," said Neugebauer.

He could really call him "Doctor," thought Liselotte and got up to fetch a vase.

Feldhusen did not sit down until she returned. "I want to thank you again, Mrs. Neugebauer," he said. "I never accepted an invitation with such alacrity. But your voice on the phone is something very special. If I were in your place, Neugebauer, I'd spend the whole day talking to my wife on the phone."

"Don't put ideas into her head," said Neugebauer. "The phone bill's high enough as it is." He poured wine into the glasses.

"You get ideas when you're a summer bachelor," teased Feldhusen. He went on looking at Liselotte. In his glance she detected frank, unobtrusive admiration, and she liked it.

"Well, cheers," said Neugebauer. "Welcome to our house."

Feldhusen clinked glasses with both of them. Then he took a cautious sip. "H'm," he said. "Excellent. Fifty-one, *Spätlese*, at a guess."

Neugebauer was astonished. "Absolutely right. How did you know?"

"It took years of practice," smiled Feldhusen, "and cost an awful lot of money." He noted Liselotte's admiring glance, set his glass down on the table, and looked around the room. Then he sighed gently. "It depresses me to look at this and then think of my own miserable little hotel room. What a nice place you have, Mrs. Neugebauer."

The poor man, thought Liselotte. We really should have invited him long ago.

He's using his bedside manner, thought Neugebauer.

"We only just finished paying for it," said Liselotte.

Feldhusen made a gesture of tolerant understanding. "That's nothing. Everybody's a bit behind nowadays. Look at me. If all the unpaid-for cars had to carry a white stripe, mine would be one of them. And how do you think it's going to be when we start furnishing our place? We've got an apartment already. In a couple of weeks my wife will be here and then things are going to get moving. And if I know her, it won't come cheap." He laughed. "Let's hope the bailiff's wife needs hospitalization. No, no, you're lucky to be as far along as you are. How many children do you have, Mrs. Neugebauer?"

"Guess."

Feldhusen knew from Neugebauer's personal file. "Guessing games too? Let's see." He looked her over again. "Well, I'd say —two?"

"No."

"Three then?"

"No."

"Still more? Four?"

She nodded. The surprise on his face was so effortless that she took it for genuine. He gave his thigh a resounding slap. "Can you beat that? A figure like Mata Hari and four children! What's happened to my professional eye?" He raised his glass to her. "Now I get it. Wife of a gynecologist—has to set a good example. To you, Mrs. Neugebauer! And to your children!" They drank.

Neugebauer remained silent. He was slowly beginning to enjoy watching Feldhusen. And poor old Liselotte! Feldhusen had half conquered her already. In response to his question she was telling him the children's names. He was trying to remember them, asking all kinds of details. Nothing in the world seemed to be of more interest to him than Mrs. Neugebauer's children.

Lilo was expanding. She was drinking more and more, speaking faster. And at the same time her annoyance at her husband's silence was growing. The bottle was emptied, and he went to fetch another. Feldhusen watched him until the door closed behind him. He bent forward and took Liselotte's hand. "I'm so glad to be here, Mrs. Neugebauer."

She gave him a beaming smile. "We're so glad you came."

"And," he continued, "I'm even more glad that I have your husband as a colleague. He's a wonderful man. I hope you appreciate him. But of course you do. I've never seen a surgeon to equal him in my life. I'm almost jealous! I've performed plenty of operations, but compared to him . . ." He leaned back and watched her closely.

She was twisting her empty glass around on the table and looking at the floor. "Yes, I know. I've often been told that. Professor Weinreich said so too. If only he weren't so awkward in other things."

Feldhusen looked astonished. "Awkward? What do you mean?"

"Well—I mean . . . in human relationships . . . He makes so many mistakes. He can't handle people the way—the way you can, for instance. He makes things hard for himself."

"Leave him the way he is," said Feldhusen benevolently. "The leopard can't change his spots. I have my weaknesses too and I'm provoked by them every day. You and I know how to take him, and that's the main thing."

She looked at him gratefully. "He can be such a queer bird sometimes," she said. "But I think he's well fixed with you."

Feldhusen had no chance to answer because Neugebauer came back. Liselotte was asking without any shyness: "Have you any children?" Feldhusen smiled sadly. "Yes, two. But unfortunately I don't see as much of them as you do of yours. I'm divorced. The children—unfortunately—live with my first wife in the Eastern zone."

"Oh, how sad!" she said. "Don't you miss them sometimes?"

"Terribly. But it's so difficult to bring them over. In the fall I want the boy at least to . . ."

"How old are they?"

"Let's see. I have to think. Peter's taking his ninth-year high school exams. He's seventeen. And Annelie—now she came along while I was doing research. She's fourteen. Shedding tears already over her first boy friend, her mother wrote me recently. Like father, like daughter!"

Liselotte laughed. "At least you have a sensible relationship with your first wife."

"Of course. Of course. Why not, after all? Are we supposed to bear a grudge forever? H'm—a divorce like that . . . But I can't complain. I've been terrifically lucky with my second wife. This time I'm really happily married. But it's a hard decision—on account of the children. It's a serious problem. So if you're ever considering it, Mrs. Neugebauer—but with your husband I certainly don't advise it."

"For goodness' sake," she laughed, "I don't think either of us is that type, Dr. Feldhusen." She glanced at her husband. "Do you, Grandpa?"

Neugebauer smiled painfully. What a stupid question! He was annoyed with his wife. She was drinking far too much. She wasn't used to it and she was falling for Feldhusen's line like any half-witted patient.

Liselotte noticed his sour mood and was annoyed with him for sitting there in silence making such a taciturn impression. What a chance he was missing to do them both a good turn!

Feldhusen seemed aware of her thoughts. He began to engage Neugebauer in the conversation and draw him out of his isolation. Quickly and apparently unintentionally he arrived at the topic of their work.

"There's something I'd like to take this opportunity of telling you, Neugebauer. When I began here I felt a bit uneasy. It was my first job as Head Physician. If I've managed to establish myself to some extent, it's been entirely because the whole show has run so smoothly and faultlessly. And because everybody has co-operated with me. And it's you more than anyone else, my dear fellow, that I have to thank for both these factors."

Neugebauer wanted to disclaim it, but Feldhusen gave him no chance to speak. "No, no. Let me finish. You were running the department before I came, and it functioned. No two ways about it. You backed me up in every way you could. And I want to thank you. Your health, Neugebauer."

Neugebauer drank and didn't know what to think. There sat the man to whom, three days ago, he had presented a perforated uterus, and he was praising him and thanking him for his support.

Liselotte, however, was happy. "Don't praise him too much," she said. "He'll get conceited."

"Truth must be served," said Feldhusen, drinking to her.

Now I'll have to thank him, thought Neugebauer. That's all I needed. He could get a man to applaud at his own execution. He said awkwardly: "I'm glad you're so satisfied with my work, Feldhusen. Nothing's further from my intentions than to make things hard for you. Whatever I do, I do for the sake of the hospital."

"He never thinks of anything else," interrupted Liselotte. "He sometimes gets to be quite a bore about it."

"The right attitude," said Feldhusen. Neugebauer fell silent. He didn't want to say anything insincere.

Later Feldhusen danced with Liselotte. Neugebauer noticed with pleasure how well she danced, and it struck him that he himself knew almost nothing about this. He noticed how Feldhusen kissed her hand. He himself would never be able to do it so unassumingly, so much as a matter of course. Did he satisfy all Liselotte's needs?

Feldhusen left at midnight.

"Come and see us any time you're lonesome and can't stand your hotel room," said Liselotte. "You're always welcome."

"Thank you very much, Mrs. Neugebauer," he replied. "Fortunately my bachelor days are nearly over. Then you must come and see us. I'm sure you'll get on magnificently with my wife. She's about your age. And next time—please wear this same dress again."

She blushed just as she had at first.

Neugebauer accompanied Feldhusen down to the street door. He watched the dark, noiseless car until it was out of sight. He went back upstairs thoughtfully.

Liselotte was clearing away. The windows were open, and the curtains were wafting in the night breeze. Neugebauer sat down and took a cigarette. Liselotte did not speak.

"Well, go ahead," he said good-humoredly.

"What with?"

"Bawling me out. What did I do wrong?"

"Nothing at all," she said. "Except that sometimes it looked as if you were about to fall asleep." She carried out the glasses, then came back for the coasters and the bowl with the remains of the salted almonds. On her way to the door she stopped in front of him. "But if you want my opinion, Hans, I really don't see what you have against him."

Neugebauer blew a delicate smoke ring. "He hasn't operated on you, has he?"

She banged the coasters and the bowl down on the table.

"Don't keep harping on that," she said vehemently. "There's more to life than just surgery."

She picked up the dishes again and went out. He could hear her moving around in the kitchen. He knew she was the only person in the world who really had his welfare at heart, and for that reason he thought over what she had said.

Sure, he might be wrong. No one is entirely good or entirely bad. Everyone is a mosaic of qualities, strong points, weaknesses, longings. Hardly anybody knows himself. How can he know another person then? One's own values aren't necessarily the true ones, nor one's own way the best.

He hadn't heard Liselotte come back. He felt her hands, cool from the water, on his forehead. She was stroking his temples.

"Try to get along with him," she said softly behind his ear. "Just try. It won't cost you anything. He'll be happy if you don't bother him, and he'll let you alone too."

He drew her head down until their lips touched.

"You know," she said, "when his wife comes we'll have to invite them both. I'd like to see her."

"I would too," he said.

7

Feldhusen's visit seemed to have had a salutary effect. They were getting along well together. Their work was proceeding without friction, their conversations without acrimony. Feldhusen was operating passably well. No blunder cast its shadow over the department. Feldhusen moved among the doctors and nurses with self-confidence and an air of settled security. He had every reason to be content. Gina was back, happy and constantly busy with fixing up the new apartment. It looked as though from now on everything he took up was to be successful.

This Tuesday too, four days before the housewarming for the new apartment, Feldhusen was in an elated mood—quite the opposite of Warzin, the intern, whose freckled face was pale and troubled. But no one paid any attention to that.

Feldhusen was leading the procession around the wards, like a prince followed by his suite. This performance took place twice a week. He himself was the main attraction. His coat was immaculately white, half open, the collar turned carelessly up. He was witty, clever, and kind. Every case suggested to him a detail, an allusion, a fresh point of view, which had escaped the others and which set him apart from them as the Head Physician, someone far superior to them.

Neugebauer walked behind him. Since Feldhusen's visit he had been determined to be objective and fair. He kept quiet, did his work with unfailing attention to detail, and when the voice inside him tried to cry out he silenced it.

Warzin was presenting the patients; this was his ward. But his mind was not on it. Behind all the dates, notes, and case histories lurked the thought of Brigitte and the talk he had had with her the night before. Feldhusen was examining the woman by whose bed they were standing. He asked a question over his shoulder. Warzin did not answer.

Feldhusen straightened up. He turned around with a friendly smile. "Well, Doctor? A bit absent-minded, eh? I'd like the blood count, if you don't mind."

Warzin jumped. He caught Krüger's ironic look. There you go, he seemed to be saying, loafing on the job again. "Excuse me, Doctor." He pulled himself together.

They went on to Dr. Florstedt's ward. Warzin went along, participating in the group, outwardly interested but inwardly indifferent. Behind the reports and Feldhusen's questions, behind the women's low answers, he was constantly hearing Brigitte's voice on the telephone. "Werner?"

"Brigitte darling! What a surprise! I'm glad to hear your voice. What's new?"

"Is anyone else listening?"

"Could be. But nobody would. Why?"

She hesitated. He could hear her breathing, quite near, as though she were standing beside him. Then the words, faint and worried: "Nothing's happened, Werner."

He knew instantly what she meant, and fear clutched at his heart. "You mean . . ."

"Yes."

"But, Brigitte darling, are you sure?"

"Yes, Werner. Usually it's absolutely . . ."

"Yes, I know. But you may have made a mistake. It's going to be all right, you'll see."

"I don't think it is, Werner. I'm—I'm scared." She sounded desperate, and all his confidence evaporated. Suddenly he couldn't laugh and act unconcerned any more. "We can't talk now, Brigitte. I'll call you back."

"When?"

Just that one word. But even that was too much. He could visualize her, with her gentle eyes, in a public telephone booth, hurried and frightened.

"Soon. From home."

"Okay."

For the first moment he had been furious. Was this a trick? Was this her retaliation for his refusal to marry her? She'd be surprised!

But it wasn't quite that simple. He had brooded over it the whole night long, without any sleep. And now here he was, and his thoughts were going round and round in his brain like a child's top throwing out sparks. He had put off telephoning and hadn't gotten in touch with her. But her despairing words were everywhere; every pregnant woman reminded him of her; every newborn baby's crying was unbearable to him. A child! He didn't want a child! His whole life would be changed; his freedom would be gone; he wouldn't be Werner Warzin any more. He wanted to remain free.

There must be some way out. He was a gynecologist. He'd find one.

The others suspected nothing. Krüger, the resident, smiled at him when their eyes met. With an effort Warzin smiled back. He would have been glad to change places with Krüger now. Krüger had the right attitude to things. Nothing like this would ever happen to him.

The procession of white coats moved on to the next room. Krüger followed, slightly aloof, relaxed, good-humored, imperturbable as usual. He had less to do with the private ward than the rest of them, and that suited him. He didn't want to work himself to death or die of worry. He had to get through the four years that would make him a specialist somehow, and the smoothest, most effortless way seemed to him the best. He told no one about his own affairs and paid no attention to anyone else's. Feldhusen was the chief, and he had to get along with him. Everyone had his peculiarities. Different men had different faults. Feldhusen wasn't a slave driver; he wasn't a troublemaker; and he wasn't a fanatic about his work. Things would have been far more difficult under Neugebauer as Head. Krüger was content.

Regina Florstedt was content too. Feldhusen had praised her and her work as anesthetist. Neugebauer had never done that; he had seldom been satisfied with anything. Regina was insignificant; no one paid any attention to her; she needed praise as much as she needed air to breathe. Feldhusen gave it to her. She was important; they couldn't get along without her. What a good thing he had been made Head!

And all around him the nurses and the rest of the group were thinking the same thing. He was a born Head. The hospital needed a man like him. He and Neugebauer—what a difference! Where Neugebauer shouted, he made his corrections in a quiet, considerate voice; where Neugebauer callously kept silent, he found the appropriate words. Those were their thoughts, and Feldhusen, the victor, walked ahead of them with their admiring glances focused on him.

A woman approached from the other end of the corridor and walked past them with an embarrassed good morning. She was plump and rosy. Her hair was blond, bright but colorless, a mass of tight curls. She was wearing a far too stylish spring coat. It was impossible not to see that she was in an advanced state of pregnancy, and after one hasty glance Feldhusen stepped slightly aside, as if to avoid any contact with her. Women in this condition made him uncomfortable. They were unprepossessing, clumsy, and devoid of charm, and they made him think of pain and blood.

A young student nurse was walking behind the woman, carrying a bulging carryall.

Feldhusen saw Neugebauer nod at the woman. It was this woman who was to determine his fate, and later he was to remember the meeting. But for the time being he knew nothing of this and went on to the next room.

As they were passing through the door he asked over his shoulder: "A new case, Neugebauer?"

"Yes. Mrs. Ingeborg Roth. Shoulder presentation. Due in eight days. I told her to check in today just to be on the safe side."

"Oh yes." Feldhusen had been listening with only half an ear. He wasn't interested in obstetrics. A minute later he had forgotten both the woman and her name.

That was how Ingeborg Roth entered the building she was never to leave again alive. She was embarrassed by so many eyes watching her. She was glad when she had passed the procession. She walked on to her own room beside the young nurse, holding herself straight, perspiring, clumsy.

Room 8 was on the second floor overlooking the garden. It had two windows, four beds with four bedside tables, a table with four chairs, a washbasin, and a big white wardrobe, which stood slightly crooked on its legs. The walls were painted dull yellow, the ceiling a shade lighter, and between the two, instead of a molding, was a disused gaspipe dating back to the time when the building was still lit by gaslight. Now two white globes of opaque glass hung from the ceiling with a thin layer of blackish dust on their upper surfaces. This was wiped away and immediately accumulated again, year in, year out, to the eternal despair of the cleaning women.

Three pictures hung on the walls. The head of a child by Rubens, Dürer's praying hands, and opposite these a landscape with young birch trees swaying in a summer wind along a road. Most women liked this one the best.

The walls of Room 8 had witnessed many things: pain and joy, tears and laughter, death and new life.

Only two of the four beds were occupied. In the left-hand corner near the door lay a woman with a sour-looking face and dark, stringy hair done in two braids—Betty Ahlers, twenty-nine years old. She looked as though she were in her late thirties.

The other occupied bed was the one by the window on the same side of the room. Gerda Holtmann was younger and more cheerful than her roommate. She was awaiting her first.

"Men have it easy," Betty Ahlers was saying. Her voice was pitched high, with a penetrating tone as if she were shouting over a fence. Her bed was creased and mussed, because she was always fidgeting and could not lie still. "They're all alike. First they promise you the moon, and then you're nothing but a scrubwoman for them. And that apartment! Like an oven in summer and in winter the windows covered with frost so you can't see through them. We've been pestering the Housing Department for three years. Nothing doing."

Betty Ahlers lived in a shack on a truck farm just outside the city, surrounded by a neglected vegetable garden and other lots with similar ramshackle dwellings. Her husband received a pension for a war injury and also delivered a circulating library's magazines and books in a yellow, two-wheeled trailer pulled by a motor scooter. Her neighbors had never seen Betty Ahlers when she wasn't expecting, and the only events that introduced any variety into the family's existence were her confinements at regular intervals. Four days ago she had had her fourth, a six-and-a-half-pound girl. She didn't have enough milk, and it was getting a supplementary bottle after each breast feeding.

"What are they there for anyhow," said Betty, "those jackasses in the Housing Department, if they can't find you a decent place to live?" She looked at the others inquiringly.

Gerda Holtmann found the incessant complaining of her roommate hard to put up with, but just the same she was glad not to be alone. She was scared of what lay ahead, and the older woman's vast experience was a comfort to her in her suspense. Her husband was a junior bank clerk and didn't earn much. She worried about making ends meet. He didn't want her to work, wanted to manage on his own. For that reason no babies had been scheduled just yet. But one came along anyway.

At first Gerda did not dare to tell her husband. She went to their family doctor. Sitting facing him, she was ashamed of her lie and could not look him in the face. Hesitantly she said: "I haven't been having my periods regularly, Doctor." She stopped and kept her eyes on her hands.

"Is that so?" The doctor's voice did not betray his thoughts. "Not regularly or not at all?"

She ventured a shy glance. "Not at all."

"H'm. Does that happen often? I mean, do you often miss?"

Gerda was grateful for this straw to clutch at, although she sensed immediately that he knew the whole story. "Oh yes, they're always irregular—sometimes just a bit, sometimes quite a lot——"

"Aha. You ought to keep track of them, Frau Holtmann. Well, let's see what we can do about it." He stood up and went over to his instrument cabinet.

How kind he is, she thought. He's not going to ask any more questions.

At one time he had asked questions, given long lectures and appealed to women's consciences. Unborn life, marital happiness, and so on. Now he was older and had seen more. He had given it up. He had found what seemed to him the best way. He gave them hormones, saturated the body with the substances which normally brought about the monthly bleeding. If it recurred—so much the better—if not, he had done what he could. The decision was left to fate, to nature, to God, or to whoever wished to make it.

"I'll give you an injection, Frau Holtmann," he said. "Another one tomorrow and another the day after. If you begin, let me know. If not, we'll try again in four weeks' time. At exactly the time you would be due."

She looked anxiously at the needle. "It won't do any harm, will it?"

"No, it won't do any harm."

She didn't inquire any further. She was relieved and worried at the same time. Both of them knew that behind the innocent words and commonplace procedure lay an attempted abortion, and both of them would hold their tongues—accomplices in a secret conspiracy, criminal from the outset, and by no means certain of success.

Time passed. Gerda waited with a heavy heart. Four weeks later she received the next injection. Nothing happened. The decision had been made.

Once more she was sitting facing him. "What shall I do now?" she asked timidly.

He smiled behind his twinkling glasses. "Have a baby," he said. "You've still got seven months to get used to the idea. You'll be glad in the end."

Gerda spared him and herself any attempt to appear surprised. It wouldn't be fair to make a scene. He had tried to help her and hadn't succeeded. He was a human being too.

Before leaving she asked: "The shots didn't do any harm, did they? I mean . . . the baby . . ."

"The baby was stronger than the shots," he said. "And that's a good sign. Don't worry. Come back if you think anything might be wrong."

And now here she was in Room 8, and in a few days the child would be born and be theirs for keeps. If only she hadn't been so scared.

"Everything takes time," she said peaceably to Betty. "The construction of new apartments can't keep up with the need for them."

"Is that so?" said Mrs. Ahlers balefully. "And yet they're building palaces, employment offices, social insurance offices, even churches, all over the place. But nothing at all for the likes of us. Anyhow, the main highway's supposed to be coming through our place now so they'll finally have to . . ." She stopped talking and sat up slightly.

The door opened and Ingeborg Roth entered. "Good morning," she said softly.

"Good morning," came the response from both beds. Betty Ahlers was staring at the elegant spring coat with unconcealed curiosity. Gerda Holtmann gave the newcomer a warm, intimate glance. Here was somebody waiting just as she was. Perhaps it would be the same day; perhaps she wouldn't have to go all alone up to the high-ceilinged, ugly room which Mrs. Ahlers had told her so much about.

The student nurse put the calfskin carryall down on the table. "This is your bed, Mrs. Roth. But you can have the other one if you'd rather."

Ingeborg Roth looked around. She glanced swiftly at her two roommates. She'd rather be near the one with the nice face who was still waiting for her baby.

"No, no. I'd like the one by the window, thank you."

"Whichever you like," said the student nurse in a friendly voice. "Make yourself at home. I'll come back for your things later."

"Thank you, Nurse." Slowly Ingeborg Roth took off her coat. Then she sat down on a chair. "I'll have to sit down a bit," she said apologetically. "It's so hot."

"Take your time," said Betty Ahlers. "You'll have plenty of time to lie in bed."

Ingeborg was undecided. A private room would be nicer, she thought. Or—no, it wouldn't either. Two's all right. Six or seven would be terrible. I'd better shake hands, or they'll think I'm stuck up.

She saw the two names over their beds. Slowly she stood up and walked around the table to Gerda Holtmann. "I'm Ingeborg Roth," she said shyly.

Gerda did not conceal her delight at the newcomer's arrival. Even the face of the sulky Betty lighted up for a moment. "It's a good thing you've come," she said. "We were running out of things to talk about."

Ingeborg smiled shyly. Then she undressed. Everything she took off seemed to weaken the tie linking her with the outside world. She thought of her husband, who hadn't been able to get time off to bring her here. Now he seemed so terribly far away, as though they were worlds apart. Suddenly she was so over-whelmed with homesickness and loneliness that she sat down on the edge of the turned-down bed and burst into tears. Her unseeing hands groped for her handkerchief.

"Now, now," said Betty Ahlers. "Don't start crying right away. You haven't any call to yet. You can get used to anything, you know. If you're looking for your hanky it's on the bed table."

"Thanks," whispered Ingeborg. She found her handkerchief and dried her wet face. "Thanks. So silly of me . . . I'm not usually . . ." Her tears were starting again. She made a great effort to stop, sobbing convulsively. Then she remembered that the nurse would be coming back. She mustn't see her in this state. She took a few deep breaths. Whatever do I look like? she thought.

The others did not speak. She went on undressing. She turned to the wall and slipped on her nightdress. Then she lay down in bed and pulled the sheet up to her chest.

Betty Ahlers waited a decent interval, but then she could contain herself no longer. "When's it due?" she asked.

Ingeborg didn't understand. "Pardon?"

"I mean when are you going to have it?"

"Next week probably," said Ingeborg in a quiet voice.

"Your first?"

"Second."

"Your second? What are you doing here then?"

"They made me." Ingeborg Roth was really speaking to the other woman, although she was not the one who had asked. "The doctor wanted me to come in ahead of time. It's not in the right position."

"Oh. Or maybe it's twins?"

"No. That's what I thought at first. It's in a crosswise position."

Betty's face looked as though she had caught sight of some monster. "Crosswise? Oh my Lord! I can tell you something about that. Frau Kremer who lives out at the truck farm, she had one of them crosswise babies. She wouldn't go to the hospital, and the doctor came every day and tried to make her, but she wouldn't. What a fuss! Suppose we was to carry on like that! Well, her husband, he couldn't stand it any longer. Anyhow he'd already taken up with someone else. Nice neighborhood, eh? Well anyhow, when her time came the doctor and the midwife came, and they stayed with her four hours, and when it finally came it couldn't breathe and it was all blue. The poor little wretch finally pulled through, but she had a terrible time, and she had to go to the hospital in the end anyway. And ever since she'd had a pain in her back day and night, and she wants to sue the doctor." She stopped to catch her breath.

Gerda Holtmann looked over at the newcomer with a quiet smile.

"It won't be like that with you. You've come in in good time. It's always wiser to go to the hospital. Maybe it will turn around and be born normally. Then you'll be home before me."

Ingeborg was grateful for her words. "Is it your first time here too?"

"Yes. First time anywhere."

"Your first baby?"

"Yes."

Ingeborg was growing more cheerful. Although the story of the woman by the door hadn't alarmed her unduly, the words of the second one had calmed and comforted her. Her feeling of being abandoned vanished when she realized that this woman was even more inexperienced and insecure than herself. She felt obliged to say something comforting in her turn.

"Everything went smoothly with my first one. I had it at home with the midwife, and the doctor didn't even come. You've no need to be worried at all."

Gerda Holtmann smiled. "I'm not."

Betty Ahlers' discordant voice interrupted them. "Two! One! I've got more than the both of you put together. Five! What have you got to say to that?" She looked at Ingeborg Roth in triumph.

"Really?" said Ingeborg politely. She didn't like the woman, but she felt a certain respect for her such as one soldier feels for another who has distinguished himself more often under fire.

The young nurse returned. She took away Ingeborg's clothes and asked if she wanted anything. She opened the window a little wider before leaving the room. Ingeborg's eyes followed her until the door closed behind her. As though she were saying good-by to all her belongings.

In the afternoon the Senior Physician came to see her.

"Good afternoon," he said. Then he went up to Ingeborg Roth's bed.

By now all trace of her tears had vanished. Her face was pink and fresh, framed by her thick, curly hair. She was wearing a batiste nightdress. On the table beside the bed Neugebauer saw a rosy-cheeked apple and beside it two paper-back novels with colorful covers. "Are you all set?"

"Yes, Doctor," she replied.

"Everything all right?"

"Yes, thank you."

"That's fine." He looked around. "The three bears! Mrs. Holtmann's the baby bear. You're next; you're the middle-sized bear. But you'll never catch up with Mrs. Ahlers here."

"I know that," said Ingeborg. "Unless . . ."

"Unless what?"

"Unless I have quadruplets."

The others laughed. "Don't talk so big," said Neugebauer. "Who put that into your head?"

She lowered her eyes and plucked at her sheet. "My husband."

"How about that? He wants to get it all over with at one time. Mass production, we call that. No, I'm sorry to disappoint you, Mrs. Roth. You've only got one."

"How can you know for sure?" cried Betty raucously from her corner.

"We do know for sure," said Neugebauer without taking his eyes off Ingeborg. "We listen in to their conversation. Yours is all alone. Just talking to itself."

His glance met Gerda's smiling one and Betty's dubious one. "Good-by, my three pretty bears," he said.

Their laughter followed him out into the hall.

"He's all right," exclaimed Betty. "Listening in to their conversation! Of all things!" She began to giggle again.

"He's here every day," said Gerda. "Even if it's late at night. He really knows his stuff."

"That's right." Betty sat up. "He attends to everything. You don't need to be scared of him. Ugh, when the Head Physician comes sweeping in with his whole gang, that's a different story. They look at you as if you were a dead fish and mutter those long words. I'm always glad to see the last of them."

The next morning Dr. Warzin made his rounds, together with Sister Eva, the floor nurse. He asked how she was, looked at her chart, felt her abdomen a bit, and left her with the impression of a scatterbrained young man with his mind on something else. A little while later Eva returned with Betty Ahlers' baby. Ingeborg Roth had not seen it yet; she had been still asleep when they brought it in that morning. The child had a yellowish, wrinkled face and wailed angrily on its pillow.

"Come on, come on!" said Betty in a matter-of-fact voice. "And don't be so clumsy this time."

It waved its arms impatiently and didn't stop wailing until it had found the breast. The other two watched reverently. It nursed with its eyes closed. The women could hear the faint sucking and lip-smacking sounds, and they saw how Betty's hard face grew soft, and tenderness spread across it like the green of spring over a stony field.

When the child had finished nursing Betty was allowed to hold it for a few minutes. She looked at it for a long time and then glanced wryly at the others. "It's no beauty," she said to Ingeborg as if in answer to some disparaging remark. "But there's plenty of time. She's got a touch of jaundice. It won't last long, the doctor says."

Ingeborg kindly came to her help. "My first one looked like a beet," she said, laughing. "I was horrified the first time I saw her. Yours is a pretty little thing already."

"Do you really think so?" Betty asked dubiously, but Ingeborg's gentle eyes seemed to reassure her, and she was content.

Later Ingeborg showed them her layette, which she had had for a long time. Pale blue for a boy, pale pink for a girl, in secret but foresighted provision for the possibility of twins. Gerda was filled with admiration, Betty with violent envy, which became even more intense when the hospital cart was brought in and Ingeborg alone bought herself a bag of Spanish grapes.

"What does your husband do?" she asked.

"He's a machine shop foreman," said Ingeborg proudly.

"Really? A machine shop foreman? Where does he work?"

"Manders Incorporated. He's been with them eight years."

"He must be a good worker," said Betty.

Ingeborg nodded. "They've just elected him shop steward."

Betty looked at her in silence. Manders Incorporated was a name that meant something in this town. Everybody knew that firm. Even her own husband had worked there once, temporarily, but her husband always quit his jobs. Now he was delivering magazines. At one time she had dreamed of seeing him become a doorman behind Manders Incorporated's gleaming plate glass. He didn't make it. She had often seen the vast parking lot in front of the factory full of rows of new cars and motorcycles belonging to the employees, and the envy she had just experienced flared up again. Why should other people be so much better off? Why didn't she have a husband who was hard-working and ambitious?

Ingeborg Roth, too, was thinking of her husband and of how well off she was with him. They were happy; nothing was lacking in their life. When the baby came—and perhaps it would be a boy—that would make two. Oh, her little girl . . . what would she be doing now? She was three, a tiny little thing as full of life as a spinning top, always happy and hardly ever crying. My little angel, her husband called her. She had had to leave the child with her mother-in-law, but she was very fond of her, thank goodness, and there was nothing to worry about. Yes, she had every reason to be happy.

And her husband would be coming this very day at visiting time. She wasn't abandoned. She could no longer understand her sadness of the day before and didn't know what she had been crying about. The room was cheerful; she felt quite at home in it now. Bright right-angled sunbeams moved across her bed, bringing nearer with every inch they covered the time when she could go back to him.

Anton Roth was the first visitor. He entered the room on the dot of three. He was broad-shouldered, stocky, self-possessed, without a trace of embarrassment at being in this room full of women. He wore a lightweight topcoat thrown over his shoulders and a hat of quite as good quality as his boss could afford. An executive hat, thought Betty. He probably had a car. A Goggo or maybe even a secondhand Volkswagen.

"Good afternoon, ladies," he said in his deep voice. "Good afternoon." Then he went over to his wife's bed. "Well, how are you doing?"

Her face beamed with happiness. She held out her arms to him. He hugged her. Their kiss wasn't a quiet one. Then he stripped the paper from a bunch of white carnations.

"But, Tony . . ."

"Do they smell good?"

"Marvelous."

"The nurse will bring you a vase later. I've brought you two more books."

"I haven't finished these yet."

"Never mind. You'll have some in reserve." He tossed his hat to the foot of the bed. "Can I smoke in here?"

"I don't know. I don't think so."

"Oh well, it doesn't matter." In a lower voice he asked: "How are things going?"

"Just the same," she replied. "It hasn't turned around."

"H'm." He took hold of her chin and looked at her sternly. "I'd like to know where it gets its pigheadedness."

"From you."

"No, I've still got all mine. It can only get it from you."

"I'm not pigheaded."

"No, you really aren't. You're a good girl."

"How's Ingrid?" she asked.

"Fine. She keeps her grandma on her toes from morning to night. Yesterday she took everything out of the china cabinet."

Ingeborg clapped her hand to her mouth. "For heaven's sake! Did she break anything?"

"No. She arranged everything neatly in a row on the rug. Figurine parade."

"Was your mother mad?"

"No. She was full of admiration. She thinks the kid's got a sense of order."

They laughed in an intimacy which needed no words. Behind them the door opened. Gerda Holtmann's husband came in. He said good afternoon shyly and went over to his wife's bed less self-confidently than Anton Roth. They kissed, modestly and cautiously. Then they chatted quietly.

Betty Ahlers wasn't expecting anyone. Her husband could only come on Fridays, and she might be home by then.

She had leaned back and was pretending to be asleep, but she was following every word that was said; nothing escaped her. In this way visiting hours made a nice break in routine for her too.

Time passed quickly. Sister Eva stuck her head in at the door. "Time to kiss your wives good-by, gentlemen. The doctor will be here in a few minutes." The husbands took their leave, Anton Roth noisy and self-assured, Mr. Holtmann, the bank clerk, quiet and embarrassed.

Outside the door they ran into the Senior Physician. Neugebauer took a step backward. "Aha," he said. "The prospective fathers. How do you do. Sorry I have to chase you out." Anton Roth introduced himself. "Could I speak to you a minute, Doctor?"

"Certainly. Come along." Neugebauer gave the shy Mr. Holtmann a nod and walked with Roth a little distance down the corridor. "Well, what's on your mind?"

"The—the . . ."

"You mean the shoulder presentation?"

"Yes. That's not normal, is it?"

"No, it's not normal. But it's much more common than you'd think. Don't worry, Mr. Roth, we'll take care of it."

"Without any complications?"

"Without any complications. Leave it to us. That's what we're paid for. And we know our stuff." He laughed.

Anton Roth laughed too. We know our stuff. That was the kind of language he liked and understood. No five-syllable words. He liked everything about this man. "That's fine. I hope you don't mind my asking. I just wanted . . ."

"Of course," said Neugebauer. "Everyone wants to know what's ahead of them, don't they? I always like to be clear about things too." He held out his hand to Roth, who gripped it firmly.

Anton Roth left the hospital quite satisfied.

On Friday morning there was a thorough house cleaning. Not a wrinkle in the sheets, the case histories ready to hand in a folder on the table.

"Head Physician's rounds," said Betty Ahlers, who knew everything. She would have liked to take a look inside the folder, but she didn't dare to. Despite her ample hospital experience she was secretly scared of the indomitable Sister Eva, who seemed able to see through her to the very fiber of her being.

The women could hear the group approaching. Distant footsteps were heard and indistinct voices. A door closed, and all was quiet; a door opened, and the voices came closer. The tension increased as the number of walls the sound had to penetrate decreased.

"Now they're in Room 6," said Betty. "Now Room 7." Their words drifted faintly in, indistinguishable, slightly uncanny.

Ingeborg Roth felt insecure. She would have liked to pull the sheet over her head and pretend to be asleep, the way she used to as a child when it was dark and menacing voices seemed to fill the air.

But it wasn't bad. The door was thrown open abruptly. Ingeborg Roth saw the beaming eyes of the man she had passed the first day in the corridor. Head Physician Feldhusen.

"Good morning to you all, ladies."

They answered quietly, one by one. Betty was first. Feldhusen smoothed her stringy hair as though he really enjoyed doing it. "Well?" he said over his shoulder.

Warzin made his report conscientiously. "Fourth day post-partum. Second occipital presentation. No complications. Lochia slight. Fundus not palpable."

"Fine!" exclaimed Feldhusen. "Music to our ears, Mrs. Ahlers. How about nursing?"

"Not quite adequate," said Warzin in a businesslike tone. "Supplementary formula."

Feldhusen wagged his finger at her. "My dear Mrs. Ahlers, that's not so good. Your milk is the best food in the whole world for the baby. No doctor and no drugs can replace it. Beer comes later."

Restrained laughter broke out dutifully, and Feldhusen waited for it to die down. "So you really must get on the ball. At least for the first two or three months. Will you promise?"

"Yes, Doctor," said Betty quietly. Her voice was free from its usual sharpness, and a faint blush crept up her neck and tinged her ears.

Feldhusen went over to Gerda Holtmann. Warzin began his report but Feldhusen interrupted. "I know, I know." He pinched her cheek. "Well, madam? Nothing doing?"

She couldn't speak.

"Never mind, never mind. No baby ever got stuck yet. They all come out in the end. What are you going to name it?"

Gerda swallowed several times. "If it's a boy—Peter."

"Excellent." Feldhusen glanced around the group as if awaiting their approval of this suggestion. "Peter, the First. And if it's a girl?"

"Lisa. Elizabeth."

"Elizabeth? The First too. You like royalty, don't you? Well, let's hope the little prince or princess doesn't keep us waiting too long." He nodded. Then he came over to Ingeborg.

What nice eyes, she thought. And he's not a bit pompous. Feldhusen shook hands with her. She felt the dry coolness of his hand and was ashamed of her own damp fingers. "A new face!" He glanced at the chart above her bed. "Fine, fine, Mrs. Roth. Are you related to the poet?"

"No, Doctor." She had made up her mind to express herself a little better than the other two, but she didn't succeed.

"Oh well, everyone can't be related to him. But you know his works, don't you?

"A man who broiled himself a chop . . ."

"Oh yes, I know that. My husband bought that book."

"Then you must have a husband with good taste." He turned his head. "Anything special, Warzin?"

Neugebauer answered instead. "The shoulder presentation, Doctor. I told you about it briefly on Monday."

Feldhusen remembered the plump, clumsy woman with the perspiring face as if it had been a bad dream. So this was she! H'm. She looked a bit better now.

Sister Eva had been waiting for his glance. She turned down the sheet. All those present saw the arching abdomen, bulging sideways, its skin stretched taut.

Feldhusen palpated briefly, without really feeling anything. This was none of his business. "H'm, h'm," he muttered in Neugebauer's direction. "This won't cause any complications."

Neugebauer realized that with these words Feldhusen was relinquishing the case to him. He wasn't going to have any more to do with it himself.

"Fine, Mrs. Roth." Feldhusen stretched out his hand. "I'm very pleased with you. A week from today we want to see you back here with a baby. Remember:

"A human being sees the light of day.

"Well, let him come on out and see it!" He laughed and turned away. Behind him the white-coated figures made for the door.

"He's really very nice," said Ingeborg quietly.

Betty propped herself up. "I never said he wasn't. But I like Dr. Neugebauer better. He's not such a man of distinction."

The next two days went by, and the last week of Ingeborg Roth's life began.

On the Tuesday of this last week Gerda Holtmann had her baby. She was gone for three hours, in the high-ceilinged, ugly labor room, on one of the delivery tables separated by white partitions. She groaned and heard other people groaning. Her time came and she thought she could not bear it now or ever again. But then she heard the cry of her baby and forgot all her pain.

Ingeborg Roth and Betty Ahlers lay in Room 8 and although they knew that no sound from the delivery room could reach them here, they were listening tensely. "I wonder if it's very bad," said Ingeborg.

"It's always bad," said Betty in a funereal voice. "Especially when it's the first." And she gave a complete and detailed description of what she had gone through herself the first time until Ingeborg could stand it no longer and began to talk of something else.

Then Gerda came back, and their gloomy mood vanished instantly. They laughed and congratulated the new mother, both chattering at the same time. Gerda laughed too and began to tell them about it, but she fell asleep in the middle of a sentence. The other two waited awhile until they heard her breathing deeply. They whispered good night, and then all was quiet in Room 8.

The next day Gerda Holtmann was a heroine. She had refused an anesthetic; she had wanted to experience the birth of her baby in complete consciousness and not miss it on account of pain. Even Betty Ahlers could not withhold a few words of congratulation.

Later, after twenty-four hours had elapsed, Gerda was allowed to put the child to her breast for the first time. It was a boy weighing almost ten pounds. He cried loud enough for two and nursed eagerly without any trouble. Gerda held him tight. She didn't want to part with him, although he had relinquished the breast and was sleeping peacefully. Her happiness infected her roommates. They became a high-spirited group. Betty Ahlers told stories about her fellow shack dwellers, though she herself failed to recognize their comic element. Their laughter rang out, until Gerda and Ingeborg begged her with tears in their eyes to stop.

Betty should have been discharged during this last week, but fate decided that she too was to witness Ingeborg Roth's death. Her breast became infected. It didn't need surgery, but she had to stay there and she was glad of it. Every day away from the miserable truck garden and the tiny dilapidated shack was to her a vacation to be treasured. Her conscience didn't bother her. Her neighbor was taking care of the children—she'd do the same for her sometime. Her husband could look after himself. She'd go back to her old life in good time, and she'd have to put up with it for many a long year, with plenty of shadow and not much sunshine.

Something else happened during these few days, and if it had not happened Ingeborg Roth would have remained alive. This event set the stage for the tragedy: the roles were cast, and the actors began inexorably to play their parts.

8

In Neugebauer's room at home a letter from his old college fraternity had been lying around for a week. It was an invitation to their annual reunion. Neugebauer was not one of those uninhibited old boys who will go to any lengths to recapture the carefree fun of their fraternity days, but three years ago he had attended a reunion for the first time since the beginning of the war and enjoyed it more than he had expected. Since then he had been a regular participant.

He wanted to go this time too, the more so as this was the special big reunion held only once every ten years. But what about Mrs. Roth? He was expecting her to have her baby on Monday, in which case he'd just be back in time. But suppose it came earlier, what then? He hesitated and could not make up his mind.

It was almost as though Liselotte guessed his thoughts. "When are you leaving for your reunion?" she asked that evening.

"I don't know. Should I go or not?"

His undecided expression surprised her. "Don't you want to?"

"I want to all right. But we've got a shoulder presentation coming up and . . ."

"And what?"

"I've just told you. We've got a——"

"A shoulder presentation!" She was suddenly transformed in the most extraordinary way. She put her hands on her hips and looked at him furiously. "And for that reason you can't go away! You're the only man in the whole hospital who can handle a shoulder presentation! The others are going around without ever having heard of one in their lives, I suppose. Without Dr. Neugebauer it can't be done. No one else can manage it, is that it? I'll tell you what's wrong with you, Hannes. To put it mildly, you're nuts."

Taken aback by her outburst, he stared at her. "But, Lilo——"

She didn't let him finish. First she had to get rid of her anger, and she lapsed into a kind of language he was not accustomed to hearing her use. "I think it's time for you to come down to earth," she said. "I just can't take any more of this. Feldhusen can't operate. Okay, you've told me that often enough, and I just about believe you. But what about the rest of them? Are they all half-wits? And you're the big specialist? You and you alone!"

"Lilo, don't get so upset about it."

"It's time I did get upset about it!" she shouted. "I'm absolutely fed up with you calling yourself indispensable. Today it's a shoulder presentation. Tomorrow it'll be something else. Millions of children are born every day without your help, but here in your hospital you've got to be in attendance. If things go on like this, I'll have to pack up and go on vacation by myself with the children because the hospital would go to blazes without you."

He had fought down his amazement; now he would have liked to get angry himself, but his understanding and sense of humor triumphed. He smiled. "Finished?"

"Yes. You can have your say now."

"I don't want to." He pulled her toward him. "You're perfectly right."

She was still on the defensive. "You're just saying that."

"No, really. What you say is right." He pulled her still closer. "I'm a bit wacky sometimes, that's all there is to it."

She stopped resisting and put her arms around his neck. "Oh, Hannes," she said with a dry little sob. "I'm sorry I—shouted at you. I only want you to . . ."

"That's okay. I know what you want. You're absolutely right."

"So you'll go?"

"Yes. They'll manage."

"Fine," she said with relief and kissed him.

At visiting time on Friday all the participants in Room 8 met again.

It was a good day.

Anton Roth was the first, as usual. Little did he know how close he was to tragedy. Nothing dampened his high spirits.

Soon after him came Gerhard Holtmann, who had not been able to come on Wednesday and whose only news of his wife and child was derived from feverish telephone calls. He came slowly in at the door and halfway across the room. Then he dropped his flowers on the table, walked quickly over to his wife's bed, and bent over her with embarrassed tenderness.

Paul Ahlers was the last to enter, an insignificant little man, dragging one leg. He hadn't been told of Betty's setback, but it didn't upset him. He had been transferred to the office, with more pay. They'd be better off; perhaps they could soon move out of the shack.

They spoke quietly, each to his own wife, privately. After a while the Holtmanns' child was brought in for a moment, though the father wasn't allowed near it. All conversation stopped. Holtmann stood with his arms hanging loose, not saying a word. The other two turned around and looked up, then they got up on tiptoe and formed a reverent semicircle around the nurse, the same distance away as the father.

When the baby had been taken out they shook Holtmann's hand, and at that moment none of them gave Gerda a thought. They were the fathers; only they themselves could really appreciate their achievement; they would have to congratulate themselves, since no one else would do it for them.

A little while later Ahlers was also allowed to see his daughter, and now he held the center of the stage. The piddling little man, who had nothing to show for himself except his five children, enjoyed being patted admiringly on the shoulder by the big, aggressive Roth. For the first time for years—actually since he got out of the army—Paul Ahlers felt on an equal footing with men of higher social standing, and he was overcome with affection for Betty.

They laughed and chatted and were happy together like a big family, and Anton Roth could tell from the joy of the others how great his own would be.

The time flew by.

Sister Eva's stern face appeared in the doorway. They immediately said good-by and all left at the same time. Chance had thrown them together in similar worries and common happiness.

Anton Roth was the last. As he stood in the doorway he glanced back. He saw that Inge was sitting up straight, following him with her eyes. In one moment of silence he registered this mental picture, and his heart was filled with love for her. He waved, and she waved back, and he did not know that she was already on a distant shore, far away from him. The door of Room 8 closed.

When evening came Neugebauer made two visits. The first took him to Inge Roth's bed. Nothing had changed. The baby was lying crosswise; the uterus was completely relaxed. "Yes ma'am," said Neugebauer, "if nothing happens next week we'll have to do something about it. But you keep quiet until Monday. I won't be here this weekend, and I want to be the first to see your baby."

Terror crossed her round face. "You won't be here? Suppose it—starts?"

"The Head will take care of you personally." For a moment he

could visualize—Feldhusen: "Fine . . . everything's going very
nicely . . . everything's going to be all right, Mom . . ." The
voice inside him struggled, but he immediately silenced it. Self-
conceit, vanity, that's all it was. Lilo was absolutely right. He
smiled reassuringly. "This whole place is lousy with good obste-
tricians. No need at all to worry, Mrs. Roth. See you on Monday."

His next stop was at Feldhusen's office.

"Yes, Neugebauer. Do come in." Feldhusen was just taking off
his white coat. Neugebauer helped him on with his suit coat.

"Thanks. What's on your mind?" As he was saying these words
Feldhusen's brain was working like lightning. What did Neugebauer want? The operations had been going well. Nothing had
happened. But these visits alarmed him.

"It's about my fraternity reunion, Doctor. I mentioned it to
you. I'd like to attend. You never know when you'll get another
chance."

So that's all, thought Feldhusen, relieved. "Why, of course,"
he exclaimed. "Of course you must go. I couldn't understand
why you were in any doubt. You can't miss a thing like that.
Which fraternity?"

"Franconia at Marburg."

"Fine. I was a member of a dueling society myself. Holsatia at
Tübingen. Active member for four semesters. Thirteen duels. I
wasn't much of a fencer, but I was a good loser." He laughed
and fingered the scar on his cheek. "Fellow named Raukens gave
me this. A nice chap. He's Head Surgeon of his own hospital
now, somewhere in the south. He wore an eye patch and never
had to worry about that part of his face. Those were the days—
when we didn't know what to do with our surplus energy! Things
are a bit different today. But it didn't do us any harm."

"I enjoyed it," said Neugebauer, "in spite of all that's been
said against us."

"Yes, but who hasn't had bad things said against them? That's
always the case. Today they're more taken up with football and
motor scooters. Oh well, everyone to his taste. But it's wonderful
to meet your old fraternity brothers again at a reunion like this.

Dignified civil servants with potbellies and a sense of responsibility, telling their sons cautionary tales about the seriousness of life."

Neugebauer laughed. "Mine aren't old enough yet."

"So it's still ahead of you. Okay, Neugebauer. Have a really good time. See if you can hold as much as you could in the old days without ending up under the table. I've been disillusioned already myself. We're not the men we used to be—unfortunately. It's a sad story. Everyone wants a long life, but no one wants to get old."

"I'll do my best. Thanks, Doctor."

"You're entirely welcome. Anything else?"

"Warzin's on duty. There's nothing much doing—except the shoulder presentation in Room 8."

"The—er—oh yes, Mrs. . . ."

"Roth."

"That's right." Feldhusen's eyes wandered about the desk. "Where did I . . . ah yes, here we are." He folded a few sheets of paper together and brandished them. "Bills," he said. "A whole stack of them. All for the apartment. Not counting the carrying charges. My dear Neugebauer, if you had my worries! People used to complain about us specialists charging so much. Nowadays skilled labor's much more exorbitant." He laughed. "All the same I'm glad I have a place to live again. It's really very nice. We're having a housewarming tomorrow."

"Congratulations."

"Thanks. You'll have to come over sometime with Mrs. Neugebauer. You really must. Just at present—well, you know how it is. Until the very last detail's complete the ladies don't want anybody to see it."

"I know." Neugebauer turned to leave. "By the way, Mrs. Roth isn't doing anything yet. I'm not expecting anything before Monday."

"What? Oh yes, Mrs. Roth. Well, if it comes earlier we'll manage. I'll be here. Everything else under control?"

"Yes."

"Fine. Well then, have fun and don't get carried away. Goodby, old chap."

Feldhusen shook hands with Neugebauer and accompanied him to the door.

Neugebauer went home in a good temper. He was looking forward to meeting his old friends, and he was looking forward to seeing Lilo. His relationship with Feldhusen was good; they had even been quite friendly in their conversation just now. It would keep on improving. The clouds had dispersed.

The day had been hot, but the cool of evening bore a hint of departing summer and of fall. Later he was often to remember this evening. Here he had come to the parting of the ways.

At 9:10 P.M. on Saturday Ingeborg Roth felt her first labor pain.

It came from deep within her, like a bubble of gas rising to the surface from infinite depths. Inge lay still; her hands tightened on the edges of the sheet. She waited until the sensation of red-hot pincers gripping her body went away. Betty Ahlers, who had been expecting an answer to her last question and hadn't received one, glanced sharply at the other bed. "Anything wrong?"

Inge managed a half-smile. "I think—I think it's beginning."

The other two sat bolt upright in bed. "Lord, Lord!" said Betty. "And Dr. Neugebauer's not here."

Gerda gave Betty an accusing look. Betty regretted her gaffe and wanted to make up for it. "Now the Head will take care of you. Are you lucky!"

Lucky! thought Ingeborg in her pain, but she couldn't say anything. She heard Gerda's voice. "You ought to tell them right away."

She knew she should. But now that the time of decision was at hand she wanted to put it off, wanted a last short respite, like a condemned man begging the executioner for a few extra minutes. "Yes," she said. "But perhaps there won't be any more. I don't want to make any unnecessary fuss." She lay motionless, her eyes turned to the ceiling. The others watched her and saw her relax. Time passed. And then the pain came back and showed in her face as in a mirror.

"Shall I ring?" asked Betty. Inge nodded.

Sister Eva was still at the nurses' station. She could have left long ago, but the night nurses didn't write up the charts the way she wanted them. Nobody could do it properly except herself. She heard the bell, saw the black figure 8 on the indicator. Deliberately, in no hurry, she filled in the last few strokes on the curve to complete it. Then she went in.

She saw at first glance that there was something the matter. Betty Ahlers was sitting at the foot of her bed like a child waiting for Santa Claus. "She's having pains," she whispered audibly.

"Lie down, ladies," ordered Eva and went over to the bed in the corner. "Are you getting started, Mrs. Roth?"

"Yes, I think so."

"Then we'd better get Doctor. Now, now, what are you making that face for? Soon you'll have your baby, and then you'll really have something to brag about."

When she had gone Gerda said: "If yours weighs ten pounds too I'll be jealous."

"Don't worry," replied Inge. "I'll be satisfied with half that."

Five minutes later Warzin arrived. He examined her. He saw that her abdomen was beginning to bulge more pronouncedly in one place. There was no doubt that labor had begun. He'd have to call Feldhusen.

Warzin was tired. The thought of Brigitte weighed heavily on him and absorbed all his energy. He had been looking forward to a night's sleep. Here we go, he thought. There'll be no sleep for us tonight.

"I'm awfully sorry to bother you at this time of night," said Inge softly.

Warzin pulled himself together. "That's all right," he said emphatically. "That's what we're paid for, Mrs. Roth. And this way there's a chance that we'll have a Sunday's child."

"Is it going to take that long?" she asked in dismay.

"I said a chance. It may not take so long. Saturday's not a bad day either. It's always been my favorite."

Warzin went back to his office. Everything was happening at once, as if fate were working against him. He found Feldhusen's home number in his list and dialed. The dialing tone buzzed endlessly in his ear. Finally an affected voice said: "Hotel Grün."

"Dr. Feldhusen, please."

"He doesn't live here any more. Who's calling?"

Damnation! Of course the Head had moved, and his new number was written down on a pad somewhere. He looked around but couldn't find it. "This is the Gynecology Department, Paul Ehrlich Hospital," said Warzin. "I wonder if you have his new number handy. I'm not sure . . ."

"Just a moment." He heard paper rustling and heavy breathing. "Here you are: 32-9-51."

His hand hurriedly wrote down the figures. "Thanks," he said. "Thank you very much. Good-by." He disconnected and waited a moment. Then he dialed Feldhusen's new number.

Feldhusen was standing in the kitchen, pouring champagne into the punch. Fehling, in a black suit and a silver-gray tie, was watching him, a cigar between his teeth.

Feldhusen felt the agreeable carefree sensation which the first few glasses of good alcoholic drinks bring. He put the empty bottle aside, dipped the silver ladle into the punch, and offered it to Fehling half full. "Have a taste." Fehling took the cigar out of his mouth and tasted it. "Is it good?"

"First class. Excellent. Even better than the first batch."

"Punch," said Feldhusen, "is the best drink for occasions like this. You don't get high so fast, or, if you do, only very slightly, and the ladies can keep up with you. Wine's no good for women in the long run. Very few of them know anything about it."

"That's true," said Fehling, although he knew nothing about wine either. He liked hard liquor, straight.

Feldhusen took the ladle from his hand and tasted it himself. "H'm. I think it's all right. Perhaps a tiny bit more . . ."

Gina appeared in the doorway. She was wearing a cocktail dress the color of anthracite, which went well with her hair. Her face had a pale pink glow; her eyes were shining. She looked stunning. "Will," she called gaily. "I have to interrupt you in this important business. Telephone."

"Oh no! Who is it?"

"Dr. Warts or something."

They laughed.

"Warzin," said Feldhusen, feeling gratified at Fehling's obvious admiration for Gina.

"Yes, that's probably it. He wants to speak to you. Professionally."

"These young men," said Feldhusen to Fehling. "The minute you leave them on their own they start calling you up. Say, where's the sugar?" he asked Gina.

"In the wall cabinet, on the left."

Feldhusen went over to the pale blue enameled wall cabinet and took out the sugar sifter.

"What are you doing?" asked Gina. "Are you coming?"

Feldhusen was standing over the punch bowl with the sugar sifter. "Yes, darling. Just a minute. Or—no, tell him I'll call him back in five minutes."

Gina disappeared. Feminine laughter drifted in from the next room until she closed the door.

Feldhusen cautiously added a pinch of sugar to the punch, stirred it, and tasted it again.

"How's your friend Neugebauer getting on?" asked Fehling.

Feldhusen looked up. "You'd be surprised. We've actually become what you might almost call friends. Everything's going very well indeed. A frank talk worked wonders. I'm glad I have him."

"Well, good," said Fehling in a pleased voice. "I always said you'd be able to handle him." He looked around at the brand-new kitchen equipment.

"Nice, isn't it?" said Feldhusen. "And convenient too. Everything in its place, all perfectly worked out, so that by turning on your own axis you can lay your hand on anything. Almost like a modern operating room. Only thing missing is the reflector."

"It looks a bit more homelike than an operating room," said Fehling. "The colored doors, for instance."

"Oh, those. That's the latest fashion. But have you any idea what a setup like this costs?"

"What?"

"Three thousand. Just imagine! Three thousand marks for some kitchen furniture."

"Yes," said Fehling. "Convenience and attractiveness come high. You could do with a few more private patients, eh?"

Feldhusen laughed nonchalantly. "Don't hesitate to send me one or two. It's not only the kitchen that costs money." He picked up the punch bowl, and Fehling opened the door for him.

There were only a few guests: the Fehlings with Daughter Jutta, a friend of Gina's, newly married, and her husband, an architect. The young woman was enchanted with Feldhusen, and it had already been agreed that her first child was to be born in his hospital. Her husband, for his part, was being very nice to Frau Fehling. It wasn't every day that a young architect got to meet a city councilor, even though the latter was unfortunately not a member of the Building Committee. But why shouldn't he provide contacts in the Department of Public Works?

Feldhusen set the punch bowl down on the table. The young man helped him serve. Frau Fehling watched him benevolently, regretting that he was already married.

When the glasses were full again Fehling tapped with his signet ring against the bowl. Everybody stopped speaking.

"But nothing to do with the war, Max," said his wife, and there was general laughter. Fehling gave his wife a conciliatory nod and began on the little speech he had prepared in the kitchen. Feldhusen listened with appropriate seriousness. He had forgotten Warzin's call.

Ingeborg Roth's baby lay crosswise in the womb, slightly tilted, its head turned to the left and its back forward. This one particular baby out of over a hundred to be in this unusual position

—just on the very night when Neugebauer could not come to its help.

Sometimes nature comes to the rescue. The child may turn around, either immediately before birth or a good while before. In the absence of nature's help there is only one recourse: the obstetrician's hands, which may be able to breach the gap in the normal process of birth.

Ingeborg Roth's baby was awaiting Feldhusen's helping hand.

With every contraction the muscular structure tightened, slowly imprisoning the child in its inexorable grip, like a steel vise. The amniotic fluid surrounding the tiny body absorbed some of the pressure, but the stronger the resistance opposing it, the more violently did nature's mighty machine exert itself.

Warzin had returned to Room 8. Looking into the patient's frightened eyes, he found himself unable to tell her the truth. "The Head will be here right away," he said. "In the meantime let's take another look."

He felt the muscles stiffen under the contraction. It's never going to rotate by itself now, he thought. The Old Man will have to take over and do a rotation or she's done for. What a nerve he's got!

He slid the bell of his stethoscope over the shiny skin, inch by inch, until he heard a fast hammering infinitely far away. The baby's heart. It was beating; there was still time.

Ten minutes went by in fruitless waiting. Warzin remained sitting by the bed. He was expecting Feldhusen's call any minute, but it did not come. He watched pain transforming the young woman's face, and he shared her suffering at the helplessness she was condemned to.

Fear seized him. He said over his shoulder: "Would you please ring for Sister Eva, Mrs. Ahlers. Thanks."

When Sister Eva came up to the bed his smile cost him an effort, and she understood why. "Let's take Mrs. Roth upstairs," he said. Then he went over to the doctors' office and hastily dialed Feldhusen's number once again.

In Room 8 they lifted the bed onto its wheels, pushed it slowly forward and out into the center aisle. In one glance Ingeborg took in again all her surroundings of the last few days: the yellow walls and the white ceiling, with the dead gaspipe separating them. The window through which the sun had shone so brightly. She saw her bedside table with the pictures of Anton and little Ingrid. Remember me, she wanted to call to them, remember me for always.

"Will someone let my husband know?" she asked Sister Eva.

"Yes, of course."

She raised her hand and waved. "Good-by, Mrs. Holtmann."

"See you soon," called Gerda.

The bed rolled toward the door.

"Good luck!" called Betty Ahlers. "Good luck! We'll keep our fingers crossed."

Ingeborg Roth's last glimpse of Room 8 was the picture above her bed of the folded hands raised toward heaven.

Fehling's amusing speech was nearing its end. "And so, my dear Dr. and Mrs. Feldhusen, I want to wish you once again happiness and success in your beautiful new apartment. I hope you will stay here a long time—if possible until you leave this world forever."

"Now, Max!" said his wife reproachfully.

"What's wrong? We've all got to go sometime. Now stop interrupting me just at the most solemn point. But may that day not dawn until the next century, for the sake of the hospital and for the sake of all the suffering women and mothers-to-be in our town. I drink to that."

Fehling raised his glass, and they all clinked glasses.

"Now it's your turn, Will," said Gina.

Feldhusen wrinkled his forehead with mock seriousness. "I'm not such a good speaker as Herr Fehling . . ."

"But you can operate instead," Frau Fehling consoled him.

Feldhusen laughed this off with a smile. "Well, let's make it short. My dear Herr Fehling, my dear guests . . ."

The telephone shrilled. Gina rushed to answer. "The Feld-husen residence." She had the receiver to her ear.

"Oh damn!" said Feldhusen. "That must be the hospital. Please excuse me." He stood up.

"You poor man," said Frau Fehling.

Gina put her hand over the mouthpiece and looked at her husband.

"It's Dr. Warzin again. Shall I . . ."

"No, no. Let me have it." He took the receiver from her hand. "Feldhusen speaking. Well, Warzin, what's on your mind?"

The others remained in their chairs in silence, watching Feld-husen: Gina full of pride, Frau Fehling full of admiration, and the city councilor with a trace of envy. They could all hear his answers. Clear, calm answers, which inspired confidence. "You're quite sure? H'm—h'm. Well, don't get excited, son. Obstetrics consists to a large extent in waiting. Yes, I know, but just the same . . . I'll be right there. Have everything ready. And don't be in too much of a hurry. Yes. Don't worry. Anything else? Okay, fine. Good-by." He hung up.

"And now you're going to tell us you've got to leave right away," said Frau Fehling.

"Unfortunately I have. That's the disadvantage of this pro-fession."

"But can't this Dr. Warzin . . ."

"I'm afraid not. It's a complicated case. My Senior Physician is away. And Warzin's a bit young and excitable, like all young kids. There's nothing else for it, Frau Fehling. The Old Man will have to go in."

"You poor man," repeated Frau Fehling.

"When will you be back?" asked Gina.

He shrugged his shoulders. "I haven't the faintest idea, darling."

"In that case you should at least finish your speech," said Frau Fehling.

Feldhusen sank into his chair. "Very well. I won't try to get out of that." He looked at the clock. "Five minutes. You can't keep sick people waiting."

"All right," exclaimed the ladies.

He took his glass and surveyed them all in turn. He sensed their admiration and sympathy. It did him good. He took Gina's hand in his left one. It made a charming impression on the others, and it was genuine.

"Actually the speech is finished," he said, smiling. "But before leaving you, in the service of Aesculapius and in the spirit of old Hippocrates, to help bring a new citizen of this fine town into the world, I would just like"—his eyes caressed Gina—"we would both like to thank you from the bottom of our hearts for . . ."

It was a clever, witty and urbane speech, and the ladies were enchanted.

The Head Midwife, Sister Thea, was waiting in the delivery room. Very few people knew her full name, which was Sophie Thea Countess von Rossfeld-Wernitz. She never spoke of her family and rarely of her past. During the First World War, when blood and tears were stifling the joys of youth, she had put on the habit of a religious order, never to take it off again. She did not regret it. She would never ask any other place than this, never hope to hear any sound more beautiful than the cry of newborn babies, whom she had been helping bring into the world for thirty-seven years.

"Don't go to sleep, Helga," she said to the student midwife who was making up one of the beds. Her voice was harsh and brusque, and so was her whole manner, outwardly at least. She was as much respected as the Head Physician himself, and she considered that his authority alone outranked hers. Neugebauer would consult her cordially and discreetly, like a colleague of equal standing. She thought more of him than anyone else did because he was a better doctor, but she never let him see it. The interns accepted her opinion without resistance. The nurses' faces took on a worried look whenever she appeared.

At the moment all was quiet. The last baby had been born

two hours ago. The room was neat and still. They all turned their
heads as the swing doors flew open and Ingeborg Roth's bed appeared.

A moment later Warzin entered. "Good evening, Sister Thea,"
he said. "Our good Frau Roth wants a weekend baby. And she
insists on coming in here to you. Can't talk her out of it."

Sister Thea's face did not change. Jokes and flattery had no
effect upon her. Besides, she could feel his uncertainty. Her clear,
hard eyes saw the pregnant woman's face lined with pain. She
came up to her and shook hands. "Good evening," she said in a
gravelly voice.

Ingeborg Roth looked up at her shyly.

"Sister Thea won't bite," said Warzin in the cheerful tone he
had heard Feldhusen use. "She only looks as if she might." Sister
Thea did not answer. To her, interns weren't much more than
student nurses, except that they had "Doctor" before their name.
She waited until the patient had been transferred and then bent
over her.

Sister Thea had seen more shoulder presentations than anyone
else in the room. At one glance she realized what was going on.
A pain gripped the swollen body. With both arms Sister Thea
took hold of Ingeborg by her shoulder and thigh, and as she held
her body in this position she seemed to be taking part of the pain
upon herself and helping her to bear it.

When the pain subsided she pulled up the sheet without speaking, glanced at the intern, and left.

Warzin knew what was ahead. Without a word he followed her
into the doctors' office adjoining the delivery room, where no one
could overhear them. Sister Eva stayed beside the bed. Warzin
closed the door. Thea's eyes were giving off sparks. "Where is the
Head Physician?"

"He's on his way. I just called him."

"You did? Just now? Why not earlier?"

"I tried earlier, but I couldn't get him."

"Did you tell him the situation?"

"Yes."

"What did he say?"

"We're to get everything ready. He'll be here right away."

"Right away," she said with contempt. "He should have been here long ago. The waters are going to break any minute. If something isn't done in the next half hour we can make arrangements for the funeral."

Warzin turned red around the ears. "I did my duty," he said sharply. "The Head's on his way."

"Very decent of him!" she exclaimed. "Let's hope he's quick. The baby will have to be rotated and extracted as soon as possible. Did you tell him so?"

"I really have to leave the decision to him."

"Decision? Pah! What is there to decide? You know that perfectly well."

Warzin shrugged his shoulders. "I'm not you, Sister Thea. And I'm not the Senior Physician."

She did not speak. Her lips were a narrow line. All was still. The clock on the wall ticked. Time went by. Sister Thea opened the door to the delivery room and glanced at the patient. Then she turned to Warzin. "You do the rotation," she said. "You've watched a dozen of them."

"Not likely. If anything goes wrong I'll be through as a doctor."

"It's much more likely to go wrong this way."

"That's a different matter, Sister Thea. If the woman dies under the care of the Head Physician, all help was in vain despite the dedicated efforts of the doctors, as they so nicely put it. If I'm in charge, there'll be talk of a young, inexperienced doctor. No sense of responsibility. Fire him!"

"Nonsense," she said scornfully.

He became annoyed. "I might just as well tell you to do the rotation."

"You're the doctor, not me," she barked.

"You're the Head Midwife. You've seen more rotations than I have, and you're certainly more capable of doing one."

Sister Thea was about to give him a bitter answer. There was a knock at the door. Sister Eva appeared. "Dr. Warzin, the waters . . ."

They rushed out and bent over the patient. "There we have it," said Sister Thea softly, and looked at Warzin with angry eyes.

They moved Inge over to the operating table. Warzin auscultated. The child's heart was still beating. How much longer? He saw that the woman was at the end of her rope. She had been brave, but now the gnawing pain in her body was beginning to get the better of her.

Warzin felt cold sweat on his forehead. The Head Midwife drew him aside. "You'll have to get a metreurynter in," she whispered in his ear. He nodded. It should have occurred to him to introduce the rubber bulb to hold back the child until Feldhusen's help arrived.

"Anesthetic," he said quietly. "I'll scrub up fast." He went back to Inge and patted her hand. "Now we're going to get to work, Mrs. Roth. You'll be asleep in a few minutes. See you when it's all over." They all looked at Ingeborg Roth, smiling, reassuring, and they were all afraid of the next hour.

Warzin scrubbed up apprehensively and hurriedly. While he was standing at the basin Ingeborg Roth was strapped down and prepared by Sister Eva. Warzin rinsed the lather from his hands. They stung as he dipped them in the dish of alcohol. He nodded to Sister Eva. Confidently and swiftly she stuck the needle in the vein. The narcotic streamed into Ingeborg Roth's blood. Her groaning diminished, and her eyelids dropped.

Warzin pulled on his gloves. Sister Thea handed him the metreurynter. The rubber bulb lay limp in his hand, and the hand was trembling slightly. He pulled himself together. A lot depended on the kind of showing he made now, and he wanted to make a good one.

It seemed, however, that everything was conspiring against him and that this child was fated to die and to carry its mother along with it to death. As Warzin bent over, a violent pain contracted the patient's body and icy terror came upon him.

His groping finger felt a tiny hand. He knew what that meant.

The child was caught, shoulder-first, inextricably. Every contraction would increase the fatal twist of its body. The dreaded impaction had occurred, with cruel swiftness. It was too late for him to do anything.

He saw the eyes of the Head Midwife and the nurse upon him. He clenched his teeth. A hot, red wave of helpless anger overwhelmed him. Why didn't Feldhusen come? Why did he leave him here in the lurch, with no help and with all the responsibility?

At that moment Feldhusen was standing in the open door of the apartment. He pushed up his cuff and looked at his watch. "Oh dear, it took more than five minutes. Keep the party going as long as you like. I don't know when I'll be back. I may be late." He kissed Gina. "Be a good hostess," he whispered with a smile.

The elevator descended with him. His quick steps carried him out into the street to his car. He was in high spirits in spite of being called away. He was still conscious of the sympathy and admiration in the eyes of his guests, and he felt strong and capable of mastering all difficulties.

In the car he let the top down, switched on the radio, and drove off. The gentle air of late summer caressed his forehead. Softly he hummed the tune the radio was playing, without the faintest inkling of what was to befall him.

In the Head Midwife's office Warzin was standing by the telephone. "This is Dr. Warzin. Excuse me, Mrs. Feldhusen, but is the Head Physician . . . Oh, he's left already? Yes. Yes. I'm sorry to disturb you, but I thought . . . Yes, thank you." Drawing in his breath, he put the receiver down and hurried back.

In the operating room adjoining the delivery room they were waiting in speechless despair. The useless anesthetic was still in effect. There was only one thing to do: the child would have to be sacrificed to save the mother's life. Warzin could no longer hear any heartbeat; it was probably dead already, though he might be mistaken as in this position the heart was sometimes inaudible.

"Is she coming to?" he asked.

"It won't be long," Sister Eva answered softly.

"Carry on with ether," he said. "The Head ought to be here any minute."

Sister Eva wiped the perspiration from Inge's exhausted face. Then she put the mask over it. The woman's breathing rattled; her pulse was fast and faint. The contractions were getting stronger, the intervals between them shorter and shorter.

At this point the child that Anton Roth and his wife had wanted so much was still alive. It had been a very healthy, strong baby, and its little heart had been full of energy. But now it was failing. The constant pressure was blocking the blood stream and closing the umbilical cord.

Just as Feldhusen's car drew up at the entrance the little heart gave its last beat. As he entered the main door it stopped.

They all turned round as he burst in at the door. His face was flushed and cheerful, his coat unbuttoned. They saw his elegant vest, the dark suit, the formal-looking tie. He came up to them with quick steps. No trace of confusion showed in his face when he saw the silent group surrounding the groaning woman.

"Good evening. How far along are we, Warzin?"

We're at the end, Warzin felt like saying. "Impaction, Doctor. Arm presentation. Child probably dead. Danger of rupture of the uterus."

Yet this report, the most sinister a gynecologist can hear, did not seem to disturb Feldhusen. "Come, come, Warzin. Why so pessimistic? While there's life there's hope, as Schiller or somebody said. Well, let's have a look."

He felt the abdomen, quickly checked the pulse. Any other time he would have thought it over more carefully, would have been more cautious and critical and more alive to the presence of death. But he was elated, his heart was full, his brain was working effortlessly. It was so long since he had performed this obstetrical operation that its limitations were vague in his memory. "Yes. Then we'll rotate and extract it."

All three of them froze. Sister Thea was the first to speak. "Rotate, Doctor? A rotation now, at this point?"

He looked into her haggard face and smiled. "Yes, Countess. Have you any major objections? Sister Eva, get me an apron."

"Then the uterus will rupture," said Sister Thea aloud and without a trace of respect.

"Oh, will it? Are you sure?"

"Yes, Doctor," said Sister Thea. She knew she was right, and she was not afraid of anything. "You'll have to decapitate."

"What? Decapitate?" He had taken off his coat and jacket and rolled up his sleeves. Sister Eva was holding the apron for him while Warzin continued the anesthetic. "And suppose the child is still alive?"

"The mother comes first."

Her words re-echoed. A difficult person, thought Feldhusen. One of those old maids who's given up all hope of getting a man. But he kept on smiling. "Shall we leave it to God to decide who comes first, Sister Thea? We have a good chance of saving them both. Why shouldn't we take it?"

"The chance came half an hour ago. It's too late now."

Her words spurred Feldhusen's will instead of curbing it. He was the Head Physician. Was he to take orders from his midwife? "In obstetrics it's hardly ever too late. Alcohol?"

"There's the dish, Doctor," said Sister Eva.

Feldhusen prepared himself hastily. He's going to do it, thought Warzin. He's actually going to do it. "Gloves," said Feldhusen. Warzin held them for him, and he worked them on. "Everything ready? All right, then let's take a look."

They stepped over to the table. Their heads were close together. Warzin could smell the alcohol on Feldhusen's breath now despite the ether in the air. Aha, he thought, so that's why he's so sure of himself.

And then Ingeborg Roth was put to death, though she had committed no crime and no sentence had been passed.

No one protested. No one tried to stop Feldhusen. His hand slipped past the presented arm, his fingers penetrated further and found room to spare. "Plenty of room," he said in the silence. "Excellent."

He felt the child's shoulder. He groped further, hoping to find a foot and pull down on it. If he succeeded he might be able to turn the child around and deliver it, head last.

He did not succeed. Around the dead little body the muscle was stretched taut, seriously overstrained, paper thin; it was holding by its last fibers. And Feldhusen's hand destroyed its last hold. The wall ruptured and with it the major artery which supplied it with blood. Labor stopped like a terrific storm suddenly dying down.

All of a sudden Feldhusen felt that he had more room. The baby was moving. He could reach higher. The baby was turning easily in his grasp.

For one brief moment he felt the joy of triumph. The rotation was a success. He had brought it off. He had won out over all their opposition. All by himself!

The baby's head resisted slightly at the last, but he overcame its resistance, and the child was free.

And then disappointment overwhelmed him like a terrible, stupefying blow. A great wave of blood gushed forth, covering the baby, the table, Feldhusen's arms. Instinctively he stepped back. With wide eyes he stared at his bloody hands.

The midwife pushed him aside. She seized the baby, tied the cord, and cut it. Even before she laid it down on the other table she knew that it would never come to life.

The blood was flowing in a warm torrent. It covered the table and dripped to the floor. They could not stop it.

The patient's face turned pale. Her rattling breathing ceased. Warzin thought he could still feel her pulse, but it was his own, hammering fast in his finger tips.

Then Ingeborg Roth died. She was twenty-five years old. Only her ravaged body remained. Her soul had departed to the eternal stars which were to keep watch over her grave.

"How's the baby?" asked Feldhusen in an expressionless voice. The midwife's voice, harsh and dry, answered him: "The baby's dead."

They turned their heads toward her and saw that it was a boy.

Feldhusen got home at one o'clock. The guests had left. Gina had carried the glasses into the kitchen and tidied up a bit. She was already in bed, relaxed and comfortable against the clean pillows.

As he came in she reached for the switch at her shoulder and turned on the ceiling lights. "Hello." She was shocked. His face was gray, old, and haunted. "For heaven's sake," she said. "Is anything the matter, Will?"

He quickly extinguished the ceiling light, then smiled. But even by the light of the reading lamp she could see that it cost him an effort.

"Tell me, Will. Is something wrong?"

"Wrong? Wrong? Yes, there certainly is. I had bad luck. That woman tonight—she was past help."

"Did she die?"

He took off his jacket, unbuttoned his vest, loosened his tie, and undid his shirt buttons with nervous hands. "Yes."

She took a deep breath. Good God, she had been expecting something worse! A car wreck or something like that, for which he was to blame. But a patient who had died—after all, these things happened. But he was upset, she could see. He would be. She was overwhelmed with sincere affection for him. "Come here, Willem," she said gently. "Sit down here by me."

He sat down heavily on the edge of her bed, and she took his hands and stroked them. "Tell me all about it."

"It was a neglected shoulder presentation. I got there too late. I did everything I could . . ."

"Too late? That wasn't your fault. You left as soon as they called up."

"Yes, I know," he said. "But just the same . . ." He knew she was trying to comfort him. In fact, he had not left immediately;

he had hung around a good twenty minutes longer. Could he have saved her if he had got there earlier?

"What about the doctor on duty? That Dr. Warzin? He was there the whole time."

"The baby had to be rotated, Gina. Inside the womb. That's not easy. Warzin didn't dare to do it. By the time I came . . ."

"And the baby?"

"It was dead anyhow." He rested his elbows on his knees and held his head in both hands. "It's terrible when a thing like this happens," he murmured as though speaking to himself. "Even if it's not your fault . . ."

She looked at him, at his hands, his profile, and his dark hair. He's wonderful, she thought, absolutely wonderful.

It did him good to be able to talk to her in the semidarkness.

Suppose he were to tell her the whole story, wouldn't that make things easier? Then she wouldn't regard him as a great gynecologist any more; he would be able to talk to her about everything—his worries, the panic that came back every time he found himself in the operating room with the scalpel in his hand, his secret fear of Neugebauer. She would help him simply by listening to him, and perhaps then it would be easier for him to achieve the goals he had set himself. While he was wondering how to begin he felt her hand on his neck. "Will! My dear old Willem!"

Slowly he turned around.

She was smiling. "I'm so proud of you."

"Proud?"

"Yes, proud. Because you're taking it so hard. You of all people. A first-class doctor. I'm absolutely certain that if this could happen to you it could have happened to anybody. I'm sure anyone else would have dismissed it with a shrug of his shoulders. 'What can't be done can't be done. I did my best.' I know doctors well enough to know that. All except you, and you're worrying your head about it when it's not your fault. It's all that Dr. Warzin's fault."

"He couldn't——"

"Go on, take his side! That's what you always do. Oh, Willem,

I'm glad you're like that. But don't take it too hard." She pulled his head down between her neck and her shoulder. He could smell her fragrance and felt secure in her admiration, her confidence, and her love.

Later, as he lay beside her in the darkness and heard her light breathing, his doubts returned, taking his thoughts back to the past. He thought of the oath he had solemnly pronounced: *I swear by Apollo . . .* How did it go now? He couldn't remember the words properly any more; only fragments occurred to him. *I will carry out regimen for the benefit of the sick and will keep them from harm and wrong . . . With purity and with holiness I will pass my life and practice my art. . . .* It was all a long way back—such a long way. So many oaths and promises. But of one thing he was certain: he had always taken his profession seriously. And hadn't he been successful all along the line? Hadn't he always been one of the most outstanding and the most popular? Even in school everything had come easily to him; he had passed his final high school examination with distinction. Then college, without having to repeat a single semester, and with all the prestige and glory of the moribund dueling fraternities. The years of specialization. The friendship with his chief, who had quickly recognized his intellectual perceptiveness and his intelligence, who advised him to go into teaching and suggested the subject for his research thesis: *The Unborn: a problem of the new Republic.* A good subject. Just the right one for those times. And in between, like brief, enjoyable adventures, maneuvers with the army reserve. After this, shortly before the war, many things happened in quick succession: his commission as an army reserve doctor, admission to the university faculty, appointment as assistant professor. And always there had been a friend, a mentor, to help him and to take an interest in his career. First Professor Klein, then Divisional Surgeon Schmidtmann, whose aide he had been throughout the war, and finally Gina's father, whom he had got to know during the war and for whom he had done many favors at that time.

All those years there had been little time for surgery. Later, in the POW camp in England, they had no use for gynecologists, and when he returned to the Russian zone he had his hands full building up a modest practice. He would still be there if he had been just an average man. But he had always wanted more than other people. He had left Trude, whose lack of sophistication dragged him down like a weight. Leaving everything behind, he had crossed the frontier and started anew. And he had succeeded! Despite all obstacles he had made it—Head Physician of the Paul Ehrlich Hospital.

And now this woman who had died under his hand three hours ago. Did this mean the end of everything? Gina's right: one mustn't take these things too much to heart.

Gina was lying beside him. He could hear her breathing, feel her smooth skin. *She believes in me. I won't disappoint her.*

Next day the sun shone upon everyone, the living and the dead.

Ingeborg Roth lay in a narrow little cubicle next to the bath-room of Ward 3. The room was tiled right up to the ceiling. Pushed up against the wall opposite the door was a wheeled stretcher. A long sheet, which had been patched many times, was stretched over it and hung down all around. It lay softly over the contours of the stiff body. The sun, halfway to its zenith, slanted in, and its light made gleaming reflections on the tiles. Before long it would touch the still bier, linger awhile, and then pass on.

In the next room but one, separated from this little cubicle by the bathroom, Warzin and the floor nurse were sitting. Sister Eva made the last entry on the dead woman's chart. Carefully she ruled a straight line. The blue temperature curve hardly deviated from normal, but the red pulse line shot sharply upward. At the point where it stopped Sister Eva made a red cross with thick strokes of her pen; it had short crossbeams. "Died, 12:20 A.M." she wrote beside it.

"What was the exact time?" Warzin called across from the other desk.

"Have you got second sight?"

"Why?"

"I've just written it down."

"Homework," said Warzin. "Everybody copies from his neighbor." His pen scratched on the paper. The ink dried quickly; he had to keep dipping his pen, and his fingers had dark blue smears.

Not so simple, the last entry. What should he write? He stuck the end of the worn green fountain pen between his lips and thought so intensely that he did not become aware of the disgusting taste for quite a time. It would be best to keep it quite factual and objective, without any trace of personal bias.

. . . a rotation to foot presentation was performed, followed by extraction (Head Physician Feldhusen). Delivery of a seven-and-a-half-pound boy showing normal signs of maturity. Death apparently intrauterine. Resuscitation attempts unsuccessful. Massive hemorrhage in the mother. Death in state of collapse with circulatory failure at 12:20 A.M. Autopsy requested.

There. That would do it. Feldhusen or Neugebauer could worry about the final version once the autopsy report was to hand.

"Dr. Warzin, Intern," he added.

Then he put down his pen and rubbed his fingers dry on the surface of the blotter. "That's that," he said and leaned back. "Now give me the number again. What did he tell us about it?"

Sister Eva handed him a tiny scrap of carelessly torn paper. "It's a grocery store downstairs in his building. We're to call there in an emergency."

"It's an emergency all right," said Warzin. He laid the scrap of paper down in front of him and reached for the telephone. The fireworks are only just beginning, he thought. He dialed the number.

When he heard the voice at the other end he felt as if he had been through this same situation once before but this time he knew where and when. Last night, when he was trying to reach Feldhusen at his hotel.

"Hello," said a high, squeaky voice.

"This is the Paul Ehrlich Hospital, Gynecology Department. Dr. Warzin speaking. Can I get Mr. Roth at this number?"

"What? Oh, Mr. Roth? Oh, the lying-in hospital? Yes, I can . . . shall I . . . I mean, I'm not . . ."

No, it doesn't sound as if you were, thought Warzin. "Never mind. Please ask him to come over here. Could you do that?"

"Yes, yes. I'll go right up. Karl, do be quiet. . . . Are you still there? I'll go right up. What is it? Is it a boy?"

Yes, it's a boy, thought Warzin. "I'm sorry I can't give out any information on the telephone, but please give him the message as soon as possible, will you?"

"Yes, certainly. Right away. Thank you."

"Good-by," said Warzin.

He stood up and picked up his packet of cigarettes.

"I'll be in my office," he said and went out.

Sister Eva folded the chart and laid it in the patient's folder. Warzin's writing was already almost dry.

Room 8 looked much as it had the previous Sunday. Ingeborg Roth had not come back; her bed was empty, and they were alone. They had waited for her a long time and hadn't gone to sleep until late. They had talked together like children in the dark when the light has been put out and they've been told to be quiet. Now it was day, and no one had come to satisfy their curiosity. A maid had brought their breakfast, but she had no information and couldn't answer their questions.

"She's probably in a private room," said Betty Ahlers. "She must have had a bad time. She'll come back here later. If she wants to . . ."

This time, though, Gerda Holtmann was unconvinced by her roommate's words. There was something in the air—something strange and disquieting. For the first time she felt a desire to get home as soon as possible.

"I'll die laughing if her baby weighs more than yours," said Betty. She received no answer. Gerda had linked her hands underneath her head and was gazing at the ceiling.

At this time the man who had killed Ingeborg Roth was still asleep. He was lying still now, in a deep sleep. Gina had not awakened him; she had got up and dressed quietly. Now she was making toast in the kitchen and pouring boiling water at regular intervals into the filter top of the coffeepot. She was thinking of him. Of his desolate face when he came home and of his grief over the death of this unknown woman. And she was thinking of how she had comforted him and restored the peace of mind he so urgently needed in his profession.

He's still asleep. Later I'll wake him, take him his coffee in bed, and watch him enjoy it.

Smiling, she watched the water seeping continuously through the coffee.

Anton Roth took the last few strides more quickly. The sand crunched under his soles. For a moment he had considered calling back, but there was no point in that. The doctor might not be available, and in the time it would take he could easily reach the hospital. Why waste any more time? No wonder old Frau Vieh-weg hadn't been able to get anything out of them. They'll never tell a third party anything on the telephone.

It was still early. All the stores were closed. For this reason he had got out at the main railroad station and bought a few roses from a vending machine—terribly expensive but never mind.

He pushed the door open. The doorman returned his greeting with a deliberate nod. A new father, you could tell by looking at him. They always came at odd times.

Roth took two steps at once. By the time he got upstairs he was out of breath, and he waited outside the glass door a moment so as not to enter the room panting. Then he walked softly along the corridor to the door of Room 8. He knocked. A voice called: "Come in," but it wasn't Inge. He opened the door cautiously.

His first glance took in the empty bed. But the photographs on the bedside table, his carnations and the novels—all were just as before. She was probably still in the delivery room.

"She's not back yet?" he asked.

"No, Mr. Roth," said Betty. "She's been gone since last night. They took her away soon after nine . . ." His look caused her to stop speaking.

Gerda Holtmann said calmly: "She must be in a different room."

"A different room," he repeated. Then he bared his teeth in a smile. "I'll go find her then. Thank you. Good-by."

But they never saw him again.

With a quiet knock he entered the examination room. Sister Eva was writing. She turned around and saw the dead woman's husband. She had been through this often enough, but it had never lost any of its frightful horror. "Here I am, Sister Eva," he said, holding up his flowers.

She looked him in the face and managed to control her own. She stood up quickly, just to be doing something. "Good morning, Mr. Roth. The doctor's waiting for you."

She preceded him to the door. He had no chance to ask her anything. She hasn't congratulated me, he thought. Or hasn't the time come yet? Or is anything . . .

She knocked at the door and opened it. Roth entered. Young Dr. Warzin stood by the window looking out.

Sister Eva closed the door. Warzin turned slowly around. He nodded without smiling and motioned toward a chair by the desk. Roth sat down slowly and laid down his flowers. Warzin remained standing, doing nothing and saying nothing. He had spent his sleepless night preparing what he was going to say, but no words came to him.

Suddenly from the depths of Anton Roth's body sprang a suspicion, overwhelming him without warning, like a stroke or a torrent of dirty water. They were afraid, he could tell—nakedly, physically afraid. They were trying to keep something from him, the cowards. He jumped up and took two strides to the window. He clutched at the lapels of Warzin's white coat, shaking the doctor back and forth like a rag doll. "Tell me, man, for God's sake. What's wrong?"

Warzin looked at him with pitiful, helpless eyes. For a few seconds they stood facing one another, paralyzed. Then Roth let go of him and stepped slowly backward as if trying to escape from some deadly peril. His voice sounded strangled by frantic terror. "Has something happened?"

"Yes," said Warzin.

"Is she . . . is she . . . ?"

"Yes," said Warzin. What's he going to do now? he thought. What would I do in his place? Lord knows.

Roth retreated again with groping steps. He stumbled into the chair he had been sitting on. He grew smaller and smaller, crumpling, until he was sitting down again. His mouth opened; from his forehead downward an ugly, yellowish pallor suffused his face.

He's going to pass out, thought Warzin. I've got to do something. He hastily opened his cabinet and poured some brandy into a mug, spilling half of it in his hurry. He put the mug down on the desk in front of Roth. It was a coffee mug of enameled tin.

Roth reached for it but did not drink. His head fell forward onto the desk. And then Warzin saw the man's fist clench and crush the mug as if it had been paper. The brandy ran down his fingers and over the desk. A shallow cut just below the knuckles began to bleed.

An endless eternity elapsed. Roth raised his head. "Where is she?"

"We can go to her," said Warzin.

Anton Roth walked bolt upright like a drunken man who is afraid of losing his balance. They went through the bathroom into the tiny cubicle.

The sun was higher now. It was shining brightly on the bier, and when Warzin pulled back the sheet the sunlight bathed Ingeborg Roth's face and the child she held in her arms.

Warzin could not bring himself to look at Roth. At this moment something reminded him of Brigitte. This was a hellish day, despite the sunshine.

Roth was standing close up against the bier.

Warzin went back to the door, then glanced swiftly around. There was nothing with which the man could harm himself. The window? I must watch him, he thought.

Tenderly Anton Roth stroked his dead wife's curly hair as if she could feel it and as if it were hurting her.

"Inge," he said. "My girl."

Warzin felt a salty taste in his mouth. He grasped the door handle behind his back and slipped silently out the door. He let it close and stood outside with his head against the panel. No sound came from within.

9

On Monday morning when Neugebauer followed Feldhusen into Room 8 he saw in Ingeborg Roth's bed a woman he didn't recognize.

For a moment he thought he was in the wrong room, but there were Betty Ahlers and Gerda Holtmann. It was Room 8 all right.

He glanced toward the window again. A new patient, a stranger to him, was sitting on the edge of the bed with an open suitcase in front of her. She was stylish and dark, the very opposite of Ingeborg Roth, with whom she had nothing in common but her protruding abdomen. Now she stood up and looked shyly across the room at the group which was beginning to fill it.

The group assembled around the first bed. There was silence for a moment, and in this silence Neugebauer asked: "Where is Mrs. Roth?"

Warzin and Sister Eva looked at one another. Nobody answered. The patients in both beds began to cry, turning their faces away and trying to stifle their sobs.

Feldhusen took no notice. He turned to Neugebauer and said

in an undertone: "We'll talk about that later, Neugebauer. Let's get through here first." After a hasty glance at the charts he walked quickly past the two beds. He shook hands with the new patient and greeted her with a few of the friendly phrases they were all familiar with.

Neugebauer was listening, but not a single word penetrated his consciousness. He followed the Head Physician through the other wards in a state of crushing, gnawing anxiety.

After his rounds Feldhusen took him along to his office. "Sit down, Neugebauer."

"Thanks," said Neugebauer, but instead of sitting down he remained standing, still and straight.

Feldhusen walked around him with nervous steps. "I'm awfully sorry, Neugebauer. I know how concerned you were about this case. But it was just one of those things. It was simply too late, that's all. I did everything I could. I'm especially sorry for Warzin."

"What?" said Neugebauer. "Did Dr. Warzin do the rotation?"

"No. Good heavens, no. That would really be the limit—for me to try to put the blame on him. Only—well, he waited rather a long time, couldn't make up his mind, called me too late. He meant well, of course—didn't want to alert me too early. And then—well . . ." He stopped and waited for a reply, but Neugebauer's mouth did not open, and his face remained hard and dark, and confronted by this silence Feldhusen's usual self-confidence deserted him. For the first time he felt powerless and insecure. Even the thought of Gina and her comforting words did not help him in the presence of the Senior Physician.

He took the few steps to his chair and sank into it. He put his hand on his forehead and closed his eyes. "That's it, Neugebauer. What more is there to be said? Everyone has his setbacks, and this is a damned bad one. All the same I'm glad the responsibility doesn't fall on Warzin or on you. I have broader shoulders. I'll carry it."

Neugebauer's eyes were cold. He recognized Feldhusen's fear, and contempt overcame any other emotion. "Then I can go now, Doctor?"

"Yes, certainly. Certainly." Feldhusen drew back the hand he had offered and watched the Senior Physician leave the room. There was no doubt about it: today he had been beaten. The last word had not yet been spoken; this was only the beginning of his danger. He must go forward to meet it before it ruined him. He took a cigarette and sat meditating. He was thinking about Neugebauer's eyes and his menacing silence.

Neugebauer was standing beside Sister Eva in the floor nurse's office. He was holding Ingeborg Roth's file in his hand and reading Warzin's final entry:

A rotation to foot presentation was performed . . . (Head Physician Feldhusen). . . . Death apparently intrauterine. . . . Massive hemorrhage in the mother. Death in state of collapse with circulatory failure. . . .

"H'm," muttered Neugebauer and dropped the sheet of paper on the desk. "Thanks, Sister Eva."

"You're welcome," she said, and as he left the room she carefully put the file back in the cabinet. Neugebauer went over to the delivery room. He crossed it, glanced quickly around, but did not stop. He knocked at the Head Midwife's door.

"Come in," she called.

"Good morning, Sister Thea." Neugebauer shut the door and walked over to the desk where she was sitting. "I'm glad to see you looking so well."

She raised her head. The eyes, set among the myriad tiny wrinkles, looked him over sharply but not unkindly. "That's nice of you. And also you'd like to know what happened to Mrs. Roth, wouldn't you?"

Neugebauer knew her. He wasn't surprised. "Yes."

"Sit down. What happened is exactly what the record says. And that's all."

Neugebauer let his hand drop on the desk, gently, without pressure. "Your opinion isn't in the record."

"My opinion is of no account," she said with a slight edge to her voice.

"Isn't it?" Neugebauer smiled. "That sounds as though no one in this hospital had ever paid any attention to your opinion."

She made no answer. He leaned toward her. "Sister Thea, are you trying to tell me that you stood by without saying a word and watched this—this rotation done?"

"I'm not trying to tell you anything," she said. "But if you insist on knowing, I advised Dr. Warzin to do the rotation himself while there was still time. He refused. He was afraid to. I advised the Head Physician not to do a rotation. It was too late. He did one. That's all."

Neugebauer nodded. "That's all," he said bitterly. "And then she was dead. No one prevented it."

The Head Midwife darted her head at him like a bird of prey. "You're the one who could have prevented it. If you'd been here!" She saw her words go home, and she felt sorry.

"I know," he said. "Ever since this morning a thousand voices seem to have been telling me so. The nursemaid turns her back, and the child immediately falls out of the window." Suddenly he exploded, almost shouting at her: "But you—the whole lot of you —you were all here! You stood by and watched him, all three of you. Messing up a shoulder presentation! Just about the last thing that ought to happen. Why didn't *you* do a rotation? In the most primitive village they wouldn't have waited until the medicine man found it convenient to show up."

Sister Thea remained unmoved. "This isn't a village."

Neugebauer drew a deep breath. "No, this isn't a village," he said hoarsely. "This is a gynecology department. Here we wait till it's too late to do anything. It's the simplest way."

She made no answer.

He grew calmer and stood up. "Thank you, Sister Thea. And forgive me for shouting. I wanted to find out what happened from you. Not from anyone else."

He turned to leave. In a hard voice from behind his back she asked: "What are you going to do?"

He looked back at her. "What would you do?"

"Conform to discipline."

Neugebauer looked at her in deadly seriousness. "Discipline," he said, "a fine word!" and went out.

Ten minutes later he was in the Pathological Anatomy building. The room in which he was standing had dead white walls, high arched windows with frosted glass panes which chilled the warm light. The floor was of marble, and four marble tables with wooden racks on them stood there, clumsy and gray. The air was heavy with a stale, hostile odor which never dispersed but to which anybody who worked there for any length of time soon became immune.

Neugebauer was standing near the door beside a plump man with hanging cheeks, the left one scarred with numerous dueling cuts. His jolly face looked out of place in the dismal surroundings. He looked more like a well-established country veterinary than a professor of pathological anatomy. Everyone who died in the hospital came to him; he pronounced the final word of their case histories, and from his lips Neugebauer learned the naked truth he had dreaded.

"Unsuccessful attempt at rotation," said the pathologist. "Violent rupture. Uterus torn. Massive hematometra. Looked pretty ghastly. It's ages since I saw a case like that. Who did it?"

"The Head Physician," said Neugebauer.

The fat man's face underwent a sudden change; it was no longer jolly. "Really? Well, well! Yes . . . well, we'll send the report over as usual. You'll excuse me, won't you, Doctor. I have a lot to do."

"Certainly, Professor," said Neugebauer automatically. Although he had nothing else to do there, he stayed for a little while. He glanced across the room to the table on which Ingeborg Roth's body lay beneath a patched sheet, in the rear by the window—the same position as her bed had occupied in Room 8. She was finished with. No doctor wanted any more to do with her. Soon she would leave this room and set off on her last journey.

In these few brief moments he came to a decision. He went out quickly, breathing deep and fast to expel the remains of the stale, dead air from his lungs.

That evening he stayed at the hospital longer than usual. He was writing a letter to the Health Department, first in rough, with many changes and revisions, then a clean copy on his personal letterhead.

Without one single unobjective word he reported Feldhusen's incompetence in surgery. One after the other, in logical sequence, he listed the four cases: the last and most serious being Ingeborg Roth's, with the pathologist's report. He wrote down the names of the eyewitnesses: Dr. Warzin, Floor Nurse Eva Hübner, Operation Room Nurse Sieglinde Stolp, Head Midwife Thea Countess Rossfeld. He tried to get it all on two pages, knowing from experience that only the first page is read with interest, the second reluctantly, and the third not at all. He crossed out everything superfluous, every inessential word, until there was nothing left but a bare report suitable for an official department or for the record. He concluded:

> May I assure you that the sole motive behind this letter is concern for the patients who are every day exposed to this danger. I consider it criminal to keep silent any longer, and I do not wish to be involved in the suffering caused to families and relatives.

He read it through again. Then he signed the original and the two copies in firm, legible writing. He addressed the two envelopes. The first to City Councilor Scharff, Director of the Health Department, New City Hall. The second to Dr. Feldhusen, Department of Obstetrics and Gynecology, Paul Ehrlich Hospital. He wrote his full name and address on the back. The last copy he carefully locked away.

On his way home he felt easier in his mind than he had for many a long week. He had done what he had to do. He was himself again.

That was why Liselotte did not notice that anything had happened to upset him. She was in the best possible mood, had him tell her all about the fraternity reunion, and then talked about Feldhusen and his new apartment. She was eager to meet Feldhusen's wife. "When do you think he'll invite us?"

"Not just yet," he said shortly.

"Why not?"

He had to steel himself against the pressing temptation to tell her everything, to blurt out that all his fears had been realized, that it was too late for tolerance and reconciliations—irrevocably and permanently too late. He controlled himself. It would be better to wait until some decision had been made. "I don't think they're getting on as fast as they'd like to with the decorating. Maybe he wouldn't care, but she wants to show off her palace in all its glory." He managed to give Liselotte a genuine smile. "If I know you, you'd feel the same way, wouldn't you?"

She nodded, but looked at him as if she were not quite convinced.

"And now," he said, "I'd like to know what we're having for supper."

By the next day the news of Neugebauer's letter had already got around. No one knew anything definite, but that made it all the more interesting, for details could be invented. It was supposed to have arrived in the mail that morning. Fräulein Rieck had seen the sender's name and given it to Feldhusen unopened.

Feldhusen too had read the sender's name, and Fräulein Rieck had noticed that he had frowned and turned pale.

Later, when he came out through the outer office, his face bore its usual friendly expression, but it was still pale. Fräulein Rieck drew her own conclusions and as soon as she had a chance told Sister Louise about them.

References were made to it in the delivery room and in the obstetrical ward too. They seeped through walls and rooms and came to rest in people's minds. And when the news got out about Feldhusen's confrontation with the Senior Physician, which was said to have been formal and icy, with the Head barely responding to Neugebauer's greeting, the situation became pretty obvious, at least to the junior employees: a declaration of war between the Head and the Senior.

"Nice goings on down your way," said Krüger sarcastically to Warzin when he met him in the hall. "Soon the newspapers will be screaming: 'Delivery Room Full of Corpses.' Fine publicity for the department!"

"For God's sake shut up," replied Warzin sulkily. "I've got worries enough of my own."

"Aha. Warzin, the merry old soul, has his worries! Didn't I tell you? What's her name this time?"

Warzin made no reply.

"No doubt she comes of a respectable family. Do you know anything about the letter?"

"What letter?"

"The Senior's supposed to have written one to the Head."

"Who says?"

"I have my sources. My Private Eye Waltraudt got to hear it someplace. From Louise, the Grandmother of God, I think."

Warzin's gesture made it plain what he thought of items of this kind. "Are you starting to believe women's gossip? You get too much coffee from your friend Waltraudt, that's the trouble."

"You never get anything for nothing," said Krüger. "At least you have to be able to use your ears. I'm not sure that I believe it, though it certainly sounds likely. If I know Neugebauer, that business with the shoulder presentation has turned his stomach. He's going to make a stink. You can count on that."

When Warzin did not answer he went on unconcernedly: "Well, it's not going to affect me. I'm going on vacation."

"When?"

"Tomorrow, brother. And you're taking over for me. A nice surprise for you, eh? It was all arranged at the last minute. Come over after a while and I'll hand over the dames in the private ward. One of them knows some fantastic jokes."

"I can hardly wait," said Warzin. "Something to laugh at for a change."

Krüger looked him up and down, smiling. "You do seem to be

a bit shaken by the performance last Saturday. I hope I'll see your ugly face again when I come back—seeing you're so deeply implicated in the business. Well, so long, old pal."

"So long." Warzin walked on, feeling depressed. It was true: he was implicated; he had been on duty, even if the responsibility had rested with Feldhusen. It might get damned embarrassing. But this wasn't the worst of his worries. The trouble with Brigitte bothered him more and haunted him incessantly.

All day long he worried about it. If something wasn't done immediately Brigitte would have the child, and in that case she would obviously expect him to marry her. His fate stretched before him like a dark street with high walls offering no exit.

There was nothing else for it but to have another talk with her—a calm, sensible, determined talk. Otherwise it would be too late.

That evening he felt he must go and see her. On the way he went over and over it in his mind. He was approaching her street, her house. No solution. He was dreading the conversation. What should he say? How should he behave? Friends of his had often asked his advice in similar trouble, in the same fix. Now he was in it himself.

They would have to get rid of the child. The first thing was to talk her into that. The second thing was how. Two stages of a plan which absolutely must work out.

Or should he give in? Say amen, get married, acquire a wife and family? Not on your life!

Deny it? Simply say: it wasn't me. You do whatever you like. No, she could prove it. There would be more of a scandal, and the result would be the same.

Just let it ride? Wait, do nothing, pay the bills when the time came? And have that load on his neck forevermore, the claim on him, those people with their middle-class morality? No, they'd have to get rid of the child.

Warzin turned into her street. The hell with it, why couldn't I have gone home that night instead of . . . Damn it!

As he came up to the house, the door was opened from inside.

Alwin Leonhard, the baker, came out. Warzin looked at him as if he were a bad omen. Her old man. That's all he needed.

Alwin Leonhard's appearance was not what one would have expected from his station in life. He looked haggard rather than well nourished. His deeply lined face was pale from the constant dry dustiness of the air in the bakery and rather unhealthy-looking, and his eyes were unfriendly. Warzin waited for him to speak and mobilized all his defenses. People of this type had a way of doing and saying *en passant* disagreeable things that people higher up the social scale, sitting comfortably in their armchairs, wouldn't even mention until after two o'clock in the morning. He knew the old man had been expecting him to marry Brigitte for some time. Was he going to say so now?

Nothing happened. The old man stepped aside slightly against the closed panels of the door and blinked at him without smiling.

"Good evening, Baker," said Warzin, as if he had never been in better spirits. "Is Brigitte upstairs?"

The old man did not answer immediately. He looked Warzin over. "Good evening, Doctor. She's upstairs." He turned around without a single friendly or courteous word and walked slowly on.

I wonder if she's said something, thought Warzin. What's wrong with him? Oh well, he's been impatient for a long time now. Oh, of course, it's Thursday. His night for playing cards with the boys in the beer joint. My future father-in-law!

Warzin pushed the door open. Hell, no!

He went up the winding stairs in semidarkness. Where am I to do the curettage? he thought. Here? I can't do it here. These people all know what everyone else had for dinner three days ago. She can't have it done here. An hour later her mother will know the whole truth, and after twenty-four hours it will be all over the neighborhood.

He visualized his own little bachelor apartment. There? Impossible. The walls were too thin. Too many people who knew him. And Tilly in the same building—Tilly who came up almost every evening and made more racket than two other girls put together.

Then, three short flights of stairs from Brigitte's door, Warzin stopped. An idea was germinating in his mind. He rejected it, but it would not go away. Was this the answer? Warzin stood still, examining it for weak points, trying to make it seem ridiculous so he could discard it. He felt glad when he wasn't able to do so.

Feldhusen.

The hospital.

The egg of Columbus.

All the circumstances were favorable: Krüger on vacation, leaving him in charge of the private ward himself. Nobody there need know a thing about it. Not even Neugebauer. Only Feldhusen, who was fretting about the bungled shoulder presentation and— if the gossip was true—about the Senior Physician's letter.

I'll tell him straight out, thought Warzin. Take the bull by the horns. He needs me. This is nothing new to him. God knows, he's probably feathered his own nest a bit with this kind of thing in the past.

Warzin climbed one step, then another. The idea was good— daring and simple. A last-minute reprieve. Admission to the private ward of the hospital for observation. Back home again after three days. Absolutely foolproof, according to all the rules of the game. Foolproof? Fabulous. Maybe camouflage it as a tubal insufflation so she can have babies. Warzin smiled and hurried upstairs, taking the last two steps together.

Then he gave his usual ring. Short, short, long, short.

When Brigitte opened the door she saw the last traces of his elation in his face. She had expected him to be gloomy and depressed. A fleeting hope rose in her that he might perhaps be glad about it and that she might still be happy.

In the room everything was as usual, although it was not Monday. The plates, the teacups, the bottle of brandy. Tied to the lamp was a little doll from the Black Forest which he had once given her; it had beady eyes and a chubby face.

Warzin drank three shots of brandy while she was out of the room. Good for you. Loosened your tongue and got rid of your inhibitions. He'd better not have any inhibitions.

He ate quickly, without talking. Brigitte served him, asked no questions, kept quiet. She cleared away. When she came back he was sitting by the window smoking.

"Come over here to me," he said.

She sat down beside him. He took her hands. "See, Brigitte darling, that's what love does to you. We're old enough to be sensible about this. I explained to you the other day why I can't get married yet. And then this had to happen—and on the very same day too. Funny, isn't it?"

He waited to see if she would say anything. She didn't.

"I know you, Brigitte dear. I know you didn't do it on purpose. It's my fault. That's what I'm here for, so we can find a way out of this together."

She still did not speak.

After a pause he continued: "I can't get married until I finish my training. Then we can have all the children we want. But not now. You understand that, don't you, Brigitte?"

He held her hands tight to prevent her from getting excited. But she kept perfectly still. Then he went on quickly: "We'll do something about it. I know it doesn't sound very good to a girl, but it's really not bad. I'm in a position to know. It's my business. It's not dangerous. After all we know what we're doing."

In the twilight he couldn't see the expression in her eyes. Her head dropped slightly; this was her only movement. She said quietly: "You don't have to marry me. Not right away anyhow."

Deep inside he trembled. Not right away, no, but in a year or two. He did not betray his impatience. "No, Brigitte," he said calmly. "We're not going to do that. That's not good enough for us. We're going to do things properly. You know what people are like. We'd have a dog's life. Just imagine your father."

She slipped lower in her chair and pulled his hands up to her face. "I wouldn't care," she said through his fingers, barely audibly. "I wouldn't care a bit. But if I'm sure you don't want to get married now—then I don't want to either."

Warzin breathed carefully so as not to show his relief.

"Werner," she asked as quietly as before, "will I—still be able to have babies?"

That does it, thought Warzin. I've got it made. "Of course, darling. If girls couldn't have babies afterward the world would soon be a damned empty place."

She looked up, straight into his face. She saw only the face she loved, not the trap and not the deception. "Werner, I hope you don't mind my saying this, but you're only young . . . I mean it's still pretty new to you. Can you really . . . have you done so many operations?"

He sat up straight, secure in his certainty of victory. "Don't worry, baby. Don't let that bother you."

"And where do you want to . . ."

"That's perfectly simple. In the hospital. Only just keep quiet about it. Not a word to anyone. You'll be admitted as a private patient for a few days' observation. That's all there is to it. When you come home again it will all be over."

She couldn't believe it. Bewildered surprise came over her face. "Yes, but . . . your Head? Will he allow it?"

"In my case he will," said Warzin.

The next morning Dr. Warzin, Intern, asked to see the Head Physician. Feldhusen was speaking on the telephone to Brütsch when Fräulein Rieck came in. He put his hand over the mouthpiece. "What is it?"

"Dr. Warzin would like——"

"Warzin?"

"Yes."

"Just a moment. Ask him to wait a minute."

Feldhusen brought the conversation to an end with a few cheerful phrases. Slowly he replaced the receiver. Warzin! What a stroke of luck.

Since Neugebauer's letter had arrived Feldhusen had been incessantly racking his brain about the stand he was to take in the coming battle. His first reaction had been to get in touch with Fehling, but he was out of town on business. A good thing too, for it would have been a mistake to bother him. Fehling was too high up; he should be held in reserve. In a matter like this Dr. Scharff, the director of the Health Department, was the appropriate person, but he must be allowed to take the initiative. Who else was there? He hadn't exchanged a single word yet with Neugebauer. He would take care not to. And the others? He had thought of Warzin, who was also involved, but he had hesitated to send for him. Wouldn't it look as if he had a guilty conscience? And for all he knew Warzin might be on Neugebauer's side.

And now here he came of his own accord. This was how it was meant to be.

Feldhusen told him to come in. "Good morning." He came toward him from behind his desk and sat down by him in one of the chairs near the window. This made everything seem less formal and reduced the distance between them, which was of no advantage to him at present. "Nice of you to drop in, Warzin. I'd probably have asked you to in any case. Well, the sooner the better." He pressed his finger tips together and paused, searching for the right words.

Warzin saw his chief's outstretched hands. He remembered them bloody and trembling.

"About that case on Saturday," Feldhusen began. He was making an effort to keep his tone casual. "Mrs. . . ."

"Roth," said Warzin dutifully.

"Roth, that's right. Thanks. Yes. My colleague Neugebauer has . . ." Feldhusen pulled a face as though he had noticed an unpleasant smell. "Well, he's seen fit to send a report on the case to the Department of Health."

So it's true, thought Warzin. A dirty business.

"We won't . . ." Feldhusen continued. "That is . . . it makes no difference at the moment what we think of this action. The point is that it has been taken, and I think that you, as one of the people most directly involved, should be informed. I don't know what will happen—possibly nothing at all—but we may be questioned in some detail on it again."

Warzin conjured up an expression of consternation. Feldhusen noticed it with satisfaction. "Now don't get worried over nothing, my dear fellow. There isn't an obstetrician alive who hasn't had something like this happen to him at some time or other. As my old professor used to say: 'Sooner or later you'll have a lawsuit on your hands just as surely as you'll have to deliver twins.' And anyhow this isn't a lawsuit yet by any means."

"No," said Warzin absently, thinking of Brigitte.

Feldhusen bent forward and looked the intern straight in the face. "And now the thing I want to make absolutely clear, Warzin, is that you can rely on me a hundred per cent. I am perfectly satisfied with you, and I shall make this plain to the appropriate authorities. I'm not the type to put the blame for a misfortune on the people who work for me. You and I both know the course of events. Labor began; you sent for me; I came. We tried to deliver the child and did not succeed. Not the first time that's ever happened, not by any means. Everyone has bad luck now and again. But we seem to have ended up with three strikes against us." He leaned back again. His face bore the hurt expression of a man who receives nothing but ingratitude for his trouble.

Warzin still did not speak, but he felt that it was his turn; he would have to say something.

He said: "Thank you for those words, Doctor. I know what I owe to you."

Let's hope you do, thought Feldhusen, and debated whether it would be advisable to run through the course of events once more so that they could tell the same story when the inquiry started. On the other hand that might look too much like trying to influence him.

While he was still trying to decide Warzin went on speaking. "Doctor, I came to see you about something else."

Feldhusen looked at him attentively and alertly. What's on his mind? he thought. It would be marvelous if he needed something. "Well?"

Warzin took the plunge. He was staking everything on one card. "I wanted to ask you if you could help me."

Feldhusen did nothing and said nothing. Now he could wait.

"It's—it's about a friend of mine."

Feldhusen felt inclined to smile, but he suppressed it. So that was it. Always the same old story. It would never end as long as the world went round. He'd been through it himself.

"A baby?"

"Yes."

Feldhusen did not speak, but left the young man to stew in his embarrassment.

After a painful pause Warzin said: "I wanted to ask you if I . . . if I could have the girl admitted here—to the private ward."

Feldhusen looked him up and down from beneath lowered eyelids, imperturbably. What a colossal nerve the kid had! Proposing to do an abortion as if he were some hole-and-corner midwife—and in his hospital too. He actually had the gall.

"Yes . . ." said Warzin. "That's—that's what I wanted to ask you, Doctor."

After a sinister pause Feldhusen asked: "Do you realize exactly what kind of suggestion you're making, Warzin?"

"Yes, I do, Doctor."

"You do, do you? Criminal abortion."

"Yes, Doctor. She asked me to do it."

"Aha. She asked you to. Never heard of Section 218, I suppose?"

"Plenty of requests for termination of pregnancy are granted, Doctor. In that case it's all right. If not, it's a crime. Who draws the line?"

"The law, my friend," said Feldhusen dryly.

"Doctor," said Warzin, amazed at his own courage, "the law is made by a bunch of anonymous bureaucrats. They aren't the ones to have the babies. And Section 218 is already shaky anyhow."

Feldhusen leaned back and slapped a plexiglass ruler against his knee. What do you know, he thought, just look what I've got here in my own house!

A late summer fly buzzed stupidly and desperately against the windowpane.

"Very interesting opinions you're expressing," said Feldhusen.

Warzin did not speak. There was nothing to say. Inwardly he was trembling, but outwardly he was calm. The Head would have to give him an answer. Yes or no.

Perhaps it's all for the best, thought Feldhusen. Perhaps it's a sign from heaven. I need every man I can get to fight Neugebauer. I need him on account of the Roth woman. And I'll know nothing about it. "Warzin, this conversation has never taken place. You understand?"

"Yes, I do, Doctor. Can . . . Can Fräulein Leonhard be admitted?"

Feldhusen rose. He went over to the window and closed it slowly. "For observation?" he asked without turning around.

"Yes."

"H'm."

He's going to do it, thought Warzin with a violent surge of happiness. He's going to do it. "Thank you very much, Doctor. Thank you very much indeed."

Suddenly Feldhusen turned round, with a hard expression on his face. "We understand each other, don't we, Warzin? In every respect?"

"Yes, Doctor."

"Fine. And—if Senior Physician Neugebauer should get in touch with you please keep me informed."

"Yes, Doctor."

Warzin left. They had become allies. It was not a good alliance.

IO

Anton Roth was awakened by the sounds coming from the kitchen. He sat up suddenly and glanced at his wrist watch. Five past eight. He'd overslept. He jumped to his feet unsteadily and caught sight of the other empty bed with its plump, shiny white comforter, its silky coverlet, and the embroidered pillowcase at its head. Ingeborg's dead! Grief overwhelmed him like leaden gloves pressing on his chest and stomach. He did not need to go to work today or tomorrow or the day after, not until after Ingeborg had been buried.

He would have liked to go back to bed, close his eyes, not think of anything. But he couldn't. He had to take care of so many things. He could hear his mother's footsteps across the hall and from the kitchen the little girl's chattering. The other one would have been a boy, he thought. There was a knock. "Tony?"

"Yes, Mother."

"Are you coming?"

"Yes."

"Your coffee's getting cold."

"Yes."

He dressed slowly, putting on the trousers of his dark suit and a white dress shirt. When he entered the kitchen he saw his mother at the table with the little girl on her lap; she was feeding her the last bites of her breakfast. She put the child down on the floor and gave her a wooden spoon to play with. She wiped her hands on her apron and pulled up the chair for her son. She was a strong, buxom woman, full of energy and always on the go.

He sat down heavily on the chair and rested both arms on the table.

She poured his coffee and passed him the plate of bread. For a moment she watched the child playing at her feet, then she looked up. "I've just thought of something."

He took a slice of bread. "What?"

"The baby carriage. We ought to advertise it right away. It's brand new, unused. We wouldn't lose more than thirty marks. And it's so nicely fixed up. What do you think?"

He put back the slice of bread. "Later on, Mother," he said with an effort. "Later on."

"Tony," she said, "you really ought to eat something. You look terrible already. Yesterday you didn't eat either . . ."

Without a word he took back the piece of bread and buttered it.

"We can easily get a hundred marks for the carriage," she went on. "That would cover the mourning. I'll have to have a lot of things dyed. Including my coat."

He made no answer, choking down his bread.

"And the child?" she asked. "What should she wear?"

"What do you mean? When?"

"For the funeral?"

He laid down the bread he had been eating on his plate. Quite suddenly he lost control of himself. He stood up, and the chair fell over backward noisily. "The child's staying home!" he shouted. "Don't keep bothering me about it. Stop bothering me."

He went out and back to his bedroom. Behind him he heard the frightened child begin to cry. He slammed the door.

He went over to the wardrobe to take out his coat and black tie. It was a big, handsome wardrobe with a wide middle section of the same shiny blond wood that the beds and bedside tables were made of. They had picked out the furniture together.

He stroked the smooth surface with his hand. The doors opened easily and soundlessly. A faint scent of fabric and lavender water came out, a breath of the life that was no more. He saw Ingeborg's dresses on their narrow hangers, silk and a confused array of colors and patterns. He came closer, and his fingers caught hold of one or two sleeves that were turned toward him. His grief overcame him again with irresistible force and enveloped everything. He buried his face in the cool, empty cloth.

From the kitchen he could hear his mother sobbing, restrainedly but loud enough for him to hear. He slipped his black tie out of the rack, tied it around his neck, put on his coat, shut the wardrobe doors, and went back to the kitchen.

His mother was sitting at the table crying into her apron, and the child was watching her with interest. He walked up behind her and laid his hand on her shoulder. "I didn't mean it, Mama."

She raised her head and sniffed. "Oh . . ."

"I'm sorry, Mama," he said and bent down to the child and kissed her. She ran her hand over his face. He straightened up. "I've got to go now," he said and went out.

He went to the funeral director's.

He saw the sign a long way off. It had black letters on a white background, and the words were framed with feathery, upright palm leaves and a black border.

HEAVENLY REST
FUNERAL HOME

Beside the door was a display window, a square of glass like a dark mirror. In the center two slanting gold chains supported an oval glass panel with elegant gold writing, and Roth read again: *Fritz Laternser, Funerals and Cremations. All Arrangements.*

On the floor beneath the panel stood a huge, solidly built coffin. A half-withered wreath with dead flowers lay across one end;

its ribbon curved over the polished wood and trailed on the floor.

Anton Roth entered.

From above his head came a harmonious chime. He saw a vibrating ring of dull brass cylinders of various lengths. The chimes rang out again when he shut the door, then died away. There were three steps down. Each step took Roth deeper into cool, motionless air, which seemed to be as old as time yet still not used up. Along the walls in back of the dim semidarkness were heavy coffins stacked up in brazen stillness. At the bottom of the steps stood a fragile table draped in black, with matching chairs.

From the darkness of the rear wall the figure of a man detached itself. At first it was nothing but a white face with heavy eyelids and grave eyes. A high forehead projected the face upward and a stiff pointed collar downward. Then came a black velvet jacket, striped trousers, and above the well-polished shoes a pair of spats of the same color as the face.

Herr Laternser made his living from death.

Concealing his uneasiness, Anton Roth said good morning to this man, who formally returned his greeting and urged him to be seated. Then Roth began to speak, and out of his vast experience Herr Laternser immediately knew what line to take with him. He offered his suggestions diffidently and unobtrusively. Even in this situation people wanted good advice. Where was the deceased to be laid to rest? The East Side Cemetery? An admirable place to be sure, sunny and quiet. The gentleman had burial insurance no doubt. Yes, indeed. Of course a casket with reinforced corners would last much longer than an ordinary one, and the difference in price was really almost negligible.

Then Anton Roth chose a coffin for his Inge. His fingers stroked the wood and the cool metal trim. He did not hurry and he examined everything carefully. She would have to lie in it a long time.

The formalities were quickly disposed of. Oh yes, the death certificate. Anton Roth didn't have it. Would it do later? Yes, certainly—but by tomorrow if possible. Yes, by tomorrow morning for sure. Anton Roth remembered that he wanted to go to the hospital in any case to talk to the Head Physician, whom he had met in the hall long ago and who had told him not to worry about his wife.

Herr Laternser gave him the address of a flower shop near the cemetery too. He knew the proprietor; they recommended customers to each other. Anton Roth thanked him. He went up the steps and out into the light. The summer air drove away the coolness, and the chimes of the brass tubes at the door rang out behind him like joyful bells. He took the next streetcar to the Paul Ehrlich Hospital.

At this time Dr. Scharff, member of the City Council and director of the Health Department, was sitting in his office. He had spent many years in this room and would spend many more, even if there should eventually be a political shift; this he could count on. He was not a party man; he was a specialist, indispensable.

The parties valued him, and the department needed him. He always managed to get what was required, and he was a good trouble shooter. His name appeared frequently in the medical journal; he had recently been publicly honored at a celebration:

> . . . our beloved and respected colleague, Dr. Scharff, whose initiative, vision, good will, and foresight have erected out of rubble a new edifice—the public health administration of our city, to which we look today with, if I may say so, justifiable pride. We wish you, Dr. Scharff, my esteemed colleague, many more years of . . .

and so on. Oh yes, his position was perfectly secure.

He had been away on a business trip with Councilor Fehling, whom he valued despite his political affiliations. On his return he had as usual found a stack of mail on his desk, among it the letter of the Senior Physician of the Paul Ehrlich Hospital, Dr. Neugebauer. This letter he now held in his hand. Every line increased his ill humor. He had had plenty of experience with doctors' quarrels; he had come to realize that jealousy was usually at the bottom of them, and he was convinced that this one was caused by the same thing. He knew that Neugebauer had also applied for the job without any prospect of getting it. Same old story, he thought. Nobody's willing to live and let live.

This concerned him personally too. He too had supported Feldhusen's application, not from any personal motive but for purely practical considerations. On the one hand Councilor Fehling had recommended him, and he had good judgment in matters of this kind; secondly he liked Feldhusen's manner. His surgery? Scharff had his own point of view so far as that went. There were some first-class surgeons who were by no means automatically qualified to be Head Physicians.

This man Neugebauer, for instance. He just wasn't up to a position like that. Feldhusen was a Head Physician after his own heart. The department was functioning well; people spoke highly of it. Where would we be if a Head Physician's position was so insecure that anyone who wanted to could topple him?

He laid down the letter, the two sheets side by side. Then he asked for a number and waited with the receiver to his ear until he heard Neugebauer's voice.

"Scharff speaking," he said in an official tone. "Good morning, Herr Neugebauer. I have your letter of the twenty-seventh. To be quite frank, it seems to me a bit peculiar. The whole thing sounds rather like informing."

At the other end of the line Neugebauer turned pale. He tried to find a swift, telling retort, but none came to him. "I don't quite understand you, Councilor," he said hoarsely.

"Come now, it's absolutely obvious. Everybody will say: 'Neugebauer's jealous, that's all.' In all seriousness do you really expect me to look into these—these charges?"

"Councilor," said Neugebauer. It took enormous self-control not to shout. Anger was burning in his throat. "I'd like to ask you most emphatically to note the last paragraph of my letter. The matter has absolutely nothing to do with me. The only people to be considered are the patients—nobody else. It would be criminal . . ."

The councilor's furious voice interrupted him. "But, my dear sir, those are just phrases. Every one of these letters I get on my desk ends like that. That sort of talk doesn't cut any ice. When one man has his eye on another man's job he's always motivated by his deep concern for the patient; he always considers it criminal on principle to keep silent. I'm not a greenhorn, Herr Neugebauer."

He heard Neugebauer breathing heavily and fast. His voice was barely recognizable. "If you take that attitude, Dr. Scharff . . ."

Scharff shifted the receiver to his other hand and sighed faintly. "Now listen, Herr Neugebauer," he said in a conciliatory voice. "Don't you want to think it over again? I've had a lot of experience in affairs like this. It's all in my day's work. You'll get into an awful lot of unpleasantness."

"I'll have to put up with that."

"Ah, that's easily said." Dr. Scharff went on speaking persuasively, like a teacher to an obstinate pupil. "Take my advice. Forget the whole story and I'll do the same. We'll put the letter away in the files. Someday there'll be an opening for you as Head Physician, then you can do whatever you want and operate the way you want to. And until then just go along. Everybody has to. There's plenty going on here that I don't like, but that's no reason for me to tear the place apart. Think it over for a day or two and you'll see that I'm right."

Scharff was in the habit of ending his conversations when he thought fit. "And now excuse me—I'll have to hang up. The Mayor is expecting me. Good-by."

Neugebauer heard the click. He sat motionless, then hung up. Yes. This was how it had begun, and this was how it would go on. What a fool he had been to expect understanding and support! They were against him from the very outset. Nothing would be done, nothing at all. The battle was lost the very moment he had begun it. Unpleasantness! He laughed bitterly. He'd heard about unpleasantness of this sort. Perjured testimony, distortion of the truth, vanishing documents. They would all abandon him, one after the other. Suddenly and with painful clarity he saw himself defeated. Nobody would come to his help; nobody and nothing. Not even Liselotte.

There was a knock at his door. He raised his head. "Come in," he said in a tired voice.

Anton Roth entered the room.

The dark suit emphasized the pallor of his face. He looked as if he had aged ten years since his wife's death.

Neugebauer stood up and walked toward him. He wanted to say something, something simple, from the heart, but nothing occurred to him. "Sit down, Mr. Roth," he said.

"Am I disturbing you, Doctor?" asked Roth quietly. There was none of his former energy left in his voice.

"We have all the time we need," replied Neugebauer.

Roth sank into the chair. He rested his elbows on the arms and did not raise his eyes from the floor as he began to speak. "I came for the death certificate, Doctor, for the undertakers. So many errands. I'd never have believed there'd be so many errands."

He spoke monotonously, without emphasis, as though he were relating something that had happened to a stranger. "It's funny when you're suddenly so—so alone. Sometimes I think she's still there, talking to me. Last night for example. And then it's not her after all. Yes. Now I've talked to everybody but you. I wanted to come to see you too, Doctor. Ingeborg always talked about you when I came here."

Neugebauer remained silent.

With groping hands Roth pulled out his wallet, searched through his papers and photographs until he found the death certificate and unfolded it. "It says here: 'Neglected shoulder presentation. Rupture of the uterus. Fatal hemorrhage in abdominal cavity.' I've been told so many different things that my head's going round and round, but I still don't know anything at all. I can't make any sense of it."

The voice tortured and hurt Neugebauer. What was he to answer? Tell the truth? Explain the whole thing to him? What good would that do the poor devil?

"You told me yourself there was no danger," Roth went on quietly. "You said I shouldn't worry. And you said: 'We know our stuff.' Do you remember that? Were you lying to me? I mean, were you just telling me that to . . . to make it easier for me?"

"No," Neugebauer heard himself say.

Roth dropped the death certificate and looked into the Senior Physician's face in bewilderment. "No? But then it must have been . . . then it shouldn't have happened . . ." He stopped speaking, his mouth open.

Neugebauer bit his lips. Should he lie, cover up? Yet he himself had made a stand against the unfairness of it, had written his letter to the Health Department. "It's possible to get the baby into the right position if you do it in time," he said.

Roth stared at him without blinking. His hands slowly folded the death certificate.

"In time?"

"Yes."

"And if you don't?"

"If you don't do it in time the child dies. If you attempt it too late the uterus ruptures."

"The uterus," said Roth, pronouncing the Latin word thoughtfully. "Like it says on the certificate."

"Like on the certificate."

Suddenly Roth straightened up. The dull apathy dropped from him. The old Anton Roth, the experienced machine shop foreman of Manders Incorporated, elected plant union leader, was still there; he had not been destroyed. The question shot out like an arrow: "Who left it too late? Did you leave it to some beginner who didn't know what he was doing?"

Neugebauer felt perspiration on his forehead. I've taken the first step, he thought. I can't stop now. "It wasn't a beginner, Mr. Roth. It was the Head Physician."

"The Head Physician?"

"Yes."

"And he got here too late?"

"I suppose so."

"What do you mean, you suppose so?"

"Judging by the way things went. I wasn't present myself."

Roth stood up abruptly. His face was distraught. "Where's his office?"

Neugebauer rubbed his hand over his forehead. Tiny sticky droplets stuck to his palm. "Listen, Mr. Roth. That's no good. You won't change anything by calling him to account. You're far too upset right now. Go home and calm down and then decide what you want to do."

Roth rubbed his heavy hand over his face. "Upset? Yes, I am. Not surprising, is it?" He grew calmer. "I know now what I've got to do," he said. "I know now. Thank you for not lying to me."

Neugebauer gripped his hand. "Apart from yourself I'm the one who feels sorriest about this, believe me. But don't do anything rash."

Anton Roth nodded and went out.

From the Paul Ehrlich Hospital he went directly to the courthouse. He walked unhurriedly down the long corridors until he came to a dingy brown door to which was attached with thumbtacks a cardboard sign reading: *Office of Public Prosecutor II.*

Anton Roth looked around. Two men and a woman were sitting on the wooden bench opposite the door. There was still one place free for him. He sat down.

The air here was different from the air in the hospital. Dry as dust and smelling like old yellowed newspapers. It constricted the chest and made one feel tired. Roth glanced at the people ahead of him. They sat in silence, staring straight ahead. Not one of them seemed inclined to speak. People came and went. Most of them had obstinate faces and spoke together in undertones; others were embarrassed and went off quickly with lowered heads.

Anton Roth waited patiently until his turn came.

The room had high windows with unwashed panes and ugly faded green curtains. The walls were piled high with dusty gray filing cabinets full of folders and dossiers, stacks of papers, millions of words, thousands of cases, countless destinies. A desk stood exactly parallel to the left-hand wall. The man behind it had close-cropped gray hair, a round skull, and eyes full of his own importance. He was wearing a shabby alpaca jacket and a plastic tie which revealed a large collar button. On the desk, among the folders, stood a thermos bottle and an incredibly tasteless statuette of the goddess of justice with her scales and blindfold. Red rubber bands were twisted around her neck, and she also functioned as a paperweight; the Prosecutor's clerk was a practical man; everything had to serve a purpose. "Sit down," he said. The chair creaked as Anton Roth sat down. The Prosecutor's clerk looked at him passively, without any sign of anticipation.

"I want to bring a charge," said Anton Roth.

"Against whom?"

"Against Head Physician Feldhusen of the Paul Ehrlich Hospital."

The clerk did not react. No name could move him, no title. Charges were brought every day, by all and sundry against all and sundry. They took their course, and the vast majority was soon forgotten. Of recent years doctors were being reported to his office more and more frequently. The clerk did not object to this; they had failed to diagnose his father-in-law's illness and given him the wrong treatment until he died. It was quite right to keep a close check on them.

Roth told his story. But although all his grief was implicit in his words, here, in this sober, dusty atmosphere, they sounded stiff and empty. His suffering, his loneliness, his vanished happiness were turned into a few sentences written on cheap paper.

"I don't want to do him any injustice," he said. "I just want it investigated."

"You just want it investigated," the clerk repeated. He always repeated people's words; it involved less effort.

Roth read the charge and signed it. Then he left.

Public Prosecutor Brandis, to whom the file happened to be assigned, was an aggressive young man. "Public Prosecutor's Office Number Two is the best," he was always saying. "You can't get away with anything here. Not with Two!" This had earned him the nickname "Not with Two." A slightly disabled war

veteran, he was alert and intelligent. Justice and the law were his
life, but this included his career too, and at times it was necessary
to keep that fact in mind.

He read the Feldhusen case, and his forehead above the bridge
of his nose wrinkled with distaste. Not very nice. An old story.
People couldn't come to terms with death; they argued and complained and finally had a brain wave: take it to court—a criminal
charge.

Nowadays every layman thought he knew it all, expected the
same precision in medicine as in technology: one shot and I'm
well again—and if I'm not you'd better look out!

And besides—a municipal hospital. A man backed by the Department of Health, the City Council, the whole electorate. A
case like this was always unrewarding, never led anywhere. Brandis sent for the investigator, Inspector Hennings. They were old
acquaintances, having worked together on several cases, both
tragic and comic. They made no attempt to fool one another.
"Looks like the usual trumped-up business," said the Prosecutor.
"I don't think much will come of it."

"There are some sorry specimens among doctors, too, Prosecutor Brandis."

"I know that. Still, this isn't just anyone, after all. Oh well, I
know I can rely on you, Hennings. You have a good nose in matters of this sort. If there's nothing to it we'll dismiss it."

Eleven days went by before Public Prosecutor Brandis held the
Roth-Feldhusen file in his hand again. It had grown fatter, bulging and weighty. Sworn reports and statements and the full case
history were all contained in the folder. It had become a case, a
legal process, which would still exist long after the protagonists
were dead. The Public Prosecutor turned the rustling pages and
read the whole thing carefully through. Then he raised his hand
and let it drop on the desk as though a witness were sitting opposite him who was supposed to confirm his opinion. Nothing
wrong here. Three hours and ten minutes from the onset of labor
until her death. Why, that was no time at all. Just think how long

it took when his Ursula had Hans-Dieter. Seven hours of labor pains. And what pains! No one could accuse anyone of negligence here.

Moreover there was not an unkind word against Feldhusen in a single one of the statements. The Head Midwife—well, yes, a bit dry and short-spoken but nothing that conflicted in any way with what Warzin had said. ". . . the Head Physician came and attempted a rotation. The child was dead. The mother died shortly afterward."

Here was the autopsy report. Perfectly clear and unequivocal, no hint of an accusation or of professional incompetence. Public Prosecutor Brandis did not know the pathologist, who was an easygoing, even-tempered man who enjoyed life. He liked peace and quiet; he had a deep-rooted German aversion to trouble, and he did not feel responsible for other people's stupidity, least of all for that of a colleague of equal standing, a Head Physician. Anybody who liked could take pot shots at him; he wanted no part in it himself.

And now this fellow Neugebauer! He had already turned in a report to the Health Department about alleged blunders on the part of the Head Physician. Nothing had come of that; they had known what to make of him. So now he had got the husband, Roth, all stirred up. Not very nice behavior in a professional man, to say the least of it. Had his eye on the boss's job, that's all there was to it. There were people like that in the legal profession too, unfortunately.

The Public Prosecutor closed the dossier and pushed it aside. This wasn't going to do anything for his reputation. He knew how cases like this came out. One expert said one thing, another something different. No one wanted to hurt anyone else. And it would end with everybody going home looking foolish.

No. This wouldn't wash. Not with Two.

Public Prosecutor Brandis slept on the Feldhusen case one more night. The next day he sent for Inspector Hennings. He had a long talk with him, and Hennings made a full report.

Feldhusen had been overwhelmingly co-operative. He had

given an exhaustive account of the whole affair without the least reticence. He showed every consideration for the husband, had full understanding for him, would probably have acted the same way himself under such a staggering blow. His Senior Physician —a first-class man, really first-class, but . . . a certain degree of rivalry . . . well, the inspector knew how things were. The inspector had nodded—sure he knew. Feldhusen had helpfully put all the documents in the case at his disposal. The inspector had been given a room in which to interrogate the people involved. He had rarely had things made so easy for him. Nobody was hiding anything; nobody seemed to have anything on his conscience. Only the old Head Midwife was a bit taciturn. He had to wring every word out of her individually.

"*Noblesse oblige,*" muttered the Public Prosecutor.

"That's right," nodded Hennings.

"Well," said Brandis, "just as I thought. There's nothing at all behind the whole thing. The autopsy report is perfectly clear. Thanks, Hennings."

The inspector left.

The next day the roundheaded Prosecutor composed a letter to Anton Roth. It stated that the departmental investigation of the Roth case had produced no evidence to suggest that anyone had been guilty of a criminal offense or of culpable negligence. No indictment could therefore be made. The case had been dismissed. A carbon copy would be sent to the Municipal Health Department for their information.

Then the dossier was closed and filed, neatly and efficiently, as such things should be done. It was placed in one of the filing cabinets under the letter F and there it remained. Soon its edges were covered with fine dust.

For the authorities the case was closed. It was closed for Anton Roth too, for he had resigned himself to the inevitable, and for Feldhusen, who was infinitely relieved. Not, however, for Dr. Scharff, the head of the Health Department. He would not put up with this. He kept order in his department. There were limits which were not to be exceeded. In this case they had been exceeded by Troublemaker Neugebauer. This was the last straw. After a conference, to which Brütsch, the Administrative Director, and Head Physician Feldhusen were invited, Scharff dictated a letter, brief and to the point, like the man himself. The letter went out that same day, by registered mail, to the private address of Senior Physician Hans-Heinrich Neugebauer. It was delivered the next morning.

11

Liselotte was cleaning house. It didn't take her very long—nothing ever did.

From the kitchen window she saw the postman approaching. She knew him quite well; he had been delivering their morning mail for years. He was an old man, dating back to a day which had ceased to exist. Sometimes he used to talk to her about those days or about his vegetable garden on the edge of town.

"Guess how big my strawberry crop was this year."

"Let's see, it's a good year. Fifty pounds?"

"Don't make me laugh, Mrs. Neugebauer. Three times that. And the size of them! As big as potatoes."

He grew flowers too, which he spoke of as if they had been living creatures, and he liked it when Liselotte asked his advice about her window boxes.

She went out when she heard his heavy, slow steps on the stairs. "Good morning, Postmaster General. Anything for us?"

"Good morning, Mrs. Neugebauer. I think I've got something."

He pushed his glasses closer to his shortsighted eyes and rummaged in his scuffed leather pouch, deliberately, without hurrying. There it was. Liselotte recognized the writing. A school friend of hers on vacation. She read it while the old man went on searching. The card was from a sunny resort on the Adriatic. They had all signed it—the husband and the children. There was even a postscript, and while Liselotte was trying to decipher this the postman said suddenly: "Your husband's not home, is he?"

Liselotte raised her head and gave him a mocking look. "No, my husband's not home. I send him out to work during the day, you know."

"I've got a registered letter," he said.

She saw a large blue envelope. The address was written in tiny, angular, pinpoint writing the size of five-point type. *Registered*, it said in big letters twice underlined. *To be delivered personally*. In the lower left-hand corner was an uncompromising official seal.

Municipal Department of Health, read Liselotte. Her heart began to pound. What was it? A registered letter from the Health Department. This could only be a professional matter. Could Hannes—could he have been promoted to Head Physician? "Do you have a pencil?" she asked. "For the receipt."

The old man shook his head. "I've got a pencil all right, but the doctor'll have to sign for it himself."

"Oh no," she said. She was aflame with curiosity. "I've often accepted things for my husband before."

"Maybe," said the old man. "But this is official."

"Well, so what? From the Health Department. We get mail from them all the time. Be a sport and let me have it. If you don't my husband will have to go fetch it. He hates unnecessary errands. He's so busy at the hospital."

The old man hesitated, then relented. "But you'll give it to him today, won't you?"

"Of course I will. He'd chew me out if I didn't." She signed hastily. As she handed him back the receipt and pencil she stepped close to him. "If it's what I think it is," she whispered, "I'll make it worth your while."

He beamed. "Okay. Then I'll keep my fingers crossed. Good morning, Mrs. Neugebauer."

His slow steps died away on the stairs. She stood in the hallway, the letter in her hand, fighting a little battle with herself. Hans didn't like her to open his professional mail. But in this case . . .

She suddenly made up her mind and tore the envelope open. Her eyes skimmed over the lines written in the same pinpoint writing as the address on the envelope. Icy shock gripped her, penetrated her heart, paralyzed her breathing. She staggered into the kitchen and dropped into a chair. And as her heart began to hammer like mad she read it again:

. . . you have irresponsibly destroyed the confidential relationship between Head and Senior Physician. You made a libelous accusation against Head Physician Feldhusen to the Health Department and through untrue statements you induced the husband of a deceased patient to bring a charge against Dr. Feldhusen. In the latter case the investigation proved Dr. Feldhusen's conduct to have been impeccable.

In the light of these occurrences you are no longer regarded as eligible for the position of Senior Physician of the Department. You are dismissed, without notice and effective immediately. You are requested henceforth to enter the premises only to remove your personal property. Your salary will cease with the check you will receive at the end of this month.

An appeal against this decision may be made to the Department of Labor within the appropriate time limit.

It was signed: Dr. Scharff, City Councilor and Director of the Health Department.

At six o'clock, after his evening rounds, Neugebauer signed the usual routine papers in his office. Then he washed his hands, exchanged his white coat for his suit coat, and left.

Feldhusen appeared at the other end of the hall. Neugebauer hesitated for a second, then walked on, not wanting to avoid him.

He had nothing on his conscience, but the icy politeness with which Feldhusen had treated him since his letter was beginning to get on his nerves. He had still heard nothing from the Health Department. It was just about time, and he was expecting something. This uncertainty was disagreeable. They would have to come to some decision in the end.

Feldhusen approached, but just as Neugebauer was getting ready to say good evening to him the Head Physician turned to his left and disappeared behind one of the white doors.

Neugebauer shrugged his shoulders. He didn't care if Feldhusen was avoiding him. As he was going past the doorman and out of the hospital he thought about the Health Department and the conversation with Scharff. They were probably waiting for the result of the police investigation of the Roth case. Neugebauer had heard about the inquiry but had kept aloof and not mentioned it to anybody. It was not a very pleasant situation, but he would have to see it through.

When he found himself outside the door to his apartment he summoned up all the cheerfulness he could. He entered the front hall and as usual whistled the first measure of the old song hit which dated back to the time he had first met Liselotte—"Come back . . ."

There was no sound. He couldn't even hear the children. They must still be out at the playground. On the little table in front of the closet lay a letter. Blue, official. He picked it up. Ah, the Health Department. At last! Why didn't they send it to the hospital? Liselotte had opened it. Registered too!

Suddenly he was overcome with a gnawing uneasiness. Registered? To his private address? He tore the sheet of paper out of the envelope. His eyes flew over the lines, faster than his brain. Then the truth penetrated his mind like lightning. He stood motionless, without thinking. "Well, well," he said emptily. "How about that!"

He did not hear the apartment door open. When he looked up Liselotte was facing him. She was pale but smiling. "Have you read it? It's all nonsense, isn't it? Some mistake . . ."

He shook his head.

"Hans," she said, and her voice was trembling, "it can't be true. You never told me anything about it. You wouldn't do a thing like that."

He took her arm. "Where are the children?"

"Outdoors. The baby's in bed already."

He pushed her into the living room. He went over to a chair, sat down, the letter in his hand, and leaned back as though he had a long, exhausting road behind him. "No, Liselotte," he said. "It's not a mistake."

She had been worrying all afternoon over the letter and had persuaded herself that it was an error, a stupid, idiotic error. She had felt like calling him up, but had not done so because she knew he didn't like to be disturbed at work. In the end she had convinced herself that he would be able to explain the whole thing away in a few words. A joke. A silly mix-up. Something to laugh yourself sick about. Now she heard his words, and their meaning was expanding in her consciousness with increasing clarity and frightfulness. "Why?" she asked softly. "What are they thinking of? Libel, it says. They say you've made untrue statements. Hans, that's absolutely insane."

"Yes, it is insane," he said. "But it depends which side you look at it from."

"What do you mean by that now?" she exclaimed brusquely. "Why didn't you mention a single word about this? You could really tell me how things reached this point."

He began to tell her, repeating what he had seen, how he had reacted, and how he had finally not been able to tolerate it any longer. "I couldn't stand by and watch that bungling any more, you understand? When he murdered that woman that was the limit. The very limit."

"Don't exaggerate," she said violently. "Murdered!"

He slapped his palm on the table. "My dear Lilo, he did." He lowered his voice as if there were a risk of eavesdropping and went on to tell her about the Roth case, about his conversation with the Head Midwife, the pathologist's report, and finally about

Roth's visit. "I told him the truth, after all the rest of them had lied to him. He wanted to go straight to Feldhusen. He was about to blow his top. I told him not to do anything foolish but to go home and calm down first. It's absolutely untrue that I encouraged him to bring a charge, and that's all there is to it."

She snatched the letter from his hand. She had read it so many times already that she almost knew it by heart. "Oh," she said. "Is that all there is to it? Then how come nothing showed up in the investigation? No suggestion that he was to blame. Wholly impeccable conduct. Can you explain that?"

"I haven't had time to think about that yet," he said in a depressed tone. "But I know how a business like this works, and you do too. They're not going to hurt one another. How would it look if they dismissed a Head Physician they'd only just appointed? They'd be utterly discredited. Everyone would be asking——"

She interrupted him, furious. "If you know all that so well, then I don't understand why you started the whole thing in the first place. I simply don't believe it was as bad as you make out. You're —you've gone mad with jealousy and envy."

She saw him turn pale, but she did not stop. "Absolutely mad. How can you endanger our whole existence? How are we going to make out now? Can you tell me that?"

In spite of his indignation he had to admit to himself that he had not given this a thought. He had considered only Feldhusen and his surgery, his hospital, and nothing else. "I'll appeal to the Department of Labor."

"Appeal! How long do you think that will take? And what are we to do in the meantime? Who's going to pay the lawyer? Before you even get into his office you'll have to put down a deposit." She stopped. She had just realized that he would receive only one more month's salary. She could see herself borrowing money, begging, humiliated. Everything would go to pieces—everything. She put her hands over her face and began to cry. "Whatever are we going to do?" she whispered.

There was nothing for him to do but go over to her. He took

her head in his arm and stroked her hair. He spoke soft, comforting words which he didn't believe himself.

She shook off his hand.

The doorbell rang. "The children," he said. But she did not react and went on crying. He went to open the door for the children, and managed to force a smile for them. "Be quiet," he said. "Mommy doesn't feel well. Go to your room until I call you." The three of them tiptoed past him to their room.

When the alarm rang the next morning Neugebauer rolled over on his side and turned it off as he had done every weekday for the last nine years. He sat up, threw back the covers, and put his feet on the floor. Everything was normal. Then memory stabbed suddenly through his brain. He didn't need to go to the hospital any more. He could go back to sleep. He'd been fired. He sat there for a few minutes, undecided, and his face was hard and dark with thought. Then he got up and went across to the bathroom.

Just as he was about to leave Liselotte appeared in her bathrobe. Her face showed traces of tears. "Are you going back?"

"Yes, to fetch my things."

"And then?"

"You know, don't you? To the lawyer's."

"Get yourself a good one," she said.

"I will. Good-by."

He took the same route as usual. The city was awake; bustling people were crossing the streets. The hospital chimney was spewing forth a pale gray cloud of smoke. The doorman greeted him, and Neugebauer nodded to him as he did every morning. It smelled the same as ever; it was the same as ever. Only he didn't belong there any more.

By the staircase leading to the upper floor and the operating room Sister Sieglinde came toward him. "Good morning, Doctor. Are you on your way up?"

"Oh no," he said. "Quite the contrary."

His tone startled her. "What do you mean—quite the contrary?"

He tapped her arm. "Come into my office a minute."

She followed him in bewilderment. He did not speak until they reached his office. He unlocked the door and let her in. "Yes, little Sister Sieglinde," he said, "it's a good thing I met you. I can say good-by to you now without facing the whole crowd."

She did not understand a word. "Say good-by? Are you going on vacation?"

"No. For good."

She flinched. "Why?"

"I've been dismissed."

"Dismissed!" Blood rushed to her cheeks and her voice was full of indignation. "Dismissed—you? Who's responsible for that?"

He smiled but did not answer.

"I know," she exclaimed belligerently. "I know perfectly well. The big——"

"Take it easy now, little Sister," he said. "Excitement's bad for the digestion. If anyone should be excited it's me, and I'm through with it."

"Aren't you going to do anything?"

"Yes, the case is being appealed. To the Department of Labor."

"That's good," she cried. "I'm glad of that. If you need me as a witness . . . any time at all . . ."

"That's nice of you. I may take you up on it." He stretched out his hand. "And now good-by, Sieglinde. There's not much to be said. You've always been a help to me. If it weren't for you . . . well, anyhow, thanks for everything."

She was close to tears.

"And now get out of here," he cried with a show of cheerfulness, "or you'll be late in the operating room and you'll get fired too."

She turned quickly and hurried out.

Then Neugebauer packed. What had accumulated during the four years he had been Senior Physician and inhabited this office was not very much. A few books, publications, periodicals. Most of it belonged to the hospital, to the institution, and he realized that he had only been a guest here, nothing more. The next man would come along, somebody new, and someday he too would pack his things. The institution, this office, the furniture, would outlast them all.

He glanced around before leaving, as he used to do as a boy when he was leaving one classroom after being promoted to another. "Well, that's that," he said softly and closed the door.

He didn't want to see any of them again, didn't want to meet anyone. Except Sister Thea. What Sieglinde had meant to him in surgery Thea had meant in the delivery room. He wanted to say good-by to her—and he wanted to hear what she had to say.

She was at her station, writing. He set down both his briefcases and smiled at her. "I want to say good-by to you, Sister Thea. I've been dismissed."

She looked him up and down with her ice-blue eyes without disapproval. "You have chosen a hard road, Doctor," she said. "And the wrong one."

"I had to," he said. "I couldn't stand it any longer. There has to be someone who'll follow things through to their logical conclusion, Sister Thea."

"Is that so?" she said, and her voice sounded sharper. "You had to, did you? And now you want me to tell you how right you are. What good have you done with your logical conclusions? No good at all. Maintain order, that's what you should have done. Where would we be if everybody tried to defy his boss? You aren't his judge. God judges."

Anger rose in him but he suppressed it. He had come to her, not she to him. He had wanted to hear her opinion, and she had given it to him. He smiled. "Suppose He were to do it! The courts would be out of business. Are we to leave it all to Him? Isn't it also His will that we should act on our own responsibility?"

"And submit," she said. "There has to be order. You should have upheld it instead of undermining it. As it is, this is an era of shaken confidence, of weakened prestige, of authority scorned."

He made a gesture in the air. "I didn't come here to argue with you, Sister Thea. If everybody were like you I wouldn't be leaving. I believe I'm doing the right thing. Perhaps you, too, will come to realize it. And perhaps"—he smiled—"someday you'll begin do-

ing the rotations yourself after all. Good-by. Thank you for your
work—and for everything else."

The hard expression vanished from her face. She came around
the desk and offered him her hand. For the first time he saw her
smile. "All the best, Dr. Neugebauer. I—I'm very sorry. Because
you're the man we're going to need here. More than ever. Good
luck."

He walked quietly through the halls. In the office of the department supervisor there was nobody but a junior clerk. He
turned in his key with a word or two. Then he went downstairs.
The doorman looked after him in amazement until the swing door
closed automatically behind him.

During the next few days Neugebauer was not especially conscious that he was freewheeling, that he was superfluous. He did
not even miss his work. It was like a brief, clearly defined interlude, a vacation from which he could return at any time. And he
had a great deal to do.

He went to see a lawyer he knew slightly and outlined the case.
He would have liked to go into as much detail as possible, but the
lawyer was in a hurry and by interpolating questions continually
held him down to the essentials. He didn't think much of his
chances and saw no hope of winning. Since the Public Prosecutor's office had dismissed the inquiry, the Department of Labor
would be skeptical from the outset. No, the prospects were very
poor.

Neugebauer left feeling much less confident than he had when
he arrived. He had had the same experience as Anton Roth at
the courthouse. In this dry atmosphere of legal justice things
looked different; emotional values became imperceptible; human
reactions meant nothing; passionate involvement did not count.
All that was left was naked, dull facts which spoke a barren language without a spark of life.

That same day he set to work to write his first job applications.
He looked in the medical journal. Openings were more plentiful
again, even for people of his age and experience. He got together
his testimonials. He hadn't had occasion to look at them for

ages; they were buried under old papers, and he read them with fresh interest.

Half his life, his joys and disappointments, were contained in these lines. Work and slow progress. With a smile of satisfaction he saw the grades he had made in his final high school examinations; he found his medical diploma with its elaborate seal, and while he was reading the testimonials he was thinking of the people who had written them. No, they weren't Feldhusens. And yet one man had had one particular failing and another man something else. There was hardly anybody one could respect totally.

He typed out the testimonials on his old portable machine, making four copies of each. They would hardly go under the platen. Occasionally he made a typing mistake and had to erase or start over.

Then the notarizations. Everything had to be notarized; he couldn't get all this done at the police station. He waited long and patiently in a notary's elegant office with the well-groomed secretaries and the deep-pile carpet and then he paid and was horrified at what it cost and thought of Liselotte, who would have to feed the family for at least two months on his last pay check.

He mailed the applications with all the supporting documents. He waited. He still had plenty to do—letters which ought to have been answered long ago; jobs which had been put off again and again. But at last everything was done, yet time still went by at its normal pace. Neugebauer sat at home. He read books and professional journals. He sorted out and reclassified his medical files. Then that, too, was finished, and he had more and more time to spare and thought more and more often of the hospital and the still, white operating room. He began waiting for the postman and watching for him from the window when he was due.

At last the first reply arrived. He was apparently qualified for the position and was among the final candidates. He would be informed soon of the decision. No personal interview until they wrote again.

The next day the second letter arrived with almost identical contents. Among the final candidates. Decision to be announced shortly. He took both letters to Liselotte in the kitchen. "Here, read these."

She dried her hands, and while he was waiting for her to get through he secretly imagined himself winning his appeal and icily declining to take back his old job since he had a new one lined up—much to the annoyance of Feldhusen and Scharff.

Liselotte handed him the letters back. "They're still not acceptances."

"But they may turn out to be. Of course I'll have to have a personal interview first. They want to know exactly who they're dealing with."

"Sure," she said. "They'll also check references. At the Paul Ehrlich for instance."

"They may not. And what if they do? Anyone will testify that I'm not exactly a beginner or a bungler."

"Yes. Feldhusen especially."

"What do you mean by that?" he asked crossly.

"Oh, never mind," she said gently. "Hans, I just wish you had five acceptances." He left the kitchen in a more sober frame of mind. Of course they would check his references. His last testimonial was missing. They'd write to Feldhusen or call him up. No department head was willing to take a chance.

He imagined Feldhusen speaking. He could picture him—the face with the glamorous scars; the coat casually unbuttoned. He could hear his voice, full of cheerfulness and optimism, and his words, which sounded so sincere. Feldhusen the winner. Liselotte was right to be skeptical. The two rejections arrived close together, just as the original letters had.

Neugebauer did not give up.

He had advertised in the medical journal. He had bought other publications, and he sent off more applications that same day. He did not mention his dismissal, and in his advertisement he avoided the phrase "not under notice." So long as his appeal was pending this was perfectly justifiable.

But it did no good. Rejection followed rejection. The same wording, the same formulas. The day arrived when all his documents had been returned, and on this day Neugebauer realized that he would never get another hospital position. All roads led past Feldhusen, and Feldhusen would keep them all closed to him.

During this period he got into the habit of taking long walks. He would take the streetcar out to the city limits and keep on walking until he was tired. It was a substitute for work. On one of these excursions he found himself near the subdivision where his friend Brinkmann had his practice. Why not drop in? It couldn't do any harm.

He would be disturbing his friend, he reflected. So what? He'd spare ten minutes for him. Besides, it was just beginning to rain.

He rang the residence bell. Rosel opened the door. "Hans! What are you doing here? Are you on vacation?"

"No, my good girl. I'm here professionally, in a manner of speaking. Could I disturb Helmut for five minutes?"

"Of course you could." She put him in the X-ray room and disappeared. After a while Brinkmann appeared in a white coat, his stethoscope hanging around his neck. "What an honor, Doctor! Come on in, kid. You're not sick, are you?"

"Never better. Are you terribly busy?"

"Up to my ears. But the folks will just have to wait when I have such an eminent visitor. Have a seat."

As Neugebauer was sitting down Brinkmann glanced at him sharply. "Say, is anything wrong?"

"Depends how you look at it," said Neugebauer. "I'm through."

"What? Quit? On account of that . . . Feldhusen?"

"Quit, nothing. Fired," said Neugebauer. "On account of that Feldhusen."

"Good God, Hannes!" Brinkmann was absolutely flabbergasted. "Tell me about it."

Neugebauer told the story briefly. "But I didn't come here to give you a long lecture."

"It's sensational enough," said Brinkmann. "You could go on a lecture tour. Subject: How to Be and Remain a Senior Physician."

"I'm through as a Senior Physician," said Neugebauer. "And that's what I'm here for. I've got to earn some daily bread for my family. My appeal to the Department of Labor comes up next week. If it doesn't come off, then . . ."

"What do you have in mind? A practice?"

"Not until later. At present I need a temporary substitute job. As soon as possible. I just dropped by to see if you'd keep your ears open among your numerous well-disposed colleagues . . ."

"Sure," said Brinkmann. "I certainly will. That ought to be possible. I'll take care of it." He glanced at the clock.

Neugebauer stood up. "Thanks. And now I must go."

"Excuse me, Hans. I'd love to have a drink with you, but just at the moment—you know how it is. Say, couldn't you come over some evening?" He reached for his appointment book. "Tomorrow for instance. Bring Lilo too. Like last time. Then we can talk in peace."

"Thanks. Thanks, but just now—I'd like to get the appeal over with first. And if you have anything for me . . ."

"I'll call you. Right away. I don't think it will take long."

Brinkmann escorted his friend through the X-ray room to the front door. "Say hello to Lilo and tell her not to worry. They can't get a man like you down."

Neugebauer took the streetcar back to town for a final consultation with his lawyer. It lasted a long time although no new points came up. Still, this time the lawyer was in less of a hurry; he seemed optimistic, and fresh confidence rose in Neugebauer.

It was already dark by the time he got home. The children were in bed, except for Uli, who was hunched over his father's desk, frowning over his math homework. Neugebauer did not interrupt him.

The light was on in the bedroom. He went in and stood still in surprise. On the bed were open, half-filled suitcases. The closets were open. Liselotte was packing. She hardly turned around.

"What's going on here?" he asked.

She carefully folded a dress before she answered. "Mother wrote that I should come and bring the children. She has room. Her tenants have left. I'm going to stay with her."

Neugebauer leaned against the doorframe. His mouth opened but he made no sound. He had already envisaged all possible eventualities. Except for this one.

"Your mother?" he finally asked.

She bent over a suitcase. "Yes. I wrote her. I can't stay here. Do you want me to run up bills all over the place?"

He stood still and saw her slender back and the nape of her neck where her hairline began. She had never been away from him before. This arrangement was a good one and a sensible one, and he didn't know himself how they were to manage, but nevertheless he felt deserted and abandoned. Why didn't she stay and face things with him? "And the children?" he asked. "What about school?"

"I'll transfer them."

"Oh. How long for?"

"I don't know," she said hesitantly. "The transfer would have to be worth while. And you have no idea when you'll . . ." She fell silent.

He was silent too. Strange how everything had changed. Only a couple of weeks ago he would have taken her by the shoulder, turned her around, and laughed in her face: "Are you out of your mind, sweetheart?" Or he would have shouted at her, turned the suitcases upside down, lectured her on what he expected of his wife. Now, however, he stood still and did nothing, because a letter from a municipal office had reduced him to a nobody.

"Yes, of course," he said. "It would have to be worth while. Can I help you?"

"No, thanks. Your supper's in the kitchen."

He went out without speaking.

Later, when they were lying side by side in bed, Neugebauer's bedside lamp was the only light. He was reading the latest copy of the medical journal, but his mind was not on the print and he had been staring at the same line for several minutes. Liselotte was lying with her eyes closed, but her breathing was not that of sleep. Across the room, beside the closet, stood the three suitcases. She still has time to unpack and stay, he thought, and turned the page.

An advertisement caught his eye—a very striking one with a heavy black border. Absent-mindedly he began to read. At the first line his interest was aroused, and he read on quickly:

> . . . modern hospital in the Sudan offers position with good prospects to experienced gynecologist. Good salary. Several years' contract. Accommodation for family. Apply, with usual documents, to the Legation of the Republic of the Sudan, Bonn, Coburger Strasse.

Neugebauer read the advertisement through several times. The Sudan, he thought. Darkest Africa! Exactly what I need. Can't be dark enough. Even Feldhusen's white arm can't reach me there. He searched his mind for geographical knowledge. The Sudan? Right next to Egypt. Not so dark after all. And the family could come on. This was the solution, damn it! He'd write tomorrow. What documents would they need? The usual ones. Including a testimonial from the Paul Ehrlich. So what? Feldhusen couldn't put anything damaging in writing, and they wouldn't be calling him up. The solution!

Liselotte's voice scared him out of his wits. "Won't you stop reading?"

He turned his head on the pillow. Her eyes were open now. "What's the matter?" he asked.

She looked at him, and now he noticed that she had been crying again, inaudibly. "Say something."

She sounded as though she needed help, and he couldn't give her any. "What do you want me to say?"

She spoke in a dead voice toward the ceiling. "This is terrible. Your applications are all rejected. It's no use thinking about a practice without money. I never realized how insecure our position was. As if we'd been walking along the edge of a cliff the whole time without knowing it."

"Most people's position is a bit shaky," he said. "And a storm knocks them over. It's not good to feel completely secure."

"That's what you say. You think only of yourself and your so-called principles."

"Lilo," he said quietly. "Do you think it's easy for me to be left alone at this time?"

"I can't stay here," she exclaimed.

He stroked her arm. "Yes, I know. I understand that. Go ahead and leave and don't worry." He did not say any more, thinking of the advertisement he had just read. Those chickens weren't hatched yet, though. She'd really carry on if he got that job. For the time being he'd better stick to reality. He said: "I went to see Helmut today. He's going to get me a temporary substitute's job."

"You're going to substitute? Here?"

"Why not? I don't care what people say. And I'm not going to do Feldhusen the favor of simply running away. Who knows how long it will be before this is cleared up and settled? So I'll work as a substitute. And you can stay with Mother. I'll send you all the money I can spare."

"Do you think she's going to charge me board?" she asked indignantly.

"Of course she is," he said dryly. "Not now, but later. And me, not you. But it'll work—perfectly well." He wanted to take her in his arms and kiss her, but she slipped out of his grasp and turned her back on him. There had been a glass wall between them since the letter had arrived, and he could not jump over it.

He let the magazine drop to the floor and switched off the light. He lay awake for a long time. Tomorrow I'll write to Bonn, he thought, and if they accept me I'll show those guys what a gynecologist is. But then his dreams of the future faded, and his thoughts returned to the hospital as if to a lost love. Now he was shut out and ostracized, and they were still carrying on without him. He thought of his office. Was his successor installed already? Probably. And he would be more sensible. More sensible but more of a coward. He would watch Feldhusen operate, keep silent, and do nothing. And one day be kicked upstairs with the reputation of being an outstanding doctor, universally respected.

Neugebauer was getting tired. His thoughts were becoming muddled and losing their logical continuity. Just one more question occurred to him before he fell asleep: how can they manage without me?

12

They were still managing all right. Neugebauer's departure had been a shock, but it had worn off. New matters came up; the talk died down.

Feldhusen was supreme. He directed the department effortlessly and with self-assurance. He operated as brashly, as fast, and as inaccurately as before. But there was nobody he needed to be afraid of. Victory had increased his self-confidence, and he went home to Gina every evening like a victor.

She smiled at him. "How are you feeling, Will?"

"Fine. Too much to do, though. I'm tired."

"Come on and sit down. I'll make you a cocktail."

She mixed him a martini.

"Cheers, darling. A nice fat fee came in today. If the private practice keeps on like this for Christmas I'm going to get you . . ."

"Let me guess." She sat down on his knee. "A—fur coat?"

He nodded and laughed.

She rubbed her nose tenderly against his cheek. "But you mustn't wear yourself out, Willem. Haven't you got a new Senior yet?"

"No. These things take time. Besides, Neugebauer's appealed."

"What? Appealed? To whom?"

"The Department of Labor. For reinstatement."

"What a nerve!"

"Now look here, darling. He's within his rights."

"Oh, you're so broad-minded and charitable! Will you have to be there?"

"Heavens no. Not likely."

"I'd like to go, though. I'd like to see what he has to say for himself."

"Don't get mixed up in it, baby. Anyway I want all your attention for myself."

She put her arms around his neck. "If I didn't have you! We're really going places, aren't we, Will?"

"I hope so," he smiled.

Yes, he was going places. And he wanted to prove that he was capable of surmounting any obstacle. He spent twelve hours or more in the hospital every day, for Krüger was still on vacation and they were short-staffed. An admirable Head Physician, absolutely indefatigable—that was the general opinion. The gap left by Neugebauer would soon be imperceptible. And despite the extra work he was heartily glad of it.

So were Louise, the Head Nurse, and Brütsch, the Administrative Director. The troublemaker, with his rigorous watchfulness and his rude behavior, was gone; they could relax. They were more appreciative than ever of Feldhusen, who had brought this about.

The happiest of all was Warzin, although he groaned under the extra load of work that Krüger's vacation meant for him. The dismissal of the Senior Physician seemed to Warzin a sign from heaven.

One day during this period Brigitte Leonhard was admitted to the hospital.

Warzin was waiting for her at the main entrance. They went up to the gynecology department without arousing any interest—a doctor and a patient walking side by side—nothing out of the ordinary. And then, as it happened, just outside the last swing door Feldhusen crossed their path.

He looked up sharply, about to ask a question. Then he realized who the girl at Warzin's side was. He stood still. Warzin said good morning; he nodded courteously and walked on.

"Who was that?" whispered Brigitte.

"Our Head Physician," replied Warzin softly. "Feldhusen. Everything's okay."

He took her to the floor nurse, to whom he spoke briefly when Brigitte had gone to her own room. "Strictly private," he said. "D and C. The Head knows all about it. We'll do it tomorrow. I may do it myself."

On the third day, after some preliminary treatment, Brigitte was taken to a small, still operating room. Warzin was the only person with her. She saw the painful smile with which he tried to cheer her up, then the injection put her to sleep.

Two days later she was released.

13

After the departure of Liselotte and the children Neugebauer sat around for almost a week feeling lonesome and useless. He had sent off his application to the Sudanese Legation in Bonn the very next day, but had received no answer yet, not even an acknowledgment. He wrote a few more applications, but halfheartedly, for he knew nothing would come of them.

Brinkmann's call found him in that mood. "Hello, Hans. Have you got anything lined up yet?"

"No, nothing definite." Neugebauer was annoyed at himself for the prevarication and knew that Brinkmann saw through it.

"I think I have something suitable for you," said Brinkmann. "A man by the name of Paulig with an up-to-date practice on the south side. He needs someone to take over for him for the next four weeks starting immediately. Would you be interested?"

Neugebauer had a hard time hiding his eagerness. "Sure," he said. "When can I see him?"

"I'd do it today if I were you."

"Fine. Thanks, Helmut."

"You're welcome. Say hello to Lilo. How's she doing?"

"Fine, thanks. She's away. At her mother's."

"Oh. Well, when she gets back come over. Will you do that?"

"We certainly will."

Dr. Paulig was a shapeless man, with restless gestures despite his stoutness. One could make a guess at his income but not at his ability. "Yes, my dear colleague, I'm sorry to have kept you waiting. Big crowd today."

"That's nice for you," said Neugebauer.

Paulig made a gesture in the air. "Sometimes it's almost too much. Oh well. I know you by name. You're not at the Paul Ehrlich any more?"

"No." The last thing in the world Neugebauer wanted at this point was to go into the reasons.

But these reasons were of no interest at all to Dr. Paulig. He was interested in something else. He rubbed his earlobe between two fingers with a trace of embarrassment. "Do you—er—intend to start a practice? Here?"

Neugebauer couldn't help laughing secretly. Always the same thing on their minds. Keep out competition. "No," he said. "I'm certainly going to stay in hospital work. I'm still looking around."

It took some time for his suspicious expression to disappear. "Oh—research?"

"Possibly. If I can manage it."

"Ah. You know, people like you belong in hospital work. The rest of us are satisfied with private practice. Seriously, Doctor, the prospects here aren't too good. A small town is the place to go. You can pick up money in the streets there. Here . . . no." He shook his head regretfully.

Neugebauer made no reply. He knew what was on his mind. Always complaining about overwork, but just let any other doctor try to butt in!

"Well, fine," said Dr. Paulig. "Let's make it snappy. Can you start Monday?"

"I certainly can."

"Excellent. And—would forty be all right?"

Forty marks a day, thought Neugebauer. More than he had expected. That was roughly what he'd made at the hospital. Fine, fine. Liselotte would be surprised. They could manage on that for some time to come. There would always be openings for temporary substitutes. No need to despair so long as you didn't mind working for strangers, like a day laborer.

"Yes," he said.

"It's settled then." Paulig stood up quickly, pleased that he hadn't had to haggle over money. "Perhaps you'd like me to show you around a bit."

When Neugebauer got home he found two letters in the hall. One was a notice to appear before the Department of Labor. The case was to come up on the Friday of the following week. The other letter was from the Sudanese Legation: a short, extremely courteous acknowledgment of his application and a request to be patient.

So I've still got a chance, he thought. Two chances, in fact: Africa and a favorable verdict in the appeal.

That evening he treated himself to a bottle of wine and dreamed about the future. The African project was very much on his mind. He took out his atlas and looked up the Sudan, but he saw nothing but a few perfectly straight boundaries, the names of one or two towns, and a lot of yellow desert. Nevertheless this fresh hope excited him. There would be no Feldhusen there and no Department of Health. There the only things that counted would be ability, staying power, strength, patience. These were not new to him. He would make out. He went on drinking and dreaming. If he won his case they'd really sit up when he promptly gave notice and went off to Africa.

He stayed up late that evening, and when the bottle was empty he went to bed feeling almost cheerful.

The next morning he took over from his colleague Paulig. He soon began to feel at home. He got along well with the receptionist-nurse, who was efficient and reliable even if she did consider herself the guardian of the practice and keep a suspicious eye on everything he did.

His days were now fully occupied. He had less time to think of Liselotte and everything else, so it did not seem long until Friday came around, the day his appeal to the Department of Labor was to be heard.

A clear, cool autumn wind was blowing as he took the streetcar to the courthouse. The hearing was to begin at eleven. He had had to leave the office early and switch a few appointments.

His lawyer arrived shortly after him and gave him a hasty, absent-minded greeting. They walked up and down the dim lobby with its arched roof. "How do you think we're going to make out?" asked Neugebauer.

The lawyer shrugged. In his ballooning robe he looked like a big, blown-up raven. "It's hard to tell. It all depends on the judge. I don't know this man. I don't get over here very often. Don't say anything unless he asks you a question, and whatever happens don't get excited. Apart from that we'll just have to wait and see and trust in the Lord."

"I hardly think He's going to be much interested," said Neugebauer with a touch of annoyance.

They paced the floor for quite a long time before their case was called.

The courtroom was large, almost like a public hall. The heating system was inadequate. It was lighted by three wide windows facing the door. To the right, on a low dais, stood a long, desklike table. At right angles to it on either side stood two smaller wooden cabinets, blocking access to the table. The left-hand wall was taken up by rows of chairs crowded together in disorder. Neugebauer glanced in that direction first and saw a few people whom he didn't recognize staring at him with curiosity.

No one from the hospital.

Three judges sat behind the table on the platform. The one in the middle was the judge who specialized in labor disputes. The others were deputy judges and laymen: one an employer, the other an employee. Everything had to be fair, both in fact and in appearance.

A third man had entered behind Neugebauer and his lawyer. He had a scarred face and a long saber cut on his cheek. He wore a dark, custom-made suit and a dove-gray vest. He looked extremely well groomed, alert, and composed. He was the opposing counsel, *Oberregierungsrat* Dr. Dietrich, attorney for the Department of Health. Rarely lost a case. A civil servant with life tenure, successfully married to the daughter of a wealthy textile manufacturer, free of worries, secure—absolutely unassailable.

One more person came in before the first words were spoken. A young woman, blond and strikingly beautiful. She was wearing a moss-green doeskin coat and a dull red scarf with rich, glowing tones. All the men looked up at her. She said good morning quietly and walked quickly over to the last row of chairs. The judge watched her with a benevolent smile.

Neugebauer looked at her too. He had the feeling that he had seen her face before, but he couldn't place it.

Gina Feldhusen recognized Neugebauer immediately from their brief encounter in the hospital corridor. She was here without her husband's knowledge, driven by an inner uncertainty which she had not been able to shake off since the night Will had come home from the hospital so upset. Here the whole business of what had happened to that patient would be discussed. Gina wanted to hear it all.

The judge looked up. All sounds in the room ceased. "I declare the proceedings open." He glanced around at every face. "Gentlemen, Dr. Dietrich, Attorney for the plaintiff, you are familiar in full detail with the case to be decided. The plaintiff's case has been presented to us."

His eyes came to rest on Neugebauer.

"Dr. Neugebauer—you may remain seated—the fact is that you feel the dismissal without notice imposed upon you by the Department of Health to be unjust. I think the best thing will be for you to run through your point of view again. Will you do so?"

Neugebauer looked at his lawyer. He nodded and shrugged imperceptibly just as he had out in the lobby. Neugebauer felt uncertain. He had expected questions—short, factual questions, and now he was supposed to tell his story, unrehearsed, in front of all these people.

His words came out slowly and heavily; even to himself they seemed clumsy and unconvincing.

Gina thought: How awkward he is! Exactly the way Will described him.

Neugebauer was saying: "I had been at the Paul Ehrlich Hospital for nine years. Five as resident and four as Senior Physician. I consider it unjust after all this time to dismiss me without notice and without even hearing my side of the case."

He was beginning to get worked up.

"We are hearing your case now," said the judge in a friendly voice. "Please go on."

Neugebauer spoke faster. "In all those years I never had a single major disagreement either with Professor Weinreich or with anybody else. I was ready to continue this same friendly co-operation with Dr. Feldhusen when he succeeded Professor Weinreich."

The judge raised his left hand slightly in Neugebauer's direction. "In your opinion why did this co-operation not succeed?"

Neugebauer thought over his reply. Perhaps everything hinged on this reply, which was going to sound too brash and arrogant. But he could do nothing except stick to the unvarnished truth. "This co-operation did not succeed because I did not agree with Dr. Feldhusen's surgical technique." Neugebauer had raised his voice. His eyes searched for the protest he expected.

But none came. The judge still wore his friendly expression. The lawyer, however, turned to Neugebauer. "Make it short," he whispered.

Neugebauer moistened his lips. "I kept a record of the cases and brought them to the attention of the Health Department when I felt I could no longer tolerate it."

Once again there was silence. Only the *Oberregierungsrat*

at the other table was making a note. "I sent a carbon copy to the Head Physician for his information. I am not in the habit of intriguing behind a person's back——"

The judge interrupted him. "After receiving this carbon copy did Dr. Feldhusen mention it to you?"

"No. Since that time we have confined ourselves to the bare essentials of professional contact."

"And before that? While your—your objections to Dr. Feldhusen's surgical technique were growing did you ever talk to him about it?"

"Yes, I did," said Neugebauer. "I never made any secret of my attitude. After nearly all the cases I noted and reported on I had a talk with him. After the fourth case I took the pathological specimen to him, a uterus which he had perforated while operating."

"And what did he say?"

"He admitted his mistake. He regretted it." Neugebauer stopped. He realized that here he was speaking for Feldhusen. "Then he had the specimen destroyed."

He was expecting another question, but none came. Everyone was listening to his words. "After the fifth and last case we had a talk too. He tried to excuse himself on the grounds that the case represented a misfortune which might have happened to anybody. I didn't say any more. After this fifth case I sent in my report to the Health Department."

The presiding judge was riffling through his papers. "Ah, this fifth case—that's the one that gave rise to the charge against Dr. Feldhusen. What can you tell us about that?"

"I was not responsible for that charge. I gave the husband, who came to me in desperation, not knowing where to turn, a full account because he had not been told the truth and because . . ."

"Has that always been your policy, Dr. Neugebauer?"

Neugebauer hesitated. "Whenever possible," he said quietly. "I have tried to tell the truth as far as possible without hurting anybody, and in this case—this was a sheer medical blunder . . ."

"Dr. Neugebauer," said the judge forcefully, "before we continue may I remind you once again that we do not have to determine Dr. Feldhusen's competence in surgery. The only thing we have to determine is whether your dismissal without notice was justified under the applicable labor legislation or not. That is to say, we must examine in this connection not Dr. Feldhusen's conduct but yours."

"I know that, Your Honor," said Neugebauer. "My lawyer has instructed me. But my conduct was the result of that of the Head Physician." Sudden annoyance flashed through Neugebauer. "If he could operate I wouldn't be here."

Everyone was quiet. The judge waited for the plaintiff's anger to subside.

Gina Feldhusen sat still on her chair. What a nerve he has! she thought. Yet at the same time the uncertainty was troubling her again. This man Neugebauer didn't make a bad impression in spite of everything, and Will himself had always admired his ability. Was it possible that after all . . . ? The idea made her feel ill.

Then came the next question. "So in the next case of a similar kind, Dr. Neugebauer, you would have done the same thing? You would have given your point of view to a relative and exposed the Head Physician in just the same way?"

The lawyer gave Neugebauer a warning glance. He paid no attention to it. "In such a flagrant case I would. I can't watch people being slaughtered without doing something about it."

Slaughtered! thought Gina and flushed with indignation.

"Now, now," said the judge, and for the first time his voice held reproof, "that seems to me rather a strong word. I think we'll hear what the representative of the Health Department has to say now. Or do you wish to say anything else?"

"Yes," said Neugebauer, "I named Operating Room Nurse Sieglinde Stolp as a witness."

The judge leafed through the dossier, then he nodded assent. Neugebauer waited for him to say something, but the judge didn't seem to want to. He nodded in the other direction. "Dr. Dietrich, please."

The *Oberregierungsrat* drew his notes toward him with a languid movement, without changing his comfortable position. He spoke easily and urbanely without hesitating. His words cut the silence like knife blades.

"Your Honor, the Court, I shall be brief. There has seldom been a more open-and-shut case than this one. A Senior Physician applies for the job of Head Physician in his own hospital. The position goes to another man. Jealousy is aroused. Personal antipathy grows stronger. Cases are collected and recorded in which the Head Physician in question is supposed to have committed surgical blunders. These are passed on to the Health Department. When nothing comes of this a husband whose wife has just died—and I should like to take this opportunity of expressing our deep sympathy for him—is incited and subtly encouraged to file a charge against the Head Physician, in violation of medical secrecy and in disregard for the most elementary rules of professional etiquette."

He made a pause for his words to take effect. Neugebauer was choking with outrage and fury. Gina Feldhusen sat with flashing eyes.

Dr. Dietrich continued. He made a face as if he were speaking against his will and with contempt of something unsavory. "Needless to say, nothing came of this either. You are familiar with the finding of the Public Prosecutor's office. So far as Sister Sieglinde Stolp, whose name has just been brought up, is concerned, I hardly think she can carry much weight as a witness in this matter since during one of the operations to which Dr. Neugebauer took exception this particular nurse was guilty of an act of distressing carelessness: she left a so-called abdominal sponge in the—er—surgical opening. A momentous error, gentlemen, as Dr. Neugebauer will confirm. It was necessary for Dr. Feldhusen, who was operating, to administer a sharp rebuke to Sister Sieglinde." He stopped speaking and looked at Neugebauer.

"Yes," said Neugebauer weakly, "but . . ."

"Thank you," said the judge.

Dr. Dietrich continued, raising his voice slightly: "And now we are told that Dr. Neugebauer feels he has been unjustly treated. We hear that in all his years of service at the Paul Ehrlich Hospital he never had a single major disagreement. Gentlemen, we have heard differently. Former Senior Physician Neugebauer was regarded in the institution as impatient, brusque, a trouble-maker, a fanatic. Everybody avoided him as far as possible; no one ever had a good word for him; he picked quarrels wherever he could. We know he had frequent differences of opinion with the Administrative Director of the institution and with the Head Nurse of his own department, and we are in a position to give the court more instances of this kind."

Another pause.

"Head Physician Feldhusen, on the contrary, in his relatively short period of service has proved himself to be a man of exactly the opposite qualities. He directs the department admirably. His staff is devoted to him. His practice is constantly growing. And now co-operation between the two gentlemen has been destroyed by the fact that Dr. Neugebauer did not approve of his Head Physician's manner of operating. With the best will in the world, he felt he could no longer stand it! A Head Physician who has been active in the profession almost twice as long as he, who was appointed to a university medical faculty fifteen years ago, and whose clinical experience far exceeds his!"

He waited. Not a sound was to be heard in the room.

He's done for. That was what they were all thinking, including Neugebauer himself. He wanted to jump to his feet but controlled himself. This blow to his hopes paralyzed him.

"The director of the Health Department, Dr. Scharff," said Dietrich with compressed lips, "made it unequivocally clear to Dr. Neugebauer what he thought of his so-called report. He considered it a denunciation! And we have just heard from Dr. Neugebauer's own lips that on the next occasion he would expose and libel the Head Physician in exactly the same way as in the Roth case. Because women are being slaughtered. 'Slaughtered' was the word he used, gentlemen!" He stopped for a moment to let his indignation die down.

"Your Honor, the Court, we are glad to have put an end to this situation and barred the way to these intentions. It was impossible to tolerate Dr. Neugebauer one day longer. The Health Department is determined to fight with all the means at its disposal any decision that would counteract that step."

His glance swept the room, as it had at the beginning, and his eyes did not flinch from Neugebauer's. He dropped his pencil on the desk with a faint rattle. "That's all, Your Honor."

Neugebauer sat numb. All of a sudden he was reminded of Brinkmann and his comfortable fireplace and of what he had said. Whoever came in conflict with the unwritten laws of established order was forced to the wall. Brinkmann had been proved right—a thousand times right!

The judge was addressing him. He roused himself from his dazed immobility. "Dr. Neugebauer, we have heard you and the other gentleman. We can, of course, continue these proceedings as long as seems necessary, but one thing seems to me certain: the confidential relationship between Dr. Feldhusen and yourself has been irreparably destroyed. Whatever our decision may be, this rift is beyond remedy. Therefore I would like to ask you a question before we go on with the case. Do you wish to return to the Paul Ehrlich Hospital—and to Dr. Feldhusen?"

All eyes were turned upon the man sitting at the table. Neugebauer thought of his past four years' work. He had been satisfied, happy, and completely engrossed in it. But to go back? To Feldhusen? He couldn't make up his mind so quickly. "I want my rights," he said.

"You will get your rights," said the judge, knitting his brows as though he were displeased. He glanced across to the defending counsel. "Dr. Dietrich, in view of this situation I suggest a compromise. Despite all the pros and cons, the dismissal without notice does not seem to be justified. Further collaboration is—and I think that on reflection Dr. Neugebauer will agree with this opinion—out of the question. I therefore suggest that the dismissal be made subject to the usual notice. Dr. Neugebauer is to stay away from the institution. His salary will continue to be paid to him for the normal period of notice . . ." He glanced at his papers. "In this case six months. Dr. Neugebauer, would you agree to this arrangement?"

Neugebauer made an effort to pull his thoughts together. Instead of a clear-cut decision; a settlement, a compromise, of the kind he hated! His soul revolted against it. But what could he do? Six months' salary. For Liselotte and the children. They needn't accept charity; they could come home to him. Would she come back?

The lawyer was speaking to him softly. "Accept it by all means, Dr. Neugebauer. No question at all. It's the utmost we could hope to get. The utmost. Accept it."

"Yes," said Neugebauer. "I agree."

"That's very sensible of you, and I hope we shall meet with the same good sense and judgment on the part of the defense."

Dr. Dietrich concealed his feeling of triumph. He had won: they were rid of Neugebauer for good. What remained was just a lawyers' haggle over the price. He resisted for a few moments, then gave in with a lavish gesture: All right, gentlemen, we're not bloodsuckers. Six months. Agreed. Neugebauer found this almost more humiliating than all that had gone before.

The judge announced the decision.

The room emptied quickly. The first to leave, with noiseless footsteps and a whispered good morning, was the blond woman, still unrecognized, and the men stared after her.

As Neugebauer left the courthouse he took deep breaths of fresh air. Finished. Over and done with. He mustn't think about it. Nothing would change it now.

He went into the nearest restaurant and had lunch. Then he asked for a sheet of paper and wrote a letter to Liselotte. He told her all about the hearing, his temporary job, and how much he missed her and the children.

He filled three pages, and when he read it through he realized that he had written a begging letter in the hope of softening her heart.

He mailed it just the same.

He was back in his practice at four o'clock. His mind was still on Liselotte and his letter as he entered the office.

The receptionist greeted him with her usual expression of forced friendliness and secret suspicion. As he was sitting down at the desk and glancing through the patients' file she had put out for him, she stood by the instrument cabinet, rummaging in it noisily and aggressively, and taking an unnecessarily long time. Her behavior irritated him. A lot of patients were waiting; he had to pull himself together and forget the hearing and his letter to Liselotte.

He stood up, put on his white coat, went over to the basin, and washed his hands. Suddenly she asked: "You don't know what's happened to the Hegar's dilators that were in here, do you, Doctor?"

"No, I don't, Fräulein Seinig."

She went on rummaging. "That's funny," she said with emphasis. "I know for certain that they were still here yesterday."

Neugebauer turned around slowly. His hands moved under the towel. "Fräulein Seinig," he said with ominous calm, "you've asked me at least eight times already if I know what's happened to something or other. I'd like you to know that I haven't taken anything of yours and that I'm not using my temporary position here to steal from the practice."

She whirled around. Her voice was as pointed as her nose. "There's no harm in asking, is there?"

"It would be better to look for them. I haven't got your dilators in my pocket. And now please send in the first patient."

She left the cabinet open and went out quickly, a deep flush on her face, and when she reappeared her eyes were swollen.

Handled it badly again, he thought. Liselotte's right. Will I ever change? He began his work feeling depressed.

The first hour passed. He listened to complaints, made examinations, wrote prescriptions, and filled out forms. The examinations absorbed him completely.

Then came Mrs. Kudritzki, a fairly young woman, married for two years and so far childless. The general practitioner's diagnosis she brought with her indicated an extrauterine pregnancy—a dangerous matter if something was not done about it in time. Neugebauer questioned her carefully and examined her extremely thoroughly. He reached the same conclusion. "Mrs. Kudritzki," he said, "your family doctor is right."

Fear showed in her eyes. "You mean I can't have the baby?"

"No."

She began to cry, and he consoled her and explained what was wrong. She found it quite interesting and dried her tears.

"Everything's sure to be all right next time," he smiled.

"And—what do I have to do?"

"You'll have to go to the hospital, Mrs. Kudritzki, and as soon as possible."

"For an operation?"

"Yes."

Her head dropped, but she did not shed any more tears. A few moments went by. Then Dr. Neugebauer realized that in this town he would never escape his past, that its shadow was omnipresent and would never leave him. "Doctor," said Mrs. Kudritzki, "if I have to have an operation I'd like to go to the Paul Ehrlich Hospital."

Neugebauer sat perfectly still. The Paul Ehrlich. Feldhusen. He could see the scalpel and the hands wielding it. Was it any business of his now?

Yes. It would always be his business. He would never be able to act as though he had seen nothing and knew nothing. He said calmly: "In your case, Mrs. Kudritzki, I think the Catholic Hospital would be better."

She wouldn't agree. "No, no. I don't want to go there. They messed up a friend of mine there good and proper. And all that rigmarole—I'm not a Catholic, you see. No, I don't want to go there."

"H'm," said Neugebauer. "Then perhaps the Deaconesses'."

"Oh, that's such a long way. The Paul Ehrlich's so much nearer for them—I mean when they come to visit me. It would be much better. Or do you—have any objection to it, Doctor?"

Did he have any objection to it? Good God! He said: "Look here, Mrs. Kudritzki, of course I have no objection to the Paul Ehrlich. I'm just considering your special case, and in my opinion the Deaconesses' would be better for you." He smiled. "Much better."

She looked at him skeptically. "Well, if you really think so."

"I do, Mrs. Kudritzki. So we'll decide on that, shall we?"

"Yes," she said, unconvinced. She didn't want to get into an argument with him. He didn't make a bad impression, and he talked as if he knew a whole lot.

"Good." He filled out her admittance form, thinking as he did so that he would have to leave this town, for everywhere he would come up against Feldhusen, directly or indirectly, even if he had a practice of his own. No, it was impossible. He would have to leave.

Gisela Kudritzki took a taxi home. She was the wife of the butcher Joseph Kudritzki, and they had a prosperous business in the Kirchstrasse. Her husband was a lot older than she, almost twenty years. This was his second marriage. Gisela had been his prettiest shopgirl, but they were happy together despite the difference in age. She found her husband drinking coffee in their tiled kitchen. He pushed out a chair for her.

"Well, what did the doctor say?"

"I'll have to go to the hospital. I have to have an operation."

He was quite overcome. "What? An operation? What in the world's wrong with you, sweetheart?"

She dropped her voice. "An abdominal pregnancy. It's not where it ought to be, you see. Not in the right place. That's why they have to operate."

"So it was . . . you were going to have . . ."

"Yes, if it had been in the proper place." She laughed, pleased at the worried expression on his face. "The operation isn't too bad, the doctor said, but it has to be done right away."

He put his beefy arm around her. "Poor baby. Are you scared? We'll come and see you every day. You'll be at the Paul Ehrlich, won't you?"

"No, the Deaconesses'. He didn't want me to go to the Paul Ehrlich."

"Whyever not? Dr. Paulig?"

"No, he's away. It was his substitute."

"That's funny, though. The Deaconesses' is such a long way off. It's ridiculous. No, sweetheart, you have hospital insurance and plenty of it, and no one's going to boss you around. Go to the Paul Ehrlich."

"But he's filled out the admission form already."

"That doesn't make any difference. He's only a young doctor anyhow. Maybe what he says isn't so."

"He wasn't so young."

"That makes it worse. A doctor who's getting on and still taking substitute jobs can't be up to much. No, sweetheart, I'll tell you what you're going to do. You're simply going to make an appointment with the Head Physician at the Paul Ehrlich. That's the safest way. Nobody can tell you which hospital to go to. You're a private patient—with a private room. What do you think!"

The next day Gisela Kudritzki sat in Feldhusen's private office. "I have to have an operation, Doctor."

Feldhusen gave her a cheerful look. "Well, it's nice of you to tell us. Saves us the trouble of examining you. Whereabouts?"

The young woman blushed. "Excuse me, but the doctor said so."

"Oh, he did, did he? And he sent you over here?"

"No, he sent me to the Deaconesses'."

"But this is the Paul Ehrlich you're at now. And in the private ward too."

"Yes, that's where I want to be."

"Then why didn't you tell the other doctor so?"

"I did. But he wouldn't agree."

"Really?" said Feldhusen. "Who is this doctor?"

"I don't know."

"Well, how about that!" exclaimed Feldhusen playfully. "This gets better and better."

"He's substituting for Dr. Paulig."

"Oh, that explains it. Well, let's have a look at his note. He must have given you one."

She fumbled in her handbag for the admittance to the Deaconesses' Hospital and passed it across the desk.

When Feldhusen saw Neugebauer's signature his face darkened. "No wonder," he said.

"Is there anything wrong?" she asked.

He was smiling again. "Let's make sure right away. I don't think there's anything wrong. Shall we go ahead?"

He examined the young woman very carefully. When he had finished he took hold of her hand. "Yes, my dear Mrs. Kudritzki, what the two other doctors found was absolutely right. But we'll take care of it. Tomorrow. You'd better go home now, fetch your things, and come right back. And if possible take a taxi."

"Is it serious, Doctor?"

"If you'd waited any longer it would have been serious. But as it is you don't need to worry."

"Will you perform the operation yourself?"

"In person." He smiled.

She smiled back and felt glad she had come to him and not to the Deaconesses'.

She went downstairs lightheartedly. In front of her was a sister wearing the cloak of her religious order and carrying a suitcase. It was the operating room nurse from gynecology, Sieglinde Stolp. She was leaving, never to return. She had been transferred to the convent. No one had actually said so, but everyone knew that Feldhusen was behind it. Thus it happened that Sieglinde never met the new Senior Physician.

He arrived a few hours after Sister Sieglinde had left the institution. A thin man with glasses and nervous hands, who had been resident in a provincial hospital in northern Germany for many years. Feldhusen had deliberately selected him from all the candidates. He needed a youngish man without too much experience, not another Neugebauer.

They were sitting in Feldhusen's office. His introduction to the staff director was over with. It had reminded Feldhusen pleasantly of his own. Things looked different now.

The new man sat bolt upright on the edge of his chair. His hands were stretched out along his thighs. The frames of his glasses were not of the latest fashion, nor his suit of first-class quality. He had three children and needed every penny. This had also carried some weight with Feldhusen. He didn't want a financially independent man who could throw up the whole business any time he pleased.

"Do you smoke, Dr. Scholz?"

The upper part of his body tipped forward slightly. "No, thank you, Doctor. I'm a non-smoker."

"Aha. Very commendable. You're one up on me then."

The newly appointed Senior Physician hastily fumbled for matches.

"Thanks." Feldhusen blew smoke into the air. "Well, my dear Scholz, where shall we start? You've already seen the setup here, as far as one can see anything on such a quick tour. You'll find your way around soon enough, don't worry."

The new doctor gave an alert nod.

"But something else. I selected you from a large number of candidates—a very large number. You had been at a good institution for a long time, under an excellent teacher who gave you a good recommendation. You've done a lot of research work. We are under no misapprehension as to the relative value of research projects, as I'm sure you'll agree. But I do like my staff to go beyond daily routine and take an interest in the theoretical side of our noble profession. That's why I'm pretty sure, by and large, that I've struck it lucky with you, as they say."

The thin cheeks of the new doctor glowed. "I hope that your confidence will always . . ."

Feldhusen raised his hand, and he stopped. "That's mighty nice of you, my dear fellow, but I'm not through yet. There's one more thing I must tell you. Dr. Scholz, you are succeeding an extraordinarily competent man. Senior Physician Neugebauer was an outstanding man in every respect. I was very sorry to see him go. Unfortunately he got himself into an unfortunate misunderstanding with the Health Department—a stupid business, I don't want to go into it. He had to leave, and I was left on my own. I was terribly sorry about it, apart from the extra work it meant for me. Yes."

He passed his hand over his eyes and looked deserving of sympathy. "So now, my dear Scholz, it's up to you to prove yourself a worthy successor to Dr. Neugebauer. It won't be impossible, but it won't be exactly easy. He had a very good reputation here. Oh, he had his peculiarities—who doesn't?—but apart from that he was absolutely first class."

Scholz did not venture a word. He was thinking: decent of him to speak so well of the fellow. What I heard can't be true.

"Yes," said Feldhusen and smiled. "That's about all for the present. I can't tell you any more now. Except about myself. I'm said to be pretty easy to get along with. Well, you'll have to judge for yourself. But in one respect I won't stand for any nonsense— not for any nonsense at all. And that is in respect to the women patients entrusted to us here. They count above everything else. They come first, then nothing, and then the patients again." He had assumed a fierce expression, and now his smile returned like the sun emerging from clouds. He stood up.

Scholz jumped from his chair. "I'll try my best not to disappoint you, Doctor."

"Fine, fine. So we'll start tomorrow. And my very best wishes."

Feldhusen remained standing, staring at the door through which Scholz had left. He was satisfied. This man was no threat to him. A timid little employee for whom his word would be the ultimate law. A good choice, a really good choice. He stubbed out his cigarette and went over to the private ward.

The next day the new Senior Physician saw his Head in action in the operating room. On Gisela Kudritzki, private patient. Dr. Scholz had often performed this operation himself; he was familiar with it down to the last detail. Here, under the brilliant lights, in his white gown and cap and mask, he felt more sure of himself than he had at the interview the day before. He stood facing Feldhusen with alert attentiveness. He wanted the Head to be pleased with him.

Feldhusen began calmly and confidently, but as usual he tired quickly. The new operating room nurse irritated him. She wasn't broken in yet and lacked an intuitive sense of what was needed, and her movements were not precise. He did so badly that even Warzin was alarmed.

Feldhusen resected only part of the left Fallopian tube, disregarding the principle that the whole tube should be removed to prevent subsequent tubal pregnancies. He removed the left ovary although it might easily have been saved. He operated sloppily and nervously.

Neugebauer's right, thought Warzin. He'll never learn. Like a butcher. Thank the Lord I took care of Brigitte myself.

When it was all over the new Senior Physician left the operating room behind Feldhusen. He had watched attentively, and during the last half hour his self-confidence had increased appreciably. When Feldhusen shook hands with him his bow was not quite so formal as it had been the day before. He watched the Head until he disappeared around the first turning of the corridor. I could have done better, he thought—a lot better. But he took care not to mention such a thing to anyone else. He would never breathe a word of it. He knew now that he would be with this institution for a long time. He would get along with this Head.

Ten days later young Mrs. Kudritzki was released. She went to say good-by to Feldhusen personally and took him a big bunch of yellow roses for his desk. She blushed with pleasure when he escorted her to the door with compliments and cheerful remarks.

For a long time she sang the praises of the Paul Ehrlich Hospital and its head physician. And when, three weeks later, a bill arrived for over six hundred marks her husband said in a satisfied tone: "You get what you pay for."

William Feldhusen was contented and happy. Not so Werner Warzin. A few days later these two, the Head and the young intern, met in the hall. Warzin's face was pale and worried.

Feldhusen stopped. "So gloomy? Go and have a drink. That always helps." He waved his hand and walked on.

It's all very well for you to talk, thought Warzin. He went into his office and closed the door behind him. For a few moments he stood still, staring ahead, his hands in his pockets. Then he pulled off his white coat and threw it on the bed. Brigitte. Now, just when he had thought everything was over and done with, the trouble was just beginning.

He hadn't been to see her since she left the hospital. He had made some excuse for the first Monday. The second Monday he hadn't bothered. Now she had called up. "Werner, if you don't show up I'm coming to the hospital."

He might have laughed off other threats but not this one. That was all he needed. A scene here, in front of everybody.

He tied his tie before the mirror. What a blessing the other business is taken care of, he thought. That would have been the last straw. If she wants to make a bit of a scene now, let her. It will die down after a while and that will be the end of it. Damn these women! Always the same thing. Easy to get, hard to get rid of. Always thinking about marriage. And today of all days, just when Tilly was expecting me. Oh well, can't be helped. I'll try to make it short. He left.

As he was going upstairs to her apartment—for the last time, he hoped—the smell of the bakery almost made him sick. A ghastly house. A ghastly neighborhood. How did I stand it so long?

He took the last few steps more slowly. Then he rang the bell. He heard her footsteps coming from the rear of the apartment.

"Hello, Brigitte."

She looked at him, searching his face for a sign of pleasure. He smiled, but he felt as though he had put on a grinning mask and then taken it off again. He hung his overcoat on one of the hooks. She took it down again and carefully straightened it on a hanger. In the meantime Warzin went into the living room.

The table was set, as usual. She'll set the table this way all her life, he thought. She came in and sat down beside him.

"How're you doing?" he asked. "Everything all right again?"

"Yes."

"There you are, you see. It was the best thing to do, wasn't it?"

"Why didn't you come on Monday?" she asked without any transition. "Why didn't you want to come today?"

Warzin took short, hurried pulls on his cigarette. He had come determined to make an end, to be honest, and to risk her tears and fuss. But he couldn't. He would have to get out of it gradually, with subtlety. "Why, darling? Because of all the work. Since Neugebauer left we all have a double load. I simply couldn't manage it. I only forgot to let you know last time."

She remained silent, and he went on speaking, with some irritation. "Anyhow last week we got a new man, but he's not really got the hang of things yet. And Krüger will be back tomorrow. Things don't look too good, though. Seems to me the Old Boy's trying to turn the joint into an exhibition model, citations and all."

He laughed openly, just as he used to. But her suspicions did not go away. A horrible, agonizing feeling had overcome her. She fought it, but it would not go away. She had done everything for him that a woman could do. Did he want to leave her now? Could a man act like that? "Is it really only your work?" she asked softly.

Warzin looked up, frowning. "What else could it be?"

She did not answer. He felt uncomfortable. Out, he thought. Just let me out. He crushed out the last third of his cigarette. "It's nothing but the work," he said. "Even now I've still got a stack of case histories to finish. I'll have to be getting along. Could we have supper?"

"Do you have to leave so soon?" she asked. "I thought you might take me to the movies."

He raised his arms and laughed. "The movies, for Pete's sake! I haven't seen a movie for weeks. No, baby, it can't be done. I've got to finish it up. Some other time. But I'm not going to skip supper for anything in the world."

She brought the potatoes. He ate quickly, in silence. When he had finished he offered her a cigarette. "That was delicious, madam. How about another cigarette?"

He gave her a light. After taking a few pulls he said suddenly: "By the way, I'm sorry I can't manage next Monday either. Professional meeting."

She tried to banish her disappointment with a new hope. "Can't you come on Saturday then? It's your day off. You were on duty last weekend." She reached for his hand across the table. "Then we'll go to the movies. You'll come, won't you?"

He pressed her fingers, pretending to think it over. "Saturday? Maybe. But I don't know what time yet."

"You'll be free in the evening."

He sat up straight, braced his elbows on the surface of the table. He was smiling, just as before, and Brigitte clung to this smile. "Look here," he said. "Call me up Friday at the hospital. I'll know definitely by then and I'll be able to tell you. Shall we leave it like that?"

"What time?"

He clasped his palms together. "Lunchtime would be best." He stood up quickly and glanced at the clock. "Darling, I absolutely must go. Don't be cross. We'll finish the wine another time. Keep it for Saturday."

He already had his coat in his hands. Brigitte followed him to the door. She held his hand tight. She looked at him again with the expression he couldn't stand. "Saturday then, Werner?"

"Okay. Call me."

He brushed her cheek with his lips, casually, without feeling.

She stood there stiffly, looking after him as he went to the door and closed it behind himself. She heard the diminishing sound of his steps on the stairs, and from behind the curtain she watched him leave the house and walk off with long strides, his collar turned up.

He knew perfectly well that he wouldn't show up.

Liselotte Neugebauer was troubled and had been for days—troubled in spirit, her mother would have said. It was about her husband's letter, which was lying in her handbag unanswered. That is to say, she had answered it, twice even, but she hadn't mailed either of the answers. The first had been cool and reserved, and when she read it over she had felt sorry for him and torn up the letter. The second time her feelings had shown through, and that was worse, because they were really too estranged for her to write him such an affectionate letter. She had been reduced to a subterfuge, and a pretty poor one at that. Uli had written to his father:

Dear Daddy,

Mommy received your letter and was very pleased with it. How are you? We are getting on fine . . .

and so on.

She was dissatisfied with herself and with the whole world, although she had no reason to complain. She was living with the children at her mother's house. There was enough room, and her mother was glad to have them.

The house was set back slightly from the street, by itself, inside a square garden with old-fashioned serpentine paths and yew hedges. It dated back to a time when money was still coined of gold and the tempo of life was more leisurely. There was a sign under the eaves that said *Villa Irma* in rounded letters and, underneath, the date 1904. The house was ringed with curved bow windows surmounted by pointed turrets, and at night, when the moon was behind it, it looked like a romantic little castle. The bow windows and the many tiny rooms were the delight of the children, and, of course, the garden. And they were allowed to do all kinds of things at their grandmother's that they weren't allowed at home.

Liselotte was sitting downstairs in the living room in one of these bow windows, reading her husband's letter for the third time. When her mother came in she hastily folded the paper.

"You can keep on reading, Lilo. The letter's from Hans, isn't it? Seems to be something very special."

Liselotte's mother was one of those women whose activities increase with age and who at seventy are still making plans as though they were forty. She was now harboring for her daughter the same plans that had been thwarted thirteen years ago by Assistant Field Surgeon Neugebauer. She had never been crazy about him, and it was mutual.

"Oh, Mama," sighed Liselotte. "If only everything were as simple as you think!"

"I know, I know. Whatever he does to you, you're still under his spell."

Anger rose in Liselotte, and it was hard for her to restrain her tongue. "For goodness' sake, stop talking like that. That's what you've always said. I can't listen to it any more."

"I know, I know, but I have to say it. I saw it coming."

"Oh no, you didn't see anything coming."

The old lady stopped talking and took a swipe with a dust rag at the edges of the china cabinet. She certainly had seen it coming. Everything might have been different if Liselotte hadn't been so obstinate about her wretched army surgeon. She had been almost engaged to young Windheim. An old merchant family, well established, with a gilt-edged fortune, and the young man was deferred from army service not because he wanted to shirk but because he was simply indispensable to the war effort. But Liselotte wouldn't have him; she was absolutely under the spell of this arrogant, penniless Neugebauer. Young Windheim had married someone else but hadn't been very happy with her, although his manufacturing business had grown fantastically in the postwar boom. He had been divorced for the last two years. Now he lived all by himself in his newly built dream house in the Humboldtstrasse. The old lady was sure he would be only too glad to have Liselotte even now, and her four children as well. They could have a car and nothing to worry about financially any more, and they could live on a grand scale. And what was she doing? Fiddling about with a letter this incompetent, obstinate character had written her. It was true: she was under his spell. The Lord alone knew what was so special about him.

The old lady ceased her attentions to the china cabinet and turned around. "What does he say anyhow? Has he at least been reinstated?"

"No, but he's substituting for another doctor. A very good practice."

"Oh really? Of all things! Substituting is what unemployed beginners do."

"What do you expect him to do?" cried Liselotte in anguish.

Her mother came over to her. "Lilo," she said gently, "you'd better think what you're to do. Write the whole thing off. It's never going to work properly. He could have been a Head Physician long ago if he didn't always rub people the wrong way. He'll do exactly the same in his next job, and then he'll be running around substituting again. You have to think of your children. He has absolutely no feeling of family responsibility or else this unpleasant business could never have happened. Write the whole thing off and tell him so."

"No," said Liselotte. "I can't do that. I'm not going to write him at all. I'm . . ."

"You're what?"

"I'm going to see him."

"And be taken in again?"

Liselotte jumped up. "He never managed to take me in yet. He never even tried to."

The old lady stepped back, hurt. "Very well. Do whatever you feel you have to do. Only I think you could save yourself the train fare."

"It's his money. He sent me enough."

"That's no reason to speak to your mother in that tone."

Suddenly Liselotte began to cry. Love and triumph arose in the old lady. She took her daughter in her arms. "My poor child," she said. "Go back. But think things over carefully before you talk to him. The children can stay here, can't they?"

Liselotte nodded. "If you want them."

Certainly the old lady wanted the children. As long as they were living with her, her secret plans might still work out. At the moment she even felt pretty confident that they would.

14

At lunchtime on Friday Brigitte Leonhard dialed the number she had dialed so often before. She had never done so with such apprehension, and she suddenly realized that she had nearly always been apprehensive when she dialed this number, hardly ever happy, as if she had always known that the whole thing was hopeless, a failure.

The dial purred softly and then was still. The ringing tone sounded very far away. It took forever for the brittle voice to answer: "Paul Ehrlich Hospital. Good morning."

"Good morning," said Brigitte. She was holding the receiver in both hands. "I'd like to speak to Dr. Warzin in Gynecology. He's probably in his office."

"I'll connect you." There was a click.

Brigitte waited. She could hear strange sounds in the distance. They reminded her of the never changing, seething sound of an old spiral-shaped sea shell which had belonged to her as a child and which she used to like to hold to her ear. Where was it now?

Unexpectedly a voice emerged from the receiver. "Dr. Warzin's not in his office. Who is calling, please?"

"Fräulein Leonhard."

There was a slight pause. "Just a minute. I'll try again." Again she waited, but she wasn't thinking about her sea shell any more. Her fear was growing worse and her suspicions too. Was he really not in?

"Hello."

"Yes?" Her hands clutched the receiver.

"I can't find him right now. He's somewhere in the building. Could I take a message?"

"No," said Brigitte weakly, "thank you."

She hung up and waited. It was half past one, and she kept looking at the clock. Once or twice she picked up the receiver and put it down again. Another fifteen minutes, she thought. There's more chance of getting him later. Only not too late.

Then suddenly she could wait no longer. She dialed in a desperate hurry.

It was the same voice as before. Unexcitable and insensitive as the result of hundreds of calls a day. "Dr. Warzin? Dr. Warzin's busy at the moment. Would you please call back in half an hour."

The receiver went dead before she could answer a word.

Again she waited.

Her despair deepened like a wall of gray fog. She tried to talk herself out of it and find excuses. Perhaps he really was tied up, in the operating room, with the Head, with a delivery. In half an hour, he'd said. He wouldn't have said that if he didn't want to speak to her. That would have been stupid and pointless. In half an hour.

Now she realized how much she loved him. She would never love anybody—no other man, no other human being—as much as she loved him.

The minutes went by unbearably slowly.

When thirty had gone by Brigitte dialed for the third time. Third time lucky, she encouraged herself. It'll work this time. He'll be in. They said in half an hour.

This time a different switchboard operator answered—older,

easygoing, hoarse from smoking. "Yes, Fräulein. What? Yes, certainly."

She heard a faint, restrained buzz. His office, she thought. I recognize it. But there was no answer.

"Hello," said the operator. "I'll call the ward."

Exactly one minute elapsed.

"Hello."

"Yes?"

"Dr. Warzin left fifteen minutes ago."

For the first half of that night Brigitte cried until she had no tears left. Then she was able to think more clearly, and she mulled everything over. The next morning at eleven o'clock she called the hospital, and this time she gave a false name, Dr. Arnold. He answered immediately.

Her heart was pounding in her throat.

"Hello, Werner."

"Brigitte?"

She heard his angry intake of breath.

"When did you take to using an assumed name?"

"When you took to not accepting my calls."

"I was busy. I have something else to do besides run after you, you know."

"I know. You were so busy that you'd left fifteen minutes after I'd been told to call back in half an hour."

He didn't speak.

"What about Saturday?"

"I can't make it."

"Oh? You can't make it?"

"No. Anyhow I don't like tricks of this kind. And I don't like girls running after me either. I'm sorry, I have to go."

Suddenly she saw everything clear, and the veil of self-deception, vain hope, and torturing doubt was torn away. He was through with her. "When can you come, Werner?" she asked.

"Not for the present. You know . . ."

"Werner," she said calmly and distinctly, "listen carefully now. You can't just throw me over like your other girls. I got rid of my child for your sake and by your own hand. Don't forget that, Werner. If you don't see me again I'll tell the whole story. To the right people. I swear I will."

He laughed grimly. "You're going to try that, are you? There's an ugly name for that in the penal code."

"There are ugly names for some other things too in the penal code."

His laughter vanished. He went on, with sullen anger in his voice: "I'm not interested in scenes, Brigitte. And you'd better quit threatening me. You're the one who'll get hurt. If that's the way things are it's certainly better for us not to meet any more. So good-by."

He caught her last words just before he hung up. Distance made them sound more menacing than they would have close to:

"I'm not kidding, Werner."

Brigitte stayed in her room the whole weekend. She went downstairs to her parents' only for coffee, but left again immediately, pleading a headache. She had lost the last glimmer of hope that Warzin might come or call up, and in the loneliness of this long afternoon her decision became definite.

She did not eat supper. Instead she did something she had never done before: she finished the bottle of wine she had intended for Warzin, all by herself, glass after glass. But her mood became no more cheerful. Everything looked blacker, more hopeless, more threatening. Before going to bed she went downstairs to the shop, took the classified telephone directory, and looked under "Law Courts" for the address of the Public Prosecutor's office. She made a note of it and went quietly back upstairs.

The next morning she helped in the shop until ten o'clock. Then she went to her mother in the kitchen. "I have to go out for an hour, Mother."

"Right now, dear, just when we're so busy? You don't look too well. Are you sick?"

"I don't know. I don't feel well. I think I need a bit of fresh air."

Frau Leonhard looked at her daughter suspiciously. Brigitte had been acting so strangely recently—ever since that examination at the hospital as a matter of fact. Could there be something wrong with her after all? "You ought to go back to the doctor," she said.

"Oh, nonsense. I'm perfectly all right."

"All right, dear. Bring three dill pickles. And I need a pound of cottage cheese too, for your father."

"Three dill pickles and a pound of cottage cheese," repeated Brigitte mechanically. She took her coat and went out.

Later, outside the big building, she stopped and looked up uncertainly and with secret fear at the stone façade. Was she doing the right thing? Was it a good thing to do? Even now she sensed that someday she would regret this action.

But her injured pride and her determination to get Werner back were stronger than the vague feeling of anxious uneasiness, and she could always deny everything, she thought, once her purpose had succeeded.

She had to wait. She sat on the wooden bench facing the ugly sign on the door. People passed by; she cast shy glances at them and was furtively appraised herself. What a dreadful place! Then a pale young man called her in and directed her to the desk on the left.

The chair creaked and shook as she sat down. This was where Anton Roth had sat when he had tried to bring Feldhusen to justice. Within these walls it had been decided that Feldhusen had not committed murder, that he was an honorable man, conscientious and correct.

The man behind the desk was looking at her, not unkindly. "Well, Fräulein?"

"I have . . . I want to bring a charge."

"Aha. Against whom?"

"A Dr. Warzin." She would have liked to run away and hide. "Werner Warzin."

"Yes. What for?"

She replied in a whisper so that the people behind her shouldn't overhear. Shame colored her cheeks bright red.

"For—abortion."

The senior Prosecutor's clerk was an experienced man. He knew she would begin to cry any minute. This would only delay matters. He made a sign to the young man, and they were left alone in the room. "Tell me all about it from the beginning. What's his name?"

She repeated the name she loved. Oh, Werner, why does it have to be like this?

"Where is he employed? Or is he in practice?"

She shook her head. "No, he's at the Paul Ehrlich Hospital. Under Dr. Feldhusen."

At this name the clerk pricked up his ears. His memory was comparable to the filing cabinets behind him, and it came into play like a light going on. Feldhusen? Something had come up involving Feldhusen. Not long ago either. Fishy. The prosecutor's clerk was like the justice he administered. The first time can be overlooked; it might happen to anybody. The second time is suspicious. One previous conviction, and the man is lost.

He asked: "And Dr. Feldhusen—is he also involved in this matter?"

Feldhusen? What did she care about Feldhusen? It was Werner she was after, and nobody else. "No," she said. "He's not involved."

The clerk took down the charge. The girl spoke faster and faster, spilling out her words so as to get through and get out.

She was home again by twelve. She didn't forget the dill pickles and cottage cheese. "Thanks, Brigitte," said her mother. "Do you feel any better?"

She nodded with a smile.

"You still look pale, though. You ought to lie down after lunch."

"Oh, I'm all right, Mother."

Public Prosecutor Brandis, nicknamed "Not with Two," read the charge that same day. His reaction was just like that of his clerk in the outer office. Works under Feldhusen, this man? Yes, of course, that business with the wife who died. And now another charge. Funny!

He called the criminal police.

"Listen, Hennings. A girl's bringing a charge—her name's Brigitte Leonhard—against a Dr. Warzin. Warzin, yes. Works under Feldhusen at the Paul Ehrlich. You remember? Sure. The same guy who was on duty when that Mrs. Roth . . . yes, that's right. The whole thing's a bit odd. The Leonhard girl says Feldhusen didn't know anything about the business. Sounds funny to me. Head Physician and didn't know anything about it. . . . That's right. Could happen, I suppose. What? Yes, revenge—yes, yes. Abortion, love affair over, and so on. The usual story. The fellow talked her into it, did it himself in the private ward at the hospital. Nice thing, eh? I'd like to know how much of this goes on without our hearing anything about it. Well, check into it yourself, will you? But really get to the bottom of it this time. Especially whether Feldhusen has anything to do with it. Yes. You'd better bear down on Warzin first. He'll be easier to break down. Yes. Okay. Fine. Good-by."

Public Prosecutor Brandis put down the receiver and remained seated. He looked with distaste at Brigitte Leonhard's charge lying on his desk before him.

At this time Neugebauer was sitting at his desk at home. His surroundings were warm and comfortable, but the warmth did not drive away his loneliness; only work did that—for a few hours at least. Neugebauer was working with tense concentration. Before him lay a sheet of paper, beside him a German-English dictionary, and on the other side an issue of the weekly medical journal. The article Neugebauer was translating into English was called "The Suture of an Infected Wound." He consulted the fat dictionary frequently, noted down a whole list of words and, after thinking for a while, wrote the sentence. Then he started looking up words again. When he had filled two pages the doorbell rang.

It was an unusual ring, two short rings in succession, almost without an interval. Neugebauer listened and waited, and it came again, impatient and urgent.

He laid down his pen and stood up. When he opened the door he was looking into Liselotte's eyes.

His hand let go of the doorknob. His arm dropped. He stared at his wife as if he were memorizing her features anew. He could not speak.

"Wake up," she said. "Or aren't you going to let me in?"

"Darling!" he said. "Lilo! What are you doing here? Why didn't you write?"

She held her head on one side. "Am I disturbing you? Have you got company?"

"You idiot! Don't hang around here on the stairs. Come in."

He pulled her inside and closed the door. Then he embraced her.

He kissed her mouth, her eyes, her whole face. She dropped her suitcase and handbag. Suddenly she began to respond to his embrace and his kisses. "I couldn't stand it any longer," she whispered.

"Lilo darling! I—I don't know how I stood it." He looked at her. There was fear in his eyes. "Are you staying?"

She nodded.

"Oh, Lilo!" He kissed her again violently before helping her take off her coat.

In the living room she saw his desk, the pages covered with writing, the journal, and the fat red dictionary.

"Are you writing applications?"

"Not any more."

"Have you found something?"

"It's not definite yet." He looked for disappointment in her eyes but did not find any. "But it won't be long now. In the meantime I'm learning English."

"English? You know English, don't you?"

"Yes. I can order a drink, buy a railroad ticket, or make a bit of conversation at a cocktail party, but to explain to an intern, for instance, how to put in a suture—there I'm lost."

"Explain to an intern . . ."

He smiled. "For example, how would you say: *Die Naht der infizierten Wunde?* You're a pretty good interpreter yourself."

She shook her head, completely at a loss.

"The suture of an infected wound," he said proudly.

"And just why do you want to explain that to your intern in English in future?"

"Because they don't speak German in the Sudan. Arabic at best, and I don't know Arabic."

"Hans," she exclaimed, "what is all this nonsense about?"

He drew her to him. "Don't get excited. How would you like to go to the Sudan? Two thousand marks a month, tax exempt. Free housing and servants. Three months' leave a year with air transportation to Germany furnished. Family to join me later. Well?"

She was bewildered. "Have you applied?"

"Yes. And I even think they'll accept me, in spite of my bad character. They need good people as badly as they need food. Especially surgeons and gynecologists. Well? For goodness' sake, say something."

"Oh, Hans, what do you want me to say? I just don't know . . . The Sudan? That's somewhere back of Egypt, isn't it?"

"Quite right," he said. "A in geography. I had to look it up."

"Isn't it terribly hot?"

"Comfortably warm. Fur coats not necessary."

"Aren't there an awful lot of bugs and things? I mean scorpions and snakes and so on?"

He laughed. "I'll buy a pistol."

"For heaven's sake! I'd pass out if I so much as set eyes on one."

He became serious. She noticed a strange expression in his face which she had never seen there before. "It's the only thing to do, Lilo," he said. "Or am I to stay here forever, substituting for other doctors and asking for charity? Look, over there I've got a real opportunity. They'll judge me only on what I can do. I'll be my own boss, with no Health Department to write me nasty letters, and things are certainly too tough out there for people like Feldhusen. Only you'll have to stand by me. I won't go without you."

She looked at him. "If you're set on it, Hans. I don't know . . . But what else can I do?"

He kissed her. "It'll work out, I'm sure, Lilo. I'll go for a trial period first, and you can come and visit for a trial period and look things over. I'm sure it will be just the thing for us. I'll never get anywhere here. Maybe three years from now. But right now no one's going to give me a job. They're all hand in glove."

"Have you—have you heard anything of Feldhusen?"

"Feldhusen? He's sitting back in his chair, basking. Oh yes, he's supposed to have a new Senior—Schulze or Scholz—never heard of him before. He's sweating it out, and I get paid anyhow. Not bad, eh?"

She knew he wasn't serious, but she didn't want to make his heart any heavier. "No. Tell me all about it."

"Tell me how the children are first."

"They're fine. Mama's willing to keep them as long as necessary."

"How very nice of her! I'd never have expected it."

She smiled. "She's a lot nicer than you think. And now it's your turn."

"Not unless you make some tea. And I'll go and get cigarettes. There aren't any left."

In the kitchen she thought about him. Her heart was too full for words, and she felt ashamed of having gone away and left him all alone in his distress. How stupid it had been and how pointless! He had taken it so quietly, too, so bravely and well. He's worth more than I am, she thought. I'm nothing without him. I'll do anything for him—anything at all. And I'll go with him wherever he likes, even if there are snakes. I'll never leave him alone again. Only I won't tell him so.

She grew worried because he was gone so long. When he rang

she rushed to the door. He had a big bunch of yellow roses and a bottle of champagne in his arms.

"Hans! You shouldn't."

"Where's the tea?"

"It's just about ready."

"Take the flowers. I'll put the bottle to chill."

Later they sat down with their glasses. The pearly bubbles rose to the surface in a constant stream. Neugebauer told her everything. It grew dusk and then dark. They talked and sat in silence, and their hearts rejoiced.

"Maybe you still don't believe me," he said, "but I'm right. One day he'll go too far. Oh, I know what you're going to say. So many men are no good, but they hold their jobs until they're old and gray so long as they don't pinch the silver. But this is something else again."

She shook his hand. "Do you hate him now?"

"No, darling. I hated him for a short time, when everything went to pieces and . . ."

"And?"

"And when you left me."

She lifted his hand to her face. "I'm back."

"Yes. And I don't hate him any more. Sometimes I even think they were right."

"Who?"

"The others. Sister Thea, for instance. I've thought about her a lot. She's a sensible old soul. She said: 'Everyone has to obey discipline and do his duty. We're not supposed to judge: God judges' . . . or something of that sort. I shouldn't have told Roth. People haven't much faith in us any more anyhow. And faith is half the battle in medicine."

"Is that so?" she said. "That Mrs. Roth had faith, didn't she? She died just the same. Maybe even because she had faith. You're a funny character! First you tear the whole hospital apart, run to a lawyer and bring a suit, and then you say the others were right."

He smiled because she was getting so worked up. "And you're

a funny kid. First you tell me to hold my tongue and put up with it all without saying a word, and now that they've chucked me out you say I was right."

She leaned against him. "Oh, Hans, it's not always easy to get on with people. Even with me. Right?"

"Me too," he said, and to hide his emotion he reached hastily for the bottle. "Come on, there's still a drink left."

Later he helped her unpack. Then they went to bed. "Gosh," he said, "I'm not used to this any more—having somebody in bed with me. I don't know if I'll be able to sleep like this."

She turned around and propped herself on her elbows. "Haven't you had anybody in bed with you the whole time?"

"Believe it or not, I missed my chance. Wasn't I a fool?"

She laughed and snuggled against him. "Hans, I'm not going away any more. I can't stand it without you."

"And suppose I go where the black men live?"

"I'll go with you."

"Really?"

"Yes. What do you expect me to do here alone, stupid?"

"Stupid yourself! You'll like it out there where the black men live." He touched her neck under her hair. "Oh, Lilo."

"What?"

"We're all alone, Lilo baby. Just the way we were the first time we ever went away together, the time I got a furlough from the front. Your mother didn't like it a bit."

"It was fun though. Naughty too."

He turned her head around and kissed her the way they had kissed then.

15

The next morning Inspector Hennings set out for the Paul Ehrlich Hospital. Inspector Hennings was forty-seven years old. He was broad-shouldered, heavy, and quiet, and he was through with all unnecessary ambition and with keeping busy for the sake of being busy. He did not permit himself the luxury of sympathy, for no one had shown him any.

He entered the hospital and followed the corridors he had taken before. His plan was made. "Not with Two" was right: take Warzin first. Didn't seem too stable, that fellow. Maybe he could railroad him. It was against the rules, but sometimes you had to go against the rules when you were dealing with people who didn't observe any.

He waited in the ward office, patient and unobtrusive. The nurses would come in from time to time and then leave him alone again. Warzin was still busy. It was close to lunchtime. Hennings could smell the aroma of gravy and potatoes boiled in their jackets.

After he had waited twenty minutes he heard a man's footsteps in the corridor. Warzin entered the room.

The inspector stood up slowly. He recognized the doctor immediately; he never forgot a face. Warzin returned his gaze and frowned. He felt vaguely that he had seen this man before, and at the same time he was reminded of something unpleasant, something dangerous. "You wanted to speak to me?"

"Yes, Doctor. I don't know . . . maybe you remember me. I came to see you once before."

That very moment Warzin recognized him: the man from the police who had questioned him about Ingeborg Roth, about her last hours and her death. What did he want? Was that still not finished with?

Then, with sudden terror, he thought of Brigitte's final words on the telephone. He felt his face changing, and he was afraid that the inspector's searching eyes would notice and recognize the truth.

He tried to smile. "Yes, that's right. You're the gentleman from the police. Mr.—I'm sorry I don't remember your name."

"Hennings."

"Yes, of course, Hennings. My memory's not what it used to be either. Excuse me, Mr. Hennings. Shall we go into my office?"

"Yes, please."

On the way over Warzin reassured himself with some hasty thinking. It was impossible. He knew Brigitte and had known her for ages. She couldn't have done it, not conceivably—and certainly not so quickly. Impossible. It must be something else.

He opened the door. His room was a mess. Smiling, he apologized, while his heart fluttered.

The inspector wasn't friendly any more. "A charge has been filed at the Public Prosecutor's office, Doctor."

"Yes, I know," said Warzin. "I thought it had already been . . ."

"This is nothing to do with the Roth case."

Warzin sat in a stupefying vacuum. So it was Brigitte after all.

The inspector saw the fear in his face. This fellow was a pushover, tottering already. He wouldn't hold out long. "Do you know a Fräulein Brigitte Leonhard?"

Warzin did not move, but his brain was working vigorously. Like lightning there flashed through his mind similar situations in movies and books—an official interrogating someone, asking tough questions. What should one reply? I don't know her? Ridiculous—he knows I know Brigitte. So behave quite naturally, relax, sound surprised, and see what happens next. "Yes, sure I know her. Why? What about her? I haven't seen her for ages." He tried to take a cigarette, slowly, as if unconsciously. He didn't succeed. His fingers were trembling. The match broke.

Inspector Hennings looked him in the eye. "She brought the charge. A charge of abortion. Performed in the private ward of this department on Friday, September 21."

Warzin sat motionless. His throat was dry, and he could feel the blood throbbing dully on the left side of his neck. He was not able to answer. He needed time to think—and he needed a brandy too. There were still two or three drinks in the bottle, he knew. Suppose he simply stood up, got out the bottle, and poured one for himself and one for the inspector?

Hennings watched him with his colorless eyes. "Your own child, Dr. Warzin," he said. "Do you admit it?" No! Warzin jumped. Now was the time to defend himself. He couldn't take everything lying down. "That's a lie!" He licked his lips. "It wasn't my child. How do I know whose it was? She came to me and asked me to help her. She's a former acquaintance of mine, so . . ."

The inspector raised his hand, and Warzin stopped. He's already admitted the main thing, thought Hennings. I'm having a good day today. "We'll find out about that. In any case you did perform an abortion, didn't you?"

"Only because I wanted to help her. Only because she asked me to." Warzin changed his tone. "Inspector," he said quietly, almost in tears, "you know how it is. When a girl comes to you as a gynecologist, not knowing what to do, crying and threatening to kill herself . . ."

"Did the Head Physician know about it? Was he present?"

Warzin's brain worked like lightning. "Did she say he was?"

"I'm asking you. I want to hear it from you."

She said he was, thought Warzin. She doesn't give a damn. And suddenly he thought: If Feldhusen's involved we may get out of it. "He knew about it," said Warzin. "I informed him. He wasn't present."

Hennings was writing in his notebook. A nice crew, he thought. While he was writing he was thinking about Anke, his seventeen-year-old daughter. She had a boy friend, a harmless young kid. He knew him, but he'd never taken him seriously. I'll have to keep an eye on them, he thought. It can happen so quickly. And then a business like this. And perhaps worse. I'll have to look into it.

He stood up. "We'll be asking you to come over and see us one of these days, Doctor. Good morning."

He went out. Warzin did not move.

The inspector knew the way to Feldhusen's office. It was lunch-time. From behind all doors came the clatter of plates and cutlery. The smell of gravy bothered Hennings and made him walk faster.

There was nobody in the outer office. The secretary must have been at lunch. For a moment the inspector hesitated, then he cautiously opened the outer door of the Head Physician's office. He saw the inner door, upholstered in leather, and knocked loud and clear.

"Come in, Fräulein Rieck," called Feldhusen.

The inspector slowly opened the door wide. Feldhusen glanced up in astonishment but didn't look displeased. "Hello," he said. "Who are you looking for?"

When the inspector shut the door Feldhusen recognized him. "Ah, Inspector, I thought it was my secretary. Do come in. In any case I want to thank you." Feldhusen went up to Hennings and cheerfully shook his hand. "It was mostly your doing that that recent disagreeable matter was settled in such a businesslike, unobtrusive way. There's no getting around the truth, obviously, but still . . . there might have been a whole lot more unpleasantness. Do sit down. I have a few minutes to spare before lunch. A cigar?"

Hennings declined with thanks. On the previous occasion he had easily fallen for this man's magnetism and charm. He admitted this, and it annoyed him. But today he was on his guard.

"Yes, most disagreeable." Feldhusen's face clouded. "I still haven't got over it. I don't mean the charge so much—Lord knows, that was the least of it—but that poor woman. And besides, the stupid affair cost me my best man. Unfortunately Senior Physician Neugebauer had to leave. The Health Department took a very serious view of the matter." He shook his head regretfully. "Yes, that's how things are. Has any new angle come up?" He did not know how to interpret the inspector's look. "I mean— maybe the man doesn't want to give up—the husband, Mr. Roth. That would be quite conceivable. Oh well, I don't want to seem curious."

Hennings waited a little while before speaking. "There's only a very distant connection, Doctor, between that affair and the one we're concerned with now."

Feldhusen drew back his head. He looked extremely surprised. "Oh, something else? Now I really am curious. What kind of connection?"

"Dr. Warzin, your intern, was present on that occasion too."

"I know, I know. He was on duty. Well?"

"Are you aware that about a month later he performed an abortion in your private ward?"

Fear struck Feldhusen like a shaft of lightning. But nothing appeared on the surface. The inspector saw only an expression of utter amazement which changed into indignant, righteous anger. He began to have his doubts.

"An abortion?" said Feldhusen. "In my private ward? Say, is this a joke? I've heard better ones, let me tell you."

"I wouldn't make such a questionable joke, Doctor. Do you know the name Leonhard—Brigitte Leonhard?"

That was the girl. Warzin—the damned sophomoric fool! "Leonhard? It's entirely possible. Doesn't mean anything to me at the moment. Who is she?"

"Fräulein Leonhard brought the charge against Dr. Warzin."

Feldhusen slapped his hand loudly on the leather chair arm. "That's really . . ."

"Do you know the girl?" asked the inspector point-blank.

"Yes, of course I remember. Warzin came and told me she was a friend of his who was having irregular periods. He wanted to have her admitted for observation for a few days as a favor. He asked me if we could take her in the private ward. I had no objection. If an assistant asks you a favor of that kind, why not? Happens every now and then."

"Did you know about the operation?"

"Of course I did. I had seen the girl once on my rounds. We discussed the case and decided to do a curettage—nothing out of the ordinary, we do hundreds of them. To find out what's wrong. Warzin performed it, then the girl was discharged. Nothing serious showed up, so far as I remember. And that's all."

"Were you present at the curettage?"

"Of course not. What do you think? I have far too much to do to attend every D and C in person. Only special cases."

"What about private patients?"

"She wasn't a private patient. She was in the private ward simply as a favor to Warzin." Feldhusen paused and then laughed bitterly. "A favor! And look what comes of it."

"Yes," said Hennings. "Look what comes of it."

Feldhusen bent forward. His face was earnest, imploring. "Inspector, I hope you'll believe me when I tell you that I would never countenance such an outrageous thing. Never! And in any case, is what the girl says true? If you only had my experience! Women do the strangest things. If she has knowingly infringed Paragraph 218 she'll get the same sentence as Warzin."

"Women do the strangest things," said the inspector. He got up.

Feldhusen grew more and more excited. "An abortion! In a gynecology department! In my department! Would you mind telling me whether you've already seen that miserable devil Warzin?"

"I've seen him."

"Well, what in God's name does he have to say about it?"

The inspector looked him straight in the eye. "His account differs slightly from yours."

"Differs from mine? In what way?"

"You'll find out, Doctor. We'll ask you to testify when the time comes. And now I wish you good morning."

He went out. The double doors closed. The outer office was still empty. When Hennings stepped out into the corridor the aroma of gravy was stronger. Feldhusen's not going to have much appetite, he thought. He's stewing in his own juice.

Feldhusen stood in the middle of the room for a time, alone, without moving. He looked at the motionless door. Then he turned around, went back slowly and woodenly to the desk, and dropped heavily into his chair. He lighted a cigarette, rested his head in his hands, and stared into space. Gina, he thought. Odd that he should think of Gina now. He thrust the thought aside. He must pull himself together; the danger was too great. Really! A ridiculous little episode, a small favor, a matter of no importance which he had long ago forgotten, and now it had become a tremendous danger. His glance swept the desk and was caught by the telephone. With a swift movement he picked up the receiver and dialed. "Is Dr. Warzin there? Send him up right away."

Warzin came, pale and out of breath. He walked slowly up to the desk. He couldn't manage to look assiduous. Anyhow it wouldn't have helped. "You sent for me, Doctor?"

Feldhusen looked threatening, almost evil, not a bit like his usual self. "What did you tell Inspector Hennings, Warzin?"

Warzin swallowed. "The truth, Doctor."

Feldhusen sprang from his chair. His face was distorted. The scars grew livid, like bloody weals. "You goddamn idiot! I told you beforehand that I knew nothing about it. I knew nothing at all about it. This is your affair pure and simple."

Warzin looked at him. He's scared, he thought. No more dignity. Just like me. We're both scared. A pretty pair. "I'm sorry,

Doctor," he said. "The inspector led me to believe that Brigitte—that Fräulein Leonhard had already incriminated you."

"So you promptly fall into the trap? Have you any idea if the whole thing is true? Don't you see that the girl is involving herself too?"

Feldhusen came out from behind the desk. He walked right up to the intern. Warzin could smell his breath. "The inspector learned from me that you asked me to admit Fräulein Leonhard for observation for a few days. Because of irregular periods. You did a D and C. Then she left. And if you weren't such a fool you'd have told him the same thing. Then it would have been our word against the girl's. You've made this course impossible for us. Now you can find your own way out." He went back to his chair and sat down. Slowly he changed back into the Head Physician. "That's for your information. You can expect to be suspended from duty."

A violent feeling of rage came over Warzin. There sat this man who couldn't operate, who had forced the dismissal of the only capable doctor here, who consisted of nothing but a façade and resounding words, and who now wanted to play innocent, as he had always done in the past and would keep on doing until he retired.

Warzin was saying slowly: "Can I, Doctor? I thought you might be more inclined to help me. We can still stick to that story . . ."

Feldhusen laughed scornfully. "At this point? So that they won't believe either of us? No, my good friend. Now it's my story. You'll have to think up a new one. That's all, Warzin."

Warzin drew a deep breath. "That's not all," he said with fury in his voice. "I helped you once, you know, Doctor, when we had that misfortune with Mrs. Roth. Yes, I helped you then. And now you want to leave me holding the bag. No, Doctor. If I have to go, you go too. That's for *your* information."

Feldhusen was almost at the end of his self-control. His face froze in a furious grimace. "I suppose blackmail is your second profession?"

Warzin blew his last fuse. "You'd better start worrying about what your second profession is going to be," he snapped. They stared at each other, without a word, with hate-filled eyes. Now they really knew each other for the first time.

"Get out," said Feldhusen. "Get out of here."

"Sure, Doctor," said Warzin and left. His fingers left damp, sweaty marks on the door handle. Feldhusen sat down. He held his head in his hands and closed his eyes.

So that's how it is. At the very top just an hour ago, and now at the very bottom. Right in the middle of his triumph and security. Warzin. A nobody, a nothing. And suddenly a great threatening figure. An old figure of speech occurred to Feldhusen: how can such a little fish stink so much. He groped for his silver case and took a cigarette. On the gilt inner side of the case Gina's name was engraved and the date when they had decided to get married. Oh, Gina—I should never have done it. It was madness. You can get away with a lot of things and be excused for a lot of things. But not this. They'll form a united front against me. . . . have you heard? That's really something, isn't it? Head of a gynecology department! Really, I must say . . . And yet who could ever have foreseen it? Every day they came with their veiled hints about possible abortions, glad if a welcome miscarriage solved their problem, ready to pay large amounts of money. And of all people this Fräulein Leonhard, in whose case he had agreed to it simply as an act of professional courtesy. First she wanted to get rid of the child, then she ran to the police with a complaint, probably because Warzin had left her.

Feldhusen nodded grimly. He knew that line. If I can't have the toy I'll break it. If I'm not happy nobody else is going to be. Women! All your life you're mixed up with women. They ought to have their necks wrung, all of them—except Gina.

He breathed heavily. That bastard, Warzin! First he grovels and kowtows—yes, Doctor, no, Doctor. And now he's going in for blackmail. The son of a bitch!

Feldhusen drew on his cigarette several times, calming himself as he smoked. What was he to do?

Keep on denying it, whatever happened. He was the Head Physician. His word was worth more than that of an intern and his girl friend. His relations with Scharff, the director of the Health Department, were excellent, not to mention Fehling, who was a personal friend. The thought of Scharff and Fehling suddenly restored his assurance. Take it easy! Just don't lose your nerve. He reached for the telephone and asked for the Health Department.

"Dr. Scharff's office."

"Feldhusen speaking. Good morning Fräulein. Please let me speak to Dr. Scharff."

"Certainly, Doctor. Just a moment."

Feldhusen waited. He heard voices in the receiver and thought he recognized Dr. Scharff's. Lord, what a time it was taking!

"Hello? Dr. Feldhusen? Dr. Scharff isn't in his office. May I take a message?"

"Er—not in his office? Has he left?"

"He—he had to attend a meeting. I don't know whether he'll be back today. Could I give him a message? Or would you rather . . ."

"No, no, it's not so important. I'll call back. Thank you. Good-by."

He hung up. Terror overcame him again. Had Scharff told her to say he was out? Had he heard something already? He couldn't have. The inspector had only just left. And in any case the Public Prosecutor's office wouldn't inform the Health Department right away. No, no. Take it easy. Don't imagine things.

He called the switchboard again and asked for City Councilor Fehling. But he couldn't get him either, and although Feldhusen told himself that neither Scharff nor Fehling could have heard about the affair yet, the two fruitless telephone calls made him painfully restless, and he imagined the two influential men sitting down together and discussing the case—discussing him, Feldhusen, weighing him in the balance, pronouncing the verdict and condemning him. But could they come to a decision so soon? No. Once again he began to think the whole thing through. He would have to make it up with Warzin, however hard that might be. Join up with him against the girl. But then Warzin would have to retract his statement. They would question him over and over again without stopping and gradually break him down. Warzin wasn't the type to hold out long.

Where was the path that led out of this labyrinth?

Feldhusen was tired. He had never felt so tired before. The more he thought, the more conscious he became of a paralyzing, inexorable weariness. For the first time his verve deserted him, his old cheerful optimism which had seen him through so much. His will and his power of resistance were gone. Constant over-exertion had sapped his strength like a lingering fever. Outward success had only concealed the inner weakness, not overcome it. His constant unsureness in surgery had worn him down. He sat with his forehead propped on his hands. The cigarette burned out in the ash tray.

I don't want to go on, he thought. I can't make it. I've bitten off more than I can chew. I've got to retreat. Right now. Go back of my own free will. A small practice somewhere a long way from here. It will take a year or two for me to establish myself, and then I'll be left in peace. In northern Germany perhaps, on the coast, or in Bavaria near the mountains.

Gina's image appeared before him. Gina. I'll have to tell her the truth. We'll talk it over tonight. Oh, God, tonight we're supposed to go to the theater. All the better. After the show we'll go to our night club, and then I'll tell you everything. You'll understand.

He stubbed out his cigarette and stood up. A last remnant of his old resilience had suddenly returned to him. The thought of a talk with Gina gave him the courage and self-confidence to carry on his work as usual.

As he went through the outer office he waved to Fräulein Rieck in his usual way. "I'll be in the private ward. Call me there if anything comes up. But only if it's something important. All right?"

"Yes, Doctor," sighed Fräulein Rieck.

He got home late. Gina was already dressed. She was sitting at her dressing table carefully touching up her lips. He bent over and kissed her temples. "Good evening, darling."

"Good evening, Will. It's late. You'll have to hurry."

"Okay. I'll be ready in a minute." He hurriedly changed his suit.

Critically she checked the dull polish on her fingernails, then she got up and stood in front of him. "All right?"

She looked stunning. He surveyed her with a mixture of desire and rueful sadness. "Wonderful," he said.

She stroked his forehead. "You're terribly tired again, aren't you? You poor thing. You work too hard, that's what it is."

He turned to the mirror to tie his tie. "I can't help it, Gina. I wish I had more time for you." Wasn't this his chance to tell her everything straight out? "Sometimes I really wonder," he continued, "if it wouldn't be better . . ."

"Will, we'll take a nice long vacation in the spring—oh, my rings, where did I leave them?" She dashed into the bathroom.

He finished tying his tie and put on his coat. Later, he thought. After the show.

She appeared in the doorway. "Will, we really must go."

As they went out she took his arm. "I'm looking forward to this so much, Will. It's funny how much I enjoy going to the theater. Especially with you. You too?"

"Sure. Who wouldn't enjoy taking a woman like you to the theater?"

She laughed and pressed his arm.

The play was a modern one by a foreigner, well cast, vividly acted, mordant and powerful; its theme was the process of growing old.

At first Feldhusen had trouble following the plot, but suddenly he found himself touched by the plight of the man on the stage and began to follow the play with increasing absorption.

During the intermission they strolled up and down in the foyer. They exchanged greetings with several people. Gina returned every bow with a radiant smile, keeping up a constant flow of conversation all the time. "It's an odd play, isn't it?" she said. "But it's clever. I wonder how it's going to end."

"It's going to end unhappily," he said. "Don't you see that? The man feels old age approaching. He doesn't want to admit it, doesn't want to come to terms with it. It's bound to end unhappily."

"He's stupid," she said. "He's not even your age, and yet he's afraid of getting old."

"He's a cotton picker, a pieceworker, and he depends on his physical strength. A man like that's halfway to the grave by the time he's forty."

"And you're just starting on your way up." She smiled up at him. "Aren't I lucky? Could I have a glass of champagne?"

"Of course you could." They went to the bar, and while he was waiting to be served he thought: I'll tell her afterward. I'll tell her everything.

As he turned around, a glass of champagne in each hand, he found himself face to face with Vera Manders, his first regular patient. "Nice to see you not in your office for once," she laughed.

He smiled back. "Good evening, Mrs. Manders. How's your tennis game?"

"Fine." She glanced at the second glass. "Who's that one for?"

"My wife."

"Oh, really? Won't you introduce me?" Curiosity shone in her green eyes.

Oh, not that, he thought. At least, not tonight. But Gina was already beckoning.

"Is that your wife?" asked Vera Manders.

He noticed her surprise, and for a moment he felt gratified. "It certainly is."

It didn't take Vera Manders a second to recover herself. She greeted Gina radiantly. "What does your husband mean by keeping you from us like this? For ages I've been saying to my husband: 'I'd really like to know what Dr. Feldhusen's wife's like.'

And he'd say: 'Someone to reckon with, you may be sure. Successful doctors have successful wives.'"

She's got presence of mind, thought Feldhusen, but he didn't feel as pleased as he would ordinarily have felt. Gina accepted the other woman's compliment with an unconcerned smile.

"Dr. Feldhusen," said Vera Manders, "you remember my invitation, don't you? What you said was: 'When my wife gets here.' Well, here she is. Early in November we're having a small party. Would you like to come?" She turned to Gina again. "My husband and I would be so pleased."

"We'd love to," said Gina.

Feldhusen did not say anything.

Like the experienced woman she was, Vera Manders devoted herself almost exclusively to Gina for the rest of the intermission. Her husband was sitting with some business friends in the smoking room, and she didn't seem to miss him particularly. When the warning bell rang she took both of Gina's hands. "May I call you sometime, Mrs. Feldhusen? You really must . . . we have a little group of ladies . . . In any case we'll see you at our house early in November. . . ." She touched Feldhusen's arm with a quasi-intimate gesture and disappeared in the crowding throng of the audience.

When they were back in their seats Gina leaned over to Feldhusen. "Was that Mrs. Manders of Manders Incorporated?"

"Yes."

"How many millions?"

He smiled. "I don't know."

"She's out for blood."

"You think so?"

"Yes. But interesting. My type. She's very good-looking. And when I asked you you said you didn't know whether she was pretty or not. She's not pretty; she's beautiful."

"You're more beautiful," he said weakly.

"Let's hope so. Anyhow I'm looking forward to the evening at their house. You must be sure to keep it free."

The lights went out, and the curtain rose.

Oh, Gina, thought Feldhusen, what do you want with this Manders woman? Let's move to a pretty little village where we can live in peace. I don't need any beautiful millionaires' wives. I only need you.

The play ended unhappily, just as Feldhusen had said it would. After prolonged applause the audience crowded around the cloak-rooms, talking about it both favorably and unfavorably.

They drove to the restaurant where they had dined together that first night. The proprietor greeted them like royalty; the waiters came running. The little table in the secluded corner where they generally sat was free. Candles were lighted, as usual. Gina loved them. "Thank you, Doctor . . . Certainly, madam . . . The '49 Moselle again, Doctor?"

Gina settled herself comfortably. "It's funny what a difference it makes, your being a Head Physician. If you were just plain Mr. Feldhusen, a businessman, say, or perhaps a member of the Board of Education, they wouldn't pay any special attention to you, or to me either."

"It would depend on my wallet."

"Not entirely. Head Physician is really something. They don't come a dime a dozen." She laughed. "Too bad you're not Professor Feldhusen too."

"Now really, Gina," he said. "Do you honestly attach so much importance to such trivial things?"

The waiter brought the wine, poured a small amount, and waited conscientiously for Feldhusen to taste it and nod his approval. Then he filled both glasses and withdrew.

"Do you?"

"What?"

"Attach so much importance to it? Head Physician, associate professor, full professor?"

"Oh, Will," said Gina. "What I really attach importance to is you."

"That's nice of you," he said seriously and raised his glass to the candlelight. She drank thirstily and put her glass down with a sigh. Now, he thought, now I can tell her, and he reached for her hand and held it tight. "Gina, since we're on this subject there's something I want to say to you."

"So solemnly? Go ahead."

"Gina, I've had enough."

She didn't understand him. "How do you mean?"

He did not relinquish her hand. "It's getting to be too much for me. I'm working myself to death, and we're not getting anything out of it. Just the endless paper work alone . . ."

"You mean at the Paul Ehrlich?"

"Yes."

"Why, Will! I think——"

"Let me finish. What would you say to retiring to a pretty little village? A health resort in Bavaria, for instance, or a North Sea beach. A nice practice all to ourselves. No one to interfere with me, no operations at night when we've got something planned, no . . ." The look she gave him silenced him.

"You're not serious, are you, Will?"

"Yes, indeed I am. I think you've even said yourself that I'm working too hard. It's true. I'm not the man I——"

"Will!" Her voice was sharp. "That's absolutely impossible. Didn't you notice how people greeted you just now at the theater? Don't you know the reputation you have here? Oh, what's the use of talking about it?" She laughed—a hard, unnatural laugh he had never heard before. "What kind of nonsense is this anyway? Why, for a moment I even took you seriously." She stroked his face with a brisk gesture. "Ridiculous! You're tired. Or didn't you like the play? I didn't either. I didn't understand it."

I did though, thought Feldhusen.

"Come on now, Will," she said. "Let's change the subject. You've almost ruined my evening with your little practice in a little village in Bavaria or by the North Sea. Ugh, the North Sea of all places—and in winter too! Tell me some more about Manders."

He took a drink and gave up. Hopeless, he thought. I'm not going to be able to tell her. She won't understand; she's too young. His original need to tell somebody was transformed into its direct opposite. He sat there, distracted, giving monosyllabic answers to Gina's questions about Vera Manders and her husband. Finally he pulled himself together. "Forgive me, darling," he said. "I'm frightfully tired. Let's go home."

She followed him without concealing her disappointment. They hardly spoke to each other. For the first time he was showing her no consideration. He couldn't help it. The other business lay on his mind like a ton weight, and she wasn't helping him to bear the burden—she couldn't, and there was no reason why she should.

Later, in bed, when the light was out, she moved over close to him. "Will, I'm so unhappy. The whole evening's spoiled. It's my fault, isn't it?"

He slid his arm beneath her neck, felt her soft, loose hair. "No. It's never just one person's fault. It's always both of us."

"Oh, Will, I do love you."

He pulled her closer. "Do you love me or the Head Physician?"

"I love Head Physician William Feldhusen."

He smiled in utter despair in the darkness. Tomorrow, he thought, I'll call Fehling again. There must be some way out. And suppose there isn't? An idea emerged like a message from hell. He resisted, forced it back with all his strength. Fehling, he thought. Scharff. And I'll have to speak to Warzin again. Everything may still be all right.

Feldhusen lay awake a long time, dreading the morning.

Day came ineluctably. Feldhusen had to return to the hospital. On his desk he found a letter from Trude. He left it where it was and called Fehling. The secretary's voice again: "Just a minute, Doctor." A wait. Then: "Dr. Feldhusen? Mr. Fehling just left, I'm sorry. No, he'll be out all day today. Could I take a message?"

"No, thank you. Or rather, if he happens to come back ask him to call me. It's urgent." Feldhusen hung up. He could feel cold sweat on his hands. Fehling didn't want to speak to him; that was quite clear. He must have been told of the affair. Fehling was a politician, and politicians are cautious in matters like this.

Don't get dragged into anything; keep your distance until everything's settled. He dialed Dr. Scharff's number. He wasn't available either, just the same as yesterday. Anger rose in Feldhusen, and opposition, and rage. Okay then—Warzin. I'll settle things with him. The hell with Fehling and Scharff.

He sat for a while, thinking over what he was going to say to Warzin. He considered one point after another, rejecting an idea here, searching for new ones. Yes, that's how he'd have to handle it. Then he stood up. It was time for his rounds.

There they were, already waiting for him in the hall, a swarm of white coats, the new Senior in front, greeting him deferentially. Feldhusen waved his hand: "Good morning. Good morning." His eyes hunted for Warzin but didn't find him. A burning fear stabbed through him. "Where is Dr. Warzin?"

The rest of them looked at each other. No one knew. Fear overwhelmed Feldhusen again, but he pulled himself together. He led the way just as on every other day. Where's Warzin? he thought. Could he have been arrested already? Take it easy! Take it easy!

That morning he achieved a triumph. Tormented by black fear, looking for new ways out and finding none, he was nevertheless the old jaunty Head Physician who captured every heart. He laughed, joked, held his unassailable position in the center of the stage. Nobody noticed the cloud hanging over him. Warzin. Where is Warzin?

After leaving the last patient's room they all stood around for a while in the hall. Feldhusen gave orders, made quick, confident decisions, all the time cherishing his hope that Warzin might still show up.

Warzin did not appear.

Feldhusen held out to the end. "Thank you, gentlemen," he said. Then he walked off with his springy step, joking in his usual way and waving his hand here and there. And nobody suspected that he had made his last rounds.

He paused in the outer office. "Fräulein Rieck, would you please find out where Dr. Warzin is? Send him to me right away."

"Certainly, Doctor."

He closed the door, dropped heavily into his chair, and waited. His eyes fell on Trude's letter. He opened it indifferently.

Dear William,

I wrote you back in June to tell you about my difficulties with the children. I've been waiting for an answer ever since, but I haven't heard a word . . .

The telephone rang harshly. Feldhusen jumped. Warzin! Or Fehling! His heart pounded. He wiped the palm of his hand on his snow-white coat before picking up the receiver. "Yes?"

"Dr. Feldhusen?" A man's voice, cool and unknown to him.

"Yes. Who's calling?"

"Public Prosecutor's Office Number Two. Prosecutor Brandis."

Feldhusen froze. "Yes. What can I do for you?"

"I expect you know what it's about. Inspector Hennings came to see you yesterday. Well, there are a few unsettled points I'd like to talk to you about. Would you be good enough to drop by sometime today?"

Feldhusen swallowed hard but kept his head. "Sometime today? Out of the question, sir. I'm up to my ears in work. But if you want to send someone over I'll be glad to help you . . ."

"I'm sorry, Dr. Feldhusen. You'll have to come yourself. The matter's serious enough, and your testimony is vitally important—to you too."

Feldhusen made his final protest. He took a deep breath, and his voice was loud and cutting. "Listen, Prosecutor Brandis, I must ask you once and for all to drop this peremptory manner. This whole business is absolutely outrageous. Who do you think I am? You talk about 'unsettled points.' For me there's nothing unsettled about the whole thing. Young Warzin—"

He was interrupted by the cool, polite voice of the Prosecutor. "Dr. Feldhusen, I've just had a two-hour talk with Dr. Warzin, and that's exactly why I'm urgently requesting you to come over as soon as possible. Just tell me what time will be convenient. This afternoon or tomorrow morning. I'm not suffering from too much time on my hands myself, you know."

This was clear and unmistakable. Feldhusen suddenly collapsed. Warzin. He's been interrogated for two hours. He'll have told everything. Maybe he's already been arrested. And what about me? He moistened his lips. "Very well," he said. "Tomorrow morning."

"What time would suit you? About eleven?"

Still perfectly polite, damn him. "Yes, about eleven."

"You know where to find me, don't you? Criminal Court building, second floor, Room 230."

"Yes, Room 230."

"Thank you very much. Good-by."

Feldhusen hung up the receiver. Tomorrow at eleven. Interrogation by the Public Prosecutor. Warzin had been interrogated for two hours. All perfectly clear. No way out. Not through Fehling and not through Scharff. No way out. No way at all?

Feldhusen rubbed his eyes. The idea that had occurred to him the previous evening returned—the message from hell. This time he no longer resisted, and the stronger its hold became, the less frightening it seemed. The sure way out of all trouble. The last course open to man. The step across the threshold behind which lies darkness, but a comforting darkness which closes all eyes and puts an end to all suffering.

Feldhusen sat for quite a while. Yes, he knew now what he had to do. He would be spared the trip to the Public Prosecutor's—and everything else too. His eyes fell on Trude's letter, which he had carelessly dropped. He picked it up, but instead of finishing it stared out the window. Wisps of fog were drifting about in the misty air. The sun had disappeared. Trude will have to go on waiting for her reply, he thought. And I'll never see my son again. He tore the letter into tiny pieces and threw them into the wastebasket.

Fräulein Rieck knocked and appeared in the doorway. "Dr. Warzin isn't in the building. Nobody knows where he is."

I'm the only one who does, thought Feldhusen. He smiled at the secretary. "Thank you, Fräulein Rieck. It doesn't matter."

She looked at him trustfully and disappeared.

He waited until the door had closed behind her, then picked up the receiver and called Gina. He was calm now, wonderfully calm, and his voice sounded almost cheerful as he spoke to her. "Hello, darling. Look, I can't make it for lunch today. Too much to do. It's not worth bucking the lunchtime traffic. And I'll be a bit late tonight too. Maybe not until eight or nine."

She wasn't disappointed. "You poor thing," she said. "Oh well, just wait till we go on vacation. Guess who called up today." He couldn't guess. "Mrs. Manders. The party's on November 12. It's going to be a really big affair. I'm very excited. I asked her to come over for coffee this afternoon. She's coming—even if she is out for blood!" She laughed.

He managed to laugh too. "Fine. Then you won't be bored. Till tonight then, darling. Good-by."

He knew he had heard her voice for the last time, and he was amazed how calm he felt.

He ordered lunch in his office. He ate almost nothing but drank all Head Nurse Louise's coffee. "Now, Doctor," she said reproachfully. "So much coffee and nothing to eat. That's not good for you."

He gestured with a smile. "You and I have the same vice, Nurse. There's no use trying to break each other of it."

She liked that. This was a Head Physician after her own heart. She hoped to work for him until she retired.

Feldhusen stayed in his office all afternoon. Conscientiously he dealt with outstanding mail and then dictated a few important reports to Fräulein Rieck. "That's all for today, Fräulein Rieck. And from now on please don't disturb me. I have work to do."

"Yes, Doctor."

He sat down at his desk and wrote out a power of attorney for his wife and a cash check placing the entire contents of his savings account at her disposal. A will wasn't necessary. He had no estate; he had intended to build one up. He didn't need to worry about Gina; her father would take care of her. The children would just have to get along without his help; there was nothing else for it.

He stood up and walked slowly back and forth across the room, his hands resting on his back. He had plenty of time; nobody disturbed him. His mind was working clearly and calmly. Everything was simple.

Once Fräulein Rieck knocked and came in with the last batch of letters. Feldhusen signed them without reading the text. Fräulein Rieck shyly stammered out a few more questions. He listened patiently and answered kindly. "Is that all?"

"Yes, Doctor," she sighed.

"Fine, Fräulein Rieck. Then I won't be needing you any more today."

"Good night, Doctor." Before she closed the door she glanced at him once more, just as she had always seen him, and it was like this that he remained in her memory, sitting at his massive desk, full of charm, immaculate in white.

An early twilight was settling over the city. The fog had grown thicker, and its misty veil shrouded all the lights. Feldhusen drew the curtains.

His supper was brought in. He did not touch it, though he drank the tea. Silence permeated the building. The babel of voices died away; footsteps grew softer and rarer. Feldhusen heard his secretary leave. He was completely alone. He sat for a long time irresolute. There was one more thing to do. Gina! Should he call her again? No, not now. But he must leave a few words for her.

And so he wrote his last letter. It turned out better than any letter he had ever written. It was free from lies and perfectly sincere.

. . . I have to leave you alone, he wrote, and this is the only thing that still troubles me. But there's no other way out. I wanted to be happy with you, but if I stayed alive I'd make you unhappy. I've always been selfish—I realize it at last—and what I'm about to do now may also be done out of selfishness because

it is so easy. But for you too this step is the best among many
solutions, and that consoles me.

They will attack me and condemn me, but they'll straighten it
out among themselves. In cases like this they stick together. I
know the whole lot of them through and through; I'm one of
them myself. I don't care any more what they think of me. You
shouldn't care either. You knew nothing about my faults and
weaknesses. I always kept them from you. Don't take this too
hard. It's not worth it, and I don't deserve it. You'll forget the
whole thing before long. You're so young. You can still be very
happy.

But if ever you find yourself in our night club, in the corner
at the rear, in the candlelight, perhaps with someone else who
loves you and whom you love, then think for a little while about
our time together and about your old

Willem

With an effort he suppressed the brooding sadness that was
trying to take possession of him. Mustn't get sentimental now.
This is how it had to be; too late to change things now. A ca-
price of fortune—fortune which controls everything, carrying a
man forward and then dropping him, building up and then de-
stroying, blindly, without any plan. This is what Feldhusen had
always believed, but now a doubt occurred to him and made his
heart uneasy. Is that how it is? he thought. Or is God the sum of
all the forces of chance? Is there a God? I don't know. Better
not to think about it.

As he was folding the sheet of paper his eyes fell on the letterhead. Dr. William Feldhusen, accredited to the university. Specialist in Gynecology and Obstetrics. Head Physician of the Department of Obstetrics and Gynecology, Paul Ehrlich Hospital.
Address. Hours for private consultation. Bank and credit references. All neatly printed on petal-white linen bond—utterly correct. What a hard struggle those few lines had cost him, ever since
he applied for this job in the hope of getting on, of getting ahead.

Hastily he wrote the address and sealed the envelope. Then he
stood up and took off his white coat. He went over to the little
white enamel cabinet on the wall beside the washbasin. The

morphine was in the narrow bottom drawer. Feldhusen took out the box, saw the brownish ampules, and the fine red print on the labels.

Three? Five?

Five would put him to sleep too quickly. Three might not be enough. Four. Four would be just right.

He hunted for a file, cut a groove in the glass tips, and snapped them off, one after another.

The syringes were lying on a piece of white gauze, neatly arranged, shiny and sterile. He took a 5 cc. syringe, inserted the plunger in the glass cylinder, and attached the needle. Slowly the colorless morphine solution rose against the gradations.

Four cc.

Feldhusen held the syringe up against the light. Carefully he expelled the air until a chain of tiny droplets issued from the needle. Then he pushed up his left shirt sleeve. He saw the cuff link. A blue lapis lazuli in a gold setting. It was a present from Gina, and Feldhusen thought of her once more.

He took the alcohol bottle and a swab. The gauze was quickly saturated. He rubbed the skin of his lower arm, felt the coldness of the evaporating alcohol. In spite of himself he had to smile. What was the use of antisepsis at this point? No more infections for me, he thought.

Then he stuck the needle into his skin. As he forced the plunger down, a little swollen cushion developed around the point of entry, a store of poison which would slowly be absorbed and help him to withstand the worst.

He swabbed the pinprick again, then pulled down his sleeve. From now on the clock was ticking away and his time was limited.

Feldhusen put on his suit coat and his overcoat. He picked up the letters and walked to the door. Before switching off the light he glanced back at the bookcase, the chair, the desk. He had liked his office.

He closed the doors. Then he walked along the corridor and downstairs. The night doorman said good night respectfully. "Good night, good night," called Feldhusen, waving his hand.

A nice guy, thought the doorman. And working so late again. If only my Klaus gets through high school all right. We'll manage to put him through college somehow.

Feldhusen walked fast. The mailbox was about fifty yards away. He dropped the envelopes in and felt with his fingers to be sure nothing had got stuck. The lid fell down noisily. Feldhusen shivered.

The car was parked on the other side of the street. The light from the street lamp glistened on the black finish in millions of tiny drops of fog. Feldhusen sat down and started the motor, which functioned noiselessly. Only a faint trembling of the car showed that it was running.

He switched his lights on and drove off. He stopped at the stop light at the end of the street, obeying the rules as though a traffic ticket could still affect him.

The expressway began about two and a half miles from town, but even before he left the network of city streets he felt the first dull haziness of fatigue. He opened the window wide and drove faster. He mustn't fall asleep yet.

The headlights pierced the mist. The clock on the dashboard showed half past eight. Still so early in the evening, and yet so late.

Then Feldhusen saw the first marker.

Expressway 1000 yards.

When he reached the junction his desire for sleep was so intense that he had to force himself to keep his eyes open. Four cc., he thought. No wonder. It's too warm.

He cut off the heater and rolled down the right window too. The damp coolness returned and held off sleep again for a while. And then indifference came upon him, euphoria, the sweet, blissful feeling that made life and death both easy. Feldhusen was content.

Gradually he bore down harder on the gas pedal. Farther and farther, right down to the floor. The car shot forward—an angry shadow behind a blinding cone of light. The wind whirled in through the open windows, tearing at his hair. Feldhusen could no longer feel the cold or hear the noise. From beneath leaden lids he watched the white line in the beam of the headlights.

The next bridge, he thought. It won't be long. It's not far. I'm driving so fast. Just till then. Then I can go to sleep, go to sleep at last. I'm so tired.

With a final, infinite effort he kept awake. He pulled the car over to the left until the dirty brown of the shoulder showed beside the wheels. Suddenly the fog lifted. The headlights groped for the bridge, which rose out of the darkness like a gigantic entrance. Feldhusen pulled farther to the left. The car began to shudder and bounce, but it held the road.

And then Feldhusen began to cry. Tears ran down his face and blew away in the draft from the windows. In these last few seconds Feldhusen wept for his wasted life.

The stone pier shone in the light like a gleaming pillar. Feldhusen shut his eyes. His hands clutched the wheel.

In a fountain of glass and steel the car rose up against the stone pier. The lights went out. A shattering crash tore through the night, ringing out over land and up to the stars.

Then merciful silence and darkness enveloped William Feldhusen.

16

At about nine o'clock that evening Neugebauer was called to a patient at the Palace Hotel. He didn't like interruptions of this kind and was annoyed when he set out. He did not get back until after midnight but, to Liselotte's surprise, in the best of spirits.

"Whoever was it?" she asked curiously.

He took off his coat and sat down on the edge of her bed. "Miss Ferida bind Abdallah, daughter of Emir Abdallah Mansuri, governor of the province of Kharubeh in Saudi Arabia."

She looked at him quizzically. "You've memorized that all right. And why are you in such a good mood? Was she so pretty? What was the matter with her?"

"She had a stomach-ache. I don't know whether she was pretty or not, because apart from her stomach I only saw her fingernails. They were bitten halfway down and what was left was painted red."

"How horrible! But you seem to be satisfied with the fee."

He suddenly took her hand. "Listen, Lilo baby. We're not waiting for the Sudan. We're going to Saudi Arabia instead, and very soon too."

"Hans, have you been drinking?"

"Of course not. The Emir made me an offer to come to Kharubeh. As Head Physician. A completely independent position——"

"Really!" she said. "And all because you cured his daughter of the stomach-ache?"

He got up and began to walk up and down in front of her bed with vigorous steps. "Listen to the whole story first. It was a terrific show. Father and mother in attendance, an interpreter, a coal-black personal servant and a whole crew of veiled women. I examined the kid. It wasn't much. A slight disturbance. As soon as I'd given her an injection she said she was all right again. The enthusiasm was enormous. Well, I left her a prescription and then the Emir took me into another room of his luxurious suite and made me the above-mentioned offer. I told him I'd let him know tomorrow. But on the way home I've thought it through carefully. I'm going to accept. I'll never get another chance like this." He stood still facing her. "Well, what have you got to say now?"

"Nothing at all."

He sat down again on the edge of her bed. "Listen, Lilo. I understand Kharubeh is a pretty big town in a marvelous location in the mountains. Pleasant climate. The hospital's brand new. We're to have a house to ourselves with a garden. Water and light free. I'd be crazy not to take it. And the salary—guess."

"Go on, tell me."

"Three thousand rials. That's three thousand marks a month, no deductions."

"That's impossible," she said in an excited voice. "Hans, he must be a fraud."

"We'll soon find out. I could get a visa in three days, he says. I'd only have to send my passport to the legation, and they'd take care of everything, including the airline ticket."

Liselotte shook her head in bewilderment. "What about your application for the Sudan?"

"The hell with that!" He bent over her and drew her to him.

"It's absolutely clear that I've got to accept, Lilo. A chance to get out of here at last. No more taking other doctors' calls; no more endless waiting. The man told me I could be there and start work in two weeks."

"What about me?"

"You'll come on, of course. With the children. The climate will be excellent for them. And we'll have a few weeks' vacation first."

She thought it over, sighing. He knew her. She was already half prepared to go. "Three thousand marks," she murmured. "If it's true."

It seemed to be true. The next evening there was a call from the Palace Hotel. The patient was doing extremely well; she had never felt better. Had the *Herr Doktor* come to any decision? Neugebauer accepted.

Now Liselotte was convinced too, and as usual when she had made up her mind she took a deep breath of relief and immediately began to make the necessary preparations.

Next morning after breakfast she handed him a yellow envelope. "Your passport. Don't forget to mail it right away. Registered. Special delivery."

He kissed her. "You're the best part of me. Good-by."

"When will you be back?"

"About one. Oh, Lord, I almost forgot. Today's my afternoon off. Now listen. After lunch we're going downtown to the Hofkonditorei where we'll have coffee."

She looked at him in amazement.

"After that we're going shopping."

"Shopping?" she exclaimed. "What for?"

"Anything you like. Think up something. Up to a thousand marks."

"Are you crazy? Where's that going to get us?"

He smiled. "You forget that we're extremely well off financially. In the first place I've still got four months' salary from the Paul Ehrlich coming, and secondly, from December on I'll be getting three thousand rials. Or isn't there anything you need?"

"Mercy, Hans, there's always something I need. For instance . . ."

"I don't want to know now. Think it over carefully so I don't have to hang around the stores too long."

She jumped up and threw her arms around his neck. "Oh, Hans, you're so different all of a sudden."

"That's your doing. Because you ran away from me. I made up my mind that that won't happen again. Good-by, you silly old woman."

"Good-by, you silly old man."

He turned back at the door for a last look at her. She was sitting with her feet up on the sofa, opening the morning paper. He smiled at her. "I wish I had it so good. No children. A nice warm apartment and a husband who's out all day earning money."

"Take off," she said. "For once I get a chance to read the paper in peace."

He shut the door behind himself. He put on his coat, taking his time, whistling as he did so. He even glanced in the hall mirror, smoothed his hair, noticed the gray flecks at his temples, and felt content. On the stairs he was still whistling. Just as he reached the first landing the apartment door above him was flung open.

He turned around. Above him stood Liselotte. She was holding the newspaper in her hand. She was terribly pale. He rushed back to her. "What's the matter?"

She pulled him back into the entrance hall. "Feldhusen," she said.

"What? What about him?"

"He's dead."

"When?"

"The day before yesterday."

He took the paper from her hand and read it. It was a short report on the city news page:

HEAD PHYSICIAN FATALLY INJURED

A serious accident occurred last Tuesday evening on the expressway at the 8.5 kilometer marker. For some as yet unexplained reason the Mercedes driven by the Head Physician of the Gynecology Department of the Paul Ehrlich Hospital, Dr. William Feldhusen, collided at top speed with a pier of the bridge. By the time he could be extricated from the totally wrecked car he was dead.

It is reported that a judicial inquiry is under way regarding an illegal operation on a woman patient in which Dr. Feldhusen and one of his interns were implicated. The possibility that Dr. Feldhusen deliberately sought his own death has not been ruled out.

Neugebauer dropped the newspaper. Liselotte looked at him wide-eyed. "What a terrible thing!" she whispered. "He was so nice that night he was here."

"He was always nice when there was anything to be gained by it."

"Hans, you shouldn't talk like that."

He turned her around by the shoulders and steered her into the living room. "Yes, I know. *De mortuis nil nisi bonum.* Here, sit down. You look quite green. Would you like a drink?"

"Heavens, no."

He poured her the last of the coffee. "Don't think about it any more. There's nothing to be done about it. He took the consequences. I think that was pretty decent."

"Decent? Good Lord! What about his wife? She's so young. Twenty-six."

"How do you know?"

"He told me that day on the telephone. He was so proud of her. I think they were very happy together."

"H'm—if she's so young she'll get over it all the more easily."

"Hans, do you always have to be so horrible?"

"Do you expect me to burst out crying? I've watched too many people die—people more innocent than Feldhusen—to shed any tears." He stroked her face tenderly. "Come along now, forget it. And now I've got to be going or my colleague Paulig will lose his patients."

He left. This time he wasn't whistling. The news of Feldhusen's death had affected him more than he had revealed to Liselotte. When somebody's dead, he suddenly thought, he's stripped of everything bad. He saw Feldhusen in his mind again: tall and elegant, with his wit, his charm, his carefree cheerfulness. If only he'd known how to operate, thought Neugebauer, he'd have been a first-class Head Physician. He never bore a grudge —no, he never did that. Not even where I was concerned. Pretty unusual, that. If it hadn't been for that one thing I could have worked under him for another ten years and learned something from him too. Not surgery, but the art of handling people.

Neugebauer thought about Feldhusen all morning. There was neither bitterness nor triumph in his thoughts; he had gotten over that a long time ago. He was glad of just one thing: that he was no longer Senior Physician at the Paul Ehrlich. This way he need have no part in the staff gossip, the police investigation, and the inevitable red tape. And he'd be spared a second term as Acting Head of the department, doing all the work and then having to hand it all over to a new Head without getting any thanks for it.

He stayed in the office until one o'clock. He saw more than thirty cases, listened patiently to their complaints and long descriptions of their illnesses, wrote prescriptions and referrals, and made thorough examinations. He went home in a good mood.

As he was standing outside his apartment door Liselotte opened it before he could take out his key ring. She seemed very excited. He shook his head reproachfully. "Darling, haven't you gotten over it yet? You mustn't read the papers for the next few days."

"Don't be so silly," she said emphatically. "This is something else. The Paul Ehrlich called. You're to call back immediately."

"Who?"

"Senior Physician Scholz."

"Oh? What does he want?"

"He wants to speak to you. Says it's important."

"Let's eat first. I'm terribly hungry."

She looked at him, crestfallen. "But it's urgent, Hans."

He hung up his coat. "Nothing's so urgent that you can't eat lunch first."

She reached for his shoulders and shook him. "Hans, don't be so obstinate! You must call up right away. Don't you see? They want you back."

He shook himself free, took her hand, and went into the kitchen with her. "They want me? You don't know them even yet, Lilo baby. And do you think I'd be willing to play Senior Physician there any more?"

"Not as Senior. As Head of course. They know how capable you are."

He looked at her with a smile. "As Head? What a little innocent you are! And Dr. Scholz of all people wants to break the big news to me two days after Feldhusen's death? He's hoping to be made Head himself."

"Well, what does he want you for then?"

He stepped up to the stove and raised the cover of the frying pan.

"I haven't the vaguest idea. In any case it can wait till after lunch. H'm—the sausages are a bit scorched. My fault. I should have been on time."

She turned him around to face her. "Hans, you're driving me crazy. You're just putting on an act. You think it's important yourself. Why shouldn't they offer you the headship?"

The telephone rang. "There he is," she cried. "You answer."

He went into the living room and took up the receiver. She had followed him and stood beside him, listening.

"Neugebauer speaking. Good morning, Herr Scholz. Yes. No. Yes, but I have no idea . . . What? Well, if you insist. No, I'd rather come over. It's more convenient for both of us. Today or tomorrow. All right. Good-by, Herr Scholz."

He hung up and turned to his wife. "I'm going to be made Minister of Health. They want to create a position especially for me. They'll never notice one extra among all the government brass we've got already——"

"Don't talk nonsense," she interrupted crossly. "What did he want?"

"To speak to me."

"What about?"

"Oh, in connection with the Feldhusen affair. I told him that he won't learn anything from me, but he still wants to. He even wanted to come over."

"Are you going there?"

"I doubt that I can get out of it."

"Go today, Hans."

"Then you'll have to give up our shopping trip."

"We can do that another time."

"All right." He smiled. "Shopping would be more profitable for you, though. But whatever you like. And now let's have that sausage for heaven's sake."

Two hours later Neugebauer entered the hospital. It was very strange.

The doorman greeted him just as he used to, with a slightly military air. They stared at him from behind the admitting window, then nodded their heads vigorously. The sisters and the student nurses all remembered him as though it had been only yesterday that he left. Head Nurse Louise came toward him in the corridor with a serious face and a sad smile. "Isn't it terrible?" she whispered.

"Terrible," replied Neugebauer. She still smells of valerian, he thought.

He entered the Head Physician's outer office. Fräulein Rieck was huddled over her typewriter. She had been crying and did not smile at him. She jumped up and opened the upholstered door to the Head's office.

From behind the desk at which Feldhusen used to sit rose a narrow-shouldered man in a white coat. He wore gold-rimmed glasses, and behind the lenses his eyes were shy. He stretched his hand out over the desk with a slight bow. "Scholz."

"Neugebauer."

"Won't you sit down?"

Neugebauer took a chair. Scholz sat down again at the desk. "I'm very grateful to you for coming, Dr. Neugebauer."

"Not at all. Not at all. I have more time to spare than you. Especially right now."

Dr. Scholz sat on the edge of his chair, resting his elbows on the desk and rubbing his hands nervously together. Feldhusen looked much more at home here, thought Neugebauer. Scholz seemed to read his thoughts. He rose, walked around the desk, and sat down next to Neugebauer in the other armchair. "Er—no doubt you know what's happened."

"I read it in the paper this morning. Accident on the expressway. Suspected suicide."

"Unfortunately," said Dr. Scholz, "unfortunately it's not merely suspected. Dr. Feldhusen was involved in a most unpleasant affair."

"Abortion," said Neugebauer.

Scholz seemed alarmed. "That hasn't been established yet," he said. "But the indications . . . Well——" He had suddenly found the lead he had been searching for the whole time. "That's why I wanted to talk to you, my dear colleague. The chief culprit is our intern, Dr. Warzin."

Warzin, thought Neugebauer. That idiot. Just like him.

"Now," went on Dr. Scholz cautiously. "The investigation is still in progress, but there is reason to fear that there may be a —er—a public scandal. This could be extremely detrimental to the reputation of our institution." He looked at Neugebauer with his gentle eyes. "I say 'our' institution because you served for many years as my predecessor here."

Served, thought Neugebauer. Nicely expressed. "These things are soon forgotten," he said. "Much worse things than this have happened. Our gang sticks together in matters of this sort, doesn't it?"

"Er—yes, of course. I, too, am of the opinion that such regrettable occurrences should not be thrashed out in unnecessary detail. Not for the sake of hushing up something which might be prejudicial to our professional position, but purely and simply in the interest of the patients."

Aha, thought Neugebauer, the patients all of a sudden. "You mean," he said, "their faith shouldn't be destroyed."

"That's right. I see we understand each other." Dr. Scholz became more animated. "Doubtless Dr. Feldhusen was not the right man in the right place. That has unfortunately been proved. You realized this at the outset and—ahem—drew your conclusions. Nevertheless, personally he was a very estimable man and —if I may say so—despite the serious differences of opinion in the past, he never spoke of you as a doctor except with the deepest respect."

"Very nice of him," said Neugebauer. What's he after? he thought.

"Yes, indeed," Dr. Scholz went on, "as you so rightly observed, as a result of this incident the patients' faith is in danger of— ah . . ."

". . . suffering a blow."

"Exactly. Suffering a blow. Especially if some circles or institutions which might be interested in—er—playing up certain cases for their sensational appeal . . . certain newspapers, for example —er . . ." Dr. Scholz cleared his throat, wiped his mouth with his handkerchief and, seeing that Neugebauer was watching him intently, fidgeted nervously with his glasses. "I desire," he began again, ". . . I mean my responsibility as temporary Head of the department . . . You know . . ."

Neugebauer knew. He raised his hand, and Dr. Scholz stopped speaking. "Now let's talk perfectly frankly, Doctor," said Neugebauer in a friendly tone. "You're afraid that since Feldhusen's death has, you might say, vindicated me in the public eye, I might unburden myself and let out a few interesting family secrets about this institution. Is that it?"

The thin skin covering Dr. Scholz's cheekbones colored slightly. "That's not how I would have . . ."

"Okay," said Neugebauer. "Your fears are absolutely groundless. I share your opinion that the patients' faith shouldn't be subjected to unnecessary strain. Enough incidents happen within our noble professional gang that can't be kept quiet. And I'm not concerned in any of this personally any more."

"But they'll approach you, Dr. Neugebauer."

Neugebauer lighted a cigarette. "Then I'll remind myself of your Head Midwife, Sister Thea. She's not only a capable woman, but a sensible one too, Dr. Scholz. Treat her with respect."

"Extremely sensible," said Scholz in confusion. "Was she involved in that business too?"

"Not directly. But she behaved admirably. And you don't need to worry, Dr. Scholz. I'll hold my tongue."

"Oh, excuse me," said Scholz, still slightly bewildered. "I certainly didn't expect you to—er—I'm sure you understand what I mean."

"Perfectly," said Neugebauer.

Scholz was visibly relieved. He leaned back in his chair and became quite talkative. He brought out his sentences without constantly having to clear his throat and talked about his training, his family, his children. Neugebauer listened and now he found the man quite tolerable. He'd like to be Head, he thought. They could do worse. He has my blessing.

Then he stood up. Scholz accompanied him to the door. "There's one thing I forgot to ask," he said, as Neugebauer already had his hand on the doorknob. "What are you doing now? Have you got something lined up?"

Neugebauer smiled at him. "As a matter of fact I was going to apply for the vacancy as Head Physician. In the meantime I've found something better. A gynecological hospital in Kharubeh. Eighty beds. Completely independent. Modern clinic. No Health Department and—no press."

Dr. Scholz fidgeted with his glasses. He didn't understand a word.

"Kharubeh," said Neugebauer, "is in Saudi Arabia, pretty far south. But that isn't generally known. Good-by, my dear colleague. All my best wishes for your success." He stepped into the outer office and waved cheerfully to Fräulein Rieck as he went by, just as Feldhusen used to do.

Winter had come early, gray and cold, with a biting northeast wind.

The wind shook the evergreens bordering the East Side Cemetery and tore at the frozen flowers on Feldhusen's grave. There was no snow to soften and cover the ugliness of the raised mound.

The wind swept through the city streets and was trapped, howling, in the inner courtyard of the Criminal Courts building, as though it wanted to interrupt the eternal course of justice.

In Courtroom 111 people sat whispering in the public seats, staring at the two accused who were awaiting the verdict: Dr. Werner Warzin and Brigitte Leonhard. The trial had produced nothing sensational, but the spectators were not very demanding. A young gynecologist who had run afoul of the penal code and his girl friend and accomplice—this provided enough material to keep the evening conversation going.

This Dr. Warzin with his nice freckled face was quite an attractive young man. So even a man like him was capable of making a false step. This was a comforting thought. And the pale, dark-haired girl with tear-stained eyes had been trying the whole time to take all the blame herself. Quite touching. But the law was inexorable, as they'd see when the judges came back after their deliberation, and that was the way things should be. Order must be preserved. Justice must be done. Even where an educated man was concerned. What were the two of them thinking about now? They'd been in love once.

Warzin sat motionless, staring over the almost bald head of his counsel at a dirty scrap of paper on the floor which had escaped the cleaning woman that morning. Fear paralyzed his thinking. He had told everything; kept nothing back. He had not mentioned Feldhusen. His counsel had done that for him in his brief, in full detail. If his counsel had his way he, Warzin, ought to be acquitted. But he didn't believe he would be. It was so easy to put all the blame on Feldhusen.

Brigitte's close presence was embarrassing to Warzin. Disagreeable. He would rather have been sitting here alone. Her presence, the quiet voice in which she had shielded him before the court, made it all still more unbearable.

His counsel, bored, was leafing through his brief. In the back a woman was coughing and didn't seem able to stop. Then the judges returned. Everybody rose, with a shuffle of feet. Warzin stood up. His eyes were riveted to the dirty scrap of paper on the floor. He felt Brigitte's hand on his arm and shook it off. Then he listened with penetrating attention to the voice of the presiding judge.

"In the name of the people . . ."

The one court reporter in the press box was taking everything down. Dr. Werner Warzin received a nine months' sentence, with immediate parole. Disbarred from the practice of medicine for a year. Brigitte Leonhard was given three months, with immediate parole. In Warzin's case, the summing up said, leniency was indicated because his experienced Head Physician had not only failed to prevent his action but even made things easy for the young intern so that the accused had not been able to realize the full extent of the reprehensibility of his action.

The judges took off their caps. The trial was over.

Warzin remained sitting stiffly in his place. Disbarred from the practice of medicine for a year, he thought. In a year I'd have been almost through. I'll have to find something else to do. But what? Male nurse? No! I'd rather wash dishes. Then he thought: Playing the piano. I worked my way through med school with that. Wonder if you could still do it today. Musicians are all organized now, just like doctors. I'll have to try it, though. There's nothing else to do.

He could hear Brigitte beside him, crying, "Werner!" She reached for his hand. He tore himself free and fled. He rushed down the corridor, snatched his hat and coat from the hook, ran across the echoing tiles, down the wide staircase, and through the stone lobby to the exit. Not until the icy wind struck him in the face did he stop, put on his coat, pull his hat way down on his forehead, and plunge his hands in his pockets. Then he walked aimlessly out into the city, and its frosty breath blew upon him like an enemy. Feldhusen, he thought. If it hadn't been for Feldhusen! I'd never have done it with anybody else. No . . .

Feldhusen was dead, but his tracks had not been obliterated, and Warzin was not the only person who was thinking about him.

At this time real estate agent Scheurich was having a business talk with textile dealer Lennartz about the apartment on the ninth floor of the new skyscraper. The rooms were empty. There was nothing to remind anyone of their former inhabitants. Nothing except the built-in kitchen. It was to be included in the lease, and the textile dealer was extremely pleased with it. Nice, very nice. The lady must have had good taste. Difficult to understand how she could give it all up so soon.

Ah yes, but after all that happened, interjected the agent.

What did he mean? It surely wasn't here that the fellow . . .

No, no. Of course not. All the same, the place must be full of memories.

Yes, of course. Hard for the poor woman. What was she doing now?

The agent shrugged his shoulders. Gone home to her parents. Then she'd probably take a trip abroad. Change of scene. Always the best thing. And after all, she wasn't so very old. Twenty-six. And not unprovided for. A big life insurance policy. And yet— an irresponsible fellow, that Feldhusen. A strikingly beautiful woman, by the way. She wouldn't stay a widow long.

That all sounded very reassuring, declared Herr Lennartz with a faint smile, thus giving the conversation an optimistic turn.

Exchanging remarks of this kind brought people into closer personal contact, and in these circumstances Herr Lennartz hoped they might perhaps meet halfway—come down, say, five hundred. High enough, in any case—the price. And cash too.

The broker showed the proper hesitation, then agreed.

Three weeks later Herr Lennartz was changing the name plate on the front door. He held the old one in his hand for a while. *Dr. William Feldhusen,* engraved on gleaming brass. Wonder if the young woman has any use for it? Probably not. He opened the lid of the incinerator and heard the brass plate drop, and he reflected for a moment on the transience of human hopes.

At this time Marianne Maurer, the first woman Feldhusen had operated on, was sitting at table with her husband. "Well," said Klaus. "How do you feel?"

"Fine, thanks," she said, but he could see that it wasn't true. It had been like this for months now. Every day she began to complain anew about her lot, and she was succumbing increasingly to a gnawing unhappiness. He tried in vain to cheer her up, took her to movies, to the theater, to night clubs. Nothing did any good.

He was young and full of vitality, and he enjoyed his work and life itself. He could have been happy even without children. She couldn't, though. That was just it. This was always between them and would be for the rest of their days. It can't go on like this, he thought sometimes. What am I to do? He didn't know.

They ate in silence. Marianne played around with her food. Then suddenly she stood up. "Excuse me, Klaus. I . . ." She went out without finishing her sentence. It wasn't necessary for him to hear it; what she had meant to say didn't matter. He finished his meal desultorily, without appetite. He reached in his pocket and lighted his usual cigarette. But before he had finished it he stood up and went out. He got into his Volkswagen and drove back to the office. I can't stand it any longer, he thought. If things don't change, we'll have to separate. I'll wait till spring, he thought. A lot of people change in the spring. He stopped at an intersection. A young woman was crossing, and she smiled at him gratefully for stopping. She was pretty, and she looked happy. He raised his hand, and she laughed. For the first time in ages he felt joy in his heart. Then his conscience got the better of him, and he drove on. I'll wait till spring, he thought. Neugebauer! The whole thing's his fault.

He knew nothing about the other women. Nothing about Erna Gerstenberg, whose plastic operation had not done any permanent good and who was tortured by the same old pains and even worse ones. Nothing about Ilse Zenker, living on in new pain and in new fear of the deadly cancer. Nothing about the old lady whose uterus had been perforated by Feldhusen's curette and whose infected peritoneum was a mass of stringy scar tissue.

And at this time machine shop foreman Anton Roth was standing in the East Side Cemetery before a stone statue of Christ giving his blessing, looking across at his wife's grave and her gravestone with its gilt letters. Winter had killed all the flowers; only moss and ivy wove a dark green cover over the mound. Anton Roth stood with his coat collar up, absorbed in contemplation of the grave. He came here often, nearly every day.

His friends at work shook their heads; they couldn't understand him, and his mother told him he should pay more attention to his daughter. But it didn't help. He couldn't forget his wife. She had understood him. He'd been able to talk to her so easily—sometimes far into the night. Now her photograph stood beside his bed in a silver frame, but she didn't speak any more, she only smiled. This made him unhappy and drove him back to the cemetery again and again. But he was made even more unhappy by the last image his memory held of her: Inge in her coffin, laid out by Herr Laternser with macabre tenderness, the child in her arms.

The branches over the grave were bare and swayed in the cold wind. Roth shivered. He read Inge's name once more, the dates of her birth and death. Then he went away. The frozen sand on the path crunched under his shoes.

A few rows from Inge's place, toward the exit, he saw the new grave which had been made a few weeks ago. Frost had turned the flowers brown, and the wreaths were touched with hoarfrost. Time somebody did something about it, thought Roth. It doesn't look good.

He did not know that William Feldhusen lay there, the man

who had killed first Inge and then himself. They lay barely fifty yards apart, in the same earth and at the same depth, the Head Physician and his patient, a man and a woman, two dead people, no longer distinguishable.

Perhaps he has no relatives, thought Roth. I envy him just the same. He's through with it all.

Slowly he opened the little gate in the iron grille at the end of the path. Behind a window of the gray stone house sat the old sexton in his green uniform. They knew each other and nodded.

The gate clicked behind him. Roth did not look back. He was already in the street, far from the sandy path, drawing farther and farther away. But he was still walking carefully, as if he did not want to disturb the dead—did not want to disturb Inge or the one in the new grave.